THINGS FALL APART

Chinua Achebe

WITH RELATED READINGS

THE EMC MASTERPIECE SERIES

Access Editions

EMC/Paradigm Publishing
St. Paul, Minnesota

Staff Credits

Laurie Skiba
Managing Editor

Valerie Murphy
Editorial Assistant

Brenda Owens
High School Editor

Lori Ann Coleman
Editorial Consultant

Becky Palmer
Associate Editor

Paul Spencer
Art and Photo Researcher

Nichola Torbett
Associate Editor

Jennifer Wreisner
Senior Designer

Jennifer J. Anderson
Assistant Editor

Parkwood Composition
Compositor

Things Fall Apart copyright ©1959 by Chinua Achebe. Reprinted by permission of Heinemann Educational Publishers, a division of Reed Consumer Books.

Cover Credits
Front Cover: Wall decorations in Nokwa, Nigeria. Photograph © Margaret Courtney-Clarke/CORBIS.
Back Cover: Photograph of Chinua Achebe © Steve Miller/New York Times Co./Archive Photos (also appears on page v of text).

Library of Congress Cataloging-in-Publication Data
Achebe, Chinua.
　Things fall apart / Chinua Achebe.
　　p. cm. – (The EMC masterpiece series access editions)
　　Reprint. Originally published: New York: Reed consumer books, 1959.
　　ISBN 0-8219-2412-5
　　1. Igbo (African people)—Fiction. 2. British—Nigeria—Fiction. 3. Men—Nigeria—Fiction. 4. Race relations—Fiction 5. Nigeria—Fiction. 6. Achebe, Chinua. Things fall apart. I. Title. II. Series.

　PR9387.9.A3 T5 2002
　823'.914—dc21

2001055670

ISBN 0-8219-2412-5

Copyright © 2003 by EMC Corporation

Published by EMC/Paradigm Publishing
875 Montreal Way
St. Paul, Minnesota 55102
800-328-1452
www.emcp.com
E-mail: educate@emcp.com

Printed in the United States of America.
　7　8　9　10　xxx　12　11　10

Table of Contents

THE LIFE AND WORKS OF

Chinua Achebe

Chinua Achebe (chēn´wä ä chä´bä) is widely acknowledged to be the greatest living African novelist. His first novel, *Things Fall Apart,* depicts the confrontation between the Igbo (formerly spelled *Ibo*) people of West Africa and the British who came to conquer them. Achebe tells the story from an African point of view, showing that the Igbo were not "savages" needing to be civilized, as the European conquerors believed, but intelligent human beings with a stable, ordered society and rich traditions.

Chinua Achebe

Achebe can be considered a teacher as well as a writer. In his writing, he strives to debunk racist myths about Africa and to show his people, and people all over the world, a more true picture of his homeland. "I would be quite satisfied," he writes, "if my novels (especially the ones I set in the past) did no more than teach my [African] readers that their past—with all its imperfections—was not one long night of savagery, from which the first Europeans acting on God's behalf delivered them."

Albert Chinualumogu Achebe was born in 1930 in the town of Ogidi, in Eastern Nigeria, the son of Janet N. and Isaiah Okafo Achebe. At that time, Nigeria was a British colony, and his mother named him after Prince Albert, husband of Queen Victoria of England. Although his first language was Igbo, Achebe was educated in English. He was also raised a devout Christian, as his father was a teacher at a missionary school. Achebe recalls that his family called themselves "the people of the church" and thought of non-Christians—including Achebe's uncle, who still practiced the traditional religion—as "heathen" or "the people of nothing."

As a child, Achebe looked down on other aspects of Igbo culture as well. He enjoyed listening to the folk stories his mother and older sister told him—stories he says "had the immemorial quality of the sky and the forest and the rivers"—but because of his European-influenced education, he thought of them as "primitive and heathenish." He thought the only good literature was written by Europeans, "the same ones who made all the other marvellous things like the motor car." Like many Nigerians at that time, Achebe was all too willing to accept the European judgment that Africans were too primitive to have anything like a real culture, history, or literature.

Attitudes were changing when Achebe was a young man, however. Many former colonies were becoming independent nations, and Africans felt a renewed pride in their own history. In college, Achebe became interested in the indigenous cultures of Africa and dropped his British name in favor of his Igbo name, Chinua. He also rejected the "African literature" studied in school, which was written by Europeans who portrayed Africans as primitive and socially backward. The true story of Africa could only be told by Africans like himself, he decided. He would become a writer.

After graduating from college, Achebe taught school and began a career in radio broadcasting. Meanwhile, he wrote. In 1958, he completed his first novel, *Things Fall Apart,* which was followed by *No Longer at Ease* (1960), *Arrow of God* (1964), and *A Man of the People* (1966). In 1961, he married Christie Chinwe Okoli. They went on to have four children.

In 1967, the Igbo people declared themselves independent and formed the state of Biafra, starting the Nigerian Civil War. Achebe traveled through Europe and North America to educate people about the Biafran cause. After the Igbo were defeated in 1970, Achebe wrote a book of poems, *Beware, Soul Brother,* based on his experiences during the war, and co-founded *Okike,* a magazine of Nigerian new writing. Soon after, he went on to teach at several American universities and later at the University of Nigeria. He wrote three children's books, two books of essays, and another novel, *Anthills of the Savannah* (1988), and edited several books of Nigerian poetry and short stories. After becoming involved in the election of 1983, Achebe wrote an analysis of his country's political problems, *The Trouble with Nigeria.*

In 1990, a car accident in Nigeria left Achebe paralyzed from the waist down. While recovering in a London hospital, he accepted an offer to teach at Bard College in New York. He thought he would only spend a few years in the U.S., but stayed away much longer after a military coup rocked Nigeria in 1993. When Achebe visted Nigeria again in 1999, he was saddened to find much of it in ruins, neglected by the corrupt government. Today he expresses hope for Nigeria's future, but acknowledges that considerable damage needs to be repaired.

Achebe's most recent work is *Home and Exile* (2000), a nonfiction book that is both a memoir and an exploration of Africa's relationship with the West. The title reflects the author's position today—although still living in "exile" in Annandale, New York, where he and his wife teach at Bard College, Achebe looks forward to returning home someday to Nigeria.

BOOKS BY CHINUA ACHEBE

Novels
Things Fall Apart, 1958
No Longer at Ease, 1960
Arrow of God, 1964
A Man of the People, 1966
Anthills of the Savannah, 1988

Short Stories
The Sacrificial Egg and Other Stories, 1962
Girls at War and Other Stories, 1973

Poetry
Beware Soul-Brother and Other Poems, 1971
(Published in the U.S. as *Christmas in Biafra and Other Poems,* 1973)

Nonfiction
Morning Yet on Creation Day, 1975
The Trouble with Nigeria, 1983
Hopes and Impediments: Selected Essays, 1988
Home and Exile, 2000

Children's Books
Chike and the River, 1966
How the Leopard Got His Claws (with John Iroaganachi), 1972
The Flute, 1975
The Drum, 1977

Anthologies
*Don't Let Him Die: An Anthology of Memorial Poems for
  Christopher Okigbo* (editor with Dubem Okafor), 1978
Aka Weta: An Anthology of Igbo Poetry
  (editor with Obiora Udechukwu), 1982
African Short Stories (editor with C. L. Innes), 1984
The Heinemann Book of Contemporary African Short Stories
  (editor with C. L. Innes), 1992
Another Africa (essays and poems, with photographs
  by Robert Lyons), 1998

Time Line of Chinua Achebe's Life

➤ = Historical events

1930
On November 16, Albert Chinualumogu Achebe is born to Isaiah Okafo Achebe, a Christian missionary teacher, and Janet N. Achebe in the Igbo village of Ogidi, Nigeria.

1944–1947
Achebe attends Government College, a highly selective secondary school in Umuahia, Nigeria.

1948–1953
Achebe enrolls at University College in Ibadan, Nigeria, planning to study medicine. He switches to literature, however, and in 1953, receives a bachelor of arts degree from London University.

1956
Achebe studies broadcasting at the British Broadcasting Corporation in London, England.

1958
Things Fall Apart is published. It wins the Margaret Wrong Memorial Prize the following year, and becomes a modern classic.

1960
➤ Nigeria becomes independent from Great Britain on October 1.
No Longer at Ease, a sequel to *Things Fall Apart,* is published and is awarded the Nigerian National Trophy for Literature.

1961
On September 10, Achebe marries Christie Chinwe Okoli. They go on to have four children: Chinelo, Ikechukwu, Chidi, and Nwando.
Achebe becomes Director of External Broadcasting for Nigerian radio, a position he will hold until 1966.

1962
The Sacrificial Egg and Other Stories is published. Achebe becomes the founding editor of Heinemann's African Writers Series.

1963
➤ Nigeria becomes a republic.

1964
Arrow of God is published.

1966
A Man of the People and *Chike and the River* are published.
➤ After alleged fraud in the elections of 1965, Igbo army officers stage a military coup. Johnson Aguiyi-Ironsi, a military commander and an Igbo, takes over as dictator.
➤ Hausa army officers assassinate Aguiyi-Ironsi in a counter-coup, and declare Yakubu Gowon the new dictator. Thousands of Igbo in northern cities are massacred; survivors flee to the Igbo homeland in southeastern Nigeria. Amid the political unrest, Achebe leaves his post as Director of External Broadcasting.

1967
Achebe and Nigerian poet Christopher Okigbo found Citadel Press, a small publishing company.
➤ The Igbo people declare independence as the Republic of Biafra, beginning the Nigerian Civil War (1967–1970). The Igbo are defeated by the Muslim Hausa-Fulani of northern Nigeria.
During the war, Achebe tours the United States and Europe as a diplomat for the Biafran cause. Okigbo is killed in the war while fighting on the side of Biafra.

Beware, Soul Brother, a book of poetry about Achebe's experiences during the Nigerian Civil War, is published and wins the Commonwealth Poetry Prize.

Achebe co-founds *Okike,* a leading journal of Nigerian new writing. He continues to edit the magazine today.

1971

How the Leopard Got His Claws, a children's book written with John Iroaganachi, is published.

Achebe moves to the U.S., where he teaches at the University of Massachusetts at Amherst and the University of Connecticut.

1972

Girls at War and Other Stories and *Christmas in Biafra and Other Poems* are published.

1973

Morning Yet on Creation Day, a book of essays, and *The Flute,* a children's book, are published.

➤ Gowon is overthown in a bloodless military coup. Murtala Muhammed takes power and begins reforming the government.

1975

➤ Murtala Muhammed is assassinated. Olusegun Obasanjo, next in command, takes over in the interim, promising to hold elections.

Achebe returns to Nigeria to teach at the University of Nigeria at Nsukka.

1976

The Drum: A Children's Story is published.

1977

Don't Let Him Die: An Anthology of Memorial Poems for Christopher Okigbo (1932–1967), edited by Achebe and Dubem Okafor, is published.

1978

➤ Obasanjo calls for a democratic election and steps down as interim leader. Shehu Shagari is elected president of Nigeria.

1979

Aka Weta: An Anthology of Igbo Poetry, edited by Achebe and Obiora Udechukwu, is published.

1982

Achebe serves as president of the People's Redemption Party for the election year. He writes *The Trouble with Nigeria,* a long essay detailing what he sees as wrong in Nigerian politics.

➤ President Shehu Shagari is reelected, but then toppled by a military coup. General Muhammadu Buhari seizes power, declaring that military-style discipline is needed to put Nigeria in order.

1983

Achebe founds the bilingual magazine *Uwa ndi Igbo,* a valuable source for Igbo studies. *African Short Stories,* an anthology edited by Achebe and C. L. Innes, is published.

1984

➤ General Ibrahim Babangida is military dictator of Nigeria after over-throwing Buhari.

1985

➤ Nigerian writer Wole Soyinka wins the Nobel Prize for Literature.

1986

Anthills of the Savannah, a sequel to *A Man of the People,* is published.

1987

Hopes and Impediments, a book of essays, and *The University and the Leadership Factor in Nigerian Politics* are published.

1988

1990	A car accident in Nigeria leaves Achebe paralyzed from the waist down; while recuperating in London, he accepts a teaching position at Bard College in New York.
1992	*The Heinemann Book of Contemporary African Short Stories,* edited by Achebe and C. L. Innes, is published.
1993	➤ Democratic elections are held in Nigeria. Declaring the results invalid, General Sani Abacha seizes power as dictator and jails the rightful winner, Moshood K. Abiola. During his rule, Abacha embezzles much of Nigeria's wealth and allows the roads, hospitals, and other infrastructure to crumble. Those who oppose him are beaten, tortured, and often killed.
1994	➤ Abacha drives novelist Wole Soyinka into exile in America by canceling his Nigerian passport.
1995	➤ Nigerian writer Ken Saro-Wiwa, an outspoken critic of the Abacha regime, is hanged, along with eight other activists. A massive public outcry and pressure from British leaders does not stop the execution.
1998	*Another Africa,* a book of Achebe's essays and poems with photographs by Robert Lyons, is published. ➤ Sani Abacha dies of a heart attack in June. An interim government led by General Abdulsalami Abubakar promises to return the country to democracy by holding elections. ➤ In July, Moshood Abiola, the rightful winner of the 1993 presidential election, dies just days before he is scheduled to be released from prison; his death sparks rioting.
1999	➤ Olusegun Obasanjo is sworn in as Nigeria's first democratically elected president since the military coup of 1983. Achebe visits his home country again after nine years in exile.
2000	*Home and Exile,* a book of essays and reflections, is published.

Things Fall Apart

The setting of *Things Fall Apart* is an Igbo village in West Africa in the 1890s, in the area that is now Nigeria. At that time the Igbo people, native to the Niger River region, lived in agricultural communities divided by clans, or groups of relatives. They had no central chief or leader. Many of them had never seen a white person. Little did they know that Queen Victoria of England had already claimed the land around them as part of the British Empire, and that soon the British imperial forces, with their religion, their material goods, and their military force, would change Igbo life forever.

Precolonial Nigeria: The Rise of Kingdoms and the Scourge of the Slave Trade

Today Nigeria is a vast country on the southern coast of West Africa that takes its name from the mighty Niger River (see the maps on pages xxiv and xxv). People have lived in the area since at least 9000 BC. From 1100 to 1300 AD, great kingdoms began to emerge. In the north were the Kanem-Bornu Empire and seven independent Hausa kingdoms. These kingdoms prospered through trade with north Africa, and became centers of Islamic culture. Much later, after the collapse of the Kanem-Bornu Empire in 1847, the north was united by a sultan from a group called the Fulani, who ruled from the city of Sokoto. In the southwest were the Yoruba kingdoms of Oyo and Benin. The Yoruba were highly skilled artisans who spread their political and spiritual influence all over West Africa. In the southeast were the Igbo people. They had well-developed trade links and a history of skilled artisans, but did not have the large, centralized kingdoms as the others did.

In the late 1400s, Portuguese navigators came to West Africa, followed by the British, the French, and the Dutch, in search of slaves for their plantations in the New World. Many Africans were willing to participate in the slave trade, accepting alcohol, weapons, and other goods in exchange for enemies or even people in their own groups that they considered undesirable. Some of the Igbo people, in fact, became wealthy by participating in the trade. Because the slave trade was conducted for so long on the coast of West Africa, in places like Nigeria and Cameroon, many African-Americans can trace their ancestry to Nigeria and specifically to the Igbo people.

Colonization of Nigeria: The Encroachment of Europe

The slave trade went on for nearly four hundred years. Britain formally abolished the slave trade in 1807, although it continued, since the abolishment was not well enforced, until about 1875. By this time, European nations had a different plan for Africa: they would colonize it, and use the natural resources for their industry. By 1898, France, Germany, Portugal, Spain, Italy, and Great Britain had each claimed a piece of the African continent. Great Britain claimed the area around the Niger River, where the Hausa, Yoruba, and Igbo had lived for centuries, as their own.

Although the British already had set up trade within the area, the process of colonization was not easy. It involved ruthless and bloody war. In the north, the British conquered the sultan of Sokoto, who ruled the Islamic Hausa and Fulani people, and in the southwest, they conquered the Yoruba kings. They let the sultan and the kings stay in power in name only, as long as they collected taxes for the British government. They also allowed the northern peoples to continue practicing the religion of Islam.

The Igbo were harder to control. Never having been ruled by sultans or kings, they were not used to obeying one chief and would not respect any chiefs appointed by the British. In *Things Fall Apart,* Achebe shows how the British conquered the Igbo in three stages: through missionaries, through trade, and finally, through force.

The first Christian missionaries entered Africa to convert the people to Christianity and to set up schools and churches. By the 1890s, they had established a missionary school in the city of Onitsha, on the Niger River. From there, they moved into Yorubaland and Igboland to spread their message. At first, many Christian missionaries who entered the Igbo communities were dismissed as crazy people or curiosities, but eventually, they gathered support among the outcasts of society, such as the *osu,* who were considered to be dedicated to the gods and were not allowed to mingle with the freeborn villagers. Women who had been forced to kill their twin babies, in accordance with the Igbo belief that twins were evil, also were attracted to the Christian religion, which condemned such infanticide.

The second way the British entered the Igbo communities was through trade. The Europeans bought palm oil from the Igbo, which they used in their industry. The Igbo used this oil, which is derived from the kernels, or seeds, of a certain kind of palm tree, to make soap, for lamps, as a cosmetic and hair oil, and above all in their cooking. But palm oil was never so valuable as it was when traded with the Europeans, and the Igbo were only too happy to trade.

Thirdly, the British set up their own government with the power to enforce British laws. They established the office of District Commissioner, who acted under the authority of the British Queen, Victoria. He was served by officers called court messengers, who acted as police, bringing in men for trial and imprisoning them. The Igbo did not know they were being conquered by the British until the government was already in place. By then, it was already too late.

While he clearly shows the devastating effect colonization had on the Igbo, Achebe is careful not to stereotype the Europeans as evil and ruthless conquerors. He includes sympathetic white characters and shows some of the positive results of the British influence as well.

Nigeria Today: Diversity and Adversity

Colonial rule brought to Nigeria Western technology, customs, and values that dramatically transformed the traditional lives of Nigeria's peoples. In 1960, Nigeria became independent from Great Britain, but many legacies of British rule remain, including the English language and English laws and political structures.

Today, the country is one of the largest in Africa. It covers 356,700 square miles and has a population of more than 126 million people. The country is incredibly diverse. Its major ethnic groups are the Hausa-Fulani, the Yoruba, and the Igbo, but in all there are more than 250 different groups—including the Kanuri, Edo, Nupe, Ogoni, Ibibio, and Ijo—each with its own customs, traditions, and language. Most Nigerians are either Muslim or Christian, although some still practice the traditional religions. Northern Nigeria is mainly Muslim, and the south is dominated by Christians.

Because of its diversity, Nigeria has had trouble staying together as a nation. In 1967, a civil war broke out because the Igbo people wanted to form their own separate nation called Biafra. The Igbo lost the war, but conflicts between the Igbo, the Yoruba, and the Hausa-Fulani still exist.

Igbo Culture in *Things Fall Apart*

As mentioned earlier, the Igbo people are native to southeastern Nigeria. The novel is set in the area around the city of Onitsha (see the map on page xxv), in the village of Umuofia, one of an alliance of nine agricultural communities. Umuofia, which means "people of the forest," is a fictional town, invented by Achebe to represent a typical Igbo village before the coming of Europeans. He based Umuofia on his own hometown of Ogidi.

To Westerners (such as people in Europe or the United States) many of the traditional beliefs and customs of the Igbo people in this novel may at first seem strange. However, that very strangeness makes the novel fascinating reading. Umuofia and other villages like it are agricultural communities. The men raise yams, the staple food of the people, and the women raise other crops such as cassava, a type of edible root. At the time this novel is set, successful Igbo men like the main character, Okonkwo, often have more than one wife. Each family lives in its own compound, or group of huts surrounded by a wall. The main hut, or *obi,* is the home of the man, the head of the family. His wives and the family's children live in separate huts inside the compound.

The world of *Things Fall Apart* is oppressively patriarchal. Men have all the power and women are little more than property. Women's roles include farming, tending animals, and caring for children. Wife-beating is commonplace. As Okonkwo, the main character, reflects in chapter 7, "No matter how prosperous a man was, if he was unable to rule his women and his children (and especially his women) he was not really a man." As you read, remember that the author is not in favor of this social structure; he is merely portraying things as they were, for good and for bad. In fact, Achebe himself has criticized the sexist attitudes of the Igbo. "That particular society," he said in an interview, "has believed too much in manliness. Perhaps this is part of the reason it crashed."

While Igbo society as portrayed in the novel is undeniably male-dominated, women do command respect in certain areas. For example, women act as priestesses for the Oracles, essentially serving as the mouthpieces of the gods. Women also are responsible for resolving minor disputes in the community, those that are not brought before the high court. The importance of the woman's role becomes clear in part 2, when Okonkwo is exiled to his motherland. His uncle, Uchendu, explains to the grieving Okonkwo why his motherland is as important as the land of his father: "A man belongs to his fatherland when things are good and life is sweet. But when there is sorrow and bitterness he finds refuge in his motherland . . . . And that is why we say that mother is supreme."

Igbo values are transmitted through traditional stories and proverbs. As you read this novel, you will find that these traditional people have great respect for language. Much of their way of life is guided by traditional stories and proverbs, and people who know these stories and sayings and can apply them to everyday life are highly respected. Also highly respected are orators, people who can speak well at public meetings held on the communal meeting ground, or *ilo.*

The Igbo people in this novel are a rigid, well-defined society with a government, laws, and justice system. Unlike the Muslims in northern Nigeria and the Yoruba of the west, the Igbo have no sultan or king; instead, they have a democratic form of government. Each clan is ruled by elders, or *ndichie,* and by men chosen to receive certain positions of authority, or titles. Decisions are made by the clan as a whole, as demonstrated in chapter 2, when all the men of Umuofia are called together to decide what should be done about a dispute with a neighboring village. Only male members of the clan, not the women, are called to help make the decision.

A second source of authority in the clan are the ancestors. Though dead, they still have voices and are called upon to act as judges and guides for the living. The ancestors speak through the *egwugwu,* important men of the village who are disguised by masks and elaborate costumes. Through a ritual drama, the *egwugwu* become possessed by the spirits of the ancestors and thus become vehicles for communication between the earthly and spiritual realms. As seen in chapter 10, the *egwugwu* are responsible for administering justice in the clan, resolving such problems as domestic violence cases and property disputes.

A third source of authority are the gods. The traditional Igbo are animist, meaning that they recognize a number of gods who are believed to embody the forces of nature. The Igbo worship a powerful creator god named Chukwu and many lesser gods, including the earth goddess, Ani, and the goddess of the sky, Amadiora. The gods can be appealed to through the offering of animal sacrifices at their shrines; their will can be determined by reading signs, or omens, and by consulting an oracle, or priestess, whose job it is to speak for a god. In *Things Fall Apart,* Chielo is the priestess of Agbala, the Oracle of the Hills and Caves. Agbala speaks through her, sometimes uttering solemn decrees that must be obeyed without question. Disobeying the Oracle would mean offending the earth goddess, who might then put a curse on the land so that the crops would not grow. Killing a member of one's own group, or clan, is also considered an offense against the earth goddess, as is making a disturbance during the so-called "week of peace" that follows the yearly harvest of yams. Social order is maintained because all Igbo understand and obey the rules of the gods and the decrees of the Oracle.

Achebe does not present an idealized view of the Igbo. He depicts some traditions that today might be considered shocking or offensive to a Western reader. On the whole, however, the novel shows that the Igbo had a well-developed, working society.

Things Fall Apart

Chinua Achebe believes that, just as myths in the African oral tradition were told to convey messages about life, "any good story, any good novel, should have a message, should have a purpose." In writing *Things Fall Apart,* Achebe's **purpose** was to tell the story of the colonization of the Igbo from an African point of view, something that hadn't been done before. In doing so, he wanted to show a truer picture of Africa and African people, one that would contradict the stereotypes and racist judgments held by many Europeans.

In order to gain a wider audience—and also to respond directly to those British colonial writers who depicted Africans as ignorant and uncivilized—Achebe chose to write in English rather than in his native Igbo. Other African authors have criticized Achebe's decision to use English, the language of the colonizer, rather than his own language. But Achebe points out that since he knows English, it is his language too—and he is free to use it however he pleases, even as a tool against the same British who brought the language to Africa.

Although he uses English, Achebe is successful in capturing the patterns of Igbo speech in the the dialogue, which has a very dignified tone. Igbo words and phrases, as well as Igbo proverbs and folk tales, are interspersed throughout the story. **Proverbs,** or traditional sayings, play an important part in Igbo culture, as Achebe informs us: "Among the Ibo the art of conversation is regarded very highly, and proverbs are the palm-oil with which words are eaten."

Things Fall Apart tells the story of Okonkwo, one of the most respected men of the Igbo village of Umuofia. The novel is divided into three parts. Part 1 tells of the struggles of Okonkwo to become a great man among his people. Part 2 tells of Okonkwo's exile from his village. Part 3 tells of the coming of Europeans and the destruction of the traditional Igbo way of life.

The novel has many elements of classical Greek **tragedy,** and in fact has been compared to Sophocles's *Oedipus.* Okonkwo fits Aristotle's definition of a tragic hero as one who shows courage and dignity in the face of inevitable doom, a doom brought on more swiftly because of his excessive pride.

The main **theme** of *Things Fall Apart* can be inferred from its title, which is taken from a line in the poem "The Second

Coming," written by Irish poet William Butler Yeats (see page 182). Yeats wrote his poem in the 1920s during a time of political upheaval in Europe, when old ways of life were being challenged and destroyed. In his novel, Achebe shows how the coming of the Europeans causes things to fall apart for the Igbo, destroying their unity and challenging their traditional beliefs, values, and customs.

Characters in
Things Fall Apart

Main Characters

Okonkwo (ō kōŋ´ kwō). Okonkwo is a powerful and important man, well known in the nine villages of his clan and beyond. Born into poverty, the son of a lazy and unsuccessful father, Okonkwo has built his own fortune. As a young man, he proved himself a fierce warrior and formidable athlete. Today, at around forty years of age, Okonkwo is one of the leaders of his village. He is wealthy, with three wives and eight children, a large compound, and a stock of yams. However, he is also violent, prone to outbursts that terrify his wives and children. Okonkwo exaggerates the masculine side of his character out of a fear of being seen as weak. A noble, powerful man driven by fear and anger, Okonkwo is a tragic hero on the verge of a crushing fall.

Unoka (ü nō´ kä). Unoka is Okonkwo's father. In his lifetime Unoka was poor and idle, a peaceful person frightened by war and bloodshed, and interested only in enjoying life. He had taken no titles of honor in the clan and owed many debts. Unoka had a shameful death as well: he was left to die in the Evil Forest because his illness, a swelling probably caused by heart or kidney failure, was considered an offense to the earth goddess. Okonkwo is ashamed of his father, and he strives to be everything that Unoka was not.

Obierika (ō bē´ ā rē kä´). Obierika is Okonkwo's close friend. He takes care of Okonkwo's property when Okonkwo is sent into exile, and visits him in Mbanta to bring him the money from his yams.

Nwoye (ən´ wō´ yä). Nwoye is Okonkwo's firstborn son. Okonkwo disapproves of what he sees as Nwoye's lack of manliness. Nwoye's conversion to Christianity effects a complete break with his father.

Ekwefi (āk wā´ fē). Ekwefi is Okonkwo's second wife. In her youth she was known as the "Crystal of Beauty." She could not marry Okonkwo because he was too poor to pay her brideprice, but after marrying another man, she ran away to be with him. Ekwefi has borne ten children, nine of whom died in infancy. Ezinma is her only surviving child.

Ezinma (ā zēn mä´). Ezinma is Ekwefi's daughter and only child. She causes her parents much anxiety because she is a sickly child and they fear she might be an *ogbanje,* a child who repeatedly dies and returns to its mother to be reborn. Ezinma is Okonkwo's favorite child, and he often wishes that she were a son instead of a daughter.

Ikemefuna (i kā´ mā fə nä´) is a young boy taken from the neighboring village of Mbaino as part of repayment for his father's murder of an Umuofian woman. He stays with Okonkwo's family for three years, coming to view Nwoye as his brother and Okonkwo as his father.

Mr. Brown. Mr. Brown is the first white missionary to arrive in the Igbo community. His mission is to convert the Igbo to Christianity, but he takes the time to learn about Igbo beliefs as well, and so becomes respected by the clan. Achebe based Mr. Brown on a real-life missionary named G. T. Basden.

Reverend James Smith. Reverend Smith is Mr. Brown's successor. Unlike Mr. Brown, he does not wish to compromise and accommodate the Igbo people. He condemns their customs as heathen and evil.

District Commissioner. The District Commissioner is the head of the new colonial government that the British, led by Queen Victoria, are establishing to rule all the Igbo people. He has been appointed head of the court, where according to the Igbo, he "judged cases in ignorance," imposing British law on the Igbo. The Commissioner is served by court messengers, who are African people from other regions. The court messengers, or *kotma* as they are called by the Igbo, act as policemen for the Commissioner and his new government.

Minor Characters

[in alphabetical order]

Akunna (ä kün´ nä´). Akunna is a great man of Okonkwo's clan who discusses religion with the missionary Mr. Brown (chapter 21). Neither man succeeds in converting the other, but both men learn a lot about the other's beliefs. Through their discussions, the author shows some striking similarities between Christianity and the native Igbo religion.

Chielo (chē ā´ lō). Chielo is the priestess of Agbala, the Oracle of the Hills and Caves. In ordinary life, she is a widow with two children, and a friend of Ekwefi.

Enoch (ē´ nək). A fanatical Christian convert in Umuofia who is said to have killed and eaten the sacred python. Later, he commits one of the greatest crimes a man can commit by desecrating an *egwugwu,* or in other words, killing an ancestral spirit (chapter 22).

Ezeani (ā zā´ ä nē´). Priest *(eze)* of the earth goddess *(Ani).* He comes to punish Okonkwo for breaking the Week of Peace.

Ezeudu (ā zā´ ü dü). The oldest man in Umuofia, Ezeudu is highly respected in the clan. He warns Okonkwo not to participate in the killing of Ikemefuna. Ezeudu's funeral takes place in chapter 13.

Mr. Kiaga. Mr. Kiaga, an Igbo who speaks a slightly different dialect from that of the Umuofians, is interpreter for the missionary Mr. Brown. Mr. Kiaga's unfamiliar dialect makes the Umuofians laugh, as he says "my buttocks" instead of "me." Later, Mr. Brown puts him in charge of the brand-new Christian church in Mbanta.

Nwakibie (n'wä kē´ bē ā). A wealthy man for whom Okonkwo works to earn his first seed yams.

Nwoye's mother. Okonkwo's first wife. She is never called by her own name, instead known as "Nwoye's mother" in order to indicate that she is the honored mother of a firstborn son.

Obiageli (ō bē ə gā´ lē). Younger sister of Nwoye. Although she and Ezinma are almost the same age, Ezinma has a lot of influence over Obiageli.

Ojiugo (ō jē´ ü gō). Okonkwo's third wife. He beats her during the Week of Peace because she neglects to prepare his dinner on time. When we first meet her, Ojiugo has only one daughter, Nkechi.

Okagbue Uyanwa (ō käg´ bwā ü yän´ wä). Medicine man who is an expert on *ogbanje* children. He is called upon to find Ezinma's *iyi-uwa,* the stone that links her to the spirit world.

Okika (ō kē´ kä). One of the six leaders of Umuofia who, along with Okonkwo, is imprisoned by the District Commissioner. He is a great orator and in chapter 24 delivers a powerful speech against the white men, declaring that the Igbo must "root out this evil."

Okoye (ō kō´ yä). Okoye comes to collect a debt from Unoka in chapter 1. Unlike Unoka, Okoye is a successful man: he has three wives and is about to take the Idemili title, the third highest in the land.

Uchendu (ü chen´ dü). Okonkwo's uncle, younger brother of his mother. When Okonkwo is exiled to Mbanta, he is received by Uchendu.

Places in
Things Fall Apart

Umuofia (ü mü wō´ fē ä). Okonkwo's clan. Umuofia consists of nine villages, each of which is descended from one of the brothers of a common ancestor. Achebe base Umuofia on his hometown of Ogidi. The word *Umuofia* literally means "children *(umu)* of the forest *(ofia)*."

Iguedo of the yellow grinding-stone. Okonkwo's village, one of the nine that make up the alliance of Umuofia.

Mbaino (əm bī´ nō). Mbaino is a neighboring village. In chapter 2, the people of Umuofia are at the point of declaring war on Mbaino because an Umuofian woman has been killed in the Mbaino marketplace. War is averted when Mbaino sends compensation of a young girl and a young boy; the boy is Ikemefuna.

Mbanta (əm bän´ tä). Okonkwo's mother's village, to which Okonkwo and his family flee when they are exiled from Umuofia.

Abame (ä bä´ mä). Abame is a neighboring clan whose village is destroyed by the white man. The story of Abame, told in chapter 15, is based on a real-life incident that happened in 1905.

Umuru (ü mü´ rü). Many of the missionaries and interpreters who come to Umuofia are from Umuru, a town described in chapter 20 as the place where the "white men first came many years before and where they had built the center of their religion and trade and government." Achebe based Umuru on the real-life city of Onitsha, on the Niger River, which was the seat of colonial authority in Igboland.

Echoes

Quotes on Themes from *Things Fall Apart*

Fighting a Long Tradition of Racism

"[Negroes are] a people of beastly living, without a God, lawe, religion . . . whose women are common for they contract no matrimonie, neither have respect to chastitie . . . whose inhabitants dwell in caves and dennes: for these are their houses, and the flesh of serpents their meat as writeth Plinie and Diodorus Siculus. They have no speech, but rather a grinning and chattering. There are also people without heads, having their eyes and mouths in their breasts."

—from an account of the voyage to West Africa in 1561
by English ship captain John Lok

"[T]hat was the worst of it—this suspicion of their not being inhuman. It would come slowly to one. [The Africans] howled and leaped, and spun, and made horrid faces; but what thrilled you was just the thought of their humanity—like yours—the thought of your remote kinship with this wild and passionate uproar. Ugly."

—Joseph Conrad, in *Heart of Darkness* (1901)

"[P]erhaps it may be, as some doctors have suggested, that [the African's] brain is different: that it has a shorter growing period and possesses less well-formed, less cunningly arranged cells than that of the Europeans—in other words, that there is a fundamental disparity between the capabilities of his brain and ours."

—Elspeth Huxley, in *White Man's Country* (1935)

"I would be quite satisfied if my novels (especially the ones I set in the past) did no more than teach my [African] readers that their past—with all its imperfections—was not one long night of savagery, from which the first Europeans acting on God's behalf delivered them."

—Chinua Achebe, in the essay "The Novelist as Teacher,"
from *Hopes and Impediments* (1988)

The Experience of Colonization

"Perhaps the sheer audacity of some stranger wandering thousands of miles from his home to tell [the Igbo] they were worshipping false gods may have left them open-mouthed in amazement—and actually aided their rapid conversion [to Christianity]!"

—Chinua Achebe, from the essay "My Home Under Imperial Fire,"
in *Home and Exile* (1988)

"Religion is not the same as God.
When the British imperialists came here in 1895,
All the missionaries of all the churches
Held the Bible in the left hand,
And the gun in the right hand.
The white man wanted us
To be drunk with religion
While he,
In the meantime,
Was mapping and grabbing our land
And starting factories and businesses
On our sweat."

> —from the Gikuyu play *Ngaahika Ndeenda* (1982; English version
> *I Will Marry When I Want*) by Kenyan authors
> Ngũgĩ wa Thiong'o and Ngũgĩ wa Miriĩ

The Power of Stories

". . . only the story . . . can continue beyond the war and the warrior.
It is the story that outlives the sound of war-drums and the exploits of
brave fighters.
It is the story . . . that saves our progeny from blundering like blind beggars
into the spikes of the cactus fence.
The story is our escort; without it, we are blind.
Does the blind man own his escort? No, neither do we the story;
rather it is the story that owns us and directs us."

> —Chinua Achebe, in *Anthills of the Savannah* (1988)

"Until the lions produce their own historian, the story of the hunt will
glorify only the hunter."

> —African proverb

"I personally wish this century to see . . . a balance of stories where
every people will be able to contribute to a definition of themselves,
where we are not victims of other people's accounts."

> —Chinua Achebe

Map of Africa

This map of Africa shows all the countries and their capital cities. Locate Nigeria in West Africa, on the Atlantic coast. You may find it interesting to compare this modern map with a map of Africa from colonial times, which you can find in a world atlas.

Map of Nigeria

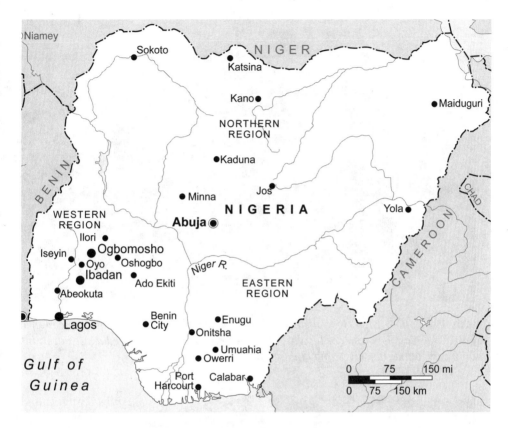

This map of Nigeria shows how the Niger River divides the country into three major regions. *Things Fall Apart* is set in the eastern region, near the town of Onitsha, which Achebe calls "Umuru" in the book. Most Igbo live in the eastern region, while the Yoruba live in the west and the Hausa-Fulani, an Islamic people, live in the north.

Images of Igbo Life

Photo: © Bettmann/CORBIS

In this 1920 photograph, Igbo men thatch the roof of an obi, *the hut of the head of a family. Like most Igbo men of his day, Okonkwo has his own* obi, *the largest hut in his family compound; his wives and children live in separate huts.*

Photo: © Margaret Courtney-Clarke/CORBIS

An Igbo woman and her daughters paint a mural on their home in Nokwa, Nigeria in this 1988 photograph. The same type of painting is depicted on the cover of this book. Okonkwo's wives decorate the walls of their home in preparation for the Feast of the New Yam (chapter 5).

Photo: © Hulton-Deutsch Collection/CORBIS

A 1956 photograph of egwugwu, ritual musicians and dancers. Okonkwo's father Unoka had his own band of egwugwu. Though Unoka's band were entertainers, egwugwu can also serve a religious function, transforming themselves through ritual dance into the spirits of the ancestors.

Critical Viewing
These photographs, taken at various times in the last century, show aspects of traditional life among the Igbo people. What are the counterparts to these activities in your community?

Photo: © Bettmann/CORBIS

A dibia, or medicine man, prepares medicines in this photograph taken in 1920. Okonkwo consults a medicine man to help his daughter Ezinma (chapter 9).

Photo: © Owen Franken/CORBIS

In this photograph from 1973, women buy yams at the market in Ibadan, Nigeria. Yams are a staple crop of Nigeria. Okonkwo's large store of yams is a sign of his wealth.

THINGS FALL APART

a novel by
Chinua Achebe

Turning and turning in the widening gyre
The falcon cannot hear the falconer;
Things fall apart; the center cannot hold,
Mere anarchy is loosed upon the world.

—W. B. Yeats, "The Second Coming"

PART ONE

Chapter One

OKONKWO WAS WELL known throughout the nine villages and even beyond. His fame rested on solid personal achievements. As a young man of eighteen he had brought honor to his village by throwing Amalinze the Cat. Amalinze was the great wrestler who for seven years was unbeaten, from Umuofia to Mbaino.[1] He was called the Cat because his back would never touch the earth. It was this man that Okonkwo threw in a fight which the old man agreed was one of the fiercest since the founder of their town engaged a spirit of the wild for seven days and seven nights.

The drums beat and the flutes sang and the spectators held their breath. Amalinze was a wily craftsman, but Okonkwo was as slippery as a fish in water. Every nerve and every muscle stood out on their arms, on their backs and their thighs, and one almost heard them stretching to breaking point. In the end Okonkwo threw the Cat.

That was many years ago, twenty years or more, and during this time Okonkwo's fame had grown like a bush-fire in the harmattan.[2] He was tall and huge, and his bushy eyebrows and wide nose gave him a very severe look. He breathed heavily, and it was said that, when he slept, his wives and children in their out-houses[3] could hear him breathe. When he walked, his heels hardly touched the ground and he seemed to walk on springs, as if he was going to pounce on somebody. And he did pounce on people quite often. He had a slight stammer and whenever he was angry and could not get his words out quickly enough, he would use his fists. He had no patience with unsuccessful men. He had had no patience with his father.

Unoka, for that was his father's name, had died ten years ago. In his day he was lazy and <u>improvident</u> and was quite incapable of thinking about tomorrow. If any money came his way, and it seldom did, he immediately bought gourds

▶ *How would you describe Okonkwo's personality? When does he "use his fists"? Why?*

▶ *How does Okonkwo differ from his father?*

---

1. **Umuofia . . . Mbaino.** Fictional Igbo villages
2. **harmattan.** Dust-laden seasonal wind on the Atlantic coast of Africa
3. **their out-houses.** Among the Igbo, women and children traditionally lived in separate quarters from the men.

words for everyday use   im • prov • i • dent (im prä´və dənt) *adj.,* failing to provide for the future. *The improvident baker used up all his flour to make muffins for breakfast and had none left to make bread for dinner.*

of palm-wine, called round his neighbors, and made merry. He always said that whenever he saw a dead man's mouth he saw the folly of not eating what one had in one's lifetime. Unoka was, of course, a debtor, and he owed every neighbor some money, from a few cowries[4] to quite substantial amounts.

He was tall but very thin and had a slight stoop. He wore a <u>haggard</u> and mournful look except when he was drinking or playing on his flute. He was very good on his flute, and his happiest moments were the two or three moons after the harvest when the village musicians brought down their instruments, hung above the fireplace. Unoka would play with them, his face beaming with blessedness and peace. Sometimes another village would ask Unoka's band and their dancing *egwugwu*[5] to come and stay with them and teach them their tunes. They would go to such hosts for as long as three or four markets, making music and feasting. Unoka loved the good <u>fare</u> and the good fellowship, and he loved this season of the year, when the rains had stopped and the sun rose every morning with dazzling beauty. And it was not too hot either, because the cold and dry harmattan wind was blowing down from the north. Some years the harmattan was very severe and a dense haze hung on the atmosphere. Old men and children would then sit round log fires, warming their bodies. Unoka loved it all, and he loved the first kites[6] that returned with the dry season, and the children who sang songs of welcome to them. He would remember his own childhood, how he had often wandered around looking for a kite sailing leisurely against the blue sky. As soon as he found one he would sing with his whole being, welcoming it back from its long, long journey, and asking it if it had brought home any lengths of cloth.[7]

That was years ago, when he was young. Unoka, the grown-up, was a failure. He was poor and his wife and children had barely enough to eat. People laughed at him

---

4. **cowries.** Shells traditionally used as money
5. *egwugwu.* Masked dancers
6. **kites.** Migratory birds of prey
7. **lengths of cloth.** The reference is to an Igbo folk tale about a bird called a kite. In their play, African children often enact scenes from traditional tales.

---

words for everyday use

hag • gard (hag´ərd) *adj.,* tired; worn. *After working for many long hours, Tina had a <u>haggard</u> expression on her face.*

fare (fer´) *n.,* food. *The Fourth of July celebrants enjoyed standard summertime outdoor <u>fare</u>: potato salad, burgers, hot dogs, chips, and dip.*

because he was a loafer, and they swore never to lend him any more money because he never paid back. But Unoka was such a man that he always succeeded in borrowing more, and piling up his debts.

One day a neighbor called Okoye came in to see him. He was reclining on a mud bed in his hut playing on the flute. He immediately rose and shook hands with Okoye, who then unrolled the goatskin which he carried under his arm, and sat down. Unoka went into an inner room and soon returned with a small wooden disc containing a kola nut,[8] some alligator pepper and a lump of white chalk.

▶ How do people in this culture show respect for their guests?

"I have kola," he announced when he sat down, and passed the disc over to his guest.

"Thank you. He who brings kola brings life. But I think you ought to break it," replied Okoye passing back the disc.

"No, it is for you, I think," and they argued like this for a few moments before Unoka accepted the honor of breaking the kola. Okoye, meanwhile, took the lump of chalk, drew some lines on the floor, and then painted his big toe.[9]

▶ To whom does Unoka pray? For what does he pray?

As he broke the kola, Unoka prayed to their ancestors for life and health, and for protection against their enemies. When they had eaten they talked about many things: about the heavy rains which were drowning the yams, about the next ancestral feast and about the <u>impending</u>

▶ What does Unoka dislike? Why?

war with the village of Mbaino. Unoka was never happy when it came to wars. He was in fact a coward and could not bear the sight of blood. And so he changed the subject and talked about music, and his face beamed. He could hear in his mind's ear the blood-stirring and intricate rhythms of the *ekwe* and the *udu* and the *ogene*,[10] and he could hear his own flute weaving in and out of them, decorating them with a colorful and <u>plaintive</u> tune. The total effect was gay and brisk, but if one picked out the flute as

---

8. **kola nut.** Bitter seed of the kola tree. Kola contains caffeine and is used to flavor cola drinks.
9. **drew some lines . . . painted his big toe.** This chalk, called *nzu* in Igbo, is a white clay used to decorate the face and body in ceremonies. When a guest is offered chalk, he uses it to mark his personal symbol on the floor. If he is a man who holds a title of honor in the village, he marks his big toe or face.
10. **ekwe . . . udu . . . ogene.** Ekwe and udu—types of drums; ogene—gong

words for everyday use

im • pend • ing (im pend´ iŋ) *adj.,* about to happen. *Sally brought the vegetables in from the garden so they would not be killed by the impending frost.*

plain • tive (plān´ tiv) *adj.,* expressing sorrow. *The puppy had become very attached to Rob, and gave a plaintive wail whenever he left the room.*

it went up and down and then broke up into short snatches, one saw that there was sorrow and grief there.

Okoye was also a musician. He played on the *ogene*. But he was not a failure like Unoka. He had a large barn full of yams and he had three wives. And now he was going to take the Idemili title,[11] the third highest in the land. It was a very expensive ceremony and he was gathering all his resources together. That was in fact the reason why he had come to see Unoka. He cleared his throat and began:

"Thank you for the kola. You may have heard of the title I intend to take shortly."

Having spoken plainly so far, Okoye said the next half a dozen sentences in proverbs. Among the Ibo the art of conversation is regarded very highly, and proverbs are the palm-oil with which words are eaten. Okoye was a great talker and he spoke for a long time, skirting round the subject and then hitting it finally. In short, he was asking Unoka to return the two hundred cowries he had borrowed from him more than two years before. As soon as Unoka understood what his friend was driving at, he burst out laughing. He laughed loud and long and his voice rang out clear as the *ogene,* and tears stood in his eyes. His visitor was amazed, and sat speechless. At the end, Unoka was able to give an answer between fresh outbursts of <u>mirth</u>.

"Look at that wall," he said, pointing at the far wall of his hut, which was rubbed with red earth so that it shone. "Look at those lines of chalk"; and Okoye saw groups of short <u>perpendicular</u> lines drawn in chalk. There were five groups, and the smallest group had ten lines. Unoka had a sense of the dramatic and so he allowed a pause, in which he took a pinch of snuff and sneezed noisily, and then he continued: "Each group there represents a debt to someone, and each stroke is one hundred cowries. You see, I owe that man a thousand cowries. But he has not come to wake me up in the morning for it. I shall pay you, but not today. Our elders say that the sun will shine on those who stand before it shines on those who kneel under them. I

◀ *How do the Igbo regard the art of conversation? What role is played by proverbs, or sayings, in their culture?*

◀ *What does this proverb mean?*

---

11. **Idemili title.** Igbo men who are wealthy and respected can take titles of honor to show that they have a higher status in the clan. Okoye is about to take a high title, which indicates that he is probably quite well-off.

words for everyday use
mirth (mərth´) n., high spirits or gladness accompanied by laughter. *The audience at the comedy club was howling with mirth.*

per • pen • dic • u • lar (pʉr´pən di´kyə lər) adj., at a right angle to a given line. *Grand Avenue is perpendicular to Main Street—Grand goes east-west and Main goes north-south.*

shall pay my big debts first." And he took another pinch of snuff, as if that was paying the big debts first. Okoye rolled his goatskin and departed.

When Unoka died he had taken no title at all and he was heavily in debt. Any wonder then that his son Okonkwo was ashamed of him? Fortunately, among these people a man was judged according to his worth and not according to the worth of his father. Okonkwo was clearly cut out for great things. He was still young but he had won fame as the greatest wrestler in the nine villages. He was a wealthy farmer and had two barns full of yams, and had just married his third wife. To crown it all he had taken two titles and had shown incredible <u>prowess</u> in two inter-tribal wars. And so although Okonkwo was still young, he was already one of the greatest men of his time. Age was respected among his people, but achievement was revered. As the elders said, if a child washed his hands he could eat with kings. Okonkwo had clearly washed his hands and so he ate with kings and elders. And that was how he came to look after the doomed lad who was sacrificed to the village of Umuofia by their neighbors to avoid war and bloodshed. The ill-fated lad was called Ikemefuna.

▶ *Why is Okonkwo ashamed of his father?*

▶ *What are Okonkwo's accomplishments? What makes him one of the great men of the village?*

words for everyday use

prow • ess (prou´ is) *n.*, bravery; skill. *The <u>prowess</u> of the fisherman was advertised by the striped bass stuffed and mounted on his living-room wall.*

Chapter Two

OKONKWO HAD JUST blown out the palm-oil lamp and stretched himself on his bamboo bed when he heard the *ogene* of the town-crier piercing the still night air. *Gome, gome, gome, gome,* boomed the hollow metal. Then the crier gave his message, and at the end of it beat his instrument again. And this was the message. Every man of Umuofia was asked to gather at the marketplace tomorrow morning. Okonkwo wondered what was amiss, for he knew certainly that something was amiss. He had <u>discerned</u> a clear overtone of tragedy in the crier's voice, and even now he could still hear it as it grew dimmer and dimmer in the distance.

◄ How are messages communicated to the entire village?

The night was very quiet. It was always quiet except on moonlight nights. Darkness held a vague terror for these people, even the bravest among them. Children were warned not to whistle at night for fear of evil spirits. Dangerous animals became even more <u>sinister</u> and <u>uncanny</u> in the dark. A snake was never called by its name at night, because it would hear. It was called a string.[1] And so on this particular night as the crier's voice was gradually swallowed up in the distance, silence returned to the world, a <u>vibrant</u> silence made more intense by the universal <u>trill</u> of a million million forest insects.

◄ Why is a snake called a string at night?

On a moonlight night it would be different. The happy voices of children playing in open fields would then be heard. And perhaps those not so young would be playing in pairs in less open places, and old men and women would remember their youth. As the Ibo say: "When the moon is shining the cripple becomes hungry for a walk."

But this particular night was dark and silent. And in all the nine villages of Umuofia a town-crier with his *ogene* asked every man to be present tomorrow morning. Okonkwo on his bamboo bed tried to figure out the nature

---

1. **A snake . . . string.** In many religious traditions, animals are believed to represent spirits or gods. Such beliefs are known as *animism*. In many religions, speaking the name of a spirit or god is forbidden.

---

words for everyday use

dis • cern (di zərn´) *vt.,* perceive or recognize. *Through the heavy fog, I could faintly* <u>discern</u> *the beam of the lighthouse.*

sin • is • ter (sin´ is tər) *adj.,* evil or dishonest. *Some people believe the deep purple light cast during a partial eclipse has a* <u>sinister</u> *aspect.*

un • can • ny (un kan´ ē) *adj.,* mysterious; unfamiliar. *It is* <u>uncanny</u> *how you called me*

right when I was about to pick up the phone and call you.

vi • brant (vī´brənt) *adj.,* pulsating with life. *She is a* <u>vibrant</u> *woman who lives her life to the fullest.*

trill (tril´) *n.,* warbling sound made by birds or insects. *Because Andrew was unused to the country, the* <u>trill</u> *of insects kept him awake all night.*

▶ How does Okonkwo feel about war? How does he differ in this respect from his father?

of the emergency, war with a neighboring clan? That seemed the most likely reason, and he was not afraid of war. He was a man of action, a man of war. Unlike his father he could stand the look of blood. In Umuofia's latest war he was the first to bring home a human head. That was his fifth head; and he was not an old man yet. On great occasions such as the funeral of a village celebrity he drank his palm-wine from his first human head.

In the morning the marketplace was full. There must have been about ten thousand men there, all talking in low voices. At last Ogbuefi[2] Ezeugo stood up in the midst of them and bellowed four times, *"Umuofia kwenu,"*[3] and on each occasion he faced a different direction and seemed to push the air with a clenched fist. And ten thousand men answered *"Yaa!"* each time. Then there was perfect silence. Ogbuefi Ezeugo was a powerful <u>orator</u> and was always chosen to speak on such occasions. He moved his hand over his white head and stroked his white beard. He then adjusted his cloth, which was passed under his right arm-pit and tied above his left shoulder.

"Umuofia kwenu," he bellowed a fifth time, and the crowd yelled in answer. And then suddenly like one possessed he shot out his left hand and pointed in the direction of Mbaino, and said through gleaming white teeth firmly clenched: "Those sons of wild animals have dared to murder a daughter of Umuofia." He threw his head down and gnashed his teeth, and allowed a murmur of suppressed anger to sweep the crowd. When he began again, the anger on his face was gone and in its place a sort of smile hovered, more terrible and more sinister than the anger. And in a clear unemotional voice he told Umuofia how their daughter had gone to market at Mbaino and had been killed. That woman, said Ezeugo, was the wife of Ogbuefi Udo, and he pointed to a man who sat near him with a bowed head. The crowd then shouted with anger and thirst for blood.

Many others spoke, and at the end it was decided to follow the normal course of action. An <u>ultimatum</u> was imme-

▶ What offense has been committed by the people of Mbaino?

---

2. **Ogbuefi.** Traditional title of respect for an affluent person, much like *Don* in Italy and Spain

3. ***Umuofia kwenu.*** Greeting to the village

words for everyday use

or • a • tor (ȯr´ət ər) *n.*, public speaker. *The activist with the melodious voice is known as a great <u>orator</u>.*

ul • ti • ma • tum (ul´tə mā´təm) *n.*, final offer or demand. *Because Mark could no longer stand his roommate, he gave him an <u>ultimatum</u>: "Shape up, or ship out!"*

diately dispatched to Mbaino asking them to choose between war on the one hand, and on the other the offer of a young man and a virgin as compensation.

Umuofia was feared by all its neighbors. It was powerful in war and in magic, and its priests and medicine men were feared in all the surrounding country. Its most potent war-medicine was as old as the clan itself. Nobody knew how old. But on one point there was general agreement—the active principle in that medicine had been an old woman with one leg. In fact, the medicine itself was called *agadi-nwayi,* or old woman. It had its shrine in the center of Umuofia, in a cleared spot. And if anybody was so foolhardy as to pass by the shrine after dusk he was sure to see the old woman hopping about.

◀ Why is Umuofia feared by its neighbors?

And so the neighboring clans who naturally knew of these things feared Umuofia, and would not go to war against it without first trying a peaceful settlement. And in fairness to Umuofia it should be recorded that it never went to war unless its case was clear and just and was accepted as such by its Oracle[4]—the Oracle of the Hills and the Caves. And there were indeed occasions when the Oracle had forbidden Umuofia to wage a war. If the clan had disobeyed the Oracle they would surely have been beaten, because their dreaded *agadi-nwayi* would never fight what the Ibo call *a fight of blame.*

◀ What is "a fight of blame"?

But the war that now threatened was a just war. Even the enemy clan knew that. And so when Okonkwo of Umuofia arrived at Mbaino as the proud and <u>imperious emissary</u> of war, he was treated with great honor and respect, and two days later he returned home with a lad of fifteen and a young virgin. The lad's name was Ikemefuna, whose sad story is still told in Umuofia unto this day.

◀ What does Mbaino do to compensate Umuofia for the loss of the murdered woman?

The elders, or *ndichie,* met to hear a report of Okonkwo's mission. At the end they decided, as everybody knew they would, that the girl should go to Ogbuefi Udo to replace his murdered wife. As for the boy, he belonged to the clan as a whole, and there was no hurry to decide his fate.

---

4. **Oracle.** A person or thing believed to have direct communication with a god or gods

words for everyday use

im • pe • ri • ous (im pir´ē əs) *adj.,* overbearing; arrogant. *No one liked Yolanda's imperious attitude; she acted as if she were better than everyone else.*

em • is • sar • y (em´i ser´ē) *n.,* person or agent sent on a specific mission. *We sent our emissary to the newly established nation to see if they wished to begin diplomatic relations.*

Okonkwo was, therefore, asked on behalf of the clan to look after him in the interim. And so for three years Ikemefuna lived in Okonkwo's household.

▶ How does Okonkwo treat his wives and children?

▶ Of what is Okonkwo afraid?

Okonkwo ruled his household with a heavy hand. His wives, especially the youngest, lived in perpetual fear of his fiery temper, and so did his little children. Perhaps down in his heart Okonkwo was not a cruel man. But his whole life was dominated by fear, the fear of failure and of weakness. It was deeper and more intimate than the fear of evil and capricious gods and of magic, the fear of the forest, and the forces of nature, malevolent, red in tooth and claw. Okonkwo's fear was greater than these. It was not external but lay deep within himself. It was the fear of himself, lest he should be found to resemble his father. Even as a little boy he had resented his father's failure and weakness, and even now he still remembered how he had suffered when a playmate had told him that his father was *agbala*. That was how Okonkwo first came to know that *agbala* was not only another name for a woman, it could also mean a man who had taken no title. And so Okonkwo was ruled by one passion—to hate everything that his father Unoka had loved. One of those things was gentleness and another was idleness.

During the planting season Okonkwo worked daily on his farms from cock-crow until the chickens went to roost. He was a very strong man and rarely felt fatigue. But his wives and young children were not as strong, and so they suffered. But they dared not complain openly. Okonkwo's first son, Nwoye, was then twelve years old but was already causing his father great anxiety for his incipient laziness. At any rate, that was how it looked to his father and he sought to correct him by constant nagging and beating. And so Nwoye was developing into a sad-faced youth.

▶ Why is Okonkwo anxious about his son?

Okonkwo's prosperity was visible in his household. He had a large compound enclosed by a thick wall of red earth. His own hut, or *obi*, stood immediately behind the only gate in the red walls. Each of his three wives had her own hut, which together formed a half moon behind the *obi*. The barn was built against one end of the red walls, and long stacks of yam stood out prosperously in it. At the

▶ Where does Okonkwo live? Where do his wives live? What other structures are in Okonkwo's compound?

words for everyday use

ca • pri • cious (kə prish´əs) *adj.*, tending to change without apparent reason. *One who has experienced disappointment in love might compare his or her fickle beloved to the capricious moon.*

in • cip • i • ent (in sip´ē ənt) *adj.*, in the first stage of existence. *Our plan for dinner is incipient; we still haven't decided exactly where we would like to go.*

opposite end of the compound was a shed for the goats, and each wife built a small attachment to her hut for the hens. Near the barn was a small house, the "medicine house" or shrine where Okonkwo kept the wooden symbols of his personal god and of his ancestral spirits. He worshipped them with sacrifices of kola nut, food and palm-wine, and offered prayers to them on behalf of himself, his three wives and eight children.

So when the daughter of Umuofia was killed in Mbaino, Ikemefuna came into Okonkwo's household. When Okonkwo brought him home that day he called his most senior wife and handed him over to her.

"He belongs to the clan," he told her. "So look after him."

"Is he staying long with us?" she asked.

"Do what you are told, woman," Okonkwo thundered, and stammered. "When did you become one of the *ndichie*[5] of Umuofia?"

And so Nwoye's mother took Ikemefuna to her hut and asked no more questions.

As for the boy himself, he was terribly afraid. He could not understand what was happening to him or what he had done. How could he know that his father had taken a hand in killing a daughter of Umuofia? All he knew was that a few men had arrived at their house, conversing with his father in low tones, and at the end he had been taken out and handed over to a stranger. His mother had wept bitterly, but he had been too surprised to weep. And so the stranger had brought him, and a girl, a long, long way from home, through lonely forest paths. He did not know who the girl was, and he never saw her again.

---

5. *ndichie*. Elders

Chapter Three

OKONKWO DID NOT have the start in life which many young men usually had. He did not inherit a barn from his father. There was no barn to inherit. The story was told in Umuofia of how his father, Unoka, had gone to consult the Oracle of the Hills and the Caves to find out why he always had a miserable harvest.

▶ Who is Agbala? Why do people come to see his priestess?

The Oracle was called Agbala,[1] and people came from far and near to consult it. They came when misfortune dogged their steps or when they had a dispute with their neighbors. They came to discover what the future held for them or to consult the spirits of their departed fathers.

The way into the shrine was a round hole at the side of a hill, just a little bigger than the round opening into a hen-house. Worshippers and those who came to seek knowledge from the god crawled on their belly through the hole and found themselves in a dark, endless space in the presence of Agbala. No one had ever beheld Agbala, except his priestess. But no one who had ever crawled into his awful shrine had come out without the fear of his power. His priestess stood by the sacred fire which she built in the heart of the cave and proclaimed the will of the god. The fire did not burn with a flame. The glowing logs only served to light up vaguely the dark figure of the priestess.

Sometimes a man came to consult the spirit of his dead father or relative. It was said that when such a spirit appeared, the man saw it vaguely in the darkness, but never heard its voice. Some people even said that they had heard the spirits flying and flapping their wings against the roof of the cave.

Many years ago when Okonkwo was still a boy his father, Unoka, had gone to <u>consult</u> Agbala. The priestess in those days was a woman called Chika. She was full of the power of her god, and she was greatly feared. Unoka stood before her and began his story.

"Every year," he said sadly, "before I put any crop in the earth, I sacrifice a cock to Ani, the owner of all land. It is the law of our fathers. I also kill a cock at the shrine of

---

1. **Agbala.** Igbo word for *woman;* the Oracle is masculine.

words for everyday use
con • sult (kən sult´) *vi.,* ask advice; refer to. *Because the singer's voice was important to her, she <u>consulted</u> a specialist when she contracted a sore throat.*

Ifejioku, the god of yams. I clear the bush and set fire to it when it is dry. I sow the yams when the first rain has fallen, and stake them when the young tendrils appear. I weed—"

"Hold your peace!" screamed the priestess, her voice terrible as it echoed through the dark void. "You have offended neither the gods nor your fathers. And when a man is at peace with his gods and his ancestors, his harvest will be good or bad according to the strength of his arm. You, Unoka, are known in all the clan for the weakness of your machete[2] and your hoe. When your neighbors go out with their axe to cut down virgin forests, you sow your yams on exhausted farms that take no labor to clear. They cross seven rivers to make their farms; you stay at home and offer sacrifices to a <u>reluctant</u> soil. Go home and work like a man."

◀ On what does the Oracle blame Unoka's lack of success?

Unoka was an ill-fated man. He had a bad *chi*[3] or personal god, and evil fortune followed him to the grave, or rather to his death, for he had no grave. He died of the swelling[4] which was an abomination to the earth goddess. When a man was afflicted with swelling in the stomach and the limbs he was not allowed to die in the house. He was carried to the Evil Forest and left there to die. There was the story of a very stubborn man who staggered back to his house and had to be carried again to the forest and tied to a tree. The sickness was an <u>abomination</u> to the earth, and so the victim could not be buried in her bowels. He died and rotted away above the earth, and was not given the first or the second burial. Such was Unoka's fate. When they carried him away, he took with him his flute.

With a father like Unoka, Okonkwo did not have the start in life which many young men had. He neither inherited a barn nor a title, nor even a young wife. But in spite of these disadvantages, he had begun even in his father's lifetime to lay the foundations of a prosperous future. It

---

2. **machete.** Large knife-like instrument used to cut plants and clear land

3. *chi.* In traditional Igbo belief, every man and woman has a personal deity that watches over him or her, the "chi." If one has a bad chi, one will have, inevitably, a bad fate.

4. **swelling.** Unoka suffered from edema, a swelling caused by the buildup of fluid in body tissues. Edema can be caused by various diseases and disorders, including heart or kidney disease.

---

words for everyday use

re • luc • tant (ri lək´ tənt) *adj.,* unwilling. *When my dog Fifi saw the deep snow, she became <u>reluctant</u> to go outside.*

a • bom • i • na • tion (ə bä´ mə nā´shən) *n.,* anything hateful or disgusting. *The new shopping mall next to the nature preserve is an <u>abomination</u>.*

was slow and painful. But he threw himself into it like one possessed. And indeed he was possessed by the fear of his father's contemptible life and shameful death.

There was a wealthy man in Okonkwo's village who had three huge barns, nine wives and thirty children. His name was Nwakibie and he had taken the highest but one title which a man could take in the clan. It was for this man that Okonkwo worked to earn his first seed yams.

He took a pot of palm-wine and a cock to Nwakibie. Two elderly neighbors were sent for, and Nwakibie's two grown-up sons were also present in his *obi*. He presented a kola nut and an alligator pepper, which was passed round for all to see and then returned to him. He broke it, saying: "We shall all live. We pray for life, children, a good harvest and happiness. You will have what is good for you and I will have what is good for me. Let the kite perch and let the eagle perch too. If one says no to the other, let his wing break."

After the kola nut had been eaten Okonkwo brought his palm-wine from the corner of the hut where it had been placed and stood it in the center of the group. He addressed Nwakibie, calling him "Our father."

"*Nna ayi,*" he said. "I have brought you this little kola. As our people say, a man who pays respect to the great paves the way for his own greatness. I have come to pay you my respects and also to ask a favor. But let us drink the wine first."

Everybody thanked Okonkwo and the neighbors brought out their drinking horns from the goatskin bags they carried. Nwakibie brought down his own horn, which was fastened to the rafters. The younger of his sons, who was also the youngest man in the group, moved to the center, raised the pot on his left knee and began to pour out the wine. The first cup went to Okonkwo, who must taste his wine before anyone else. Then the group drank, beginning with the eldest man. When everyone had drunk two or three horns, Nwakibie sent for his wives. Some of them were not at home and only four came in.

"Is Anasi not in?" he asked them. They said she was coming. Anasi was the first wife and the others could not drink before her, and so they stood waiting.

Anasi was a middle-aged woman, tall and strongly built. There was authority in her bearing and she looked every inch the ruler of the womenfolk in a large and prosperous family. She wore the anklet of her husband's titles, which the first wife alone could wear.

She walked up to her husband and accepted the horn from him. She then went down on one knee, drank a little and handed back the horn. She rose, called him by his name and went back to her hut. The other wives drank in the same way, in their proper order, and went away.

The men then continued their drinking and talking. Ogbuefi Idigo was talking about the palm-wine tapper, Obiako, who suddenly gave up his trade.

"There must be something behind it," he said, wiping the foam of wine from his moustache with the back of his left hand. "There must be a reason for it. A toad does not run in the daytime for nothing."

"Some people say the Oracle warned him that he would fall off a palm tree and kill himself," said Akukalia.

"Obiako has always been a strange one," said Nwakibie. "I have heard that many years ago, when his father had not been dead very long, he had gone to consult the Oracle. The Oracle said to him, 'Your dead father wants you to sacrifice a goat to him.' Do you know what he told the Oracle? He said, 'Ask my dead father if he ever had a fowl when he was alive.'" Everybody laughed heartily except Okonkwo, who laughed uneasily because, as the saying goes, an old woman is always uneasy when dry bones are mentioned in a proverb. Okonkwo remembered his own father.

At last the young man who was pouring out the wine held up half a horn of the thick, white <u>dregs</u> and said, "What we are eating is finished." "We have seen it," the others replied. "Who will drink the dregs?" he asked. "Whoever has a job in hand," said Idigo, looking at Nwakibie's elder son, Igwelo, with a mischievous twinkle in his eye.

Everybody agreed that Igwelo should drink the dregs. He accepted the half-full horn from his brother and drank it. As Idigo had said, Igwelo had a job in hand because he had married his first wife a month or two before. The thick dregs of palm-wine were supposed to be good for men who were going in to their wives.

After the wine had been drunk Okonkwo laid his difficulties before Nwakibie.

"I have come to you for help," he said. "Perhaps you can already guess what it is. I have cleared a farm but have no yams to sow. I know what it is to ask a man to trust

◀ For what does Okonkwo ask the prosperous farmer?

words for everyday use   **dregs** (dregz´) *n. pl.*, particles of solid matter that settle at the bottom of a liquid. *We drank the <u>dregs</u> of the orange juice, which were made up mostly of pulp that had sunk to the bottom.*

another with his yams, especially these days when young men are afraid of hard work. I am not afraid of work. The lizard that jumped from the high iroko tree to the ground said he would praise himself if no one else did. I began to fend for myself at an age when most people still suck at their mothers' breasts. If you give me some yam seeds I shall not fail you."

Nwakibie cleared his throat. "It pleases me to see a young man like you these days when our youth have gone so soft. Many young men have come to me to ask for yams but I have refused because I knew they would just dump them in the earth and leave them to be choked by weeds. When I say no to them they think I am hardhearted. But it is not so. Eneke the bird says that since men have learnt to shoot without missing, he has learnt to fly without perching. I have learnt to be stingy with my yams. But I can trust you. I know it as I look at you. As our fathers said, you can tell a ripe corn by its look. I shall give you twice four hundred yams. Go ahead and prepare your farm."

▶ Why is the farmer, Nwakibie, so generous to Okonkwo?

Okonkwo thanked him again and again and went home feeling happy. He knew that Nwakibie would not refuse him, but he had not expected he would be so generous. He had not hoped to get more than four hundred seeds. He would now have to make a bigger farm. He hoped to get another four hundred yams from one of his father's friends at Isiuzo.

Share-cropping was a very slow way of building up a barn of one's own. After all the toil one only got a third of the harvest. But for a young man whose father had no yams, there was no other way. And what made it worse in Okonkwo's case was that he had to support his mother and two sisters from his meager harvest. And supporting his mother also meant supporting his father. She could not be expected to cook and eat while her husband starved. And so at a very early age when he was striving desperately to build a barn through share-cropping Okonkwo was also fending for his father's house. It was like pouring grains of corn into a bag full of holes. His mother and sisters worked hard enough, but they grew women's crops, like coco-yams, beans and cassava. Yam, the king of crops, was a man's crop.[5]

▶ How is labor divided among the villagers?

The year that Okonkwo took eight hundred seed-yams from Nwakibie was the worst year in living memory.

---

5. **man's crop.** In many traditional cultures, the labor of men, women, and children is specialized. The author is reporting, not endorsing, such a division of labor along gender lines.

Nothing happened at its proper time; it was either too early or too late. It seemed as if the world had gone mad. The first rains were late, and, when they came, lasted only a brief moment. The blazing sun returned, more fierce than it had ever been known, and scorched all the green that had appeared with the rains. The earth burned like hot coals and roasted all the yams that had been sown. Like all good farmers, Okonkwo had begun to sow with the first rains. He had sown four hundred seeds when the rains dried up and the heat returned. He watched the sky all day for signs of rain-clouds and lay awake all night. In the morning he went back to his farm and saw the withering tendrils. He had tried to protect them from the smoldering earth by making rings of thick sisal leaves around them. But by the end of the day the sisal rings were burnt dry and grey. He changed them every day, and prayed that the rain might fall in the night. But the <u>drought</u> continued for eight market weeks and the yams were killed.

Some farmers had not planted their yams yet. They were the lazy easy-going ones who always put off clearing their farms as long as they could. This year they were the wise ones. They sympathized with their neighbors with much shaking of the head, but inwardly they were happy for what they took to be their own foresight.

Okonkwo planted what was left of his seed-yams when the rains finally returned. He had one <u>consolation</u>. The yams he had sown before the drought were his own, the harvest of the previous year. He still had the eight hundred from Nwakibie and the four hundred from his father's friend. So he would make a fresh start.

But the year had gone mad. Rain fell as it had never fallen before. For days and nights together it poured down in violent torrents, and washed away the yam heaps. Trees were uprooted and deep gorges appeared everywhere. Then the rain became less violent. But it went on from day to day without a pause. The spell of sunshine which always came in the middle of the wet season did not appear. The yams put on <u>luxuriant</u> green leaves, but every farmer knew that without sunshine the tubers would not grow.

That year the harvest was sad, like a funeral, and many farmers wept as they dug up the miserable and rotting

words for everyday use

drought (drout´) n., long period of dry weather. *The <u>drought</u> was ended by a torrential rain.*

con • so • la • tion (kän´sə lā´shən) n., comfort; solace. *Receiving a picture of his* departed friend in the mail was little <u>consolation</u> to Robert.

lux • u • ri • ant (ləg zhür´ē ənt) adj., growing in great abundance. *Have you seen the <u>luxuriant</u> growth of weeds in the flower bed?*

yams. One man tied his cloth to a tree branch and hanged himself.

▶ What sort of spirit does Okonkwo have? Is he easily defeated? Explain.

Okonkwo remembered that tragic year with a cold shiver throughout the rest of his life. It always surprised him when he thought of it later that he did not sink under the load of despair. He knew he was a fierce fighter, but that year had been enough to break the heart of a lion.

"Since I survived that year," he always said, "I shall survive anything." He put it down to his inflexible will.

His father, Unoka, who was then an ailing man, had said to him during that terrible harvest month: "Do not despair. I know you will not despair. You have a manly and a proud heart. A proud heart can survive a general failure because such a failure does not prick its pride. It is more difficult and more bitter when a man fails *alone.*"

Unoka was like that in his last days. His love of talk had grown with age and sickness. It tried Okonkwo's patience beyond words.

Chapter Four

"LOOKING AT A king's mouth," said an old man, "one would think he never sucked at his mother's breast." He was talking about Okonkwo, who had risen so suddenly from great poverty and misfortune to be one of the lords of the clan. The old man bore no ill-will towards Okonkwo. Indeed he respected him for his industry and success. But he was struck, as most people were, by Okonkwo's brusqueness in dealing with less successful men. Only a week ago a man had contradicted him at a kindred meeting which they held to discuss the next ancestral feast. Without looking at the man Okonkwo had said: "This meeting is for men." The man who had contradicted him had no titles. That was why he had called him a woman. Okonkwo knew how to kill a man's spirit.

Everybody at the kindred meeting took sides with Osugo when Okonkwo called him a woman. The oldest man present said sternly that those whose palm-kernels were cracked for them by a benevolent spirit should not forget to be humble. Okonkwo said he was sorry for what he had said, and the meeting continued.

But it was really not true that Okonkwo's palm-kernels had been cracked for him by a benevolent spirit. He had cracked them himself. Anyone who knew his grim struggle against poverty and misfortune could not say he had been lucky. If ever a man deserved his success, that man was Okonkwo. At an early age he had achieved fame as the greatest wrestler in all the land. That was not luck. At the most one could say that his *chi* or personal god was good. But the Ibo people have a proverb that when a man says yes his *chi* says yes also. Okonkwo said yes very strongly; so his *chi* agreed. And not only his *chi* but his clan too, because it judged a man by the work of his hands. That was why Okonkwo had been chosen by the nine villages to carry a message of war to their enemies unless they agreed to give up a young man and a virgin to atone for the murder of Udo's wife. And such was the deep fear that their enemies had for Umuofia that they treated Okonkwo like a king and brought him a virgin who was given to Udo as wife, and the lad Ikemefuna.

◀ *Why does Okonkwo deserve his success?*

The elders of the clan had decided that Ikemefuna should be in Okonkwo's care for a while. But no one thought it would be as long as three years. They seemed to forget all about him as soon as they had taken the decision.

At first Ikemefuna was very much afraid. Once or twice he tried to run away, but he did not know where to begin. He thought of his mother and his three-year-old sister and wept bitterly. Nwoye's mother was very kind to him and treated him as one of her own children. But all he said was: "When shall I go home?" When Okonkwo heard that he would not eat any food he came into the hut with a big stick in his hand and stood over him while he swallowed his yams, trembling. A few moments later he went behind the hut and began to vomit painfully. Nwoye's mother went to him and placed her hands on his chest and on his back. He was ill for three market weeks, and when he recovered he seemed to have overcome his great fear and sadness.

He was by nature a very lively boy and he gradually became popular in Okonkwo's household, especially with the children. Okonkwo's son, Nwoye, who was two years younger, became quite inseparable from him because he seemed to know everything. He could fashion out flutes from bamboo stems and even from the elephant grass. He knew the names of all the birds and could set clever traps for the little bush rodents. And he knew which trees made the strongest bows.

Even Okonkwo himself became very fond of the boy—inwardly of course. Okonkwo never showed any emotion openly, unless it be the emotion of anger. To show affection was a sign of weakness; the only thing worth demonstrating was strength. He therefore treated Ikemefuna as he treated everybody else—with a heavy hand. But there was no doubt that he liked the boy. Sometimes when he went to big village meetings or <u>communal</u> ancestral feasts he allowed Ikemefuna to accompany him, like a son, carrying his stool and his goatskin bag. And, indeed, Ikemefuna called him father.

Ikemefuna came to Umuofia at the end of the carefree season between harvest and planting. In fact he recovered from his illness only a few days before the Week of Peace began. And that was also the year Okonkwo broke the peace, and was punished, as was the custom, by Ezeani, the priest of the earth goddess.

▶ *How do Okonkwo and Ikemefuna treat each other?*
What relationship is developing between them?

words for everyday use
com • mu • nal (kə myü´nəl) *adj.*, shared by a group or community. *The waiters in the restaurant put all their tips in a <u>communal</u> pot and then divided them up evenly at the end of the night.*

Okonkwo was provoked to justifiable anger by his youngest wife, who went to plait her hair at her friend's house and did not return early enough to cook the afternoon meal. Okonkwo did not know at first that she was not at home. After waiting in vain for the dish he went to her hut to see what she was doing. There was nobody in the hut and the fireplace was cold.

"Where is Ojiugo?" he asked his second wife, who came out of her hut to draw water from a gigantic pot in the shade of a small tree in the middle of the compound.

"She has gone to plait her hair."

Okonkwo bit his lips as anger welled up within him.

"Where are her children? Did she take them?" he asked with unusual coolness and restraint.

"They are here," answered his first wife, Nwoye's mother. Okonkwo bent down and looked into her hut. Ojiugo's children were eating with the children of his first wife.

"Did she ask you to feed them before she went?"

"Yes," lied Nwoye's mother, trying to minimize Ojiugo's thoughtlessness.

Okonkwo knew she was not speaking the truth. He walked back to his *obi* to wait Ojiugo's return. And when she returned he beat her very heavily.[1] In his anger he had forgotten that it was the Week of Peace. His first two wives ran out in great alarm pleading with him that it was the sacred week. But Okonkwo was not the man to stop beating somebody half-way through, not even for fear of a goddess.

◀ What offense does Okonkwo commit? Why?

Okonkwo's neighbors heard his wife crying and sent their voices over the compound walls to ask what was the matter. Some of them came over to see for themselves. It was unheard of to beat somebody during the sacred week.

Before it was dusk Ezeani, who was the priest of the earth goddess, Ani, called on Okonkwo in his *obi*. Okonkwo brought out a kola nut and placed it before the priest.

"Take away your kola nut. I shall not eat in the house of a man who has no respect for our gods and ancestors."

Okonkwo tried to explain to him what his wife had done, but Ezeani seemed to pay no attention. He held a

---

1. *Things Fall Apart* chronicles the destruction of a traditional way of life, many parts of which were worth preserving; however, Achebe is a realist, and he does not shrink from depicting the darker side of life, such as the mistreatment of women. Himself a supporter of feminism, Achebe describes Okonkwo's mistreatment of his wives both because he wishes to give an unsentimentalized portrayal of Igbo life and because he wishes to illustrate Okonkwo's basic personality flaw—his need to show strength and dominance.

▶ How are people supposed to act during the Week of Peace?

▶ What awful consequences might the clan suffer as a result of Okonkwo's actions?

short staff in his hand which he brought down on the floor to emphasize his points.

"Listen to me," he said when Okonkwo had spoken. "You are not a stranger in Umuofia. You know as well as I do that our forefathers ordained that before we plant any crops in the earth we should observe a week in which a man does not say a harsh word to his neighbor. We live in peace with our fellows to honor our great goddess of the earth without whose blessing our crops will not grow. You have committed a great evil." He brought down his staff heavily on the floor. "Your wife was at fault, but even if you came into your *obi* and found her lover on top of her, you would still have committed a great evil to beat her." His staff came down again. "The evil you have done can ruin the whole clan. The earth goddess whom you have insulted may refuse to give us her increase, and we shall all perish." His tone now changed from anger to command. "You will bring to the shrine of Ani tomorrow one she-goat, one hen, a length of cloth and a hundred cowries." He rose and left the hut.

Okonkwo did as the priest said. He also took with him a pot of palm-wine. Inwardly, he was repentant. But he was not the man to go about telling his neighbors that he was in error. And so people said he had no respect for the gods of the clan. His enemies said his good fortune had gone to his head. They called him the little bird *nza* who so far forgot himself after a heavy meal that he challenged his *chi*.

No work was done during the Week of Peace. People called on their neighbors and drank palm-wine. This year they talked of nothing else but the *nso-ani*[2] which Okonkwo had committed. It was the first time for many years that a man had broken the sacred peace. Even the oldest men could only remember one or two other occasions somewhere in the dim past.

Ogbuefi Ezeudu, who was the oldest man in the village, was telling two other men who came to visit him that the punishment for breaking the Peace of Ani had become very mild in their clan.

"It has not always been so," he said. "My father told me that he had been told that in the past a man who broke the

---

2. *nso-ani.* Offense against the earth goddess

words for everyday use   **or • dain** (or dān´) *vt.,* establish; order; decree. *The king ordained that his son's birthday would be a national holiday.*

peace was dragged on the ground through the village until he died. But after a while this custom was stopped because it spoilt the peace which it was meant to preserve."

"Somebody told me yesterday," said one of the younger men, "that in some clans it is an abomination for a man to die during the Week of Peace."

"It is indeed true," said Ogbuefi Ezeudu. "They have that custom in Obodoani. If a man dies at this time he is not buried but cast into the Evil Forest. It is a bad custom which these people observe because they lack understanding. They throw away large numbers of men and women without burial. And what is the result? Their clan is full of the evil spirits of these unburied dead, hungry to do harm to the living."

After the Week of Peace every man and his family began to clear the bush to make new farms. The cut bush was left to dry and fire was then set to it. As the smoke rose into the sky kites appeared from different directions and hovered over the burning field in silent <u>valediction</u>. The rainy season was approaching when they would go away until the dry season returned.

Okonkwo spent the next few days preparing his seed-yams. He looked at each yam carefully to see whether it was good for sowing. Sometimes he decided that a yam was too big to be sown as one seed and he split it deftly along its length with his sharp knife. His eldest son, Nwoye, and Ikemefuna helped him by fetching the yams in long baskets from the barn and in counting the prepared seeds in groups of four hundred. Sometimes Okonkwo gave them a few yams each to prepare. But he always found fault with their effort, and he said so with much threatening.

◄ How does Okonkwo behave toward the boys? Why? What does he want them to do?

"Do you think you are cutting up yams for cooking?" he asked Nwoye. "If you split another yam of this size, I shall break your jaw. You think you are still a child. I began to own a farm at your age. And you," he said to Ikemefuna, "do you not grow yams where you come from?"

Inwardly Okonkwo knew that the boys were still too young to understand fully the difficult art of preparing seed-yams. But he thought that one could not begin too early. Yam stood for manliness, and he who could feed his family on yams from one harvest to another was a very great

---

words for everyday use

val • e • dic • tion (val´ə dik´shən) *n.*, farewell. *Before departing from his troops after the war, the general delivered a stirring <u>valediction</u>.*

man indeed. Okonkwo wanted his son to be a great farmer and a great man. He would stamp out the disquieting signs of laziness which he thought he already saw in him.

"I will not have a son who cannot hold up his head in the gathering of the clan. I would sooner strangle him with my own hands. And if you stand staring at me like that," he swore, "Amadiora[3] will break your head for you!"

Some days later, when the land had been moistened by two or three heavy rains, Okonkwo and his family went to the farm with baskets of seed-yams, their hoes and machetes, and the planting began. They made single mounds of earth in straight lines all over the field and sowed the yams in them.

Yam, the king of crops, was a very exacting king. For three or four moons it demanded hard work and constant attention from cock-crow till the chickens went back to roost. The young tendrils were protected from earth-heat with rings of sisal leaves. As the rains became heavier the women planted maize, melons and beans between the yam mounds. The yams were then staked, first with little sticks and later with tall and big tree branches. The women weeded the farm three times at definite periods in the life of the yams, neither early nor late.

And now the rains had really come, so heavy and persistent that even the village rain-maker no longer claimed to be able to intervene. He could not stop the rain now, just as he would not attempt to start it in the heart of the dry season, without serious danger to his own health. The personal dynamism required to counter the forces of these extremes of weather would be far too great for the human frame.

And so nature was not interfered with in the middle of the rainy season. Sometimes it poured down in such thick sheets of water that earth and sky seemed merged in one grey wetness. It was then uncertain whether the low rumbling of Amadiora's thunder came from above or below. At such times, in each of the countless thatched huts of Umuofia, children sat around their mother's cooking fire telling stories, or with their father in his *obi* warming them-

---

3. **Amadiora.** Goddess of the sky, thunder, and rain

words for everyday use

dy • na • mism (dī´nə miz´əm) *n.*, energy. *The speaker moved about the stage and spoke passionately, stirring the audience with her dynamism.*

selves from a log fire, roasting and eating maize. It was a brief resting period between the exacting and <u>arduous</u> planting season and the equally exacting but light-hearted month of harvests.

Ikemefuna had begun to feel like a member of Okonkwo's family. He still thought about his mother and his three-year-old sister, and he had moments of sadness and depression. But he and Nwoye had become so deeply attached to each other that such moments became less frequent and less poignant. Ikemefuna had an endless stock of folk tales. Even those which Nwoye knew already were told with a new freshness and the local flavor of a different clan. Nwoye remembered this period very vividly till the end of his life. He even remembered how he had laughed when Ikemefuna told him that the proper name for a corn-cob with only a few scattered grains was *eze-agadi-nwayi,* or the teeth of an old woman. Nwoye's mind had gone immediately to Nwayieke, who lived near the udala tree. She had about three teeth and was always smoking her pipe.

◀ *How do Nwoye and Ikemefuna feel toward each other?*

Gradually the rains became lighter and less frequent, and earth and sky once again became separate. The rain fell in thin, slanting showers through sunshine and quiet breeze. Children no longer stayed indoors but ran about singing:

> *"The rain is falling, the sun is shining,*
> *Alone Nnadi is cooking and eating."*

Nwoye always wondered who Nnadi was and why he should live all by himself, cooking and eating. In the end he decided that Nnadi must live in that land of Ikemefuna's favorite story where the ant holds his court in splendor and the sands dance forever.

words for everyday use

ar • du • ous (är´jü əs) *adj.,* hard to accomplish; difficult; strenuous. *Have you ever undertaken the <u>arduous</u> task of canoeing upstream against a swift current?*

Chapter Five

THE FEAST OF the New Yam was approaching and Umuofia was in a festival mood. It was an occasion for giving thanks to Ani, the earth goddess and the source of all fertility. Ani played a greater part in the life of the people than any other deity. She was the ultimate judge of morality and conduct. And what was more, she was in close communion with the departed fathers of the clan whose bodies had been committed to earth.

▶ What is the purpose of the Feast of the New Yam?

The Feast of the New Yam was held every year before the harvest began, to honor the earth goddess and the ancestral spirits of the clan. New yams could not be eaten until some had first been offered to these powers. Men and women, young and old, looked forward to the New Yam Festival because it began the season of plenty—the new year. On the last night before the festival, yams of the old year were all disposed of by those who still had them. The new year must begin with tasty, fresh yams and not the shrivelled and <u>fibrous</u> crop of the previous year. All cooking-pots, calabashes[1] and wooden bowls were thoroughly washed, especially the wooden mortar in which yam was pounded. Yam foo-foo[2] and vegetable soup was the chief food in the celebration. So much of it was cooked that, no matter how heavily the family ate or how many friends and relations they invited from neighboring villages, there was always a huge quantity of food left over at the end of the day. The story was always told of a wealthy man who set before his guests a mound of foo-foo so high that those who sat on one side could not see what was happening on the other, and it was not until late in the evening that one of them saw for the first time his in-law who had arrived during the course of the meal and had fallen to on the opposite side. It was only then that they exchanged greetings and shook hands over what was left of the food.

The New Yam Festival was thus an occasion for joy throughout Umuofia. And every man whose arm was strong, as the Ibo people say, was expected to invite large

---

1. **calabashes.** Gourds or shells used as bottles or dippers
2. **foo-foo.** Pounded yam

words for everyday use   fi • brous (fī´brəs) *adj.,* tough; stringy. *The pumpkin was filled with seeds and some sort of* <u>*fibrous*</u>*, or stringy, material that was white and wet.*

numbers of guests from far and wide. Okonkwo always asked his wives' relations, and since he now had three wives his guests would make a fairly big crowd.

But somehow Okonkwo could never become as enthusiastic over feasts as most people. He was a good eater and he could drink one or two fairly big gourds of palm-wine. But he was always uncomfortable sitting around for days waiting for a feast or getting over it. He would be very much happier working on his farm.

◀ What preparations do Okonkwo's wives and children make for the festival?

The festival was now only three days away. Okonkwo's wives had scrubbed the walls and the huts with red earth until they reflected light. They had then drawn patterns on them in white, yellow and dark green. They then set about painting themselves with cam wood and drawing beautiful black patterns on their stomachs and on their backs. The children were also decorated, especially their hair, which was shaved in beautiful patterns. The three women talked excitedly about the relations who had been invited, and the children <u>reveled</u> in the thought of being spoilt by these visitors from mother-land. Ikemefuna was equally excited. The New Yam Festival seemed to him to be a much bigger event here than in his own village, a place which was already becoming remote and vague in his imagination.

◀ Why is Okonkwo angry?

And then the storm burst. Okonkwo, who had been walking about aimlessly in his compound in suppressed anger, suddenly found an outlet.

"Who killed this banana tree?" he asked.

A hush fell on the compound immediately.

"Who killed this tree? Or are you all deaf and dumb?"

As a matter of fact the tree was very much alive. Okonkwo's second wife had merely cut a few leaves off it to wrap some food, and she said so. Without further argument Okonkwo gave her a sound beating and left her and her only daughter weeping. Neither of the other wives dared to interfere beyond an occasional and <u>tentative</u>, "It is enough, Okonkwo," pleaded from a reasonable distance.

His anger thus satisfied, Okonkwo decided to go out hunting. He had an old rusty gun made by a clever blacksmith who had come to live in Umuofia long ago. But although Okonkwo was a great man whose prowess was universally acknowledged, he was not a hunter. In fact he had

words for everyday use

rev • el (rev´əl) vi., take intense pleasure. *The students* <u>reveled</u> *in their day off.*

ten • ta • tive (ten´tə tiv) adj., timid; uncertain. *Our* <u>tentative</u> *plan is to wait until the snow melts and then to try to hike back down the mountain, but we shall have to alter that plan if the weather stays cold.*

▶ *What does Okonkwo do in his anger?*

not killed a rat with his gun. And so when he called Ikemefuna to fetch his gun, the wife who had just been beaten murmured something about guns that never shot. Unfortunately for her, Okonkwo heard it and ran madly into his room for the loaded gun, ran out again and aimed at her as she clambered over the dwarf wall of the barn. He pressed the trigger and there was a loud report accompanied by the wail of his wives and children. He threw down the gun and jumped into the barn, and there lay the woman, very much shaken and frightened but quite unhurt. He heaved a heavy sigh and went away with the gun.

In spite of this incident the New Yam Festival was celebrated with great joy in Okonkwo's household. Early that morning as he offered a sacrifice of new yam and palm-oil to his ancestors he asked them to protect him, his children and their mothers in the new year.

As the day wore on his in-laws arrived from three surrounding villages, and each party brought with them a huge pot of palm-wine. And there was eating and drinking till night, when Okonkwo's in-laws began to leave for their homes.

The second day of the new year was the day of the great wrestling match between Okonkwo's village and their neighbors. It was difficult to say which the people enjoyed more—the feasting and fellowship of the first day or the wrestling contest of the second. But there was one woman who had no doubt whatever in her mind. She was Okonkwo's second wife, Ekwefi, whom he nearly shot. There was no festival in all the seasons of the year which gave her as much pleasure as the wrestling match. Many years ago when she was the village beauty Okonkwo had won her heart by throwing the Cat in the greatest contest within living memory. She did not marry him because he was too poor to pay her bride-price. But a few years later she ran away from her husband and came to live with Okonkwo. All this happened many years ago. Now Ekwefi was a woman of forty-five who had suffered a great deal in her time. But her love of wrestling contests was still as strong as it was thirty years ago.

It was not yet noon on the second day of the New Yam Festival. Ekwefi and her only daughter, Ezinma, sat near the fireplace waiting for the water in the pot to boil. The fowl Ekwefi had just killed was in the wooden mortar. The water began to boil, and in one deft movement she lifted the pot from the fire and poured the boiling water on to the fowl. She put back the empty pot on the circular pad in the corner, and looked at her palms, which were black with soot. Ezinma was always surprised that her mother could lift a pot from the fire with her bare hands.

"Ekwefi," she said, "is it true that when people are grown up, fire does not burn them?" Ezinma, unlike most children, called her mother by her name.

"Yes," replied Ekwefi, too busy to argue. Her daughter was only ten years old but she was wiser than her years.

"But Nwoye's mother dropped her pot of hot soup the other day and it broke on the floor."

Ekwefi turned the hen over in the mortar and began to pluck the feathers.

"Ekwefi," said Ezinma, who had joined in plucking the feathers, "my eyelid is twitching."

"It means you are going to cry," said her mother.

"No," Ezinma said, "it is this eyelid, the top one."

"That means you will see something."

"What will I see?" she asked.

"How can I know?" Ekwefi wanted her to work it out herself.

"Oho," said Ezinma at last. "I know what it is—the wrestling match."

At last the hen was plucked clean. Ekwefi tried to pull out the horny beak but it was too hard. She turned round on her low stool and put the beak in the fire for a few moments. She pulled again and it came off.

"Ekwefi!" a voice called from one of the other huts. It was Nwoye's mother, Okonkwo's first wife.

"Is that me?" Ekwefi called back. That was the way people answered calls from outside. They never answered yes for fear it might be an evil spirit calling.

"Will you give Ezinma some fire to bring to me?" Her own children and Ikemefuna had gone to the stream.

Ekwefi put a few live coals into a piece of broken pot and Ezinma carried it across the clean-swept compound to Nwoye's mother.

"Thank you, Nma," she said. She was peeling new yarns, and in a basket beside her were green vegetables and beans.

"Let me make the fire for you," Ezinma offered.

"Thank you, Ezigbo," she said. She often called her Ezigbo, which means "the good one."

Ezinma went outside and brought some sticks from a huge bundle of firewood. She broke them into little pieces across the sole of her foot and began to build a fire, blowing it with her breath.

"You will blow your eyes out," said Nwoye's mother, looking up from the yams she was peeling. "Use the fan." She stood up and pulled out the fan which was fastened

◀ Traditional peoples often interpret commonplace events as signs. What interpretation is given to the twitching of Ezinma's eyelid?

◀ Why does Ekwefi answer as she does?

into one of the rafters. As soon as she got up, the trouble-some nanny-goat, which had been dutifully eating yam peelings, dug her teeth into the real thing, scooped out two mouthfuls and fled from the hut to chew the cud in the goats' shed. Nwoye's mother swore at her and settled down again to her peeling. Ezinma's fire was now sending up thick clouds of smoke. She went on fanning it until it burst into flames. Nwoye's mother thanked her and she went back to her mother's hut.

Just then the distant beating of drums began to reach them. It came from the direction of the *ilo,* the village playground. Every village had its own *ilo* which was as old as the village itself and where all the great ceremonies and dances took place. The drums beat the unmistakable wrestling dance—quick, light and gay, and it came floating on the wind.

Okonkwo cleared his throat and moved his feet to the beat of the drums. It filled him with fire as it had always done from his youth. He trembled with the desire to con-quer and subdue. It was like the desire for woman.

"We shall be late for the wrestling," said Ezinma to her mother.

"They will not begin until the sun goes down."

"But they are beating the drums."

"Yes. The drums begin at noon but the wrestling waits until the sun begins to sink. Go and see if your father has brought out yams for the afternoon."

"He has. Nwoye's mother is already cooking."

"Go and bring our own, then. We must cook quickly or we shall be late for the wrestling."

Ezinma ran in the direction of the barn and brought back two yams from the dwarf wall.

Ekwefi peeled the yams quickly. The troublesome nanny-goat sniffed about, eating the peelings. She cut the yams into small pieces and began to prepare a pottage,[3] using some of the chicken.

At that moment they heard someone crying just outside their compound. It was very much like Obiageli, Nwoye's sister.

"Is that not Obiageli weeping?" Ekwefi called across the yard to Nwoye's mother.

"Yes," she replied. "She must have broken her water-pot."

The weeping was now quite close and soon the chil-dren filed in, carrying on their heads various sizes of pots

---

3. **pottage.** Soup

suitable to their years. Ikemefuna came first with the biggest pot, closely followed by Nwoye and his two younger brothers. Obiageli brought up the rear, her face streaming with tears. In her hand was the cloth pad on which the pot should have rested on her head.

"What happened?" her mother asked, and Obiageli told her mournful story. Her mother consoled her and promised to buy her another pot.

Nwoye's younger brothers were about to tell their mother the true story of the accident when Ikemefuna looked at them sternly and they held their peace. The fact was that Obiageli had been making *inyanga*[4] with her pot. She had balanced it on her head, folded her arms in front of her and began to sway her waist like a grown-up young lady. When the pot fell down and broke she burst out laughing. She only began to weep when they got near the iroko tree outside their compound.

◀ How did Obiageli break her water pot?

The drums were still beating, persistent and unchanging. Their sound was no longer a separate thing from the living village. It was like the pulsation of its heart. It throbbed in the air, in the sunshine, and even in the trees, and filled the village with excitement.

Ekwefi ladled her husband's share of the pottage into a bowl and covered it. Ezinma took it to him in his *obi*.

Okonkwo was sitting on a goatskin already eating his first wife's meal. Obiageli, who had brought it from her mother's hut, sat on the floor waiting for him to finish. Ezinma placed her mother's dish before him and sat with Obiageli.

"Sit like a woman!" Okonkwo shouted at her. Ezinma brought her two legs together and stretched them in front of her.

"Father, will you go to see the wrestling?" Ezinma asked after a suitable interval.

"Yes," he answered. "Will you go?"

"Yes." And after a pause she said: "Can I bring your chair for you?"

"No, that is a boy's job." Okonkwo was specially fond of Ezinma. She looked very much like her mother, who was

◀ Why does Okonkwo show his fondness for Ezinma only on rare occasions?

---

4. **making *inyanga*.** Showing off

words for everyday use   pul • sa • tion (pul sā′shən) *n.*, rhythmic beating. *Through the walls of the auditorium, one could hear and feel the pulsation of the bass guitar.*

once the village beauty. But his fondness only showed on very rare occasions.

"Obiageli broke her pot today," Ezinma said.

"Yes, she has told me about it," Okonkwo said between mouthfuls.

"Father," said Obiageli, "people should not talk when they are eating or pepper may go down the wrong way."

"That is very true. Do you hear that, Ezinma? You are older than Obiageli but she has more sense."

He uncovered his second wife's dish and began to eat from it. Obiageli took the first dish and returned to her mother's hut. And then Nkechi came in, bringing the third dish. Nkechi was the daughter of Okonkwo's third wife.

In the distance the drums continued to beat.

Respond to the Selection

Imagine you were one of Okonkwo's children. How would you feel about your father, and why? What would you want him to change about his behavior?

Investigate, Inquire, and Imagine

Recall: GATHERING FACTS

1a. What accomplishments have helped to make Okonkwo a great man of the village? Okonkwo has "a slight stammer." What does he do when he cannot "get his words out quickly enough"?

2a. How does Ikemefuna come to live in Okonkwo's compound? What offense was committed by people in the village of Mbaino?

3a. What does Okonkwo do during the Week of Peace? Who visits him as a result? What penalty must Okonkwo pay for breaking the peace?

4a. Describe the living arrangement of a typical Igbo family in Umuofia. What work are the men responsible for? What work are the women responsible for?

Interpret: FINDING MEANING

→ 1b. How would you describe Okonkwo's personality? What are his positive and negative character traits?

→ 2b. How would you describe Okonkwo's relationships with his wives and children? What is revealed about Okonkwo by his actions toward Nwoye, Ezinma, Ikemefuna, and his wives?

→ 3b. Why is the priest worried about Okonkwo causing a disturbance during the Week of Peace?

→ 4b. How is a typical Igbo family different from a typical family of your own culture? In most Western countries today, men and women are treated equally under the law. In the United States, for example, the law requires that women and men receive equal pay for equal work. Is equality among men and women part of the traditional culture described in this novel? Explain.

Analyze: Taking Things Apart

5a. Compare and contrast Okonkwo with his father, Unoka. Why does Okonkwo feel as he does toward his father? Which man do you think understands more about living a good life?

Synthesize: Bringing Things Together

5b. Okonkwo spends much of his time attempting to prove that he is a strong, resourceful man. In what ways is he actually quite weak? What does he fear?

Evaluate: Making Judgments

6a. Okonkwo is admired by the people of Umuofia. Is he a great man, in your opinion? Consider how he gained his success as well as how he behaves as a husband, father, and citizen of Umuofia. What about him do you admire? What do you dislike?

Extend: Connecting Ideas

6b. Sometimes people from different cultures have a very difficult time understanding one another. What parts of the culture of the Igbo village of Umuofia are very different from the culture in which you live? What parts of the culture are attractive to you? What parts are not appealing to you? Why?

Understanding Literature

CHARACTERIZATION. **Characterization** is the use of literary techniques to create a character. Writers use three major techniques to create characters: direct description, portrayal of characters' behavior, and representations of characters' internal states. In chapters 1–5, Chinua Achebe uses all three techniques to create the character of Okonkwo. He describes Okonkwo's appearance, habits, dress, background, personality, motivations, and so on; portrays Okonkwo's behavior with his family and in the village; and reveals Okonkwo's private thoughts and feelings. Create a character chart like the one below to show examples of all three techniques. Sample answers are provided.

Direct Description of Okonkwo	Portrayal of Okonkwo's Behavior	Portrayal of Okonkwo's Internal States
Okonkwo is "tall and huge." He often pounces on people.	He insults a man at the kindred meeting by calling him a woman.	Inwardly, Okonkwo feels sorry for breaking the Week of Peace.

FORESHADOWING. **Foreshadowing** is the act of presenting materials that hint at events to occur later in a story. What is foreshadowed with regard to Ikemefuna at the end of chapter 1?

PROVERB. A **proverb,** or **adage,** is a traditional saying, such as "You can lead a horse to water, but you can't make it drink." Proverbs play an important role in the culture of Umuofia. In the words of the novel, "Among the Ibo the art of conversation is regarded very highly, and proverbs are the palm-oil with which words are eaten." Explain the meanings of the following proverbs from chapters 1 through 5:

a. He who brings kola brings life. (chapter 1)
b. [T]he sun will shine on those who stand before it shines on those who kneel under them. (chapter 1)
c. [I]f a child washed his hands he could eat with kings. (chapter 1)
d. Let the kite perch and let the eagle perch too. If one says no to the other, let his wing break. (chapter 3)
e. [A] man who pays respect to the great paves the way for his own greatness. (chapter 3)
f. A toad does not run in the daytime for nothing. (chapter 3)
g. [A]n old woman is always uneasy when dry bones are mentioned in a proverb. (chapter 3)
h. The lizard that jumped from the high iroko tree to the ground said he would praise himself if no one else did. (chapter 3)
i. Looking at a king's mouth . . . one would think he never sucked at his mother's breast. (chapter 4)
j. [T]hose whose palm-kernels were cracked for them by a benevolent spirit should not forget to be humble. (chapter 4)
k. When a man says yes his *chi* says yes also. (chapter 4)
l. [T]he little bird *nza* . . . so far forgot himself after a heavy meal that he challenged his *chi*. (chapter 4)

Chapter Six

THE WHOLE VILLAGE turned out on the *ilo,* men, women and children. They stood round in a huge circle leaving the center of the playground free. The elders and grandees[1] of the village sat on their own stools brought there by their young sons or slaves. Okonkwo was among them. All others stood except those who came early enough to secure places on the few stands which had been built by placing smooth logs on forked pillars.

The wrestlers were not there yet and the drummers held the field. They too sat just in front of the huge circle of spectators, facing the elders. Behind them was the big and ancient silk-cotton tree which was sacred. Spirits of good children lived in that tree waiting to be born. On ordinary days young women who desired children came to sit under its shade.

▶ What do the Igbo believe about the silk-cotton tree?

There were seven drums and they were arranged according to their sizes in a long wooden basket. Three men beat them with sticks, working feverishly from one drum to another. They were possessed by the spirit of the drums.

The young men who kept order on these occasions dashed about, consulting among themselves and with the leaders of the two wrestling teams, who were still outside the circle, behind the crowd. Once in a while two young men carrying palm fronds ran round the circle and kept the crowd back by beating the ground in front of them or, if they were stubborn, their legs and feet.

At last the two teams danced into the circle and the crowd roared and clapped. The drums rose to a frenzy. The people surged forwards. The young men who kept order flew around, waving their palm fronds. Old men nodded to the beat of the drums and remembered the days when they wrestled to its intoxicating rhythm.

The contest began with boys of fifteen or sixteen. There were only three such boys in each team. They were not the real wrestlers; they merely set the scene. Within a short time the first two bouts were over. But the third created a big sensation even among the elders who did not usually show their excitement so openly. It was as quick as the other two, perhaps even quicker. But very few people had ever seen that kind of wrestling before. As soon as the two boys closed in, one of them did something which no one could describe because it had been as quick as a flash. And

---

1. **grandees.** Important persons, dignitaries

the other boy was flat on his back. The crowd roared and clapped and for a while drowned the frenzied drums. Okonkwo sprang to his feet and quickly sat down again. Three young men from the victorious boy's team ran forward, carried him shoulder-high and danced through the cheering crowd. Everybody soon knew who the boy was. His name was Maduka, the son of Obierika.

The drummers stopped for a brief rest before the real matches. Their bodies shone with sweat, and they took up fans and began to fan themselves. They also drank water from small pots and ate kola nuts. They became ordinary human beings again, talking and laughing among themselves and with others who stood near them. The air, which had been stretched taut with excitement, relaxed again. It was as if water had been poured on the tightened skin of a drum. Many people looked around, perhaps for the first time, and saw those who stood or sat next to them.

"I did not know it was you," Ekwefi said to the woman who had stood shoulder to shoulder with her since the beginning of the matches.

"I do not blame you," said the woman. "I have never seen such a large crowd of people. Is it true that Okonkwo nearly killed you with his gun?"

"It is true indeed, my dear friend. I cannot yet find a mouth with which to tell the story."

"Your *chi* is very much awake, my friend. And how is my daughter, Ezinma?"

◀ *What concern do Ekwefi and the woman have with regard to Ezinma?*

"She has been very well for some time now. Perhaps she has come to stay."

"I think she has. How old is she now?"

"She is about ten years old."

"I think she will stay. They usually stay if they do not die before the age of six."

"I pray she stays," said Ekwefi with a heavy sigh.

The woman with whom she talked was called Chielo. She was the priestess of Agbala, the Oracle of the Hills and the Caves. In ordinary life Chielo was a widow with two children. She was very friendly with Ekwefi and they shared a common shed in the market. She was particularly fond of Ekwefi's only daughter, Ezinma, whom she called "my daughter." Quite often she bought bean-cakes and gave Ekwefi some to take home to Ezinma. Anyone seeing Chielo in ordinary life would hardly believe she was the same person who prophesied when the spirit of Agbala was upon her.

◀ *Who is Chielo? What job does she have?*

The drummers took up their sticks again and the air shivered and grew tense like a tightened bow.

The two teams were ranged facing each other across the clear space. A young man from one team danced across the center to the other side and pointed at whomever he wanted to fight. They danced back to the center together and then closed in.

There were twelve men on each side and the challenge went from one side to the other. Two judges walked around the wrestlers and when they thought they were equally matched, stopped them. Five matches ended in this way. But the really exciting moments were when a man was thrown. The huge voice of the crowd then rose to the sky and in every direction. It was even heard in the surrounding villages.

The last match was between the leaders of the teams. They were among the best wrestlers in all the nine villages. The crowd wondered who would throw the other this year. Some said Okafo was the better man; others said he was not the equal of Ikezue. Last year neither of them had thrown the other even though the judges had allowed the contest to go on longer than was the custom. They had the same style and one saw the other's plans beforehand. It might happen again this year.

Dusk was already approaching when their contest began. The drums went mad and the crowds also. They surged forward as the two young men danced into the circle. The palm fronds were helpless in keeping them back.

Ikezue held out his right hand. Okafo seized it, and they closed in. It was a fierce contest. Ikezue strove to dig in his right heel behind Okafo so as to pitch him backwards in the clever *ege* style. But the one knew what the other was thinking. The crowd had surrounded and swallowed up the drummers, whose frantic rhythm was no longer a mere <u>disembodied</u> sound but the very heartbeat of the people.

The wrestlers were now almost still in each other's grip. The muscles on their arms and their thighs and on their backs stood out and twitched. It looked like an equal match. The two judges were already moving forward to separate them when Ikezue, now desperate, went down quickly on one knee in an attempt to fling his man back-

▶ What metaphor is used to describe the drums?

words for everyday use   **dis • em • bod • ied** (dis´ im bä´dēd) *adj.,* freed from bodily existence. *The swamp gas hovered over the marsh like a <u>disembodied</u> spirit.*

wards over his head. It was a sad miscalculation. Quick as the lightning of Amadiora, Okafo raised his right leg and swung it over his rival's head. The crowd burst into a thunderous roar. Okafo was swept off his feet by his supporters and carried home shoulderhigh. They sang his praise and the young women clapped their hands:

> *"Who will wrestle for our village?*
> > *Okafo will wrestle for our village.*
> *Has he thrown a hundred men?*
> > *He has thrown four hundred men.*
> *Has he thrown a hundred Cats?*
> > *He has thrown four hundred Cats.*
> *Then send him word to fight for us."*

Chapter Seven

▶ To what is Ikemefuna compared? How well has he adapted to his new home?

FOR THREE YEARS Ikemefuna lived in Okonkwo's household and the elders of Umuofia seemed to have forgotten about him. He grew rapidly like a yam tendril in the rainy season, and was full of the sap of life. He had become wholly absorbed into his new family. He was like an elder brother to Nwoye, and from the very first seemed to have kindled a new fire in the younger boy. He made him feel grown-up; and they no longer spent the evenings in mother's hut while she cooked, but now sat with Okonkwo in his *obi*, or watched him as he tapped his palm tree for the evening wine. Nothing pleased Nwoye now more than to be sent for by his mother or another of his father's wives to do one of those difficult and masculine tasks in the home, like splitting wood, or pounding food. On receiving such a message through a younger brother or sister, Nwoye would <u>feign</u> annoyance and grumble aloud about women and their troubles.

▶ Why does Nwoye pretend to be annoyed? Of what is he secretly proud?

Okonkwo was inwardly pleased at his son's development, and he knew it was due to Ikemefuna. He wanted Nwoye to grow into a tough young man capable of ruling his father's household when he was dead and gone to join the ancestors. He wanted him to be a prosperous man, having enough in his barn to feed the ancestors with regular sacrifices. And so he was always happy when he heard him grumbling about women. That showed that in time he would be able to control his women-folk. No matter how prosperous a man was, if he was unable to rule his women and his children (and especially his women) he was not really a man.[1] He was like the man in the song who had ten and one wives and not enough soup for his foo-foo.

▶ What makes Okonkwo happy? Why?

So Okonkwo encouraged the boys to sit with him in his *obi*, and he told them stories of the land—masculine stories of violence and bloodshed. Nwoye knew that it was

▶ In what way does Okonkwo instruct the boys? Why does he do this? What does Nwoye prefer?

---

1. **no matter . . . really a man.** The patriarchal attitude held by Okonkwo was common in traditional African societies, as it was in Western culture throughout much of history. Today, however, many African societies encourage a more balanced relationship between the sexes.

---

words for everyday use   feign (fān´) *vt.,* pretend. *The child <u>feigned</u> sickness so that she could stay home from school.*

right to be masculine and to be violent, but somehow he still preferred the stories that his mother used to tell, and which she no doubt still told to her younger children—stories of the tortoise and his <u>wily</u> ways, and of the bird *eneke-nti-oba* who challenged the whole world to a wrestling contest and was finally thrown by the cat. He remembered the story she often told of the quarrel between Earth and Sky long ago, and how Sky withheld rain for seven years, until crops withered and the dead could not be buried because the hoes broke on the stony Earth. At last Vulture was sent to plead with Sky, and to soften his heart with a song of the suffering of the sons of men. Whenever Nwoye's mother sang this song he felt carried away to the distant scene in the sky where Vulture, Earth's emissary, sang for mercy. At last Sky was moved to pity, and he gave to Vulture rain wrapped in leaves of cocoyam. But as he flew home his long talon pierced the leaves and the rain fell as it had never fallen before. And so heavily did it rain on Vulture that he did not return to deliver his message but flew to a distant land, from where he had <u>espied</u> a fire. And when he got there he found it was a man making a sacrifice. He warmed himself in the fire and ate the entrails.

That was the kind of story that Nwoye loved. But he now knew that they were for foolish women and children, and he knew that his father wanted him to be a man. And so he feigned that he no longer cared for women's stories. And when he did this he saw that his father was pleased, and no longer rebuked him or beat him. So Nwoye and Ikemefuna would listen to Okonkwo's stories about tribal wars or how, years ago, he had stalked his victim, overpowered him and obtained his first human head. And as he told them of the past they sat in darkness or the dim glow of logs, waiting for the women to finish their cooking. When they finished, each brought her bowl of foo-foo and bowl of soup to her husband. An oil lamp was lit and Okonkwo tasted from each bowl, and then passed two shares to Nwoye and Ikemefuna.

In this way the moons and the seasons passed. And then the locusts came. It had not happened for many a long year. The elders said locusts came once in a generation,

---

words for everyday use

wil • y (wī´lē) *adj.*, sly; crafty. *The <u>wily</u> coyote finally captured the roadrunner.*

es • py (e spī´) *vt.*, catch sight of. *The eagle <u>espied</u> a mouse scurrying among the fallen leaves.*

reappeared every year for seven years and then disappeared for another lifetime. They went back to their caves in a distant land, where they were guarded by a race of stunted men. And then after another lifetime these men opened the caves again and the locusts came to Umuofia.

They came in the cold harmattan season after the harvests had been gathered, and ate up all the wild grass in the fields.

Okonkwo and the two boys were working on the red outer walls of the compound. This was one of the lighter tasks of the afterharvest season. A new cover of thick palm branches and palm leaves was set on the walls to protect them from the next rainy season. Okonkwo worked on the outside of the wall and the boys worked from within. There were little holes from one side to the other in the upper levels of the wall, and through these Okonkwo passed the rope, or *tie-tie,* to the boys and they passed it round the wooden stays and then back to him; and in this way the cover was strengthened on the wall.

The women had gone to the bush to collect firewood, and the little children to visit their playmates in the neighboring compounds. The harmattan was in the air and seemed to distill a hazy feeling of sleep on the world. Okonkwo and the boys worked in complete silence, which was only broken when a new palm frond was lifted on to the wall or when a busy hen moved dry leaves about in her ceaseless search for food.

And then quite suddenly a shadow fell on the world, and the sun seemed hidden behind a thick cloud. Okonkwo looked up from his work and wondered if it was going to rain at such an unlikely time of the year. But almost immediately a shout of joy broke out in all directions, and Umuofia, which had dozed in the noon-day haze, broke into life and activity.

"Locusts are descending," was joyfully chanted everywhere, and men, women and children left their work or their play and ran into the open to see the unfamiliar sight. The locusts had not come for many, many years, and only the old people had seen them before.

At first, a fairly small swarm came. They were the <u>harbingers</u> sent to survey the land. And then appeared on the horizon a slowly moving mass like a boundless sheet of black cloud drifting towards Umuofia. Soon it covered half the sky, and the solid mass was now broken by tiny eyes of light like shining star-dust. It was a tremendous sight, full of power and beauty.

Everyone was now about, talking excitedly and praying that the locusts should camp in Umuofia for the night. For although locusts had not visited Umuofia for many years, everybody knew by instinct that they were very good to eat. And at last the locusts did descend. They settled on every tree and on every blade of grass; they settled on the roofs and covered the bare ground. Mighty tree branches broke away under them, and the whole country became the brown-earth color of the vast, hungry swarm.

◀ Why are the people happy about the coming of the locusts?

Many people went out with baskets trying to catch them, but the elders counseled patience till nightfall. And they were right. The locusts settled in the bushes for the night and their wings became wet with dew. Then all Umuofia turned out in spite of the cold harmattan, and everyone filled his bags and pots with locusts. The next morning they were roasted in clay pots and then spread in the sun until they became dry and brittle. And for many days this rare food was eaten with solid palm-oil.

Okonkwo sat in his *obi* crunching happily with Ikemefuna and Nwoye, and drinking palm-wine <u>copiously</u>, when Ogbuefi Ezeudu came in. Ezeudu was the oldest man in this quarter of Umuofia. He had been a great and fearless warrior in his time, and was now <u>accorded</u> great respect in all the clan. He refused to join in the meal, and asked Okonkwo to have a word with him outside. And so they walked out together, the old man supporting himself with his stick. When they were out of ear-shot, he said to Okonkwo:

◀ Why is Ezeudu so well respected?

"That boy calls you father. Do not bear a hand in his death." Okonkwo was surprised, and was about to say something when the old man continued:

"Yes, Umuofia has decided to kill him. The Oracle of the Hills and the Caves has pronounced it. They will take him outside Umuofia as is the custom, and kill him there. But I want you to have nothing to do with it. He calls you his father."

◀ What has been decided by the Oracle of the Hills and the Caves? What does Ezeudu warn Okonkwo not to do?

---

words for everyday use

co • pi • ous • ly (kō′pē əs lē) *adv.*, abundantly; plentifully. *Water poured <u>copiously</u> from the fountain, filling the basin and overflowing into the street.*

ac • cord (ə kȯrd′) *vt.*, grant; give; allow. *Welcome our guest, and <u>accord</u> him all our hospitality.*

The next day a group of elders from all the nine villages of Umuofia came to Okonkwo's house early in the morning, and before they began to speak in low tones Nwoye and Ikemefuna were sent out. They did not stay very long, but when they went away Okonkwo sat still for a very long time supporting his chin in his palms. Later in the day he called Ikemefuna and told him that he was to be taken home the next day. Nwoye overheard it and burst into tears, whereupon his father beat him heavily. As for Ikemefuna, he was at a loss. His own home had gradually become very faint and distant. He still missed his mother and his sister and would be very glad to see them. But somehow he knew he was not going to see them. He remembered once when men had talked in low tones with his father; and it seemed now as if it was happening all over again.

Later, Nwoye went to his mother's hut and told her that Ikemefuna was going home. She immediately dropped the <u>pestle</u> with which she was grinding pepper, folded her arms across her breast and sighed, "Poor child."

The next day, the men returned with a pot of wine. They were all fully dressed as if they were going to a big clan meeting or to pay a visit to a neighboring village. They passed their cloths under the right arm-pit, and hung their goatskin bags and sheathed machetes over their left shoulders. Okonkwo got ready quickly and the party set out with Ikemefuna carrying the pot of wine. A deathly silence descended on Okonkwo's compound. Even the very little children seemed to know. Throughout that day Nwoye sat in his mother's hut and tears stood in his eyes.

At the beginning of their journey the men of Umuofia talked and laughed about the locusts, about their women, and about some <u>effeminate</u> men who had refused to come with them. But as they drew near to the outskirts of Umuofia silence fell upon them too.

The sun rose slowly to the center of the sky, and the dry, sandy footway began to throw up the heat that lay buried in it. Some birds chirruped in the forests around. The men trod dry leaves on the sand. All else was silent. Then from the distance came the faint beating of the *ekwe*. It rose and faded with the wind—a peaceful dance from a distant clan.

words for everyday use

pes • tle (pəs´təl) *n.*, tool for grinding or crushing. *The elderly man ground the corn with a mortar and <u>pestle</u> and then added lime juice to create corn tortillas.*

ef • fem • i • nate (e fem´ə nit) *adj.*, having female qualities. *In different cultures, different qualities are considered <u>effeminate</u>, or appropriate to women.*

"It is an *ozo*[2] dance," the men said among themselves. But no one was sure where it was coming from. Some said Ezimili, others Abame or Aninta.[3] They argued for a short while and fell into silence again, and the <u>elusive</u> dance rose and fell with the wind. Somewhere a man was taking one of the titles of his clan, with music and dancing and a great feast.

The footway had now become a narrow line in the heart of the forest. The short trees and sparse undergrowth which surrounded the men's village began to give way to giant trees and climbers which perhaps had stood from the beginning of things, untouched by the axe and the bush-fire. The sun breaking through their leaves and branches threw a pattern of light and shade on the sandy footway.

Ikemefuna heard a whisper close behind him and turned round sharply. The man who had whispered now called out aloud, urging the others to hurry up.

"We still have a long way to go," he said. Then he and another man went before Ikemefuna and set a faster pace.

Thus the men of Umuofia pursued their way, armed with sheathed machetes, and Ikemefuna, carrying a pot of palm-wine on his head, walked in their midst. Although he had felt uneasy at first, he was not afraid now. Okonkwo walked behind him. He could hardly imagine that Okonkwo was not his real father. He had never been fond of his real father, and at the end of three years he had become very distant indeed. But his mother and his three-year-old sister . . . of course she would not be three now, but six. Would he recognize her now? She must have grown quite big. How his mother would weep for joy, and thank Okonkwo for having looked after him so well and for bringing him back. She would want to hear everything that had happened to him in all these years. Could he remember them all? He would tell her about Nwoye and his mother, and about the locusts . . . Then quite suddenly a thought came upon him. His mother might be dead. He tried in vain to force the thought out of his mind. Then

◀ *Why is Ikemefuna not afraid? What feelings does he have toward Okonkwo?*

---

2. *ozo.* Title of honor among the Igbo
3. **Ezimili, . . . Abame . . . Aninta.** Neighboring villages

---

words for everyday use   e • lu • sive (ē lü´siv) *adj.,* hard to grasp. *Ponce de Leon searched for the Fountain of Youth, but, alas, it proved to be <u>elusive</u>.*

he tried to settle the matter the way he used to settle such matters when he was a little boy. He still remembered the song:

Eze elina, elina!
                    Sala
Eze ilikwa ya
Ikwaba akwa oligholi
Ebe Danda nechi eze
Ebe Uzuzu nete egwu
                    Sala

He sang it in his mind, and walked to its beat. If the song ended on his right foot, his mother was alive. If it ended on his left, she was dead. No, not dead, but ill. It ended on the right. She was alive and well. He sang the song again, and it ended on the left. But the second time did not count. The first voice gets to Chukwu, or God's house. That was a favorite saying of children. Ikemefuna felt like a child once more. It must be the thought of going home to his mother.

One of the men behind him cleared his throat. Ikemefuna looked back, and the man growled at him to go on and not stand looking back. The way he said it sent cold fear down Ikemefuna's back. His hands trembled vaguely on the black pot he carried. Why had Okonkwo withdrawn to the rear? Ikemefuna felt his legs melting under him. And he was afraid to look back.

▶ What does Okonkwo do? Why?

As the man who had cleared his throat drew up and raised his machete, Okonkwo looked away. He heard the blow. The pot fell and broke in the sand. He heard Ikemefuna cry, "My father, they have killed me!" as he ran toward him. Dazed with fear, Okonkwo drew his machete and cut him down. He was afraid of being thought weak.

▶ How does Nwoye feel about the death of Ikemefuna?

As soon as his father walked in, that night, Nwoye knew that Ikemefuna had been killed, and something seemed to give way inside him, like the snapping of a tightened bow. He did not cry. He just hung limp. He had had the same kind of feeling not long ago, during the last harvest season. Every child loved the harvest season. Those who were big enough to carry even a few yams in a tiny basket went with grown-ups to the farm. And if they could not help in digging up the yams, they could gather firewood together for roasting the ones that would be eaten there on the farm. This roasted yam soaked in red palm-oil and eaten in the open farm was sweeter than any meal at home. It was after such a day at the farm during the last harvest that Nwoye had felt for the first time a snapping inside him like the one he now felt. They were returning home with baskets of yams from a distant farm across the stream when they had heard the voice of an infant crying in the thick forest. A sudden hush had fallen on the women, who had been talking, and they had quickened their steps. Nwoye had heard that twins were put in earthenware pots and thrown away in the forest, but he had never yet come across them. A vague chill had descended on him and his head had seemed to swell, like a <u>solitary</u> walker at night who passes an evil spirit on the way. Then something had given way inside him. It descended on him again, this feeling, when his father walked in, that night after killing Ikemefuna.

◀ When did Nwoye first feel a "snapping" inside him? What caused the feeling?

words for everyday use

sol • i • tar • y (säl´ə ter´ē) adj., alone, single. *High atop a lookout station, the forest ranger keeps her <u>solitary</u> vigil.*

Chapter Eight

▶ How does the
death of Ikemefuna
affect Okonkwo?

OKONKWO DID NOT taste any food for two days after the death of Ikemefuna. He drank palm-wine from morning till night, and his eyes were red and fierce like the eyes of a rat when it was caught by the tail and dashed against the floor. He called his son, Nwoye, to sit with him in his *obi*. But the boy was afraid of him and slipped out of the hut as soon as he noticed him dozing.

He did not sleep at night. He tried not to think about Ikemefuna, but the more he tried the more he thought about him. Once he got up from bed and walked about his compound. But he was so weak that his legs could hardly carry him. He felt like a drunken giant walking with the limbs of a mosquito. Now and then a cold shiver descended on his head and spread down his body.

On the third day he asked his second wife, Ekwefi, to roast plantains[1] for him. She prepared it the way he liked— with slices of oil-bean and fish.

"You have not eaten for two days," said his daughter Ezinma when she brought the food to him. "So you must finish this." She sat down and stretched her legs in front of her. Okonkwo ate the food absent-mindedly. "She should have been a boy," he thought as he looked at his ten-year-old daughter. He passed her a piece of fish.

"Go and bring me some cold water," he said. Ezinma rushed out of the hut, chewing the fish, and soon returned with a bowl of cool water from the earthen pot in her mother's hut.

Okonkwo took the bowl from her and gulped the water down. He ate a few more pieces of plantain and pushed the dish aside.

"Bring me my bag," he asked, and Ezinma brought his goatskin bag from the far end of the hut. He searched in it for his snuff-bottle. It was a deep bag and took almost the whole length of his arm. It contained other things apart from his snuff-bottle. There was a drinking horn in it, and also a drinking gourd, and they knocked against each other as he searched. When he brought out the snuff-bottle he tapped it a few times against his knee-cap before taking out some snuff on the palm of his left hand. Then he remembered that he had not taken out his snuff-spoon. He searched his bag again and brought out a small, flat, ivory spoon, with which he carried the brown snuff to his nostrils.

---

1. **plantains.** Fruit related to the banana

Ezinma took the dish in one hand and the empty water bowl in the other and went back to her mother's hut. "She should have been a boy," Okonkwo said to himself again. His mind went back to Ikemefuna and he shivered. If only he could find some work to do he would be able to forget. But it was the season of rest between the harvest and the next planting season. The only work that men did at this time was covering the walls of their compound with new palm fronds. And Okonkwo had already done that. He had finished it on the very day the locusts came, when he had worked on one side of the wall and Ikemefuna and Nwoye on the other.

"When did you become a shivering old woman," Okonkwo asked himself, "you, who are known in all the nine villages for your <u>valor</u> in war? How can a man who has killed five men in battle fall to pieces because he has added a boy to their number? Okonkwo, you have become a woman indeed."

◄ Why is Okonkwo upset with himself?

He sprang to his feet, hung his goatskin bag on his shoulder and went to visit his friend, Obierika.

Obierika was sitting outside under the shade of an orange tree making <u>thatches</u> from leaves of the raffia-palm. He exchanged greetings with Okonkwo and led the way into his *obi*.

"I was coming over to see you as soon as I finished that thatch," he said, rubbing off the grains of sand that clung to his thighs.

"Is it well?" Okonkwo asked.

"Yes," replied Obierika. "My daughter's suitor is coming today and I hope we will clinch the matter of the bride-price. I want you to be there."

Just then Obierika's son, Maduka, came into the *obi* from outside, greeted Okonkwo and turned towards the compound.

"Come and shake hands with me," Okonkwo said to the lad. "Your wrestling the other day gave me much happiness." The boy smiled, shook hands with Okonkwo and went into the compound.

"He will do great things," Okonkwo said. "If I had a son like him I should be happy. I am worried about Nwoye. A bowl of pounded yams can throw him in a wrestling

---

words for everyday use

val • or (val´ər) *n.*, courage or bravery. *The soldier was decorated for <u>valor</u> after rescuing one of his companions.*

thatch (thach´) *n.*, woven plant material often used to make a roof. *The villagers gathered material to repair the damage done by the high winds to the <u>thatch</u> on the roofs of their huts.*

match. His two younger brothers are more promising. But I can tell you, Obierika, that my children do not resemble me. Where are the young suckers that will grow when the old banana tree dies? If Ezinma had been a boy I would have been happier. She has the right spirit."

"You worry yourself for nothing," said Obierika. "The children are still very young."

"Nwoye is old enough to impregnate a woman. At his age I was already fending for myself. No, my friend, he is not too young. A chick that will grow into a cock can be spotted the very day it hatches. I have done my best to make Nwoye grow into a man, but there is too much of his mother in him."

"Too much of his grandfather," Obierika thought, but he did not say it. The same thought also came to Okonkwo's mind. But he had long learnt how to lay that ghost.[2] Whenever the thought of his father's weakness and failure troubled him he expelled it by thinking about his own strength and success. And so he did now. His mind went to his latest show of manliness.

"I cannot understand why you refused to come with us to kill that boy," he asked Obierika.

"Because I did not want to," Obierika replied sharply. "I had something better to do."

"You sound as if you question the authority and the decision of the Oracle, who said he should die."

"I do not. Why should I? But the Oracle did not ask me to carry out its decision."

"But someone had to do it. If we were all afraid of blood, it would not be done. And what do you think the Oracle would do then?"

▶ What disagreement does Okonkwo have with his friend Obierika?

"You know very well, Okonkwo, that I am not afraid of blood; and if anyone tells you that I am, he is telling a lie. And let me tell you one thing, my friend. If I were you I would have stayed at home. What you have done will not please the Earth. It is the kind of action for which the goddess wipes out whole families."

"The Earth cannot punish me for obeying her messenger," Okonkwo said. "A child's fingers are not scalded by a piece of hot yam which its mother puts into its palm."

"That is true," Obierika agreed. "But if the Oracle said that my son should be killed I would neither dispute it nor be the one to do it."

They would have gone on arguing had Ofoedu not come in just then. It was clear from his twinkling eyes that

---

2. **lay that ghost.** Return that spirit from the past to its grave, used metaphorically to mean "put that painful memory aside"

he had important news. But it would be impolite to rush him. Obierika offered him a <u>lobe</u> of the kola nut he had broken with Okonkwo. Ofoedu ate slowly and talked about the locusts. When he finished his kola nut he said:

"The things that happen these days are very strange."

"What has happened?" asked Okonkwo.

"Do you know Ogbuefi Ndulue?" Ofoedu asked.

"Ogbuefi Ndulue of Ire village," Okonkwo and Obierika said together.

"He died this morning," said Ofoedu.

"That is not strange. He was the oldest man in Ire," said Obierika.

"You are right," Ofoedu agreed. "But you ought to ask why the drum has not been beaten to tell Umuofia of his death."

"Why?" asked Obierika and Okonkwo together.

"That is the strange part of it. You know his first wife who walks with a stick?"

"Yes. She is called Ozoemena."

"That is so," said Ofoedu. "Ozoemena was, as you know, too old to attend Ndulue during his illness. His younger wives did that. When he died this morning, one of these women went to Ozoemena's hut and told her. She rose from her mat, took her stick and walked over to the *obi*. She knelt on her knees and hands at the threshold and called her husband, who was laid on a mat. "Ogbuefi Ndulue," she called, three times, and went back to her hut. When the youngest wife went to call her again to be present at the washing of the body, she found her lying on the mat, dead."

"That is very strange indeed," said Okonkwo. "They will put off Ndulue's funeral until his wife has been buried."

"That is why the drum has not been beaten to tell Umuofia."

"It was always said that Ndulue and Ozoemena had one mind," said Obierika. "I remember when I was a young boy there was a song about them. He could not do anything without telling her."

"I did not know that," said Okonkwo. "I thought he was a strong man in his youth."

"He was indeed," said Ofoedu.

Okonkwo shook his head doubtfully.

"He led Umuofia to war in those days," said Obierika.

◄ What is strange about the death of Ndulue? Why has the drum not been beaten to tell Umuofia of his death? What does Obierika say about the relationship between Ndulue and his first wife, Ozoemena?

◄ Okonkwo seems to think that strong feelings of love are incompatible with strength or manliness. Do you agree? Why, or why not?

words for everyday use   lobe (lōb´) *n.*, rounded, projecting part. *Charlie ate one <u>lobe</u> of the grapefruit, and Jill ate the other one.*

Okonkwo was beginning to feel like his old self again. All that he required was something to occupy his mind. If he had killed Ikemefuna during the busy planting season or harvesting it would not have been so bad; his mind would have been centered on his work. Okonkwo was not a man of thought but of action. But in the absence of work, talking was the next best.

Soon after Ofoedu left, Okonkwo took up his goatskin bag to go.

"I must go home to tap my palm trees for the afternoon," he said.

"Who taps your tall trees for you?" asked Obierika.

"Umezulike," replied Okonkwo.

"Sometimes I wish I had not taken the ozo title," said Obierika. "It wounds my heart to see these young men killing palm trees in the name of tapping."

"It is so indeed," Okonkwo agreed. "But the law of the land must be obeyed."

"I don't know how we got that law," said Obierika. "In many other clans a man of title is not forbidden to climb the palm tree. Here we say he cannot climb the tall tree but he can tap the short ones standing on the ground. It is like Dimaragana, who would not lend his knife for cutting up dog-meat because the dog was taboo to him, but offered to use his teeth."

"I think it is good that our clan holds the *ozo* title in high <u>esteem</u>," said Okonkwo. "In those other clans you speak of, *ozo* is so low that every beggar takes it."

"I was only speaking in jest," said Obierika. "In Abame and Aninta the title is worth less than two cowries. Every man wears the thread of title on his ankle, and does not lose it even if he steals."

"They have indeed soiled the name of *ozo*," said Okonkwo as he rose to go.

"It will not be very long now before my in-laws come," said Obierika.

"I shall return very soon," said Okonkwo, looking at the position of the sun.

There were seven men in Obierika's hut when Okonkwo returned. The suitor was a young man of about twenty-five, and with him were his father and uncle. On Obierika's

words for everyday use   es • teem (e stēm´) *n.*, great regard or respect. *Paulo has great <u>esteem</u> for Albert Einstein, who had the courage to view the world in an altogether new manner.*

side were his two elder brothers and Maduka, his sixteen-year-old son.

"Ask Akueke's mother to send us some kola nuts," said Obierika to his son. Maduka vanished into the compound like lightning. The conversation at once centered on him, and everybody agreed that he was as sharp as a razor.

"I sometimes think he is too sharp," said Obierika, somewhat <u>indulgently</u>. "He hardly ever walks. He is always in a hurry. If you are sending him on an errand he flies away before he has heard half of the message."

"You were very much like that yourself," said his eldest brother. "As our people say, 'When mother-cow is chewing grass its young ones watch its mouth.' Maduka has been watching your mouth."

As he was speaking the boy returned, followed by Akueke, his half-sister, carrying a wooden dish with three kola nuts and alligator pepper. She gave the dish to her father's eldest brother and then shook hands, very shyly, with her suitor and his relatives. She was about sixteen and just ripe for marriage. Her suitor and his relatives surveyed her young body with expert eyes as if to assure themselves that she was beautiful and ripe.

She wore a <u>coiffure</u> which was done up into a crest in the middle of the head. Cam wood was rubbed lightly into her skin, and all over her body were black patterns drawn with *uli*.[3] She wore a black necklace which hung down in three coils just above her full, succulent breasts. On her arms were red and yellow bangles, and on her waist four or five rows of *jigida,* or waist-beads.

When she had shaken hands, or rather held out her hand to be shaken, she returned to her mother's hut to help with the cooking.

"Remove your *jigida* first," her mother warned as she moved near the fireplace to bring the pestle resting against the wall. "Every day I tell you that *jigida* and fire are not friends. But you will never hear. You grew your ears for decoration, not for hearing. One of these days your *jigida* will catch fire on your waist, and then you will know."

Akueke moved to the other end of the hut and began to remove the waist-beads. It had to be done slowly and

◄ Of what does Akueke's mother warn her? Why do you think Akueke does not listen to these warnings?

---

3. *uli.* Black dye

| **words for everyday use** | in • dul • gent • ly (in duľ jənt lē) *adv.,* kindly; leniently. *The parents <u>indulgently</u> allowed their children to stay up an extra hour to watch the fireworks.* | coif • fure (kwä fyùr´) *n.,* headdress; style of arranging the hair. *The hairstylist encouraged his customers not to ride in convertibles because the wind would ruin their <u>coiffures</u>.* |

carefully, taking each string separately, else it would break and the thousand tiny rings would have to be strung together again. She rubbed each string downwards with her palms until it passed the buttocks and slipped down to the floor around her feet.

The men in the *obi* had already begun to drink the palm-wine which Akueke's suitor had brought. It was a very good wine and powerful, for in spite of the palm fruit hung across the mouth of the pot to <u>restrain</u> the lively liquor, white foam rose and spilled over.

"That wine is the work of a good tapper," said Okonkwo.

The young suitor, whose name was Ibe, smiled broadly and said to his father: "Do you hear that?" He then said to the others: "He will never admit that I am a good tapper."

"He tapped three of my best palm trees to death," said his father, Ukegbu.

"That was about five years ago," said Ibe, who had begun to pour out the wine, "before I learnt how to tap." He filled the first horn and gave to his father. Then he poured out for the others. Okonkwo brought out his big horn from the goatskin bag, blew into it to remove any dust that might be there, and gave it to Ibe to fill.

As the men drank, they talked about everything except the thing for which they had gathered. It was only after the pot had been emptied that the suitor's father cleared his voice and announced the object of their visit.

Obierika then presented to him a small bundle of short broomsticks. Ukegbu counted them.

"They are thirty?" he asked.

Obierika nodded in agreement.

"We are at last getting somewhere," Ukegbu said, and then turning to his brother and his son he said: "Let us go out and whisper together." The three rose and went outside. When they returned Ukegbu handed the bundle of sticks back to Obierika. He counted them; instead of thirty there were now only fifteen. He passed them over to his eldest brother, Machi, who also counted them and said:

"We had not thought to go below thirty. But as the dog said, 'If I fall down for you and you fall down for me, it is play.' Marriage should be a play and not a fight; so we are

words for everyday use

re • strain (ri strān´) vt., hold back; contain. *"Please try to behave in a <u>restrained</u> manner when you meet Mr. Stewart," said Kikki's mother, knowing how she idolized the rock star.*

falling down again." He then added ten sticks to the fifteen and gave the bundle to Ukegbu.

In this way Akueke's bride-price was finally settled at twenty bags of cowries. It was already dusk when the two parties came to this agreement.

"Go and tell Akueke's mother that we have finished," Obierika said to his son, Maduka. Almost immediately the woman came in with a big bowl of foo-foo. Obierika's second wife followed with a pot of soup, and Maduka brought in a pot of palm-wine.

As the men ate and drank palm-wine they talked about the customs of their neighbors.

◄ Of what do the men talk?

"It was only this morning," said Obierika, "that Okonkwo and I were talking about Abame and Aninta, where titled men climb trees and pound foo-foo for their wives."

"All their customs are upside-down. They do not decide bride-price as we do, with sticks. They haggle and bargain as if they were buying a goat or a cow in the market."

◄ How do the men feel about customs that are different from their own?

"That is very bad," said Obierika's eldest brother. "But what is good in one place is bad in another place. In Umunso they do not bargain at all, not even with broomsticks. The suitor just goes on bringing bags of cowries until his in-laws tell him to stop. It is a bad custom because it always leads to a quarrel."

"The world is large," said Okonkwo. "I have even heard that in some tribes a man's children belong to his wife and her family."

"That cannot be," said Machi. "You might as well say that the woman lies on top of the man when they are making the children."

"It is like the story of white men who, they say, are white like this piece of chalk," said Obierika. He held up a piece of chalk, which every man kept in his *obi* and with which his guests drew lines on the floor before they ate kola nuts. "And these white men, they say, have no toes."

◄ What experience have the villagers had with white-skinned people? How do you know?

"And have you never seen them?" asked Machi.

"Have you?" asked Obierika.

"One of them passes here frequently," said Machi. "His name is Amadi."

Those who knew Amadi laughed. He was a leper, and the polite name for leprosy[4] was "the white skin."

---

4. **leper . . . leprosy.** *Leper*—person afflicted with leprosy; *leprosy*—infectious disease that causes gangrene in the limbs, ears, and nose. The patient's skin turns white as the disease progresses.

Respond to the Selection

How do you feel about the killing of Ikemefuna? Do you consider Okonkwo's action that of a strong man or of a weak one? Explain.

Investigate, Inquire, and Imagine

Recall: GATHERING FACTS

1a. What public event does everyone in the village of Umuofia come to see in chapter 6?

2a. How long has Ikemefuna been with Okonkwo's family? Who decides that he should be killed? How is Ikemefuna killed?

3a. In chapter 7, Ezeudu comes to visit Okonkwo and tells him of the Oracle's decision. What does Ezeudu tell Okonkwo not to do? Why doesn't Okonkwo follow Ezeudu's advice?

4a. What peculiar belief about white people is expressed by Obierika at the end of chapter 8? Have the people of Umuofia had any contact with white Europeans at this point in the novel?

Interpret: FINDING MEANING

1b. Why do you think the people of Umuofia prize successful wrestlers? Why is it important in this culture for young men to be trained in the skills of warriors?

2b. How do you feel about the Oracle's decision that Ikemefuna must die? Is any reason given to explain why killing him is necessary?

3b. Why do you think Okonkwo takes the lead role in the killing of Ikemefuna? How did Okonkwo feel toward the boy? What does Okonkwo's action reveal about him? How does Okonkwo's action affect his son Nwoye? How does it affect Okonkwo?

4b. What about white people's clothing might have brought rise to this peculiar belief? What does Okonkwo mean when he says at the end of chapter 8 that "the world is large"? Do you agree with Okonkwo, Obierika, and the others that some customs are bad and others are good?

Analyze: TAKING THINGS APART

5a. Analyze Okonkwo's idea of masculinity. Consider the following questions: Why does he worry about Nwoye? What pleases him about Ikemefuna's influence on Nwoye? When and why does he call himself a "shivering old woman"? Are Okonkwo's ideas of masculinity typical of Igbo society, or are they extreme? Explain.

Synthesize: BRINGING THINGS TOGETHER

→ 5b. What weakness does Okonkwo demonstrate when he takes a lead role in killing Ikemefuna? Why does he act as he does even though he does not have to do so?

Perspective: LOOKING AT OTHER VIEWS

6a. Why do the elders of Umuofia agree to follow the Oracle's orders with regard to Ikemefuna? From their point of view, what might have happened if they defied the Oracle? Use quotes from the novel to support your answer.

Empathy: SEEING FROM INSIDE

→ 6b. Imagine you are Nwoye. How do you feel about your father and about your society after what happened to Ikemefuna? You may write your answer in the form of a diary entry.

Understanding Literature

MOOD. **Mood,** or **atmosphere,** is the emotion created in the reader by part or all of a literary work. Reread chapter 7 and examine its mood. How would you describe it? At what point does the mood change, and how? What details create the mood of the second half of the chapter?

SYMBOL. A **symbol** is a thing that stands for or represents both itself and something else. Reread the following passage from chapter 7, which tells of the coming of the locusts to Umuofia. What might the locusts symbolize? Who else is coming to "settle" in Umuofia?

> At first, a fairly small swarm came. They were the harbingers sent to survey the land. And then appeared on the horizon a slowly moving mass like a boundless sheet of black cloud drifting towards Umuofia . . . . And at last the locusts did descend. They settled on every tree and on every blade of grass; they settled on the roofs and covered the bare ground. Mighty tree branches broke away under them, and the whole country became the brown-earth color of the vast, hungry swarm.

THEME. A **theme** is a central idea in a literary work. What is the theme of the conversation between the men at the end of chapter 8? Why is it so difficult for people to accept customs and beliefs that are different from their own? Should people be willing to accept all such customs and beliefs in a spirit of tolerance? Is it important for people to question traditional beliefs and customs when they violate individual conscience? Why, or why not?

TRAGEDY AND TRAGIC FLAW. A **tragedy** is a drama or other work of literature that tells the story of the fall of a person of high status. Tragedy tends to be serious. It celebrates the courage and dignity of a tragic hero in the face of inevitable doom. Sometimes that doom is made inevitable by a tragic flaw in the hero. Called *hamartia* by the Greeks, a **tragic flaw** is a personal weakness, most often pride, which brings about the character's downfall. What tragic flaw or flaws does Okonkwo have? Of what does Obierika warn Okonkwo after the killing of Ikemefuna? What is Okonkwo's response to his friend's warning? Do you agree with Okonkwo, or do you think he will pay for his actions? Explain.

Chapter Nine

FOR THE FIRST time in three nights, Okonkwo slept. He woke up once in the middle of the night and his mind went back to the past three days without making him feel uneasy. He began to wonder why he had felt uneasy at all. It was like a man wondering in broad daylight why a dream had appeared so terrible to him at night. He stretched himself and scratched his thigh where a mosquito had bitten him as he slept. Another one was wailing near his right ear. He slapped the ear and hoped he had killed it. Why do they always go for one's ears? When he was a child his mother had told him a story about it. But it was as silly as all women's stories. Mosquito, she had said, had asked Ear to marry him, whereupon Ear fell on the floor in uncontrollable laughter. "How much longer do you think you will live?" she asked. "You are already a skeleton." Mosquito went away <u>humiliated</u>, and any time he passed her way he told Ear that he was still alive.

◀ How is the buzzing of the mosquito in people's ears explained by this myth?

Okonkwo turned on his side and went back to sleep. He was <u>roused</u> in the morning by someone banging on his door.

"Who is that?" he growled. He knew it must be Ekwefi. Of his three wives Ekwefi was the only one who would have the <u>audacity</u> to bang on his door.

"Ezinma is dying," came her voice, and all the tragedy and sorrow of her life were packed in those words.

◀ What potential tragedy is the family facing?

Okonkwo sprang from his bed, pushed back the bolt on his door and ran into Ekwefi's hut.

Ezinma lay shivering on a mat beside a huge fire that her mother had kept burning all night.

"It is *iba*,"[1] said Okonkwo as he took his machete and went into the bush to collect the leaves and grasses and barks of trees that went into making the medicine for *iba*.

Ekwefi knelt beside the sick child, occasionally feeling with her palm the wet, burning forehead.

Ezinma was an only child and the center of her mother's world. Very often it was Ezinma who had decided what

---

1. ***iba.*** Malarial fever, which can be contracted through mosquito bites. The Igbo believed that *iba* was caused by the influence of evil spirits.

words for everyday use	hu • mil • i • at • ed (hyü mil´ē ā təd) part., hurt in pride or dignity. *The actor was <u>humiliated</u> when some members of the audience started booing.* rouse (rouz) vt., cause to come out of a state of sleep. *Sara had been working for*	*eighteen hours straight before she fell asleep; therefore, she was difficult to <u>rouse.</u>* au • dac • i • ty (ò das´ə tē) n., boldness; daring. *No one had the <u>audacity</u> to interrupt the president during his speech.*

food her mother should prepare. Ekwefi even gave her such <u>delicacies</u> as eggs, which children were rarely allowed to eat because such food tempted them to steal. One day as Ezinma was eating an egg Okonkwo had come in unexpectedly from his hut. He was greatly shocked and swore to beat Ekwefi if she dared to give the child eggs again. But it was impossible to refuse Ezinma anything. After her father's <u>rebuke</u> she developed an even keener appetite for eggs. And she enjoyed above all the secrecy in which she now ate them. Her mother always took her into their bedroom and shut the door.

Ezinma did not call her mother *Nne* like all children. She called her by her name, Ekwefi, as her father and other grown-up people did. The relationship between them was not only that of mother and child. There was something in it like the companionship of equals, which was strengthened by such little conspiracies as eating eggs in the bedroom.

Ekwefi had suffered a good deal in her life. She had borne ten children and nine of them had died in infancy, usually before the age of three. As she buried one child after another her sorrow gave way to despair and then to grim <u>resignation</u>. The birth of her children, which should be a woman's crowning glory, became for Ekwefi mere physical agony devoid of promise. The naming ceremony after seven market weeks became an empty ritual. Her deepening despair found expression in the names she gave her children. One of them was a pathetic cry, Onwumbiko "Death, I implore you." But Death took no notice; Onwumbiko died in his fifteenth month. The next child was a girl, Ozoemena—"May it not happen again." She died in her eleventh month, and two others after her. Ekwefi then became <u>defiant</u> and called her next child Onwuma "Death may please himself." And he did.

After the death of Ekwefi's second child, Okonkwo had gone to a medicine man, who was also a <u>diviner</u> of the Afa Oracle, to inquire what was amiss. This man told him that

▶ *What explanation is offered by the medicine man for the repeated deaths of Ekwefi's children?*

the child was an *ogbanje*,[2] one of those wicked children who, when they died, entered their mothers' wombs to be born again.

"When your wife becomes pregnant again," he said, "let her not sleep in her hut. Let her go and stay with her people. In that way she will <u>elude</u> her wicked tormentor and break its evil cycle of birth and death."

Ekwefi did as she was asked. As soon as she became pregnant she went to live with her old mother in another village. It was there that her third child was born and circumcised on the eighth day. She did not return to Okonkwo's compound until three days before the naming ceremony. The child was called Onwumbiko.

Onwumbiko was not given proper burial when he died. Okonkwo had called in another medicine man who was famous in the clan for his great knowledge about *ogbanje* children. His name was Okagbue Uyanwa. Okagbue was a very striking figure, tall, with a full beard and a bald head. He was light in complexion and his eyes were red and fiery. He always gnashed his teeth as he listened to those who came to consult him. He asked Okonkwo a few questions about the dead child. All the neighbors and relations who had come to mourn gathered round them.

"On what market-day was it born?" he asked.

"*Oye,*" replied Okonkwo.

"And it died this morning?"

Okonkwo said yes, and only then realized for the first time that the child had died on the same market-day as it had been born. The neighbors and relations also saw the coincidence and said among themselves that it was very significant.

"Where do you sleep with your wife, in your *obi* or in her own hut?" asked the medicine man.

"In her hut."

"In future call her into your *obi*."

The medicine man then ordered that there should be no mourning for the dead child. He brought out a sharp razor from the goatskin bag slung from his left shoulder and

---

2. *ogbanje*. Child who, according to Igbo belief, is repeatedly reborn to a mother and repeatedly dies. This belief may have come about as a way of explaining the high rate of infant mortality. Many children died of sickle-cell anemia, a hereditary disease common among West African peoples.

words for everyday use   e • lude (ē lüd´) *vt.,* avoid, escape. *"The escaped convict continues to <u>elude</u> our forces,"* said the sergeant.

began to mutilate the child. Then he took it away to bury in the Evil Forest, holding it by the ankle and dragging it on the ground behind him. After such treatment it would think twice before coming again, unless it was one of the stubborn ones who returned, carrying the stamp of their mutilation—a missing finger or perhaps a dark line where the medicine man's razor had cut them.

By the time Onwumbiko died Ekwefi had become a very bitter woman. Her husband's first wife had already had three sons, all strong and healthy. When she had borne her third son in succession, Okonkwo had slaughtered a goat for her, as was the custom. Ekwefi had nothing but good wishes for her. But she had grown so bitter about her own *chi* that she could not rejoice with others over their good fortune. And so, on the day that Nwoye's mother cele-brated the birth of her three sons with feasting and music, Ekwefi was the only person in the happy company who went about with a cloud on her brow. Her husband's wife took this for <u>malevolence</u>, as husbands' wives were wont to. How could she know that Ekwefi's bitterness did not flow outwards to others but inwards into her own soul; that she did not blame others for their good fortune but her own evil *chi* who denied her any?

At last Ezinma was born, and although ailing she seemed determined to live. At first Ekwefi accepted her, as she had accepted others—with <u>listless</u> resignation. But when she lived on to her fourth, fifth and sixth years, love returned once more to her mother, and, with love, anxiety. She determined to nurse her child to health, and she put all her being into it. She was rewarded by occasional spells of health during which Ezinma bubbled with energy like fresh palm-wine. At such times she seemed beyond danger. But all of a sudden she would go down again. Everybody knew she was an *ogbanje*. These sudden bouts of sickness and health were typical of her kind. But she had lived so long that perhaps she had decided to stay. Some of them did become tired of their evil rounds of birth and death, or took pity on their mothers, and stayed. Ekwefi believed deep inside her that Ezinma had come to stay. She believed because it was that faith alone that gave her own life any kind of meaning. And this faith had been strengthened

▶ *Whom does Ekwefi blame for her bad fortune?*

▶ *How do Ekwefi's feelings toward her daughter change? Why?*

▶ *How do the people know that Ezinma is an* ogbanje?

---

words for everyday use

ma • lev • o • lence (mə lev′ə ləns) *n.*, spitefulness; ill will. *The judge was particu-larly troubled by the <u>malevolence</u> shown in the vandals' actions.*

list • less (list′lis) *adj.*, spiritless; with no interest. *Because of the heat, Billy felt quite <u>listless</u> and simply sat on the front porch, fanning himself.*

when a year or so ago a medicine man had dug up Ezinma's *iyi-uwa*.[3] Everyone knew then that she would live because her bond with the world of *ogbanje* had been broken. Ekwefi was reassured. But such was her anxiety for her daughter that she could not rid herself completely of her fear. And although she believed that the *iyi-uwa* which had been dug up was genuine, she could not ignore the fact that some really evil children sometimes misled people into digging up a <u>specious</u> one.

But Ezinma's *iyi-uwa* had looked real enough. It was a smooth pebble wrapped in a dirty rag. The man who dug it up was the same Okagbue who was famous in all the clan for his knowledge in these matters. Ezinma had not wanted to cooperate with him at first. But that was only to be expected. No *ogbanje* would yield her secrets easily, and most of them never did because they died too young before they could be asked questions.

"Where did you bury your *iyi-uwa?*" Okagbue had asked Ezinma. She was nine then and was just recovering from a serious illness.

"What is *iyi-uwa?*" she asked in return.

"You know what it is. You buried it in the ground somewhere so that you can die and return again to torment your mother."

Ezinma looked at her mother, whose eyes, sad and pleading, were fixed on her.

"Answer the question at once," roared Okonkwo, who stood beside her. All the family were there and some of the neighbors too.

"Leave her to me," the medicine man told Okonkwo in a cool, confident voice. He turned again to Ezinma. "Where did you bury your *iyi-uwa?*"

"Where they bury children," she replied, and the quiet spectators murmured to themselves.

"Come along then and show me the spot," said the medicine man.

The crowd set out with Ezinma leading the way and Okagbue following closely behind her. Okonkwo came

◀ What is an iyi-uwa, and why must it be dug out of the ground? Why is this procedure not always successful?

---

3. *iyi-uwa.* Stone that is a link between an *ogbanje* child and the spirit world; finding and destroying the stone was believed to prevent the child from dying and thus repeating the cycle

words for everyday use spe • cious (spē´ shəs) *adj., not genuine. The unscrupulous art dealer made a <u>specious</u> claim that the unsigned drawing was an orginal van Gogh.*

next and Ekwefi followed him. When she came to the main road, Ezinma turned left as if she was going to the stream.

"But you said it was where they bury children?" asked the medicine man.

▶ What causes Ezinma to feel important?

"No," said Ezinma, whose feeling of importance was <u>manifest</u> in her sprightly walk. She sometimes broke into a run and stopped again suddenly. The crowd followed her silently. Women and children returning from the stream with pots of water on their heads wondered what was happening until they saw Okagbue and guessed that it must be something to do with *ogbanje*. And they all knew Ekwefi and her daughter very well.

When she got to the big udala tree Ezinma turned left into the bush, and the crowd followed her. Because of her size she made her way through trees and creepers[4] more quickly than her followers. The bush was alive with the tread of feet on dry leaves and sticks and the moving aside of tree branches. Ezinma went deeper and deeper and the crowd went with her. Then she suddenly turned round and began to walk back to the road. Everybody stood to let her pass and then filed after her.

▶ Compare the communication styles of Okonkwo and Okagbue. Which style is more likely to be effective in a confrontational situation?

"If you bring us all this way for nothing I shall beat sense into you," Okonkwo threatened.

"I have told you to let her alone. I know how to deal with them," said Okagbue.

Ezinma led the way back to the road, looked left and right and turned right. And so they arrived home again.

"Where did you bury your *iyi-uwa?*" asked Okagbue when Ezinma finally stopped outside her father's *obi.* Okagbue's voice was unchanged. It was quiet and confident.

"It is near that orange tree," Ezinma said.

"And why did you not say so, you wicked daughter of Akalogoli?" Okonkwo swore furiously. The medicine man ignored him.

"Come and show me the exact spot," he said quietly to Ezinma.

"It is here," she said when they got to the tree.

---

4. **creepers.** Plants that spread out along the ground

words for everyday use

man • i • fest (man´ ə fest´) *adj.,* apparent; obvious. *The <u>manifest</u> good will of the ambassador from the United States won the confidence of the people of the war-torn country.*

"Point at the spot with your finger," said Okagbue.

"It is here," said Ezinma touching the ground with her finger. Okonkwo stood by, rumbling like thunder in the rainy season.

"Bring me a hoe," said Okagbue.

When Ekwefi brought the hoe, he had already put aside his goatskin bag and his big cloth and was in his underwear, a long and thin strip of cloth wound round the waist like a belt and then passed between the legs to be fastened to the belt behind. He immediately set to work digging a pit where Ezinma had indicated. The neighbors sat around watching the pit becoming deeper and deeper. The dark top-soil soon gave way to the bright-red earth with which women scrubbed the floor and walls of huts. Okagbue worked tirelessly and in silence, his back shining with perspiration. Okonkwo stood by the pit. He asked Okagbue to come up and rest while he took a hand. But Okagbue said he was not tired yet.

Ekwefi went into her hut to cook yams. Her husband had brought out more yams than usual because the medicine man had to be fed. Ezinma went with her and helped in preparing the vegetables.

"There is too much green vegetable," she said.

"Don't you see the pot is full of yams?" Ekwefi asked. "And you know how leaves become smaller after cooking."

"Yes," said Ezinma, "that was why the snake-lizard killed his mother."

"Very true," said Ekwefi.

"He gave his mother seven baskets of vegetables to cook and in the end there were only three. And so he killed her," said Ezinma.

"That is not the end of the story."

"Oho," said Ezinma, "I remember now. He brought another seven baskets and cooked them himself. And there were again only three. So he killed himself too."

Outside the *obi* Okagbue and Okonkwo were digging the pit to find where Ezinma had buried her *iyi-uwa*. Neighbors sat around, watching. The pit was now so deep that they no longer saw the digger. They only saw the red earth he threw up mounting higher and higher. Okonkwo's son, Nwoye, stood near the edge of the pit because he wanted to take in all that happened.

Okagbue had again taken over the digging from Okonkwo. He worked, as usual, in silence. The neighbors and Okonkwo's wives were now talking. The children had lost interest and were playing.

Suddenly Okagbue sprang to the surface with the agility of a leopard.

"It is very near now," he said. "I have felt it."

There was immediate excitement and those who were sitting jumped to their feet.

"Call your wife and child," he said to Okonkwo. But Ekwefi and Ezinma had heard the noise and run out to see what it was.

Okagbue went back into the pit, which was now surrounded by spectators. After a few more hoe-fuls of earth he struck the *iyi-uwa*. He raised it carefully with the hoe and threw it to the surface. Some women ran away in fear when it was thrown. But they soon returned and everyone was gazing at the rag from a reasonable distance. Okagbue emerged and without saying a word or even looking at the spectators he went to his goatskin bag, took out two leaves and began to chew them. When he had swallowed them, he took up the rag with his left hand and began to untie it. And then the smooth, shiny pebble fell out. He picked it up.

"Is this yours?" he asked Ezinma.

"Yes," she replied. All the women shouted with joy because Ekwefi's troubles were at last ended.

All this had happened more than a year ago and Ezinma had not been ill since. And then suddenly she had begun to shiver in the night. Ekwefi brought her to the fireplace, spread her mat on the floor and built a fire. But she had got worse and worse. As she knelt by her, feeling with her palm the wet, burning forehead, she prayed a thousand times. Although her husband's wives were saying that it was nothing more than *iba,* she did not hear them.

Okonkwo returned from the bush carrying on his left shoulder a large bundle of grasses and leaves, roots and barks of medicinal trees and shrubs. He went into Ekwefi's hut, put down his load and sat down.

"Get me a pot," he said, "and leave the child alone."

Ekwefi went to bring the pot and Okonkwo selected the best from his bundle, in their due proportions, and cut them up. He put them in the pot and Ekwefi poured in some water.

"Is that enough?" she asked when she had poured in about half of the water in the bowl.

"A little more . . . I said *a little.* Are you deaf?" Okonkwo roared at her.

She set the pot on the fire and Okonkwo took up his machete to return to his *obi.*

▶ *What does the medicine man find?*

▶ *What does Okonkwo do for his daughter?*

"You must watch the pot carefully," he said as he went, "and don't allow it to boil over. If it does its power will be gone." He went away to his hut and Ekwefi began to tend the medicine pot almost as if it was itself a sick child. Her eyes went constantly from Ezinma to the boiling pot and back to Ezinma.

Okonkwo returned when he felt the medicine had cooked long enough. He looked it over and said it was done.

"Bring a low stool for Ezinma," he said, "and a thick mat."

He took down the pot from the fire and placed it in front of the stool. He then roused Ezinma and placed her on the stool, astride the steaming pot. The thick mat was thrown over both. Ezinma struggled to escape from the choking and overpowering steam, but she was held down. She started to cry.

When the mat was at last removed she was drenched in perspiration. Ekwefi mopped her with a piece of cloth and she lay down on a dry mat and was soon asleep.

Chapter Ten

LARGE CROWDS BEGAN to gather on the village *ilo* as soon as the edge had worn off the sun's heat and it was no longer painful on the body. Most communal ceremonies took place at that time of the day, so that even when it was said that a ceremony would begin "after the midday meal" everyone understood that it would begin a long time later, when the sun's heat had softened.

It was clear from the way the crowd stood or sat that the ceremony was for men. There were many women, but they looked on from the fringe like outsiders. The titled men and elders sat on their stools waiting for the trials to begin. In front of them was a row of stools on which nobody sat. There were nine of them. Two little groups of people stood at a respectable distance beyond the stools. They faced the elders. There were three men in one group and three men and one woman in the other. The woman was Mgbafo and the three men with her were her brothers. In the other group were her husband, Uzowulu, and his relatives. Mgbafo and her brothers were as still as statues into whose faces the artist has molded defiance. Uzowulu and his relative, on the other hand, were whispering together. It looked like whispering, but they were really talking at the top of their voices. Everybody in the crowd was talking. It was like the market. From a distance the noise was a deep rumble carried by the wind.

An iron gong sounded, setting up a wave of expectation in the crowd. Everyone looked in the direction of the *egwugwu*[1] house. *Gome, gome, gome, gome* went the gong, and a powerful flute blew a high-pitched blast. Then came the voices of the *egwugwu*, guttural and awesome. The wave struck the women and children and there was a backward stampede. But it was momentary. They were already far enough where they stood and there was room for running away if any of the *egwugwu* should go towards them.

The drum sounded again and the flute blew. The *egwugwu* house was now a <u>pandemonium</u> of <u>quavering</u>

▶ What event is being held?

---

1. *egwugwu.* Masked dancers who play the roles of ancestral spirits. The Igbo believe that during the ritual dramas they perform, the *egwugwu* become possessed by the spirits of the ancestors.

words for everyday use

pan • de • mo • ni • um (pan´ də mō´nē əm) *n.*, scene of wild noises and confusion. *When someone yelled "fire!" in the crowded theater, <u>pandemonium</u> broke out.*

qua • ver • ing (kwā´vər iŋ) *part.*, trembling; shaking. *With a <u>quavering</u> voice, the father said, "My child is still in there!"*

voices: *Aru oyim de de de de dei!* filled the air as the spirits of the ancestors, just emerged from the earth, greeted themselves in their <u>esoteric</u> language. The *egwugwu* house into which they emerged faced the forest, away from the crowd, who saw only its back with the many-colored patterns and drawings done by specially chosen women at regular intervals. These women never saw the inside of the hut. No woman ever did. They scrubbed and painted the outside walls under the supervision of men. If they imagined what was inside, they kept their imagination to themselves. No woman ever asked questions about the most powerful and the most secret cult in the clan.

Aru oyim de de de dei! flew around the dark, closed hut like tongues of fire. The ancestral spirits of the clan were abroad. The metal gong beat continuously now and the flute, shrill and powerful, floated on the <u>chaos</u>.

And then the *egwugwu* appeared. The women and children sent up a great shout and took to their heels. It was instinctive. A woman fled as soon as an *egwugwu* came in sight. And when, as on that day, nine of the greatest masked spirits in the clan came out together it was a terrifying spectacle. Even Mgbafo took to her heels and had to be restrained by her brothers.

◀ *Who are the egwugwu?*

Each of the nine *egwugwu* represented a village of the clan. Their leader was called Evil Forest. Smoke poured out of his head.

The nine villages of Umuofia had grown out of the nine sons of the first father of the clan. Evil Forest represented the village of Umeru, or the children of Eru, who was the eldest of the nine sons.

"*Umuofia kwenu!*" shouted the leading *egwugwu*, pushing the air with his raffia[2] arms. The elders of the clan replied, "*Yaa!*"

"*Umuofia kwenu!*"

"*Yaa!*"

"*Umuofia kwenu!*"

"*Yaa!*"

Evil Forest then thrust the pointed end of his rattling staff into the earth. And it began to shake and rattle, like

---

2. **raffia.** Fiber made from leaves of a palm tree

words for everyday use
es • o • ter • ic (es′ə ter′ik) *adj.*, understood by a chosen few. *Kele was involved in a number of <u>esoteric</u> studies, such as the study of the folk tales of ancient Mongolia.*

cha • os (kā′äs′) *n.*, extreme confusion; disorder. *The lights went out in the crowded train station, and <u>chaos</u> ensued.*

something <u>agitating</u> with a metallic life. He took the first of the empty stools and the eight other *egwugwu* began to sit in order of <u>seniority</u> after him.

Okonkwo's wives, and perhaps other women as well, might have noticed that the second *egwugwu* had the springy walk of Okonkwo. And they might also have noticed that Okonkwo was not among the titled men and elders who sat behind the row of *egwugwu*. But if they thought these things they kept them within themselves. The *egwugwu* with the springy walk was one of the dead fathers of the clan. He looked terrible with the smoked raffia body, a huge wooden face painted white except for the round hollow eyes and the charred teeth that were as big as a man's fingers. On his head were two powerful horns.

When all the *egwugwu* had sat down and the sound of the many tiny bells and rattles on their bodies had subsided, Evil Forest addressed the two groups of people facing them.

"Uzowulu's body, I salute you," he said. Spirits always addressed humans as "bodies." Uzowulu bent down and touched the earth with his right hand as a sign of <u>submission</u>.

"Our father, my hand has touched the ground," he said.

"Uzowulu's body, do you know me?" asked the spirit.

"How can I know you, father? You are beyond our knowledge."

Evil Forest then turned to the other group and addressed the eldest of the three brothers.

"The body of Odukwe, I greet you," he said, and Odukwe bent down and touched the earth. The hearing then began.

Uzowulu stepped forward and presented his case.

"That woman standing there is my wife, Mgbafo. I married her with my money and my yams. I do not owe my in-laws anything. I owe them no yams. I owe them no coco-yams. One morning three of them came to my house, beat me up and took my wife and children away. This happened in the rainy season. I have waited in vain for my wife to return. At last I went to my in-laws and said to

▶ How do the spirit dancers address human beings? Why do you think they do this?

▶ What is the proper response when the spirit asks, "Do you know me?"

them, 'You have taken back your sister. I did not send her away. You yourselves took her. The law of the clan is that you should return her bride-price.' But my wife's brothers said they had nothing to tell me. So I have brought the matter to the fathers of the clan. My case is finished. I salute you."

"Your words are good," said the leader of the *egwugwu*. "Let us hear Odukwe. His words may also be good."

Odukwe was short and thick-set. He stepped forward, saluted the spirits and began his story.

"My in-law has told you that we went to his house, beat him up and took our sister and her children away. All that is true. He told you that he came to take back her bride-price and we refused to give it him. That also is true. My in-law, Uzowulu, is a beast. My sister lived with him for nine years. During those years no single day passed in the sky without his beating the woman. We have tried to settle their quarrels time without number and on each occasion Uzowulu was guilty—"

"It is a lie!" Uzowulu shouted.

"Two years ago," continued Odukwe, "when she was pregnant, he beat her until she miscarried."

"It is a lie. She miscarried after she had gone to sleep with her lover."

"Uzowulu's body, I salute you," said Evil Forest, silencing him. "What kind of lover sleeps with a pregnant woman?" There was a loud murmur of <u>approbation</u> from the crowd. Odukwe continued: "Last year when my sister was recovering from an illness, he beat her again so that if the neighbors had not gone in to save her she would have been killed. We heard of it, and did as you have been told. The law of Umuofia is that if a woman runs away from her husband her bride-price is returned. But in this case she ran away to save her life. Her two children belong to Uzowulu. We do not dispute it, but they are too young to leave their mother. If, on the other hand, Uzowulu should recover from his madness and come in the proper way to beg his wife to return she will do so on the understanding that if he ever beats her again we shall cut off his genitals for him."

The crowd roared with laughter. Evil Forest rose to his feet and order was immediately restored. A steady cloud of

---

words for everyday use
ap • pro • ba • tion (aˊprə bāˊshən) *n.*, approval; act of approving formally or officially. *The governor's proposal met with <u>approbation</u> from all the members of the state legislature—not one senator said "Nay" to his idea.*

▶ How do the women react to Evil Forest? Why?

▶ What function do the egwugwu serve?

smoke rose from his head. He sat down again and called two witnesses. They were both Uzowulu's neighbors, and they agreed about the beating. Evil Forest then stood up, pulled out his staff and thrust it into the earth again. He ran a few steps in the direction of the women; they all fled in terror, only to return to their places almost immediately. The nine *egwugwu* then went away to consult together in their house. They were silent for a long time. Then the metal gong sounded and the flute was blown. The *egwugwu* had emerged once again from their underground home. They saluted one another and then reappeared on the *ilo*.

"*Umuofia kwenu!*" roared Evil Forest, facing the elders and grandees of the clan.

"*Yaa!*" replied the thunderous crowd, then silence descended from the sky and swallowed the noise.

Evil Forest began to speak and all the while he spoke everyone was silent. The eight other *egwugwu* were as still as statues.

"We have heard both sides of the case," said Evil Forest. "Our duty is not to blame this man or to praise that, but to settle the dispute." He turned to Uzowulu's group and allowed a short pause.

"Uzowulu's body, do you know me?"

"How can I know you, father? You are beyond our knowledge," Uzowulu replied.

"I am Evil Forest. I kill a man on the day that his life is sweetest to him."

"That is true," replied Uzowulu.

▶ What does the masked spirit tell Uzowulu?

"Go to your in-laws with a pot of wine and beg your wife to return to you. It is not bravery when a man fights with a woman." He turned to Odukwe, and allowed a brief pause.

"Odukwe's body, I greet you," he said.

"My hand is on the ground," replied Odukwe.

"Do you know me?"

"No man can know you," replied Odukwe.

▶ What is the decision of the court? How have the spirit dancers settled the case?

"I am Evil Forest, I am Dry-meat-that-fills-the-mouth, I am Fire-that-burns-without-faggots.[3] If your in-law brings wine to you, let your sister go with him. I salute you." He pulled his staff from the hard earth and thrust it back.

"*Umuofia kwenu!*" he roared, and the crowd answered.

---

3. **faggots.** Bundles of sticks, twigs, or branches, used especially for fuel

"I don't know why such a <u>trifle</u> should come before the *egwugwu*," said one elder to another.

"Don't you know what kind of man Uzowulu is? He will not listen to any other decision," replied the other.

As they spoke two other groups of people had replaced the first before the *egwugwu,* and a great land case began.

◀ What does one elder think of the case of Uzowulu and his wife?

words for everyday use

tri • fle (trī´ fəl) *n.,* something of little value; trivial matter. *The cost of admission wasn't much; it was a <u>trifle.</u>*

Chapter Eleven

THE NIGHT WAS <u>impenetrably</u> dark. The moon had been rising later and later every night until now it was seen only at dawn. And whenever the moon <u>forsook</u> evening and rose at cock-crow the nights were as black as charcoal.

Ezinma and her mother sat on a mat on the floor after their supper of yam foo-foo and bitter-leaf soup. A palm-oil lamp gave out yellowish light. Without it, it would have been impossible to eat; one could not have known where one's mouth was in the darkness of that night. There was an oil lamp in all the four huts on Okonkwo's compound, and each hut seen from the others looked like a soft eye of yellow half-light set in the solid massiveness of night.

The world was silent except for the shrill cry of insects, which was part of the night, and the sound of wooden mortar and pestle[1] as Nwayieke pounded her foo-foo. Nwayieke lived four compounds away, and she was notorious for her late cooking. Every woman in the neighborhood knew the sound of Nwayieke's mortar and pestle. It was also part of the night.

Okonkwo had eaten from his wives' dishes and was now reclining with his back against the wall. He searched his bag and brought out his snuff-bottle. He turned it on to his left palm, but nothing came out. He hit the bottle against his knee to shake up the tobacco. That was always the trouble with Okeke's snuff. It very quickly went damp, and there was too much saltpeter in it. Okonkwo had not bought snuff from him for a long time. Idigo was the man who knew how to grind good snuff. But he had recently fallen ill.

Low voices, broken now and again by singing, reached Okonkwo from his wives' huts as each woman and her children told folk stories. Ekwefi and her daughter, Ezinma, sat on a mat on the floor. It was Ekwefi's turn to tell a story.

"Once upon a time," she began, "all the birds were invited to a feast in the sky. They were very happy and

---

1. **mortar and pestle.** Bowl and rod used for grinding something into a paste or powder

words for everyday use

im • pen • e • tra • bly (im pen´i trə blē) adv., incapable of being passed through. *The bushes beside the road were <u>impenetrably</u> thick, so we had to go around them.*

for • sake (fôr sāk´) vt., abandon. *Do not <u>forsake</u> me, oh, my darling.*

began to prepare themselves for the great day. They painted their bodies with red cam wood and drew beautiful patterns on them with *uli*.

"Tortoise saw all these preparations and soon discovered what it all meant. Nothing that happened in the world of the animals ever escaped his notice; he was full of cunning. As soon as he heard of the great feast in the sky his throat began to itch at the very thought. There was a famine in those days and Tortoise had not eaten a good meal for two moons. His body rattled like a piece of dry stick in his empty shell. So he began to plan how he would go to the sky."

"But he had no wings," said Ezinma.

"Be patient," replied her mother. "That is the story. Tortoise had no wings, but he went to the birds and asked to be allowed to go with them.

"'We know you too well,' said the birds when they had heard him. 'You are full of cunning and you are ungrateful. If we allow you to come with us you will soon begin your mischief.'

"'You do not know me,' said Tortoise. 'I am a changed man. I have learned that a man who makes trouble for others is also making it for himself.'

"Tortoise had a sweet tongue, and within a short time all the birds agreed that he was a changed man, and they each gave him a feather, with which he made two wings.

◀ What talent does Tortoise have?

"At last the great day came and Tortoise was the first to arrive at the meeting-place. When all the birds had gathered together, they set off in a body. Tortoise was very happy and <u>voluble</u> as he flew among the birds, and he was soon chosen as the man to speak for the party because he was a great orator.

"'There is one important thing which we must not forget,' he said as they flew on their way. 'When people are invited to a great feast like this, they take new names for the occasion. Our hosts in the sky will expect us to honor this age-old custom.'

"None of the birds had heard of this custom but they knew that Tortoise, in spite of his failings in other directions, was a widely traveled man who knew the customs of different peoples. And so they each took a new name.

---

words for everyday use   vol • u • ble (väl´ yü bəl) *adj.*, talkative. *Danielle is a <u>voluble</u> child; she chatters all day long.*

▶ Why do you think
Tortoise chooses this
name?

When they had all taken, Tortoise also took one. He was to be called *All of you.*

"At last the party arrived in the sky and their hosts were very happy to see them. Tortoise stood up in his many-colored <u>plumage</u> and thanked them for their invitation. His speech was so <u>eloquent</u> that all the birds were glad they had brought him, and nodded their heads in approval of all he said. Their hosts took him as the king of the birds, especially as he looked somewhat different from the others.

"After kola nuts had been presented and eaten, the people of the sky set before their guests the most <u>delectable</u> dishes Tortoise had ever seen or dreamed of. The soup was brought out hot from the fire and in the very pot in which it had been cooked. It was full of meat and fish. Tortoise began to sniff aloud. There was pounded yam and also yam pottage cooked with palm-oil and fresh fish. There were also pots of palm-wine. When everything had been set before the guests, one of the people of the sky came forward and tasted a little from each pot. He then invited the birds to eat. But Tortoise jumped to his feet and asked: 'For whom have you prepared this feast?'

"'For all of you,' replied the man.

▶ What trick does
Tortoise play?

"Tortoise turned to the birds and said: 'You remember that my name is *All of you.* The custom here is to serve the spokesman first and the others later. They will serve you when I have eaten.'

"He began to eat and the birds grumbled angrily. The people of the sky thought it must be their custom to leave all the food for their king. And so Tortoise ate the best part of the food and then drank two pots of palm-wine, so that he was full of food and drink and his body filled out in his shell.

"The birds gathered round to eat what was left and to peck at the bones he had thrown all about the floor. Some of them were too angry to eat. They chose to fly home on an empty stomach. But before they left each took back the feather he had lent to Tortoise. And there he stood in his hard shell full of food and wine but without any wings to fly home. He asked the birds to take a message for his wife, but they all refused. In the end Parrot, who had felt more

---

**words
for
everyday
use**

plum • age (plüm´ij) *n.*, feathers of a bird. *Ducks tend their <u>plumage</u> carefully, preening and grooming often.*

el • o • quent (el´ə kwənt) *adj.*, fluent and persuasive. *The "I Have a Dream"*

speech is an <u>eloquent</u> example of oratory.
de • lec • ta • ble (de lek´tə bəl) *adj.*, delightful; delicious. *"Oh, Shana," I said, "this pecan pie is <u>delectable</u>!"*

angry than the others, suddenly changed his mind and agreed to take the message.

"'Tell my wife,' said Tortoise, 'to bring out all the soft things in my house and cover the compound with them so that I can jump down from the sky without very great danger.'"

"Parrot promised to deliver the message, and then flew away. But when he reached Tortoise's house he told his wife to bring out all the hard things in the house. And so she brought out her husband's hoes, machetes, spears, guns and even his cannon. Tortoise looked down from the sky and saw his wife bringing things out, but it was too far to see what they were. When all seemed ready he let himself go. He fell and fell and fell until he began to fear that he would never stop falling. And then like the sound of his cannon he crashed on the compound."

"Did he die?" asked Ezinma.

"No," replied Ekwefi. "His shell broke into pieces. But there was a great medicine man in the neighborhood. Tortoise's wife sent for him and he gathered all the bits of shell and stuck them together. That is why Tortoise's shell is not smooth."

◀ Why is Tortoise's shell not smooth?

"There is no song in the story," Ezinma pointed out.

"No," said Ekwefi. "I shall think of another one with a song. But it is your turn now."

"Once upon a time," Ezinma began, "Tortoise and Cat went to wrestle against Yams—no, that is not the beginning. Once upon a time there was a great famine in the land of animals. Everybody was lean except Cat, who was fat and whose body shone as if oil was rubbed on it . . ."

She broke off because at that very moment a loud and high-pitched voice broke the outer silence of the night. It was Chielo, the priestess of Agbala, prophesying. There was nothing new in that. Once in a while Chielo was possessed by the spirit of her god and she began to prophesy. But tonight she was addressing her prophecy and greetings to Okonkwo, and so everyone in his family listened. The folk stories stopped.

◀ Why do the family members stop talking?

"Agbala do-o-o-o! Agbala ekeneo-o-o-o," came the voice like a sharp knife cutting through the night. "Okonkwo! Agbala ekene gio-o-o! Agbala cholu ifu ada ya Ezinmao-o-o-o!"

At the mention of Ezinma's name Ekwefi jerked her head sharply like an animal that had sniffed death in the air. Her heart jumped painfully within her.

◀ What does Ekwefi fear?

The priestess had now reached Okonkwo's compound and was talking with him outside his hut. She was saying again and again that Agbala wanted to see his daughter,

Ezinma. Okonkwo pleaded with her to come back in the morning because Ezinma was now asleep. But Chielo ignored what he was trying to say and went on shouting that Agbala wanted to see his daughter. Her voice was as clear as metal, and Okonkwo's women and children heard from their huts all that she said. Okonkwo was still pleading that the girl had been ill of late and was asleep. Ekwefi quickly took her to their bedroom and placed her on their high bamboo bed.

The priestess suddenly screamed. "Beware, Okonkwo!" she warned. "Beware of exchanging words with Agbala. Does a man speak when a god speaks? Beware!"

She walked through Okonkwo's hut into the circular compound and went straight towards Ekwefi's hut. Okonkwo came after her.

"Ekwefi," she called, "Agbala greets you. Where is my daughter, Ezinma? Agbala wants to see her."

Ekwefi came out from her hut carrying her oil lamp in her left hand. There was a light wind blowing, so she cupped her right hand to shelter the flame. Nwoye's mother, also carrying an oil lamp, emerged from her hut. Her children stood in the darkness outside their hut watching the strange event. Okonkwo's youngest wife also came out and joined the others.

"Where does Agbala want to see her?" Ekwefi asked.

"Where else but in his house in the hills and the caves?" replied the priestess.

"I will come with you, too," Ekwefi said firmly.

▶ Why does the priestess react in this way?

"Tufia-a!" the priestess cursed, her voice cracking like the angry bark of thunder in the dry season. "How dare you, woman, to go before the mighty Agbala of your own accord? Beware, woman, lest he strike you in his anger. Bring me my daughter."

Ekwefi went into her hut and came out again with Ezinma.

"Come, my daughter," said the priestess. "I shall carry you on my back. A baby on its mother's back does not know that the way is long."

Ezinma began to cry. She was used to Chielo calling her "my daughter." But it was a different Chielo she now saw in the yellow half-light.

"Don't cry, my daughter," said the priestess, "lest Agbala be angry with you."

"Don't cry," said Ekwefi, "she will bring you back very soon. I shall give you some fish to eat." She went into the hut again and brought down the smoke-black basket in which she kept her dried fish and other ingredients for cooking soup. She broke a piece in two and gave it to Ezinma, who clung to her.

"Don't be afraid," said Ekwefi, stroking her head, which was shaved in places, leaving a regular pattern of hair. They went outside again. The priestess bent down on one knee and Ezinma climbed on her back, her left palm closed on her fish and her eyes gleaming with tears.

"*Agbala do-o-o-o! Agbala ekeneo-o-o-o! . . .*" Chielo began once again to chant greetings to her god. She turned round sharply and walked through Okonkwo's hut, bending very low at the <u>eaves</u>. Ezinma was crying loudly now, calling on her mother. The two voices disappeared into the thick darkness.

A strange and sudden weakness descended on Ekwefi as she stood gazing in the direction of the voices like a hen whose only chick has been carried away by a kite. Ezinma's voice soon faded away and only Chielo was heard moving farther and farther into the distance.

"Why do you stand there as though she had been kidnapped?" asked Okonkwo as he went back to his hut.

"She will bring her back soon," Nwoye's mother said.

But Ekwefi did not hear these consolations. She stood for a while, and then, all of a sudden, made up her mind. She hurried through Okonkwo's hut and went outside.

"Where are you going?" he asked.

"I am following Chielo," she replied and disappeared in the darkness. Okonkwo cleared his throat, and brought out his snuff-bottle from the goatskin bag by his side.

◀ *What does Ekwefi decide to do?*

The priestess's voice was already growing faint in the distance. Ekwefi hurried to the main footpath and turned left in the direction of the voice. Her eyes were useless to her in the darkness. But she picked her way easily on the sandy footpath hedged on either side by branches and damp leaves. She began to run, holding her breasts with her arms to stop them flapping noisily against her body. She hit her left foot against an outcropped root, and terror seized her. It was an ill omen. She ran faster. But Chielo's voice was still a long way away. Had she been running too? How could she go so fast with Ezinma on her back? Although the night was cool, Ekwefi was beginning to feel hot from her running. She continually ran into the luxuriant weeds and

◀ *What does Ekwefi consider a bad sign, or "ill omen"?*

words for everyday use   eaves (ēvz´) *n. pl.*, lower edges of a roof. *Sparrows built their nests in the <u>eaves</u>.*

creepers that walled in the path. Once she tripped up and fell. Only then did she realize, with a start, that Chielo had stopped her chanting. Her heart beat violently and she stood still. Then Chielo's renewed outburst came from only a few paces ahead. But Ekwefi could not see her. She shut her eyes for a while and opened them again in an effort to see. But it was useless. She could not see beyond her nose.

There were no stars in the sky because there was a rain-cloud. Fireflies went about with their tiny green lamps, which only made the darkness more <u>profound</u>. Between Chielo's outbursts the night was alive with the shrill tremor of forest insects woven into the darkness.

"*Agbala do-o-o-o!* . . . *Agbala ekeneo-o-o-o!* . . ." Ekwefi trudged behind, neither getting too near nor keeping too far back. She thought they must be going toward the sacred cave. Now that she walked slowly she had time to think. What would she do when they got to the cave? She would not dare to enter. She would wait at the mouth, all alone in that fearful place. She thought of all the terrors of the night. She remembered that night, long ago, when she had seen *Ogbu-agali-odu*, one of those evil essences[2] loosed upon the world by the potent "medicines" which the tribe had made in the distant past against its enemies but had now forgotten how to control. Ekwefi had been returning from the stream with her mother on a dark night like this when they saw its glow as it flew in their direction. They had thrown down their water-pots and lain by the road-side expecting the <u>sinister</u> light to descend on them and kill them. That was the only time Ekwefi ever saw *Ogbu-agali-odu*. But although it had happened so long ago, her blood still ran cold whenever she remembered that night.

The priestess's voice came at longer intervals now, but its <u>vigor</u> was undiminished. The air was cool and damp with dew. Ezinma sneezed. Ekwefi muttered, "Life to you." At the same time the priestess also said, "Life to you, my daughter." Ezinma's voice from the darkness warmed her mother's heart. She trudged slowly along.

▶ *What did Ekwefi encounter in the forest long ago?*

---

2. **essences.** Beings or substances in concentrated form

words for everyday use

pro • found (prō found´) *adj.*, deep; intense. *The boss's request for volunteers was met with a <u>profound</u> silence.*

sin • is • ter (sin´is tər) *adj.*, wicked; evil. *The gangster intimidated people with his <u>sinister</u> looks.*

vig • or (vig´ər) *n.*, strength; intensity. *At seventy, Ms. Smith was still a strong woman; her <u>vigor</u> was unimpaired.*

And then the priestess screamed. "Somebody is walking behind me!" she said. "Whether you are spirit or man, may Agbala shave your head with a blunt razor! May he twist your neck until you see your heels!"

Ekwefi stood rooted to the spot. One mind said to her: "Woman, go home before Agbala does you harm." But she could not. She stood until Chielo had increased the distance between them and she began to follow again. She had already walked so long that she began to feel a slight numbness in the limbs and in the head. Then it occurred to her that they could not have been heading for the cave. They must have by-passed it long ago; they must be going toward Umuachi, the farthest village in the clan. Chielo's voice now came after long <u>intervals</u>.

It seemed to Ekwefi that the night had become a little lighter. The cloud had lifted and a few stars were out. The moon must be preparing to rise, its <u>sullenness</u> over. When the moon rose late in the night, people said it was refusing food, as a sullen husband refuses his wife's food when they have quarrelled.

"Agbala do-o-o-o! Umuachi! Agbala ekene unuo-o-o!" It was just as Ekwefi had thought. The priestess was now saluting the village of Umuachi. It was unbelievable, the distance they had covered. As they emerged into the open village from the narrow forest track the darkness was softened and it became possible to see the vague shape of trees. Ekwefi screwed her eyes up in an effort to see her daughter and the priestess, but whenever she thought she saw their shape it immediately dissolved like a melting lump of darkness. She walked numbly along.

Chielo's voice was now rising continuously, as when she first set out. Ekwefi had a feeling of spacious openness, and she guessed they must be on the village *ilo,* or playground. And she realized too with something like a jerk that Chielo was no longer moving forward. She was, in fact, returning. Ekwefi quickly moved away from her line of retreat. Chielo passed by, and they began to go back the way they had come.

It was a long and weary journey and Ekwefi felt like a sleepwalker most of the way. The moon was definitely

---

words for everyday use

in • ter • val (in′tər vəl) *n.,* space; gap. *During the short <u>interval</u> between hymns, the minister took up a collection to help flood victims in Sri Lanka.*

sul • len • ness (sul′ən nəs) *n.,* resentment; gloominess. *We tried to cheer Kate up, but nothing could relieve her <u>sullenness.</u>*

rising, and although it had not yet appeared on the sky its light had already melted down the darkness. Ekwefi could now <u>discern</u> the figure of the priestess and her burden. She slowed down her pace so as to increase the distance between them. She was afraid of what might happen if Chielo suddenly turned round and saw her.

She had prayed for the moon to rise. But now she found the half-light of the <u>incipient</u> moon more terrifying than darkness. The world was now peopled with vague, fantastic figures that dissolved under her steady gaze and then formed again in new shapes. At one stage Ekwefi was so afraid that she nearly called out to Chielo for companionship and human sympathy. What she had seen was the shape of a man climbing a palm tree, his head pointing to the earth and his legs skywards. But at that very moment Chielo's voice rose again in her possessed chanting, and Ekwefi <u>recoiled</u>, because there was no humanity there. It was not the same Chielo who sat with her in the market and sometimes bought bean-cakes for Ezinma, whom she called her daughter. It was a different woman—the priestess of Agbala, the Oracle of the Hills and Caves. Ekwefi trudged along between two fears. The sound of her benumbed steps seemed to come from some other person walking behind her. Her arms were folded across her bare breasts. Dew fell heavily and the air was cold. She could no longer think, not even about the terrors of night. She just jogged along in a half-sleep, only waking to full life when Chielo sang.

At last they took a turning and began to head for the caves. From then on, Chielo never ceased in her chanting. She greeted her god in a <u>multitude</u> of names—the owner of the future, the messenger of earth, the god who cut a man down when his life was sweetest to him. Ekwefi was also awakened and her <u>benumbed</u> fears revived.

The moon was now up and she could see Chielo and Ezinma clearly. How a woman could carry a child of that size so easily and for so long was a miracle. But Ekwefi was

▶ Why doesn't Ekwefi appeal to her friend Chielo for sympathy?

words for everyday use

dis • cern (di zərn´) vt., perceive; recognize. *In the dim morning light, I could barely <u>discern</u> the outlines of the buildings against the sky.*

in • cip • i • ent (in sip´ē ent) adj., in the first stage of existence. *At ten, Jack's <u>incipient</u> skills as a performer began to show themselves in his tendency to take center stage in the living room.*

re • coil (ri koil´) vi., retreat; shrink back.

The rattlesnake struck at its victim and then <u>recoiled</u> to avoid being struck in turn.

mul • ti • tude (mul´tə tüd´) n., large number. *A <u>multitude</u> of sheep gather on the hillside, looking from a distance like hundreds of white periods on a sheet of dark green paper.*

be • numbed (bē numd´) part., deadened. *In the cold wind, Lloyd could barely feel the tips of his own <u>benumbed</u> fingers.*

not thinking about that. Chielo was not a woman that night.

"Agbala do-o-o-o! Agbala ekeneo-o-o! Chi negbu madu ubosi ndu ya nato ya uto daluo-o-o! . . ."[3]

Ekwefi could already see the hills looming in the moonlight. They formed a circular ring with a break at one point through which the foot-track led to the center of the circle.

As soon as the priestess stepped into this ring of hills her voice was not only doubled in strength but was thrown back on all sides. It was indeed the shrine of a great god. Ekwefi picked her way carefully and quietly. She was already beginning to doubt the wisdom of her coming. Nothing would happen to Ezinma, she thought. And if anything happened to her could she stop it? She would not dare to enter the underground caves. Her coming was quite useless, she thought.

As these things went through her mind she did not realize how close they were to the cave mouth. And so when the priestess with Ezinma on her back disappeared through a hole hardly big enough to pass a hen, Ekwefi broke into a run as though to stop them. As she stood gazing at the circular darkness which had swallowed them, tears gushed from her eyes, and she swore within her that if she heard Ezinma cry she would rush into the cave to defend her against all the gods in the world. She would die with her.

◄ What is Ekwefi willing to do? What does this tell us about her feelings toward Ezinma?

Having sworn that oath, she sat down on a stony ledge and waited. Her fear had vanished. She could hear the priestess's voice, all its metal taken out of it by the vast emptiness of the cave. She buried her face in her lap and waited.

She did not know how long she waited. It must have been a very long time. Her back was turned on the footpath that led out of the hills. She must have heard a noise behind her and turned round sharply. A man stood there with a machete in his hand. Ekwefi uttered a scream and sprang to her feet.

"Don't be foolish," said Okonkwo's voice. "I thought you were going into the shrine with Chielo," he mocked.

◄ Why do you think Okonkwo comes? How does he feel toward Ezinma?

Ekwefi did not answer. Tears of gratitude filled her eyes. She knew her daughter was safe.

"Go home and sleep," said Okonkwo. "I shall wait here."

"I shall wait too. It is almost dawn. The first cock has crowed."

---

3. *Agbala...daluo-o-o!* Agbala wants something! Agbala greets you! God who kills a man on his happiest day!

As they stood there together, Ekwefi's mind went back to the days when they were young. She had married Anene because Okonkwo was too poor then to marry. Two years after her marriage to Anene she could bear it no longer and she ran away to Okonkwo. It had been early in the morning. The moon was shining. She was going to the stream to fetch water. Okonkwo's house was on the way to the stream. She went in and knocked at his door and he came out. Even in those days he was not a man of many words. He just carried her into his bed and in the darkness began to feel around her waist for the loose end of her cloth.

Chapter Twelve

ON THE FOLLOWING morning the entire neighborhood wore a <u>festive</u> air because Okonkwo's friend, Obierika, was celebrating his daughter's *uri*.[1] It was the day on which her suitor (having already paid the greater part of her brideprice) would bring palm-wine not only to her parents and immediate relatives but to the wide and extensive group of kinsmen called *umunna*. Everybody had been invited—men, women and children. But it was really a woman's ceremony and the central figures were the bride and her mother.

◀ What tradition is the author going to introduce in this chapter?

As soon as day broke, breakfast was hastily eaten and women and children began to gather at Obierika's compound to help the bride's mother in her difficult but happy task of cooking for a whole village.

Okonkwo's family was astir like any other family in the neighborhood. Nwoye's mother and Okonkwo's youngest wife were ready to set out for Obierika's compound with all their children. Nwoye's mother carried a basket of cocoyams, a cake of salt and smoked fish which she would present to Obierika's wife. Okonkwo's youngest wife, Ojiugo, also had a basket of plantains and coco-yams and a small pot of palm-oil. Their children carried pots of water.

Ekwefi was tired and sleepy from the exhausting experiences of the previous night. It was not very long since they had returned. The priestess, with Ezinma sleeping on her back, had crawled out of the shrine on her belly like a snake. She had not as much as looked at Okonkwo and Ekwefi or shown any surprise at finding them at the mouth of the cave. She looked straight ahead of her and walked back to the village. Okonkwo and his wife followed at a respectful distance. They thought the priestess might be going to her house, but she went to Okonkwo's compound, passed through his *obi* and into Ekwefi's hut and walked into her bedroom. She placed Ezinma carefully on the bed and went away without saying a word to anybody.

Ezinma was still sleeping when everyone else was astir, and Ekwefi asked Nwoye's mother and Ojiugo to explain to Obierika's wife that she would be late. She had got ready

---

1. *uri.* Ceremony in which the dowry, or bride price, is paid

words for everyday use   fes • tive (fes´tiv) *adj.,* merry; joyous. *The room was decorated for a banquet or some other <u>festive</u> occasion.*

her basket of coco-yams and fish, but she must wait for Ezinma to wake.

"You need some sleep yourself," said Nwoye's mother. "You look very tired."

As they spoke Ezinma emerged from the hut, rubbing her eyes and stretching her spare frame. She saw the other children with their water-pots and remembered that they were going to fetch water for Obierika's wife. She went back to the hut and brought her pot.

"Have you slept enough?" asked her mother.

"Yes," she replied. "Let us go."

"Not before you have had your breakfast," said Ekwefi. And she went into her hut to warm the vegetable soup she had cooked last night.

"We shall be going," said Nwoye's mother. "I will tell Obierika's wife that you are coming later." And so they all went to help Obierika's wife—Nwoye's mother with her four children and Ojiugo with her two.

As they trooped through Okonkwo's *obi* he asked: "Who will prepare my afternoon meal?"

"I shall return to do it," said Ojiugo.

▶ What feelings did Okonkwo hide?

Okonkwo was also feeling tired and sleepy, for although nobody else knew it, he had not slept at all last night. He had felt very anxious but did not show it. When Ekwefi had followed the priestess, he had allowed what he regarded as a reasonable and manly interval to pass and then gone with his machete to the shrine, where he thought they must be. It was only when he had got there that it had occurred to him that the priestess might have chosen to go round the villages first. Okonkwo had returned home and sat waiting. When he thought he had waited long enough he again returned to the shrine. But the Hills and the Caves were as silent as death. It was only on his fourth trip that he had found Ekwefi, and by then he had become gravely worried.

Obierika's compound was as busy as an anthill. Temporary cooking <u>tripods</u> were erected on every available space by bringing together three blocks of sun-dried earth and making a fire in their midst. Cooking pots went up and down the tripods, and foo-foo was pounded in a hun-

words for everyday use
tri • pod (trī´päd´) *n.*, three-legged stand. *The photographer attached his camera to a tripod to avoid having it jiggle when the pictures were snapped.*

dred wooden mortars. Some of the women cooked the yams and the cassava,[2] and others prepared vegetable soup. Young men pounded the foo-foo or split firewood. The children made endless trips to the stream.

Three young men helped Obierika to slaughter the two goats with which the soup was made. They were very fat goats, but the fattest of all was <u>tethered</u> to a peg near the wall of the compound. It was as big as a small cow. Obierika had sent one of his relatives all the way to Umuike to buy that goat. It was the one he would present alive to his in-laws.

"The market of Umuike is a wonderful place," said the young man who had been sent by Obierika to buy the giant goat. "There are so many people on it that if you threw up a grain of sand it would not find a way to fall to earth again."

"It is the result of a great medicine," said Obierika. "The people of Umuike wanted their market to grow and swallow up the markets of their neighbors. So they made a powerful medicine. Every market day, before the first cock-crow, this medicine stands on the market ground in the shape of an old woman with a fan. With this magic fan she <u>beckons</u> to the market all the neighboring clans. She beckons in front of her and behind her, to her right and to her left."

◀ To what cause does Obierika attribute the success of the market at Umuike?

"And so everybody comes," said another man, "honest men and thieves. They can steal your cloth from off your waist in that market."

"Yes," said Obierika. "I warned Nwankwo to keep a sharp eye and a sharp ear. There was once a man who went to sell a goat. He led it on a thick rope which he tied round his wrist. But as he walked through the market he realized that people were pointing at him as they do to a madman. He could not understand it until he looked back and saw that what he led at the end of the tether was not a goat but a heavy log of wood."

◀ How does Obierika explain the cleverness of thieves?

"Do you think a thief can do that kind of thing single-handed?" asked Nwankwo.

"No," said Obierika. "They use medicine."

---

2. **cassava.** Edible root

---

words for everyday use teth • er (teth´ər) vt., fasten with a rope or chain. *Ralph <u>tethered</u> the dog to a stake in front of the doghouse.*

beck • on (bek´'n) vt., summon by gesture. *It's summer; the beach <u>beckons</u> to me.*

When they had cut the goats' throats and collected the blood in a bowl, they held them over an open fire to burn off the hair, and the smell of burning hair blended with the smell of cooking. Then they washed them and cut them up for the women who prepared the soup.

All this anthill activity was going smoothly when a sudden interruption came. It was a cry in the distance: *Oji odu achu ijiji-o-o! (The one that uses its tail to drive flies away!)* [3] Every woman immediately abandoned whatever she was doing and rushed out in the direction of the cry.

"We cannot all rush out like that, leaving what we are cooking to burn in the fire," shouted Chielo, the priestess. "Three or four of us should stay behind."

"It is true," said another woman. "We will allow three or four women to stay behind."

▶ How is the cow's owner punished? Whose responsibility is it to restore order and enforce the law in this case?

Five women stayed behind to look after the cooking-pots, and all the rest rushed away to see the cow that had been let loose. When they saw it they drove it back to its owner, who at once paid the heavy fine which the village imposed on anyone whose cow was let loose on his neighbors' crops. When the women had exacted the penalty they checked among themselves to see if any woman had failed to come out when the cry had been raised.

"Where is Mgbogo?" asked one of them.

"She is ill in bed," said Mgbogo's next-door neighbor. "She has *iba*."

"The only other person is Udenkwo," said another woman, "and her child is not twenty-eight days yet."

Those women whom Obierika's wife had not asked to help her with the cooking returned to their homes, and the rest went back, in a body, to Obierika's compound.

"Whose cow is it?" asked the women who had been allowed to stay behind.

"It was my husband's," said Ezelagbo. "One of the young children had opened the gate of the cow-shed."

Early in the afternoon the first two pots of palm-wine arrived from Obierika's in-laws. They were duly presented to the women, who drank a cup or two each, to help them in their cooking. Some of it also went to the bride and her attendant maidens, who were putting the last delicate touches of razor to her coiffure and cam wood on her smooth skin.

---

3. **The one that uses its tail . . . away.** Cow; a cow uses its tail to swat at flies

When the heat of the sun began to soften, Obierika's son, Maduka, took a long broom and swept the ground in front of his father's *obi*. And as if they had been waiting for that, Obierika's relatives and friends began to arrive, every man with his goatskin bag hung on one shoulder and a rolled goatskin mat under his arm. Some of them were accompanied by their sons bearing carved wooden stools. Okonkwo was one of them. They sat in a half circle and began to talk of many things. It would not be long before the suitors came.

Okonkwo brought out his snuff-bottle and offered it to Ogbuefi Ezenwa, who sat next to him. Ezenwa took it, tapped it on his kneecap, rubbed his left palm on his body to dry it before tipping a little snuff into it. His actions were deliberate, and he spoke as he performed them:

"I hope our in-laws will bring many pots of wine. Although they come from a village that is known for being close fisted, they ought to know that Akueke is the bride for a king."

◀ Why are the pots to be brought?

"They dare not bring fewer than thirty pots," said Okonkwo. "I shall tell them my mind if they do."

At that moment Obierika's son, Maduka, led out the giant goat from the inner compound, for his father's relatives to see. They all admired it and said that that was the way things should be done. The goat was then led back to the inner compound.

Very soon after, the in-laws began to arrive. Young men and boys in single file, each carrying a pot of wine, came first. Obierika's relatives counted the pots as they came in. Twenty, twenty-five. There was a long break, and the hosts looked at each other as if to say, "I told you." Then more pots came. Thirty, thirty-five, forty, forty-five. The hosts nodded in approval and seemed to say, "Now they are behaving like men." Altogether there were fifty pots of wine. After the pot-bearers came Ibe, the suitor, and the elders of his family. They sat in a half-moon, thus completing a circle with their hosts. The pots of wine stood in their midst. Then the bride, her mother and half a dozen other women and girls emerged from the inner compound, and went round the circle shaking hands with all. The bride's mother led the way, followed by the bride and the other women. The married women wore their best cloths and the girls wore red and black waist-beads and anklets of brass.

When the women retired, Obierika presented kola nuts to his in-laws. His eldest brother broke the first one. "Life to all of us," he said as he broke it. "And let there be friendship between your family and ours."

The crowd answered: *"Ee-e-e!"*

"We are giving you our daughter today. She will be a good wife to you. She will bear you nine sons like the mother of our town."

"Ee-e-e!"

The oldest man in the camp of the visitors replied: "It will be good for you and it will be good for us."

"Ee-e-e!"

"This is not the first time my people have come to marry your daughter. My mother was one of you."

"Ee-e-e!"

"And this will not be the last, because you understand us and we understand you. You are a great family."

"Ee-e-e!"

"Prosperous men and great warriors." He looked in the direction of Okonkwo. "Your daughter will bear us sons like you."

"Ee-e-e!"

The kola was eaten and the drinking of palm-wine began. Groups of four or five men sat round with a pot in their midst. As the evening wore on, food was presented to the guests. There were huge bowls of foo-foo and steaming pots of soup. There were also pots of yam pottage. It was a great feast.

As night fell, burning torches were set on wooden tripods and the young men raised a song. The elders sat in a big circle and the singers went round singing each man's praise as they came before him. They had something to say for every man. Some were great farmers, some were orators who spoke for the clan; Okonkwo was the greatest wrestler and warrior alive. When they had gone round the circle they settled down in the center, and girls came from the inner compound to dance. At first the bride was not among them. But when she finally appeared holding a cock in her right hand, a loud cheer rose from the crowd. All the other dancers made way for her. She presented the cock to the musicians and began to dance. Her brass anklets rattled as she danced and her body gleamed with cam wood in the soft yellow light. The musicians with their wood, clay and metal instruments went from song to song. And they were all gay. They sang the latest song in the village:

▶ What do the men call Okonkwo?

> *"If I hold her hand*
> > *She says, 'Don't touch!'*
> *If I hold her foot*
> > *She says, 'Don't touch!'*
> *But when I hold her waist beads*
> > *She pretends not to know."*

The night was already far spent when the guests rose to go, taking their bride home to spend seven market weeks with her suitor's family. They sang songs as they went, and on their way they paid short courtesy visits to prominent men like Okonkwo, before they finally left for their village. Okonkwo made a present of two cocks to them.

Chapter Thirteen

GO-DI-DI-GO-GO-DI-GO. DI-GO-GO-DI-GO. It was the *ekwe* talking to the clan. One of the things every man learned was the language of the hollowed-out instrument. Diim! Diim! Diim! boomed the cannon at intervals.

The first cock had not crowed, and Umuofia was still swallowed up in sleep and silence when the *ekwe* began to talk, and the cannon shattered the silence. Men stirred on their bamboo beds and listened anxiously. Somebody was dead. The cannon seemed to <u>rend</u> the sky. Di-go-go-di-go-di-di-go-go floated in the message-laden night air. The faint and distant <u>wailing</u> of women settled like a <u>sediment</u> of sorrow on the earth. Now and again a full-chested <u>lamentation</u> rose above the wailing whenever a man came into the place of death. He raised his voice once or twice in manly sorrow and then sat down with the other men listening to the endless wailing of the women and the esoteric language of the *ekwe*. Now and again the cannon boomed. The wailing of the women would not be heard beyond the village, but the *ekwe* carried the news to all the nine villages and even beyond. It began by naming the clan: *Umuofia obodo dike,* "the land of the brave." *Umuofia obodo dike! Umuofia obodo dike!* It said this over and over again, and as it dwelt on it, anxiety mounted in every heart that heaved on a bamboo bed that night. Then it went nearer and named the village: *"Iguedo of the yellow grinding-stone!"* It was Okonkwo's village. Again and again Iguedo was called and men waited breathlessly in all the nine villages. At last the man was named and people sighed "E-u-u, Ezeudu is dead." A cold shiver ran down Okonkwo's back as he remembered the last time the old man had visited him. "That boy calls you father," he had said. "Bear no hand in his death."

Ezeudu was a great man, and so all the clan was at his funeral. The ancient drums of death beat, guns and cannon were fired, and men dashed about in frenzy, cutting

▶ *What does Okonkwo remember about Ezeudu?*

---

words for everyday use

rend (rend´) *vt.,* tear; split. *The movers got one leg of the coffee table caught in the curtains, thus <u>rending</u> the delicate fabric.*

wail • ing (wāl´iŋ) *n.,* crying. *"How can I sleep with all of that <u>wailing</u>?" asked the new father.*

sed • i • ment (sed´ə mənt) *n.,* matter that settles to the bottom. *The pirate's treasure box was covered by <u>sediment</u> at the bottom of the ocean.*

lam • en • ta • tion (lam´ən tā´shən) *n.,* expression of grief. *The general was troubled by the <u>lamentations</u> of the people who had lost their sons and daughters in the war.*

down every tree or animal they saw, jumping over walls and dancing on the roof. It was a warrior's funeral, and from morning till night warriors came and went in their age groups. They all wore smoked raffia skirts and their bodies were painted with chalk and charcoal. Now and again an ancestral spirit or *egwugwu* appeared from the underworld, speaking in a <u>tremulous</u>, unearthly voice and completely covered in raffia. Some of them were very violent, and there had been a mad rush for shelter earlier in the day when one appeared with a sharp machete and was only prevented from doing serious harm by two men who restrained him with the help of a strong rope tied round his waist. Sometimes he turned round and chased those men, and they ran for their lives. But they always returned to the long rope he trailed behind. He sang, in a terrifying voice, that Ekwensu, or Evil Spirit, had entered his eye.

But the most dreaded of all was yet to come. He was always alone and was shaped like a coffin. A sickly odor hung in the air wherever he went, and flies went with him. Even the greatest medicine men took shelter when he was near. Many years ago another *egwugwu* had dared to stand his ground before him and had been <u>transfixed</u> to the spot for two days. This one had only one hand and with it carried a basket full of water.

But some of the *egwugwu* were quite harmless. One of them was so old and infirm that he leaned heavily on a stick. He walked unsteadily to the place where the corpse was laid, gazed at it a while and went away again—to the underworld.

The land of the living was not far removed from the domain of the ancestors. There was coming and going between them, especially at festivals and also when an old man died, because an old man was very close to the ancestors. A man's life from birth to death was a series of transition rites[1] which brought him nearer and nearer to his ancestors.

◀ *What do the people believe about the connection between the land of the living and that of the ancestors?*

Ezeudu had been the oldest man in his village, and at his death there were only three men in the whole clan who

---

1. **transition rites.** Ceremonies held to mark passage from one stage of life, such as childhood, to the next

<table>
<tr><td>**words for everyday use**</td><td>**trem • u • lous** (trem´yü ləs) *adj.*, shaking, quivering. *The cowardly lion spoke to the wizard in a <u>tremulous</u> voice.*</td><td>**trans • fix** (trans fiks´) *vt.*, make motionless. *The deer stood at the side of the road, <u>transfixed</u> in the headlights of the car.*</td></tr>
</table>

were older, and four or five others in his own age group. Whenever one of these ancient men appeared in the crowd to dance unsteadily the funeral steps of the tribe, younger men gave way and the <u>tumult</u> <u>subsided</u>.

It was a great funeral, such as befitted a noble warrior. As the evening drew near, the shouting and the firing of guns, the beating of drums and the brandishing and clanging of machetes increased.

Ezeudu had taken three titles in his life. It was a rare achievement. There were only four titles in the clan, and only one or two men in any generation ever achieved the fourth and highest. When they did, they became the lords of the land. Because he had taken titles, Ezeudu was to be buried after dark with only a glowing brand to light the sacred ceremony.

But before this quiet and final rite, the tumult increased tenfold. Drums beat violently and men leaped up and down in frenzy. Guns were fired on all sides and sparks flew out as machetes clanged together in warriors' salutes. The air was full of dust and the smell of gunpowder. It was then that the one-handed spirit came, carrying a basket full of water. People made way for him on all sides and the noise subsided. Even the smell of gunpowder was swallowed in the sickly smell that now filled the air. He danced a few steps to the funeral drums and then went to see the corpse.

"Ezeudu!" he called in his <u>guttural</u> voice. "If you had been poor in your last life I would have asked you to be rich when you come again. But you were rich. If you had been a coward, I would have asked you to bring courage. But you were a fearless warrior. If you had died young, I would have asked you to get life. But you lived long. So I shall ask you to come again the way you came before. If your death was the death of nature, go in peace. But if a man caused it, do not allow him a moment's rest." He danced a few more steps and went away.

▶ What terrible event happens during Ezeudu's funeral?

The drums and the dancing began again and reached fever-heat. Darkness was around the corner, and the burial was near. Guns fired the last salute and the cannon rent

<hr>

words for everyday use

tu • mult (tü´mult´) *n.*, commotion. *The dropping of the hundred-dollar bills from the tenth-story window caused a <u>tumult</u> in the street below.*

sub • side (səb sīd´) *vi.*, become less intense. *After Marcia's magnificent speech,* it took fully two minutes for the applause of the audience to <u>subside</u>.

gut • tur • al (gut´ər əl) *adj.*, harsh; throaty. *The German language is known for its <u>guttural</u> consonants like the ch in ich.*

the sky. And then from the center of the <u>delirious</u> fury came a cry of agony and shouts of horror. It was as if a spell had been cast. All was silent. In the center of the crowd a boy lay in a pool of blood. It was the dead man's sixteen-year-old son, who with his brothers and halfbrothers had been dancing the traditional farewell to their father. Okonkwo's gun had exploded and a piece of iron had pierced the boy's heart.

The confusion that followed was without parallel in the tradition of Umuofia. Violent deaths were frequent, but nothing like this had ever happened.

The only course open to Okonkwo was to flee from the clan. It was a crime against the earth goddess to kill a clansman, and a man who committed it must flee from the land. The crime was of two kinds, male and female. Okonkwo had committed the female, because it had been <u>inadvertent</u>. He could return to the clan after seven years.

That night he collected his most valuable belongings into head-loads. His wives wept bitterly and their children wept with them without knowing why. Obierika and half a dozen other friends came to help and to console him. They each made nine or ten trips carrying Okonkwo's yams to store in Obierika's barn. And before the cock crowed Okonkwo and his family were fleeing to his motherland. It was a little village called Mbanta, just beyond the borders of Mbaino.

◄ How is Okonkwo punished for his crime?

As soon as the day broke, a large crowd of men from Ezeudu's quarter stormed Okonkwo's compound, dressed in garbs of war. They set fire to his houses, demolished his red walls, killed his animals and destroyed his barn. It was the justice of the earth goddess, and they were merely her messengers. They had no hatred in their hearts against Okonkwo. His greatest friend, Obierika, was among them. They were merely cleansing the land which Okonkwo had polluted with the blood of a clansman.

Obierika was a man who thought about things. When the will of the goddess had been done, he sat down in his *obi* and mourned his friend's <u>calamity</u>. Why should a man

---

words for everyday use

de • lir • i • ous (di lir´ē əs) *adj.*, wildly excited. *The fever caused Bob to speak in a <u>delirious</u> manner.*

in • ad • vert • ent (in´ad vərt´'nt) *adj.*, unintentional. *Unfortunately, the surprise party was revealed to Morticia by George's* <u>inadvertent</u> *remark about having to pay the caterers.*

ca • lam • i • ty (kə lam´ə tē) *n.*, disaster. *The bull entered the china shop, and <u>calamity</u> ensued.*

suffer so <u>grievously</u> for an offense he had committed inadvertently? But although he thought for a long time he found no answer. He was merely led into greater complexities. He remembered his wife's twin children, whom he had thrown away. What crime had they committed? The Earth had <u>decreed</u> that they were an offense on the land and must be destroyed. And if the clan did not exact punishment for an offense against the great goddess, her <u>wrath</u> was loosed on all the land and not just on the offender. As the elders said, if one finger brought oil it soiled the others.

Respond to the Selection

Do you feel that Okonkwo deserves to be punished for the death that occurred during the funeral dance? Why, or why not? Discuss this matter with your classmates.

Investigate, Inquire, and Imagine

Recall: GATHERING FACTS

1a. What is an *ogbanje?* What does Ekwefi fear might be true of her child Ezinma?

2a. Where does Ezinma lead the medicine man? What does the medicine man find when he digs into the ground?

3a. Who conducts trials in Umuofia? Who are the *egwugwu?*

4a. What disastrous event occurs during the funeral ceremony for Ezeudu?

Interpret: FINDING MEANING

1b. According to traditional Igbo belief, what causes a mother to lose several children, one after another?

2b. Why do you think Ezinma has such an air of importance when she leads the medicine man to the forest?

3b. How do the *egwugwu* address humans? Why do you think they speak in this way?

4b. What aspects of the funeral ceremony make it possible for dangerous accidents to occur? How is this accident related to the infiltration of Western technology into a traditional culture?

Analyze: TAKING THINGS APART

5a. Describe each of the Igbo traditions Achebe introduces in these chapters. What purpose do you think he has for showing us these traditions?

Synthesize: BRINGING THINGS TOGETHER

5b. What have you learned about the values of the Igbo people in chapters 9–13? about their day-to-day realities? What role does religion play in their lives?

Evaluate: MAKING JUDGMENTS

6a. Describe the judicial system of
the Igbo of Umuofia as you
understand it. Do you think the
system is effective? As you
answer this question, consider
the case of Mgbafo and
Uzowulu as well as Okonkwo's
punishment. How would you
resolve each of these two cases?

Extend: CONNECTING IDEAS

6b. What role does religion play in
the justice system of the Igbo?
Reread the end of chapter 13. If
you could advise Obierika, what
would you tell him? How would
you answer his questions?

Understanding Literature

CHARACTERIZATION. **Characterization** is the use of literary techniques to create a
character. Writers use three major techniques to create characters: direct description, portrayal of characters' behavior, and representations of characters' internal
states. How does Achebe use these techniques to reveal more about the characters of Ekwefi and Ezinma in chapters 9, 11, and 12? What is revealed about
Okonkwo's character in chapters 9, 11, and 12, as he faces losing his daughter
Ezinma? What is revealed about his relationship with Ekwefi?

MYTH. A **myth** is a story that explains objects or events in the natural world as
resulting from the action of some supernatural force or entity, most often a god.
Myths and science have a lot in common because both offer explanations of
natural phenomena. In traditional Igbo culture, how are the deaths of children
explained? In the myth told by Ekwefi, how is the patterned shell of Tortoise
explained? How do these explanations differ from modern scientific ones?

SUSPENSE. **Suspense** is a feeling of expectation, anxiousness, or curiosity created
by questions raised in the mind of a reader. In these chapters, how does the
author create suspense about what will happen to Ezinma, and how does he
resolve the suspense? As you read these chapters, what did you predict was
going to happen to Ezinma?

PART TWO

Chapter Fourteen

OKONKWO WAS WELL received by his mother's kinsmen in Mbanta. The old man who received him was his mother's younger brother, who was now the eldest surviving member of that family. His name was Uchendu, and it was he who had received Okonkwo's mother twenty and ten years before when she had been brought home from Umuofia to be buried with her people. Okonkwo was only a boy then and Uchendu still remembered him crying the traditional farewell: "Mother, mother, mother is going."

That was many years ago. Today Okonkwo was not bringing his mother home to be buried with her people. He was taking his family of three wives and their children to seek <u>refuge</u> in his motherland. As soon as Uchendu saw him with his sad and weary company he guessed what had happened, and asked no questions. It was not until the following day that Okonkwo told him the full story. The old man listened silently to the end and then said with some relief: "It is a female *ochu*."[1] And he arranged the <u>requisite</u> rites and sacrifices.

▶ Why does Uchendu arrange for special rites and sacrifices?

Okonkwo was given a plot of ground on which to build his compound, and two or three pieces of land on which to farm during the coming planting season. With the help of his mother's kinsmen he built himself an *obi* and three huts for his wives. He then installed his personal god and the symbols of his departed fathers. Each of Uchendu's five sons contributed three hundred seed-yams to enable their cousin to plant a farm, for as soon as the first rain came farming would begin.

▶ How does Okonkwo get the seed-yams?

At last the rain came. It was sudden and tremendous. For two or three moons the sun had been gathering strength till it seemed to breathe a breath of fire on the earth. All the grass had long been scorched brown, and the sand felt like live coals to the feet. Evergreen trees wore a dusty coat of brown. The birds were silenced in the forests, and the world lay panting under the live, vibrating heat. And then came the clap of thunder. It was an angry, metallic and thirsty clap, unlike the deep and liquid rumbling of

---

1. *ochu.* Manslaughter

words for everyday use

ref • uge (ref´ yüj) *n.,* shelter; protection. *The outlaw fled across the border and took <u>refuge</u> in the mountains.*

req • ui • site (rek´wə zit) *adj.,* required; necessary. *You cannot get a job in the diplomatic corps without having studied the <u>requisite</u> foreign languages.*

the rainy season. A mighty wind arose and filled the air with dust. Palm trees swayed as the wind combed their leaves into flying crests like strange and fantastic <u>coiffures</u>.

When the rain finally came, it was in large, solid drops of frozen water which the people called "the nuts of the water of heaven." They were hard and painful on the body as they fell, yet young people ran about happily picking up the cold nuts and throwing them into their mouths to melt.

The earth quickly came to life and the birds in the forests fluttered around and chirped merrily. A vague scent of life and green vegetation was diffused in the air. As the rain began to fall more soberly and in smaller liquid drops, children sought for shelter, and all were happy, refreshed and thankful.

Okonkwo and his family worked very hard to plant a new farm. But it was like beginning life anew without the vigor and enthusiasm of youth, like learning to become left-handed in old age. Work no longer had for him the pleasure it used to have, and when there was no work to do he sat in a silent half-sleep.

His life had been ruled by a great passion—to become one of the lords of the clan. That had been his life-spring. And he had all but achieved it. Then everything had been broken. He had been cast out of his clan like a fish onto a dry, sandy beach, panting. Clearly his personal god or *chi* was not made for great things. A man could not rise beyond the destiny of his *chi*. The saying of the elders was not true—that if a man said yea his *chi* also affirmed. Here was a man whose *chi* said nay despite his own <u>affirmation</u>.

◀ *What passion rules Okonkwo's life?*

◀ *What is a person's* chi*? What does Okonkwo fear about his own* chi*?*

The old man, Uchendu, saw clearly that Okonkwo had yielded to despair and he was greatly troubled. He would speak to him after the *isa-ifi* ceremony.[2]

The youngest of Uchendu's five sons, Amikwu, was marrying a new wife. The bride-price had been paid and all but the last ceremony had been performed. Amikwu and his people had taken palm-wine to the bride's kinsmen about two moons before Okonkwo's arrival in Mbanta. And so it was time for the final ceremony of confession.

---

2. **isa-ifi ceremony.** Ceremony of confession, one of a series of marriage rituals

words for everyday use

coif • fure (kwä fyu̇r´) n., hairstyle. *The Bride of Frankenstein had a frightful* coiffure—*a huge beehive hairdo with white streaks up the sides.*

af • fir • ma • tion (af´ər mā´shən) n., positive declaration. *The prosecutor asked whether the witness was, indeed, an expert on alarm systems, and the witness made a positive <u>affirmation</u> of that fact.*

The daughters of the family were all there, some of them having come a long way from their homes in distant villages. Uchendu's eldest daughter had come from Obodo, nearly half a day's journey away. The daughters of Uchendu's brothers were also there. It was a full gathering of *umuada*,[3] in the same way as they would meet if a death occurred in the family. There were twenty-two of them.

They sat in a big circle on the ground and the bride sat in the center with a hen in her right hand. Uchendu sat by her, holding the ancestral staff of the family. All the other men stood outside the circle, watching. Their wives watched also. It was evening and the sun was setting.

Uchendu's eldest daughter, Njide, asked the questions.

"Remember that if you do not answer truthfully you will suffer or even die at childbirth," she began. "How many men have lain with you since my brother first expressed the desire to marry you?"

"None," she replied simply.

"Answer truthfully," urged the other women.

"None?" asked Njide.

"None," she answered.

"Swear on this staff of my fathers," said Uchendu.

"I swear," said the bride.

Uchendu took the hen from her, slit its throat with a sharp knife and allowed some of the blood to fall on his ancestral staff.

From that day Amikwu took the young bride to his hut and she became his wife. The daughters of the family did not return to their homes immediately but spent two or three days with their kinsmen.

On the second day Uchendu called together his sons and daughters and his nephew, Okonkwo. The men brought their goatskin mats, with which they sat on the floor, and the women sat on a sisal mat spread on a raised bank of earth. Uchendu pulled gently at his grey beard and gnashed his teeth. Then he began to speak, quietly and deliberately, picking his words with great care:

"It is Okonkwo that I primarily wish to speak to," he began. "But I want all of you to note what I am going to say. I am an old man and you are all children. I know more about the world than any of you. If there is any one among you who thinks he knows more let him speak up." He paused, but no one spoke.

---

3. *umuada.* Family gathering of daughters

"Why is Okonkwo with us today? This is not his clan. We are only his mother's kinsmen. He does not belong here. He is an exile, condemned for seven years to live in a strange land. And so he is bowed with grief. But there is just one question I would like to ask him. Can you tell me, Okonkwo, why it is that one of the commonest names we give our children is Nneka or 'Mother is Supreme'? We all know that a man is the head of the family and his wives do his bidding. A child belongs to its father and his family and not to its mother and her family. A man belongs to his father and not to his motherland. And yet we say Nneka—'Mother is Supreme.' Why is that?"

There was silence. "I want Okonkwo to answer me," said Uchendu.

"I do not know the answer," Okonkwo replied.

"You do not know the answer? So you see that you are a child. You have many wives and many children—more children than I have. You are a great man in your clan. But you are still a child, *my* child. Listen to me and I shall tell you. But there is one more question I shall ask you. Why is it that when a woman dies she is taken home to be buried with her own kinsmen? She is not buried with her husband's kinsmen. Why is that? Your mother was brought home to me and buried with my people. Why was that?"

Okonkwo shook his head.

"He does not know that either," said Uchendu, "and yet he is full of sorrow because he has come to live in his motherland for a few years." He laughed a <u>mirthless</u> laughter, and turned to his sons and daughters. "What about you? Can you answer my question?"

They all shook their heads.

"Then listen to me," he said and cleared his throat. "It's true that a child belongs to its father. But when a father beats his child, it seeks sympathy in its mother's hut. A man belongs to his fatherland when things are good and life is sweet. But when there is sorrow and bitterness he finds refuge in his motherland. Your mother is there to protect you. She is buried there. And that is why we say that mother is supreme. Is it right that you, Okonkwo, should bring to your mother a heavy face and refuse to be comforted? Be careful or you may displease the dead. Your

◀ What questions is Okonkwo unable to answer?

◀ Why does Uchendu speak to Okonkwo? What message does he convey?

words for everyday use

mirth • less (murth´lis) *adj.*, humorless; sad. *After losing the game, the members of the football team were <u>mirthless</u>.*

duty is to comfort your wives and children and take them back to your fatherland after seven years. But if you allow sorrow to weigh you down and kill you, they will all die in <u>exile</u>." He paused for a long while. "These are now your kinsmen." He waved at his sons and daughters. "You think you are the greatest sufferer in the world. Do you know that men are sometimes banished for life? Do you know that men sometimes lose all their yams and even their children? I had six wives once. I have none now except that young girl who knows not her right from her left. Do you know how many children I have buried—children I <u>begot</u> in my youth and strength? Twenty-two. I did not hang myself, and I am still alive. If you think you are the greatest sufferer in the world ask my daughter, Akueni, how many twins she has borne and thrown away. Have you not heard the song they sing when a woman dies?

> " 'For whom is it well, for whom, is it well?
> There is no one for whom it is well.'

"I have no more to say to you."

---

words for everyday use

ex • ile (eks´īl´) *n.*, state or period of forced absence from one's country or community; banishment. *After living in exile in France, Khomeni returned to Iran and led a fundamentalist revolution.*

be • get (bē get´) *vt.*, be the father of. *Kindness begets kindness.*

Chapter Fifteen

It was in the second year of Okonkwo's exile that his friend, Obierika, came to visit him. He brought with him two young men, each of them carrying a heavy bag on his head. Okonkwo helped them put down their loads. It was clear that the bags were full of cowries.

Okonkwo was very happy to receive his friend. His wives and children were very happy too, and so were his cousins and their wives when he sent for them and told them who his guest was.

"You must take him to salute our father," said one of the cousins.

"Yes," replied Okonkwo. "We are going directly." But before they went he whispered something to his first wife. She nodded, and soon the children were chasing one of their cocks.

Uchendu had been told by one of his grandchildren that three strangers had come to Okonkwo's house. He was therefore waiting to receive them. He held out his hands to them when they came into his *obi,* and after they had shaken hands he asked Okonkwo who they were.

"This is Obierika, my great friend. I have already spoken to you about him."

"Yes," said the old man, turning to Obierika. "My son has told me about you, and I am happy you have come to see us. I knew your father, Iweka. He was a great man. He had many friends here and came to see them quite often. Those were good days when a man had friends in distant clans. Your generation does not know that. You stay at home, afraid of your next-door neighbor. Even a man's motherland is strange to him nowadays." He looked at Okonkwo. "I am an old man and I like to talk. That is all I am good for now." He got up painfully, went into an inner room and came back with a kola nut.

"Who are the young men with you?" he asked as he sat down again on his goatskin. Okonkwo told him.

"Ah," he said. "Welcome, my sons." He presented the kola nut to them, and when they had seen it and thanked him, he broke it and they ate.

"Go into that room," he said to Okonkwo, pointing with his finger. "You will find a pot of wine there."

Okonkwo brought the wine and they began to drink. It was a day old, and very strong.

"Yes," said Uchendu after a long silence. "People traveled more in those days. There is not a single clan in these

◀ *What does Uchendu say about the younger generation? Do you think his idea of "the good old days" is common to all cultures?*

parts that I do not know very well. Aninta, Umuazu, Ikeocha, Elumelu, Abame—I know them all."

"Have you heard," asked Obierika, "that Abame is no more?"

"How is that?" asked Uchendu and Okonkwo together.

"Abame has been wiped out," said Obierika. "It is a strange and terrible story. If I had not seen the few survivors with my own eyes and heard their story with my own ears, I would not have believed. Was it not on an Eke day[1] that they fled into Umuofia?" he asked his two companions, and they nodded their heads.

"Three moons ago," said Obierika, "on an Eke market day a little band of fugitives came into our town. Most of them were sons of our land whose mothers had been buried with us. But there were some too who came because they had friends in our town, and others who could think of nowhere else open to escape. And so they fled into Umuofia with a woeful story." He drank his palm-wine, and Okonkwo filled his horn again. He continued:

"During the last planting season a white man had appeared in their clan."

"An albino," suggested Okonkwo.

▶ What do the people of Abame do to the white man? to his bicycle?

"He was not an albino. He was quite different." He sipped his wine. "And he was riding an iron horse.[2] The first people who saw him ran away, but he stood beckoning to them. In the end the fearless ones went near and even touched him. The elders consulted their Oracle and it told them that the strange man would break their clan and spread destruction among them." Obierika again drank a little of his wine. "And so they killed the white man and tied his iron horse to their sacred tree because it looked as if it would run away to call the man's friends. I forgot to tell you another thing which the Oracle said. It said that other white men were on their way. They were locusts, it said, and that first man was their harbinger sent to explore the terrain. And so they killed him."

"What did the white man say before they killed him?" asked Uchendu.

---

1. **Eke day.** The days of the week, in order, are Afo, Nkwo, Eke, and Oye. Eke is market day in Umuofia.

2. **iron horse.** Bicycle

words for everyday use

al • bi • no (al bī´ nō) *n.*, person whose skin, hair, and eyes lack normal coloration. *The albino fox is a rare and beautiful creature.*

"He said nothing," answered one of Obierika's companions.

"He said something, only they did not understand him," said Obierika. "He seemed to speak through his nose."

"One of the men told me," said Obierika's other companion, "that he repeated over and over again a word that resembled Mbaino. Perhaps he had been going to Mbaino and had lost his way."

"Anyway," resumed Obierika, "they killed him and tied up his iron horse. This was before the planting season began. For a long time nothing happened. The rains had come and yams had been sown. The iron horse was still tied to the sacred silk-cotton tree. And then one morning three white men led by a band of ordinary men like us came to the clan. They saw the iron horse and went away again. Most of the men and women of Abame had gone to their farms. Only a few of them saw these white men and their followers. For many market weeks nothing else happened. They have a big market in Abame on every other Afo day and, as you know, the whole clan gathers there. That was the day it happened. The three white men and a very large number of other men surrounded the market. They must have used a powerful medicine to make themselves invisible until the market was full. And they began to shoot. Everybody was killed, except the old and the sick who were at home and a handful of men and women whose *chi* were wide awake and brought them out of that market." He paused.

◀ What happened to the people of Abame?

"Their clan is now completely empty. Even the sacred fish in their mysterious lake have fled and the lake has turned the color of blood. A great evil has come upon their land as the Oracle had warned."

There was a long silence. Uchendu ground his teeth together <u>audibly</u>. Then he burst out:

"Never kill a man who says nothing. Those men of Abame were fools. What did they know about the man?" He ground his teeth again and told a story to illustrate his point. "Mother Kite once sent her daughter to bring food. She went, and brought back a duckling. 'You have done very well,' said Mother Kite to her daughter, 'but tell me,

---

words for everyday use   au • di • bly (ó´ də blē) *adv.,* loudly enough to be heard. *Please speak <u>audibly</u>. I can't hear you.*

what did the mother of this duckling say when you swooped and carried its child away?' 'It said nothing,' replied the young kite. 'It just walked away.' 'You must return the duckling,' said Mother Kite. 'There is something ominous behind the silence.' And so Daughter Kite returned the duckling and took a chick instead. 'What did the mother of this chick do?' asked the old kite. 'It cried and raved and cursed me,' said the young kite. 'Then we can eat the chick,' said her mother. 'There is nothing to fear from someone who shouts.' Those men of Abame were fools."

"They were fools," said Okonkwo after a pause. "They had been warned that danger was ahead. They should have armed themselves with their guns and their machetes even when they went to market."

"They have paid for their foolishness," said Obierika. "But I am greatly afraid. We have heard stories about white men who made the powerful guns and the strong drinks and took slaves away across the seas, but no one thought the stories were true."

▶ What stories have these people heard about white men?

"There is no story that is not true," said Uchendu. "The world has no end, and what is good among one people is an abomination with others. We have albinos among us. Do you not think that they came to our clan by mistake, that they have strayed from their way to a land where everybody is like them?"

▶ What does Uchendu mean when he says that "the world has no end"?

Okonkwo's first wife soon finished her cooking and set before their guests a big meal of pounded yams and bitter-leaf soup. Okonkwo's son, Nwoye, brought in a pot of sweet wine tapped from the raffia palm.

"You are a big man now," Obierika said to Nwoye. "Your friend Anene asked me to greet you."

"Is he well?" asked Nwoye.

"We are all well," said Obierika.

Ezinma brought them a bowl of water with which to wash their hands. After that they began to eat and to drink the wine.

"When did you set out from home?" asked Okonkwo.

"We had meant to set out from my house before cock-crow," said Obierika. "But Nweke did not appear until it was quite light. Never make an early morning appointment with a man who has just married a new wife." They all laughed.

"Has Nweke married a wife?" asked Okonkwo.

"He has married Okadigbo's second daughter," said Obierika.

"That is very good," said Okonkwo. "I do not blame you for not hearing the cock crow."

When they had eaten, Obierika pointed at the two heavy bags.

"That is the money from your yams," he said. "I sold the big ones as soon as you left. Later on I sold some of the seed-yams and gave out others to sharecroppers. I shall do that every year until you return. But I thought you would need the money now and so I brought it. Who knows what may happen tomorrow? Perhaps green men will come to our clan and shoot us."

"God will not permit it," said Okonkwo. "I do not know how to thank you."

"I can tell you," said Obierika. "Kill one of your sons for me."[3]

"That will not be enough," said Okonkwo.

"Then kill yourself," said Obierika.

"Forgive me," said Okonkwo, smiling. "I shall not talk about thanking you any more."

◄ What point does Obierika make to Okonkwo about friendship?

---

3. **I can . . . for me.** Obierika's extreme request makes the point that no reward or return is equal to an offering of friendship.

Chapter Sixteen

WHEN NEARLY TWO years later Obierika paid another visit to his friend in exile the circumstances were less happy. The missionaries had come to Umuofia. They had built their church there, won a handful of <u>converts</u> and were already sending <u>evangelists</u> to the surrounding towns and villages. That was a source of great sorrow to the leaders of the clan; but many of them believed that the strange faith and the white man's god would not last. None of his converts was a man whose word was heeded in the assembly of the people. None of them was a man of title. They were mostly the kind of people that were called *efulefu*, worthless, empty men. The imagery of an *efulefu* in the language of the clan was a man who sold his machete and wore the sheath to battle. Chielo, the priestess of Agbala, called the converts the excrement of the clan, and the new faith was a mad dog that had come to eat it up.

▶ What sorts of people are the first converts to the new religion?

What moved Obierika to visit Okonkwo was the sudden appearance of the latter's son, Nwoye, among the missionaries in Umuofia.

"What are you doing here?" Obierika had asked when after many difficulties the missionaries had allowed him to speak to the boy.

"I am one of them," replied Nwoye.

"How is your father?" Obierika asked, not knowing what else to say.

"I don't know. He is not my father," said Nwoye, unhappily.

And so Obierika went to Mbanta to see his friend. And he found that Okonkwo did not wish to speak about Nwoye. It was only from Nwoye's mother that he heard scraps of the story.

The arrival of the missionaries had caused a considerable stir in the village of Mbanta. There were six of them and one was a white man. Every man and woman came out to see the white man. Stories about these strange men had grown since one of them had been killed in Abame and his iron horse tied to the sacred silk-cotton tree. And so every-

words for everyday use

con • vert (kän´vərt´) *n.*, person who changes from one religion to another. *Perhaps the most famous <u>convert</u> in history was Paul, who converted from Judaism to Christianity.*

e • van • ge • list (ē van´jə list´) *n.*, preacher who holds public services to spread Christianity. *The <u>evangelist</u> traveled from town to town, speaking at revival meetings.*

body came to see the white man. It was the time of the year when everybody was at home. The harvest was over.

When they had all gathered, the white man began to speak to them. He spoke through an interpreter who was an Ibo man, though his dialect was different and harsh to the ears of Mbanta. Many people laughed at his dialect and the way he used words strangely. Instead of saying "myself" he always said "my buttocks." But he was a man of commanding presence and the clansmen listened to him. He said he was one of them, as they could see from his color and his language. The other four black men were also their brothers, although one of them did not speak Ibo. The white man was also their brother because they were all sons of God. And he told them about this new God, the Creator of all the world and all the men and women. He told them that they worshiped false gods, gods of wood and stone. A deep murmur went through the crowd when he said this. He told them that the true God lived on high and that all men when they died went before Him for judgment. Evil men and all the heathen who in their blindness bowed to wood and stone were thrown into a fire that burned like palm-oil. But good men who worshiped the true God lived forever in His happy kingdom. "We have been sent by this great God to ask you to leave your wicked ways and false gods and turn to Him so that you may be saved when you die," he said.

◀ What does the missionary have to say about the traditional religion of the Igbo?

"Your buttocks understand our language," said someone lightheartedly and the crowd laughed.

"What did he say?" the white man asked his interpreter. But before he could answer, another man asked a question: "Where is the white man's horse?" he asked. The Ibo evangelists consulted among themselves and decided that the man probably meant bicycle. They told the white man and he smiled <u>benevolently</u>.

"Tell them," he said, "that I shall bring many iron horses when we have settled down among them. Some of them will even ride the iron horse themselves." This was interpreted to them but very few of them heard. They were talking excitedly among themselves because the white man had said he was going to live among them. They had not thought about that.

◀ Why are the men excited?

words
for
everyday
use

be • nev • o • lent • ly (bə nevˊə lənt lē) *adv.*, in a kind or sympathetic way. *The philanthropist <u>benevolently</u> gave all his money to charities.*

At this point an old man said he had a question. "Which is this god of yours," he asked, "the goddess of the earth, the god of the sky, Amadiora or the thunderbolt, or what?"

The interpreter spoke to the white man and he immediately gave his answer. "All the gods you have named are not gods at all. They are gods of deceit who tell you to kill your fellows and destroy innocent children. There is only one true God and He has the earth, the sky, you and me and all of us."

"If we leave our gods and follow your god," asked another man, "who will protect us from the anger of our neglected gods and ancestors?"

"Your gods are not alive and cannot do you any harm," replied the white man. "They are pieces of wood and stone."

▶ Why do the men laugh?

When this was interpreted to the men of Mbanta they broke into <u>derisive</u> laughter. These men must be mad, they said to themselves. How else could they say that Ani and Amadiora were harmless? And Idemili and Ogwugwu too? And some of them began to go away.

▶ How does the music succeed where the talking failed?

Then the missionaries burst into song. It was one of those gay and rollicking tunes of evangelism which had the power of plucking at silent and dusty chords in the heart of an Ibo man. The interpreter explained each verse to the audience, some of whom now stood <u>enthralled</u>. It was a story of brothers who lived in darkness and in fear, ignorant of the love of God. It told of one sheep out on the hills, away from the gates of God and from the tender shepherd's care.[1]

After the singing the interpreter spoke about the Son of God whose name was Jesu Kristi. Okonkwo, who only stayed in the hope that it might come to chasing the men out of the village or whipping them, now said:

"You told us with your own mouth that there was only one god. Now you talk about his son. He must have a wife, then." The crowd agreed.

---

1. **It told of . . . care.** In Matthew 18:12–14, Jesus tells a parable about a lost sheep, saying that if a person has a hundred sheep and one goes astray, he will leave the other ninety-nine and go to find the one that is lost.

words for everyday use

de • ri • sive (di rī´siv) adj., scornful; ridiculing. *The comedian continued with his monologue despite the <u>derisive</u> comments from the audience.*

en • thralled (en thröld´) part., fascinated; held as if in a spell. *The children sat <u>enthralled</u> by the story of Beauty and the Beast.*

"I did not say He had a wife," said the interpreter, somewhat lamely.

"Your buttocks said he had a son," said the joker. "So he must have a wife and all of them must have buttocks."

The missionary ignored him and went on to talk about the Holy Trinity.[2] At the end of it Okonkwo was fully convinced that the man was mad. He shrugged his shoulders and went away to tap his afternoon palm-wine.

But there was a young lad who had been captivated. His name was Nwoye, Okonkwo's first son. It was not the mad logic of the Trinity that captivated him. He did not understand it. It was the poetry of the new religion, something felt in the <u>marrow</u>. The hymn about brothers who sat in darkness and in fear seemed to answer a vague and persistent question that haunted his young soul—the question of the twins crying in the bush and the question of Ikemefuna who was killed. He felt a relief within as the hymn poured into his <u>parched</u> soul. The words of the hymn were like the drops of frozen rain melting on the dry <u>palate</u> of the panting earth. Nwoye's <u>callow</u> mind was greatly puzzled.

◄ *Why does the new religion appeal to Nwoye?*

---

2. **Holy Trinity.** In Christian belief, God the Father, Christ the Son, and the Holy Spirit. In many Christian sects, these entities are viewed as three aspects of the one God. This idea that the three may in some way be one is a mystical tenet that places demands on the imagination and intelligence of the prospective convert. That is why Okonkwo, on hearing the missionary speak of the Trinity, thinks him mad.

words for everyday use

mar • row (mar´ō) *n.*, soft tissue inside bones; innermost, essential part. *The thought of reentering that cold, damp cave chilled me to the <u>marrow</u>.*

parched (pärcht´) *part.*, dried up; very thirsty. *Rain came, bringing relief to the <u>parched</u> land.*

pal • ate (pal´ət) *n.*, roof of the mouth. *Peanut butter sometimes sticks to my <u>palate</u>.*

cal • low (kal´ō) *adj.*, young; inexperienced. *The <u>callow</u> reporter had not yet learned to be sensitive to people's grief.*

Chapter Seventeen

THE MISSIONARIES SPENT their first four or five nights in the marketplace, and went into the village in the morning to preach the gospel. They asked who the king of the village was, but the villagers told them that there was no king. "We have men of high title and the chief priests and the elders," they said.

It was not very easy getting the men of high title and the elders together after the excitement of the first day. But the missionaries persevered, and in the end they were received by the rulers of Mbanta. They asked for a plot of land to build their church.

Every clan and village had its "evil forest." In it were buried all those who died of the really evil diseases, like leprosy and smallpox. It was also the dumping ground for the potent fetishes[1] of great medicine men when they died. An "evil forest" was, therefore, alive with sinister forces and powers of darkness. It was such a forest that the rulers of Mbanta gave to the missionaries. They did not really want them in their clan, and so they made them that offer which nobody in his right senses would accept.

"They want a piece of land to build their shrine," said Uchendu to his peers when they consulted among themselves. "We shall give them a piece of land." He paused, and there was a murmur of surprise and disagreement. "Let us give them a portion of the Evil Forest. They boast about victory over death. Let us give them a real battlefield in which to show their victory." They laughed and agreed, and sent for the missionaries, whom they had asked to leave them for a while so that they might "whisper together." They offered them as much of the Evil Forest as they cared to take. And to their greatest amazement the missionaries thanked them and burst into song.

"They do not understand," said some of the elders. "But they will understand when they go to their plot of land tomorrow morning." And they dispersed.

The next morning the crazy men actually began to clear a part of the forest and to build their house. The inhabitants of Mbanta expected them all to be dead within four days. The first day passed and the second and third and fourth, and none of them died. Everyone was puzzled. And then it became known that the white man's fetish had unbelievable power. It was said that he wore glasses on his

▶ What land is given to the missionaries? Why? What do the men expect will happen? How do the people of Mbanta explain the fact that the missionaries are unharmed?

---

1. **fetishes.** Objects with magical powers

eyes so that he could see and talk to evil spirits. Not long after, he won his first three converts.

Although Nwoye had been attracted to the new faith from the very first day, he kept it secret. He dared not go too near the missionaries for fear of his father. But whenever they came to preach in the open marketplace or the village playground, Nwoye was there. And he was already beginning to know some of the simple stories they told.

"We have now built a church," said Mr. Kiaga, the interpreter, who was now in charge of the infant congregation. The white man had gone back to Umuofia, where he built his headquarters and from where he paid regular visits to Mr. Kiaga's congregation at Mbanta.

"We have now built a church," said Mr. Kiaga, "and we want you all to come in every seventh day to worship the true God."

On the following Sunday, Nwoye passed and repassed the little red-earth and thatch building without summoning enough courage to enter. He heard the voice of singing and although it came from a handful of men it was loud and confident. Their church stood on a circular clearing that looked like the open mouth of the Evil Forest. Was it waiting to snap its teeth together? After passing and repassing by the church, Nwoye returned home.

It was well known among the people of Mbanta that their gods and ancestors were sometimes long-suffering and would deliberately allow a man to go on defying them. But even in such cases they set their limit at seven market weeks or twenty-eight days. Beyond that limit no man was suffered to go. And so excitement mounted in the village as the seventh week approached since the <u>impudent</u> missionaries built their church in the Evil Forest. The villagers were so certain about the doom that awaited these men that one or two converts thought it wise to suspend their <u>allegiance</u> to the new faith.

At last the day came by which all the missionaries should have died. But they were still alive, building a new red-earth and thatch house for their teacher, Mr. Kiaga. That week they won a handful more converts. And for the first time they had a woman. Her name was Nneka, the wife of Amadi, who was a prosperous farmer. She was very heavy with child.

◄ *Why does the church win new converts?*

---

words for everyday use

im • pu • dent (im′pyü dənt) *adj.*, shamelessly bold. *The impudent child was always talking back to her elders.*

al • le • giance (ə lē′jəns) *n.*, loyalty; devotion. *The sailors pledged allegiance to their king and to one another.*

Nneka had had four previous pregnancies and child-births. But each time she had borne twins, and they had been immediately thrown away. Her husband and his family were already becoming highly critical of such a woman and were not unduly perturbed when they found she had fled to join the Christians. It was a good riddance.

▶ What does Amikwu see? Why does he report this news to Okonkwo?

One morning Okonkwo's cousin, Amikwu, was passing by the church on his way from the neighboring village, when he saw Nwoye among the Christians. He was greatly surprised, and when he got home he went straight to Okonkwo's hut and told him what he had seen. The women began to talk excitedly, but Okonkwo sat unmoved.

It was late afternoon before Nwoye returned. He went into the *obi* and saluted his father, but he did not answer. Nwoye turned round to walk into the inner compound when his father, suddenly overcome with fury, sprang to his feet and gripped him by the neck.

"Where have you been?" he stammered.

Nwoye struggled to free himself from the choking grip.

"Answer me," roared Okonkwo, "before I kill you!" He seized a heavy stick that lay on the dwarf wall and hit him two or three savage blows.

"Answer me!" he roared again. Nwoye stood looking at him and did not say a word. The women were screaming outside, afraid to go in.

"Leave that boy at once!" said a voice in the outer compound. It was Okonkwo's uncle Uchendu. "Are you mad?"

▶ What happens to Nwoye?

Okonkwo did not answer. But he left hold of Nwoye, who walked away and never returned.

He went back to the church and told Mr. Kiaga that he had decided to go to Umuofia, where the white missionary had set up a school to teach young Christians to read and write.

Mr. Kiaga's joy was very great. "Blessed is he who forsakes his father and his mother for my sake," he intoned. "Those that hear my words are my father and my mother."

Nwoye did not fully understand. But he was happy to leave his father. He would return later to his mother and his brothers and sisters and convert them to the new faith.

words for everyday use

per • turb (pər tərb´) *vt.*, cause to be alarmed or upset. *Misha has nerves of steel; he was not in the least perturbed during the earthquake.*

for • sake (fȯr sāk´) *vt.*, give up; leave; abandon. *Do not forsake the ways of your ancestors.*

in • tone (in tōn´) *vi.*, speak or recite in a singing tone. *The priest intoned a prayer, and the listeners marveled at the beauty of his voice.*

As Okonkwo sat in his hut that night, gazing into a log fire, he thought over the matter. A sudden fury rose within him and he felt a strong desire to take up his machete, go to the church and wipe out the entire vile and <u>miscreant</u> gang. But on further thought he told himself that Nwoye was not worth fighting for. Why, he cried in his heart, should he, Okonkwo, of all people, be cursed with such a son? He saw clearly in it the finger of his personal god or *chi*. For how else could he explain his great misfortune and exile and now his <u>despicable</u> son's behavior? Now that he had time to think of it, his son's crime stood out in its stark enormity. To abandon the gods of one's father and go about with a lot of effeminate men clucking like old hens was the very depth of abomination. Suppose when he died all his male children decided to follow Nwoye's steps and abandon their ancestors? Okonkwo felt a cold shudder run through him at the terrible prospect, like the prospect of <u>annihilation</u>. He saw himself and his fathers crowding round their ancestral shrine waiting in vain for worship and sacrifice and finding nothing but ashes of bygone days, and his children the while praying to the white man's god. If such a thing were ever to happen, he, Okonkwo, would wipe them off the face of the earth.

◀ What is Okonkwo's first inclination? Why does he change his mind?

Okonkwo was popularly called the "Roaring Flame." As he looked into the log fire he recalled the name. He was a flaming fire. How then could he have begotten a son like Nwoye, <u>degenerate</u> and effeminate? Perhaps he was not his son. No! he could not be. His wife had played him false. He would teach her! But Nwoye resembled his grandfather, Unoka, who was Okonkwo's father. He pushed the thought out of his mind. He, Okonkwo, was called a flaming fire. How could he have begotten a woman for a son? At Nwoye's age Okonkwo had already become famous throughout Umuofia for his wrestling and his fearlessness.

◀ Why might Okonkwo have a nickname like "Roaring Flame"?

He sighed heavily, and as if in sympathy the smoldering log also sighed. And immediately Okonkwo's eyes were opened and he saw the whole matter clearly. Living fire begets cold, impotent ash. He sighed again, deeply.

---

words for everyday use

mis • cre • ant (mis′krē ənt) *adj.*, evil. *The <u>miscreants</u> were arrested and put in jail.*

des • pi • ca • ble (des′pi kə bəl) *adj.*, deserving to be despised; contemptible. *Making fun of that unfortunate person was a <u>despicable</u> act.*

an • ni • hi • la • tion (ə nī′ə lā′shən) *n.*, complete destruction; putting out of exis-tence. *The clearing of the rain forest resulted in the <u>annihilation</u> of several species of plants and animals.*

de • gen • er • ate (dē jen′ər it) *adj.*, hav-ing sunk below a normal condition; morally corrupt. *Some of the Puritans thought of dancing as a <u>degenerate</u> activity.*

Chapter Eighteen

THE YOUNG CHURCH in Mbanta had a few crises early in its life. At first the clan had assumed that it would not survive. But it had gone on living and gradually becoming stronger. The clan was worried, but not overmuch. If a gang of *efulefu* decided to live in the Evil Forest it was their own affair. When one came to think of it, the Evil Forest was a fit home for such undesirable people. It was true they were rescuing twins from the bush, but they never brought them into the village. As far as the villagers were concerned, the twins still remained where they had been thrown away. Surely the earth goddess would not visit the sins of the missionaries on the innocent villagers?

But on one occasion the missionaries had tried to overstep the bounds. Three converts had gone into the village and boasted openly that all the gods were dead and <u>impotent</u> and that they were prepared to defy them by burning all their shrines.

"Go and burn your mothers' genitals," said one of the priests. The men were seized and beaten until they streamed with blood. After that nothing happened for a long time between the church and the clan.

▶ What institution has been created by the white men in Umuofia and for what purpose?

But stories were already gaining ground that the white man had not only brought a religion but also a government. It was said that they had built a place of judgment in Umuofia to protect the followers of their religion. It was even said that they had hanged one man who killed a missionary.

Although such stories were now often told they looked like fairy tales in Mbanta and did not as yet affect the relationship between the new church and the clan. There was no question of killing a missionary here, for Mr. Kiaga, despite his madness, was quite harmless. As for his converts, no one could kill them without having to flee from the clan, for in spite of their worthlessness they still belonged to the clan. And so nobody gave serious thought to the stories about the white man's government or the consequences of killing the Christians. If they became more troublesome than they already were they would simply be driven out of the clan.

words for everyday use   im • po • tent (im′pə tənt) *adj.,* lacking strength; powerless. *The authorities felt <u>impotent</u> against the rapid spread of cholera in the population.*

And the little church was at that moment too deeply absorbed in its own troubles to annoy the clan. It all began over the question of admitting outcasts.

These outcasts, or *osu*, seeing that the new religion welcomed twins and such abominations, thought that it was possible that they would also be received. And so one Sunday two of them went into the church. There was an immediate stir; but so great was the work the new religion had done among the converts that they did not immediately leave the church when the outcasts came in. Those who found themselves nearest to them merely moved to another seat. It was a miracle. But it only lasted till the end of the service. The whole church raised a protest and were about to drive these people out, when Mr. Kiaga stopped them and began to explain.

"Before God," he said, "there is no slave or free. We are all children of God and we must receive these our brothers."

"You do not understand," said one of the converts. "What will the heathen say of us when they hear that we receive *osu* into our midst? They will laugh."

"Let them laugh," said Mr. Kiaga. "God will laugh at them on the judgment day. Why do the nations rage and the peoples imagine a vain thing? He that sitteth in the heavens shall laugh. The Lord shall have them in derision."

"You do not understand," the convert maintained. "You are our teacher, and you can teach us the things of the new faith. But this is a matter which we know." And he told him what an *osu* was.

He was a person dedicated to a god, a thing set apart—a taboo for ever, and his children after him. He could neither marry nor be married by the freeborn. He was in fact an outcast, living in a special area of the village, close to the Great Shrine. Wherever he went he carried with him the mark of his forbidden caste—long, tangled and dirty hair. A razor was taboo to him. An *osu* could not attend an assembly of the freeborn, and they, in turn, could not shelter under his roof. He could not take any of the four titles of the clan, and when he died he was buried by his kind in the Evil Forest. How could such a man be a follower of Christ?

"He needs Christ more than you and I," said Mr. Kiaga.

"Then I shall go back to the clan," said the convert. And he went. Mr. Kiaga stood firm, and it was his firmness that saved the young church. The wavering converts drew inspiration and confidence from his unshakable faith. He ordered the outcasts to shave off their long, tangled hair. At first they were afraid they might die.

◄ What saves Mr. Kiaga's young church?

"Unless you shave off the mark of your heathen belief I will not admit you into the church," said Mr. Kiaga. "You fear that you will die. Why should that be? How are you different from other men who shave their hair? The same God created you and them. But they have cast you out like lepers. It is against the will of God, who has promised everlasting life to all who believe in His holy name. The heathen say you will die if you do this or that, and you are afraid. They also said I would die if I built my church on this ground. Am I dead? They said I would die if I took care of twins. I am still alive. The heathen speak nothing but falsehood. Only the word of our God is true."

▶ What makes the two outcasts among the strongest believers in the new faith?

The two outcasts shaved off their hair, and soon they were among the strongest <u>adherents</u> of the new faith. And what was more, nearly all the *osu* in Mbanta followed their example. It was in fact one of them who in his zeal brought the church into serious conflict with the clan a year later by killing the sacred python,[1] the emanation[2] of the god of water.

The royal python was the most revered animal in Mbanta and all the surrounding clans. It was addressed as "Our Father," and was allowed to go wherever it chose, even into people's beds. It ate rats in the house and sometimes swallowed hens' eggs. If a clansman killed a royal python accidentally, he made sacrifices of <u>atonement</u> and performed an expensive burial ceremony such as was done for a great man. No punishment was <u>prescribed</u> for a man who killed the python knowingly. Nobody thought that such a thing could ever happen.

▶ Why was no punishment prescribed for deliberately killing a python?

Perhaps it never did happen. That was the way the clan at first looked at it. No one had actually seen the man do it. The story had arisen among the Christians themselves.

But, all the same, the rulers and elders of Mbanta assembled to decide on their action. Many of them spoke at great length and in fury. The spirit of wars was upon them. Okonkwo, who had begun to play a part in the affairs of his motherland, said that until the abominable gang was

▶ What course of action does Okonkwo want to follow?

---

1. **python.** Enormous nonpoisonous snake that kills its prey by constricting it
2. **emanation.** Living manifestation; physical form

words for everyday use

ad • her • ent (ad hir´ənt) *n.,* supporter or follower of a cause. *Several <u>adherents</u> of the faith traveled to faraway Nigeria to spread the gospel.*

a • tone • ment (ə tōn´mənt) *n.,* payment given for wrongdoing. *The king was required to make a pilgrimage as <u>atonement</u> for his sins.*

pre • scribe (prē skrīb´) *vt.,* set down as a rule. *After students started wearing cut-off jeans, a new school dress code was <u>prescribed</u> by the principal.*

chased out of the village with whips there would be no peace.

But there were many others who saw the situation differently, and it was their counsel that prevailed in the end.

"It is not our custom to fight for our gods," said one of them. "Let us not presume to do so now. If a man kills the sacred python in the secrecy of his hut, the matter lies between him and the god. We did not see it. If we put ourselves between the god and his victim we may receive blows intended for the offender. When a man blasphemes, what do we do? Do we go and stop his mouth? No. We put our fingers into our ears to stop us hearing. That is a wise action."

◄ What course of action does Okeke want to take and why? What decision do the men make with regard to the Christians?

"Let us not reason like cowards," said Okonkwo. "If a man comes into my hut and defecates on the floor, what do I do? Do I shut my eyes? No! I take a stick and break his head. That is what a man does. These people are daily pouring filth over us, and Okeke says we should pretend not to see." Okonkwo made a sound full of disgust. This was a womanly clan, he thought. Such a thing could never happen in his fatherland, Umuofia.

"Okonkwo has spoken the truth," said another man. "We should do something. But let us ostracize these men. We would then not be held accountable for their abominations."

Everybody in the assembly spoke, and in the end it was decided to ostracize the Christians. Okonkwo ground his teeth in disgust.

That night a bell-man went through the length and breadth of Mbanta proclaiming that the adherents of the new faith were thenceforth excluded from the life and privileges of the clan.

The Christians had grown in number and were now a small community of men, women and children, self-assured and confident. Mr. Brown, the white missionary, paid regular visits to them. "When I think that it is only eighteen months since the Seed was first sown among you," he said, "I marvel at what the Lord hath wrought."

---

words for everyday use

blas • pheme (blas´fēm´) vi., speak irreverently; curse. To _blaspheme_ against God is, in some Islamic countries, punishable by death.

os • tra • cize (äs´trə sīz´) vt., banish; exclude; reject. _In Puritan New England,_

followers of Catholicism and the Quaker faith were often _ostracized._

wrought (rȯt´) vi., (alt. p.p. of work) done. _After the new city was built, the chief architect looked out over it and said, "This is a fine thing that we have _wrought._"

It was Wednesday in Holy Week[3] and Mr. Kiaga had asked the women to bring red earth and white chalk and water to scrub the church for Easter; and the women had formed themselves into three groups for this purpose. They set out early that morning, some of them with their water-pots to the stream, another group with hoes and baskets to the village red-earth pit, and the others to the chalk quarry.

Mr. Kiaga was praying in the church when he heard the women talking excitedly. He rounded off his prayer and went to see what it was all about. The women had come to the church with empty water-pots. They said that some young men had chased them away from the stream with whips. Soon after, the women who had gone for red earth returned with empty baskets. Some of them had been heavily whipped. The chalk women also returned to tell a similar story.

"What does it all mean?" asked Mr. Kiaga, who was greatly perplexed.

"The village has outlawed us," said one of the women. "The bell-man announced it last night. But it is not our custom to <u>debar</u> anyone from the stream or the quarry."

Another woman said. "They want to ruin us. They will not allow us into the markets. They have said so."

Mr. Kiaga was going to send into the village for his men-converts when he saw them coming on their own. Of course they had all heard the bell-man, but they had never in all their lives heard of women being debarred from the stream.

"Come along," they said to the women. "We will go with you to meet those cowards." Some of them had big sticks and some even machetes.

But Mr. Kiaga restrained them. He wanted first to know why they had been outlawed.

"They say that Okoli killed the sacred python," said one man.

"It is false," said another. "Okoli told me himself that it was false."

Okoli was not there to answer. He had fallen ill on the previous night. Before the day was over he was dead. His death showed that the gods were still able to fight their own battles. The clan saw no reason then for <u>molesting</u> the Christians.

▶ *What do the villagers believe causes Okoli's death?*

---

3. **Holy Week.** Week preceding Easter

words for everyday use

de • bar (dē bär´) *vt.*, exclude. *The boys were <u>debarred</u> from going to the library because they routinely made a lot of noise there.*

mo • lest (mə lest´) *vt.*, attack; cause harm to; annoy. *In medieval times in Europe, travel between cities was dangerous because there were many thieves on the roads, waiting to <u>molest</u> unsuspecting travelers.*

Chapter Nineteen

THE LAST BIG rains of the year were falling. It was the time for treading red earth with which to build walls. It was not done earlier because the rains were too heavy and would have washed away the heap of trodden earth; and it could not be done later because harvesting would soon set in, and after that the dry season.

It was going to be Okonkwo's last harvest in Mbanta. The seven wasted and weary years were at last dragging to a close. Although he had prospered in his motherland Okonkwo knew that he would have prospered even more in Umuofia, in the land of his fathers where men were bold and warlike. In these seven years he would have climbed to the utmost heights. And so he regretted every day of his exile. His mother's kinsmen had been very kind to him, and he was grateful. But that did not alter the facts. He had called the first child born to him in exile Nneka—"Mother is Supreme"—out of politeness to his mother's kinsmen. But two years later when a son was born he called him Nwofia— "Begotten in the Wilderness."

◄ Why does Okonkwo resent his years in exile?

As soon as he entered his last year in exile Okonkwo sent money to Obierika to build him two huts in his old compound where he and his family would live until he built more huts and the outside wall of his compound. He could not ask another man to build his own *obi* for him, nor the walls of his compound. Those things a man built for himself or inherited from his father.

As the last heavy rains of the year began to fall, Obierika sent word that the two huts had been built and Okonkwo began to prepare for his return, after the rains. He would have liked to return earlier and build his compound that year before the rains stopped, but in doing so he would have taken something from the full penalty of seven years. And that could not be. So he waited impatiently for the dry season to come.

It came slowly. The rain became lighter and lighter until it fell in slanting showers. Sometimes the sun shone through the rain and a light breeze blew. It was a gay and airy kind of rain. The rainbow began to appear, and sometimes two rainbows, like a mother and her daughter, the one young and beautiful, and the other an old and faint shadow. The rainbow was called the python of the sky.

Okonkwo called his three wives and told them to get things together for a great feast. "I must thank my mother's kinsmen before I go," he said.

Ekwefi still had some cassava left on her farm from the previous year. Neither of the other wives had. It was not that they had been lazy, but that they had many children to feed. It was therefore understood that Ekwefi would provide cassava for the feast. Nwoye's mother and Ojiugo would provide the other things like smoked fish, palm-oil and pepper for the soup. Okonkwo would take care of meat and yams.

Ekwefi rose early on the following morning and went to her farm with her daughter, Ezinma, and Ojiugo's daughter, Obiageli, to harvest cassava tubers. Each of them carried a long cane basket, a machete for cutting down the soft cassava stem, and a little hoe for digging out the <u>tuber</u>. Fortunately, a light rain had fallen during the night and the soil would not be very hard.

"It will not take us long to harvest as much as we like," said Ekwefi.

"But the leaves will be wet," said Ezinma. Her basket was balanced on her head, and her arms folded across her breasts. She felt cold. "I dislike cold water dropping on my back. We should have waited for the sun to rise and dry the leaves."

Obiageli called her "Salt" because she said that she disliked water. "Are you afraid you may dissolve?"

The harvesting was easy, as Ekwefi had said. Ezinma shook every tree violently with a long stick before she bent down to cut the stem and dig out the tuber. Sometimes it was not necessary to dig. They just pulled the stump, and earth rose, roots snapped below, and the tuber was pulled out.

When they had harvested a sizable heap they carried it down in two trips to the stream, where every woman had a shallow well for <u>fermenting</u> her cassava.

"It should be ready in four days or even three," said Obiageli. "They are young tubers."

"They are not all that young," said Ekwefi. "I planted the farm nearly two years ago. It is a poor soil and that is why the tubers are so small."

Okonkwo never did things by halves. When his wife Ekwefi protested that two goats were sufficient for the feast he told her that it was not her affair.

---

words for everyday use

tu • ber (tü´ bər) *n.*, thick part of an underground stem. *Potatoes and yams are both types of <u>tubers</u>.*

fer • ment (fər ment´) *vt.*, chemically change into an alcoholic substance. *If you leave the juice sitting out too long, it will start to <u>ferment</u> and go bad.*

"I am calling a feast because I have the wherewithal. I cannot live on the bank of a river and wash my hands with spittle. My mother's people have been good to me and I must show my gratitude."

◀ Why does Okonkwo want to hold a great feast? What does his desire to do so reveal about him?

And so three goats were slaughtered and a number of fowls. It was like a wedding feast. There was foo-foo and yam pottage, egusi[1] soup and bitter-leaf soup and pots and pots of palm-wine.

All the *umunna*[2] were invited to the feast, all the descendants of Okolo, who had lived about two hundred years before. The oldest member of this extensive family was Okonkwo's uncle, Uchendu. The kola nut was given to him to break, and he prayed to the ancestors. He asked them for health and children. "We do not ask for wealth because he that has health and children will also have wealth. We do not pray to have more money but to have more kinsmen. We are better than animals because we have kinsmen. An animal rubs its itching flank against a tree, a man asks his kinsman to scratch him." He prayed especially for Okonkwo and his family. He then broke the kola nut and threw one of the lobes on the ground for the ancestors.

◀ Why are kinsmen important, according to Uchendu?

As the broken kola nuts were passed round, Okonkwo's wives and children and those who came to help them with the cooking began to bring out the food. His sons brought out the pots of palm-wine. There was so much food and drink that many kinsmen whistled in surprise. When all was laid out, Okonkwo rose to speak.

"I beg you to accept this little kola," he said. "It is not to pay you back for all you did for me in these seven years. A child cannot pay for its mother's milk. I have only called you together because it is good for kinsmen to meet."

Yam pottage was served first because it was lighter than foo-foo and because yam always came first. Then the foo-foo was served. Some kinsmen ate it with egusi soup and others with bitter-leaf soup. The meat was then shared so that every member of the *umunna* had a portion. Every man rose in order of years and took a share. Even the few kinsmen who had not been able to come had their shares taken out for them in due turn.

As the palm-wine was drunk one of the oldest members of the *umunna* rose to thank Okonkwo:

---

1. **egusi.** Watermelon seed. It can be dried and roasted and then ground for use in soups.

2. **umunna.** Wide group of relatives (all descendants of a common male ancestor)

"If I say that we did not expect such a big feast I will be suggesting that we did not know how openhanded our son, Okonkwo, is. We all know him, and we expected a big feast. But it turned out to be even bigger than we expected. Thank you. May all you took out return again tenfold. It is good in these days when the younger generation consider themselves wiser than their sires to see a man doing things in the grand, old way. A man who calls his kinsmen to a feast does not do so to save them from starving. They all have food in their own homes. When we gather together in the moonlit village ground it is not because of the moon. Every man can see it in his own compound. We come together because it is good for kinsmen to do so. You may ask why I am saying all this. I say it because I fear for the younger generation, for you people." He waved his arm where most of the young men sat, "As for me, I have only a short while to live, and so have Uchendu and Unachukwu and Emefo. But I fear for you young people because you do not understand how strong is the bond of kinship. You do not know what it is to speak with one voice. And what is the result? An abominable religion has settled among you. A man can now leave his father and his brothers. He can curse the gods of his fathers and his ancestors, like a hunter's dog that suddenly goes mad and turns on his master. I fear for you; I fear for the clan." He turned again to Okonkwo and said, "Thank you for calling us together."

▶ What does the elderly man fear? Why is it important for a people to "speak with one voice"?

Respond to the Selection

How do you feel about Okonkwo's plans at the end of part 2 of the novel? Has he changed as a result of his experience, or is he the same sort of person he has always been? Explain.

Investigate, Inquire, and Imagine

Recall: GATHERING FACTS

Interpret: FINDING MEANING

1a. Where does Okonkwo go when he leaves his village? For how long must he stay there? How does he feel shortly after he arrives?

➤ 1b. What lifts Okonkwo out of the despair that he feels after leaving his village? What does Okonkwo expect to do when he returns to his village?

2a. According to Uchendu, why do the Igbo have the expression "Mother is Supreme"? Why, when a woman dies, is she taken home to be buried with her own relatives?

➤ 2b. What does this custom suggest about the importance of mothers in Igbo culture?

3a. What does Okonkwo's friend Obierika do for him in chapter 15?

➤ 3b. Why does Okonkwo say to his friend, at the end of chapter 15, "I shall not talk about thanking you any more"?

4a. What important event has occurred when Obierika visits Okonkwo for the second time? What change has occurred in the life of Nwoye, Okonkwo's son? How does Okonkwo feel about his son's conversion?

➤ 4b. Who are the first converts to the new religion? Why are these people attracted to it? What do the Igbo expect to happen to the missionaries when they give them land in the Evil Forest? What actually happens, and how does this affect the work of the missionaries?

Analyze: TAKING THINGS APART

5a. Outline how, in these chapters, the Europeans have begun to establish themselves in Mbanta and other Igbo communities. Why do the Igbo not immediately drive them out? What does the elderly man say at the meeting at the end of chapter 19? What does he fear?

Synthesize: BRINGING THINGS TOGETHER

→ 5b. The title of this novel is *Things Fall Apart.* What is beginning to fall apart at the end of chapter 19?

Evaluate: MAKING JUDGMENTS

6a. Assess the positive and negative effects the new religion has on the community of Mbanta. What positive features does the new religion have? Why do many people find it attractive? Why might some people see the new religion as a threat?

Extend: CONNECTING IDEAS

→ 6b. Imagine that you are one of the Igbo elders and have observed and listened to the missionaries for some time. Write a paragraph in which you argue for or against accepting the new religion.

Understanding Literature

Motif. A **motif** is any element that recurs in one or more works of literature or art. The idea of a *chi,* or personal god, is one motif in *Things Fall Apart.* Find two places in chapters 14–19 where Okonkwo's *chi* is mentioned. What does Okonkwo believe about his *chi?* Do you agree with him? Explain why, or why not.

Symbol. A **symbol** is a thing that stands for or represents both itself and something else. Okonkwo's nickname is "Roaring Flame." Do you think fire is a good symbol for Okonkwo's nature? Why, or why not?

Theme. A **theme** is a central idea in a literary work. One theme of *Things Fall Apart* is that the coming of Westerners and Western civilization caused a breakdown of traditional ways of life in Africa. What evidence is offered in chapters 17–19 that such a breakdown is occurring?

PART THREE

Chapter Twenty

▶ What price has Okonkwo paid by being away from his clan for so long?

SEVEN YEARS WAS a long time to be away from one's clan. A man's place was not always there, waiting for him. As soon as he left, someone else rose and filled it. The clan was like a lizard; if it lost its tail it soon grew another.

Okonkwo knew these things. He knew that he had lost his place among the nine masked spirits who administered justice in the clan. He had lost the chance to lead his warlike clan against the new religion, which, he was told, had gained ground. He had lost the years in which he might have taken the highest titles in the clan. But some of these losses were not <u>irreparable</u>. He was determined that his return should be marked by his people. He would return with a flourish, and regain the seven wasted years.

▶ What plans does Okonkwo have for reestablishing himself after his return?

Even in his first year in exile he had begun to plan for his return. The first thing he would do would be to rebuild his compound on a more magnificent scale. He would build a bigger barn than he had had before and he would build huts for two new wives. Then he would show his wealth by <u>initiating</u> his sons into the *ozo* society. Only the really great men in the clan were able to do this. Okonkwo saw clearly the high esteem in which he would be held, and he saw himself taking the highest title in the land.

As the years of exile passed one by one it seemed to him that his *chi* might now be making amends for the past disaster. His yams grew abundantly, not only in his motherland but also in Umuofia, where his friend gave them out year by year to sharecroppers.

Then the tragedy of his first son had occurred. At first it appeared as if it might prove too great for his spirit. But it was a <u>resilient</u> spirit, and in the end Okonkwo overcame his sorrow. He had five other sons and he would bring them up in the way of the clan.

He sent for the five sons and they came and sat in his *obi*. The youngest of them was four years old.

"You have all seen the great abomination of your brother. Now he is no longer my son or your brother. I will only have a son who is a man, who will hold his head up among my people. If any one of you prefers to be a

---

words for everyday use

ir • rep • a • ra • ble (ir rep´ə rə bəl) *adj.*, unable to be repaired or remedied. *Ian was told that no matter what mistake he made, no situation was <u>irreparable</u>.*

in • i • ti • ate (i nish´ē āt´) *vt.*, admit as a member; teach the fundamentals. *Some*

cultures <u>initiate</u> youths into manhood or womanhood to mark a rite of passage.

re • sil • ient (ri zil´yənt) *adj.*, recovering strength quickly. *His thesis was that cartoon characters, who can survive almost any disaster, are more <u>resilient</u> than cockroaches.*

woman, let him follow Nwoye now while I am alive so that I can curse him. If you turn against me when I am dead I will visit you and break your neck."

Okonkwo was very lucky in his daughters. He never stopped regretting that Ezinma was a girl. Of all his children she alone understood his every mood. A bond of sympathy had grown between them as the years had passed.

Ezinma grew up in her father's exile and became one of the most beautiful girls in Mbanta. She was called Crystal of Beauty, as her mother had been called in her youth. The young ailing girl who had caused her mother so much heartache had been transformed, almost overnight, into a healthy, <u>buoyant</u> maiden. She had, it was true, her moments of depression when she would snap at everybody like an angry dog. These moods descended on her suddenly and for no apparent reason. But they were very rare and short-lived. As long as they lasted, she could bear no other person but her father.

Many young men and prosperous middle-aged men of Mbanta came to marry her. But she refused them all, because her father had called her one evening and said to her: "There are many good and prosperous people here, but I shall be happy if you marry in Umuofia when we return home."

◀ Why does Okonkwo want his daughter to wait until his return from exile in order to marry?

That was all he had said. But Ezinma had seen clearly all the thought and hidden meaning behind the few words. And she had agreed.

"Your half-sister, Obiageli, will not understand me," Okonkwo said. "But you can explain to her."

Although they were almost the same age, Ezinma wielded a strong influence over her half-sister. She explained to her why they should not marry yet, and she agreed also. And so the two of them refused every offer of marriage in Mbanta.

"I wish she were a boy," Okonkwo thought within himself. She understood things so perfectly. Who else among his children could have read his thoughts so well? With two beautiful grown-up daughters his return to Umuofia would attract considerable attention. His future sons-in-law would be men of authority in the clan. The poor and unknown would not dare to come forth.

| **words for everyday use** | **buoy • ant** (boi´ənt) *adj.,* tending to rise; not easily depressed; cheerful. *Corky was in a buoyant mood; she smiled at everyone she passed.* |

Umuofia had indeed changed during the seven years Okonkwo had been in exile. The church had come and led many astray. Not only the low-born and the outcast but sometimes a worthy man had joined it. Such a man was Ogbuefi Ugonna, who had taken two titles, and who like a madman had cut the anklet of his titles and cast it away to join the Christians. The white missionary was very proud of him and he was one of the first men in Umuofia to receive the sacrament of Holy Communion,[1] or Holy Feast as it was called in Ibo. Ogbuefi Ugonna had thought of the Feast in terms of eating and drinking, only more holy than the village variety. He had therefore put his drinking-horn into his goatskin bag for the occasion.

But apart from the church, the white men had also brought a government. They had built a court where the District Commissioner judged cases in ignorance. He had court messengers who brought men to him for trial. Many of these messengers came from Umuru on the bank of the Great River, where the white men first came many years before and where they had built the center of their religion and trade and government. These court messengers were greatly hated in Umuofia because they were foreigners and also arrogant and high-handed. They were called *kotma*,[2] and because of their ash-colored shorts they earned the additional name of Ashy-Buttocks. They guarded the prison, which was full of men who had offended against the white man's law. Some of these prisoners had thrown away their twins and some had molested the Christians. They were beaten in the prison by the *kotma* and made to work every morning clearing the government compound and fetching wood for the white Commissioner and the court messengers. Some of these prisoners were men of title who should be above such mean occupation. They were grieved by the <u>indignity</u> and mourned for their neglected farms. As they cut grass in the morning the younger men sang in time with the strokes of their machetes:

▶ *Why are the court messengers hated?*

---

1. **Holy Communion.** Christian rite in which bread and wine are consumed
2. *kotma.* Pidgin word for "court messenger" (formed by shortening and combining the words)

words for everyday use

in • dig • ni • ty (in dig′nə tē) *n.,* something that humiliates, insults, or injures self-respect. *Tony found that trying out for the play and not getting the part was not as difficult as the <u>indignity</u> of everyone knowing he had not succeeded.*

Kotma *of the ash buttocks,*
   He is fit to be a slave
The white man has no sense,
   He is fit to be a slave

The court messengers did not like to be called Ashy-Buttocks, and they beat the men. But the song spread in Umuofia.

Okonkwo's head was bowed in sadness as Obierika told him these things.

"Perhaps I have been away too long," Okonkwo said, almost to himself. "But I cannot understand these things you tell me. What is it that has happened to our people? Why have they lost the power to fight?"

"Have you not heard how the white man wiped out Abame?" asked Obierika.

"I have heard," said Okonkwo. "But I have also heard that Abame people were weak and foolish. Why did they not fight back? Had they no guns and machetes? We would be cowards to compare ourselves with the men of Abame. Their fathers had never dared to stand before our ancestors. We must fight these men and drive them from the land."

"It is already too late," said Obierika sadly. "Our own men and our sons have joined the ranks of the stranger. They have joined his religion and they help to uphold his government. If we should try to drive out the white men in Umuofia we should find it easy. There are only two of them. But what of our own people who are following their way and have been given power? They would go to Umuru and bring the soldiers, and we would be like Abame." He paused for a long time and then said: "I told you on my last visit to Mbanta how they hanged Aneto."

"What has happened to that piece of land in dispute?" asked Okonkwo.

"The white man's court has decided that it should belong to Nnama's family, who had given much money to the white man's messengers and interpreter."

"Does the white man understand our custom about land?"

"How can he when he does not even speak our tongue? But he says that our customs are bad; and our own brothers who have taken up his religion also say that our customs are bad. How do you think we can fight when our own brothers have turned against us? The white man is very clever. He came quietly and peaceably with his religion. We were amused at his foolishness and allowed him

◀ *Why, according to Obierika, is it too late to fight the white men?*

▶ What, according to Obierika, has fallen apart?

to stay. Now he has won our brothers, and our clan can no longer act like one. He has put a knife on the things that held us together and we have fallen apart."

"How did they get hold of Aneto to hang him?" asked Okonkwo.

"When he killed Oduche in the fight over the land, he fled to Aninta to escape the wrath of the earth. This was about eight days after the fight, because Oduche had not died immediately from his wounds. It was on the seventh day that he died. But everybody knew that he was going to die and Aneto got his belongings together in readiness to flee. But the Christians had told the white man about the accident, and he sent his *kotma* to catch Aneto. He was imprisoned with all the leaders of his family. In the end Oduche died and Aneto was taken to Umuru and hanged. The other people were released, but even now they have not found the mouth with which to tell of their suffering."

The two men sat in silence for a long while afterwards.

Chapter Twenty-One

THERE WERE MANY men and women in Umuofia who did not feel as strongly as Okonkwo about the new <u>dispensation</u>. The white man had indeed brought a lunatic religion, but he had also built a trading store and for the first time palm-oil and kernel became things of great price, and much money flowed into Umuofia.

And even in the matter of religion there was a growing feeling that there might be something in it after all, something vaguely akin to method in the overwhelming madness.

This growing feeling was due to Mr. Brown, the white missionary, who was very firm in restraining his flock from provoking the wrath of the clan. One member in particular was very difficult to restrain. His name was Enoch[1] and his father was the priest of the snake cult. The story went around that Enoch had killed and eaten the sacred python, and that his father had cursed him.

Mr. Brown preached against such excess of <u>zeal</u>. Everything was possible, he told his energetic flock, but everything was not <u>expedient</u>. And so Mr. Brown came to be respected even by the clan, because he trod softly on its faith. He made friends with some of the great men of the clan and on one of his frequent visits to the neighboring villages he had been presented with a carved elephant tusk, which was a sign of dignity and rank. One of the great men in that village was called Akunna and he had given one of his sons to be taught the white man's knowledge in Mr. Brown's school.

Whenever Mr. Brown went to that village he spent long hours with Akunna in his *obi* talking through an interpreter about religion. Neither of them succeeded in converting the other but they learned more about their different beliefs.

◀ In what ways do the people benefit from the coming of the white men?

◀ Why is Mr. Brown respected by the clan?

---

1. **Enoch.** Enoch is a name from the Book of Genesis in the Bible. Two of the descendants of Adam and Eve are called Enoch. One is the son of Cain, a man who was banished from God's sight after he killed his own brother (Genesis 4). The other Enoch is a holy man who "walked with God" (Genesis 5:18–24).

words for everyday use

dis • pen • sa • tion (dis´pən sā´shən) *n.,* system of management; administration. *The business's <u>dispensation</u> was praised for effectively managing so many employees.*

zeal (zēl´) *n.,* intense enthusiasm; passion. *Jacob has great <u>zeal</u> for zucchini; he has been known to eat everything from fried zucchini to zucchini pancakes.*

ex • pe • di • ent (ek spē´dē ənt) *adj.,* useful for causing a desired effect; advantageous. *Ephraim was known for finding the most <u>expedient</u> solution to a problem and never was caught in a disadvantageous situation.*

▶ What similarity exists in the beliefs of the two men? what differences?

"You say that there is one supreme God who made heaven and earth," said Akunna on one of Mr. Brown's visits. "We also believe in Him and call Him Chukwu. He made all the world and the other gods."

"There are no other gods," said Mr. Brown. "Chukwu is the only God and all others are false. You carve a piece of wood—like that one" (he pointed at the rafters from which Akunna's carved *Ikenga* hung), "and you call it a god. But it is still a piece of wood."

"Yes," said Akunna. "It is indeed a piece of wood. The tree from which it came was made by Chukwu, as indeed all minor gods were. But He made them for His messengers so that we could approach Him through them. It is like yourself. You are the head of your church."

"No," protested Mr. Brown. "The head of my church is God Himself."

"I know," said Akunna, "but there must be a head in this world among men. Somebody like yourself must be the head here."

"The head of my church in that sense is in England."

"That is exactly what I am saying. The head of your church is in your country. He has sent you here as his messenger. And you have also appointed your own messengers and servants. Or let me take another example, the District Commissioner. He is sent by your king."

"They have a queen," said the interpreter on his own account.

"Your queen sends her messenger, the District Commissioner. He finds that he cannot do the work alone and so he appoints *kotma* to help him. It is the same with God, or Chukwu. He appoints the smaller gods to help Him because His work is too great for one person."

"You should not think of him as a person," said Mr. Brown, "It is because you do so that you imagine He must need helpers. And the worst thing about it is that you give all the worship to the false gods you have created."

"That is not so. We make sacrifices to the little gods, but when they fail and there is no one else to turn to we go to Chukwu. It is right to do so. We approach a great man through his servants. But when his servants fail to help us, then we go to the last source of hope. We appear to pay greater attention to the little gods but that is not so. We worry them more because we are afraid to worry their Master. Our fathers knew that Chukwu was the Overlord and that is why many of them gave their children the name Chukwuka—'Chukwu is Supreme.'"

▶ What things does Mr. Brown learn about the religion of the clan?

"You said one interesting thing," said Mr. Brown. "You are afraid of Chukwu. In my religion Chukwu is a loving Father and need not be feared by those who do His will."

"But we must fear Him when we are not doing His will," said Akunna. "And who is to tell His will? It is too great to be known."

In this way Mr. Brown learned a good deal about the religion of the clan and he came to the conclusion that a frontal attack on it would not succeed. And so he built a school and a little hospital in Umuofia. He went from family to family begging people to send their children to his school. But at first they only sent their slaves or sometimes their lazy children. Mr. Brown begged and argued and prophesied. He said that the leaders of the land in the future would be men and women who had learned to read and write. If Umuofia failed to send her children to the school, strangers would come from other places to rule them. They could already see that happening in the Native Court, where the D.C. was surrounded by strangers who spoke his tongue. Most of these strangers came from the distant town of Umuru on the bank of the Great River where the white man first went.

In the end Mr. Brown's arguments began to have an effect. More people came to learn in his school, and he encouraged them with gifts of singlets and towels. They were not all young, these people who came to learn. Some of them were thirty years old or more. They worked on their farms in the morning and went to school in the afternoon. And it was not long before the people began to say that the white man's medicine was quick in working. Mr. Brown's school produced quick results. A few months in it were enough to make one a court messenger or even a court clerk. Those who stayed longer became teachers; and from Umuofia laborers went forth into the Lord's vineyard. New churches were established in the surrounding villages and a few schools with them. From the very beginning religion and education went hand in hand.

Mr. Brown's mission grew from strength to strength, and because of its link with the new administration it earned a new social <u>prestige</u>. But Mr. Brown himself was

◀ In what way does the school contribute to the spread of the white men's religion?

words for everyday use

pres • tige (pres tēzh´) *n.,* reputation; power to influence. *The power and <u>prestige</u> of the investment banker were lost once his illegal activities were discovered.*

breaking down in health. At first he ignored the warning signs. But in the end he had to leave his flock, sad and broken.

It was in the first rainy season after Okonkwo's return to Umuofia that Mr. Brown left for home. As soon as he had learned of Okonkwo's return five months earlier, the missionary had immediately paid him a visit. He had just sent Okonkwo's son, Nwoye, who was now called Isaac,[2] to the new training college for teachers in Umuru. And he had hoped that Okonkwo would be happy to hear of it. But Okonkwo had driven him away with the threat that if he came into his compound again, he would be carried out of it.

▶ Why does Okonkwo's plan to reestablish himself as a great man in the village fail?

Okonkwo's return to his native land was not as memorable as he had wished. It was true his two beautiful daughters aroused great interest among suitors and marriage negotiations were soon in progress, but, beyond that, Umuofia did not appear to have taken any special notice of the warrior's return. The clan had undergone such profound change during his exile that it was barely recognizable. The new religion and government and the trading stores were very much in the people's eyes and minds. There were still many who saw these new institutions as evil, but even they talked and thought about little else, and certainly not about Okonkwo's return.

And it was the wrong year too. If Okonkwo had immediately initiated his two sons into the *ozo* society as he had planned he would have caused a stir. But the initiation rite was performed once in three years in Umuofia, and he had to wait for nearly two years for the next round of ceremonies.

Okonkwo was deeply grieved. And it was not just a personal grief. He mourned for the clan, which he saw breaking up and falling apart, and he mourned for the warlike men of Umuofia, who had so unaccountably become soft like women.

---

2. **Isaac.** In the Bible, Isaac is the son of Abraham; to test Abraham, God orders him to sacrifice Isaac but at the last moment intervenes to stop the sacrifice (Genesis 22:1–19).

Chapter Twenty-Two

MR. BROWN'S SUCCESSOR was the Reverend James Smith, and he was a different kind of man. He condemned openly Mr. Brown's policy of compromise and <u>accommodation</u>. He saw things as black and white. And black was evil. He saw the world as a battlefield in which the children of light were locked in mortal conflict with the sons of darkness. He spoke in his sermons about sheep and goats and about wheat and tares.[1] He believed in slaying the prophets of Baal.[2]

◀ How does Mr. Smith differ from Mr. Brown?

Mr. Smith was greatly distressed by the ignorance which many of his flock showed even in such things as the Trinity[3] and the Sacraments.[4] It only showed that they were seeds sown on a rocky soil.[5] Mr. Brown had thought of nothing but numbers. He should have known that the kingdom of God did not depend on large crowds. Our Lord Himself stressed the importance of fewness. Narrow is the way and few the number. To fill the Lord's holy temple with an <u>idolatrous</u> crowd clamoring for signs was a folly of everlasting consequence. Our Lord used the whip only once in His life—to drive the crowd away from His church.[6]

Within a few weeks of his arrival in Umuofia Mr. Smith suspended a young woman from the church for pouring

---

1. **sheep and goats...wheat and tares.** According to Christian belief, at Judgment Day Christ would separate the believers from the non-believers, just as a shepherd divides his sheep from the goats (see Matthew 25:31–34). Christ's parable of the wheat and the tares depicts the non-believers as tares, or injurious weeds, in a field of wheat (see Matthew 13:24–30).

2. **slaying the prophets of Baal.** Baal was a god of the Phoenicians and Canaanites and, according to Judeo-Christian belief, one of the false gods. In the Old Testament of the Bible, the Lord's prophet, Elijah, carries out the death sentence for the prophets of Baal (See I Kings 18:18–40).

3. **Trinity.** In Christian belief, God the Father, His son Jesus Christ, and the Holy Spirit

4. **Sacraments.** In Christian practice, holy rites such as baptism and communion

5. **seeds . . . soil.** Christ's parable of the sower tells of scattering seed on stony ground, causing plants to spring up quickly but not grow properly (see Matthew 13:3–21 and Mark 4:3–17).

6. **Our Lord . . . church.** Christ drove merchants and moneychangers from the temple in Jerusalem (see Matthew 21:12–13).

---

words for everyday use

ac • com • mo • da • tion (ə kăm´ə dā´shən) *n.*, willingness to adapt and adjust or to reconcile differences. *A policy of <u>accommodation</u> can be more successful when reconciling differences than closed-mindedness.*

i • dol • a • trous (ī däl´ə trəs) *adj.*, blindly worshiping objects or images. *Modern religions have often condemned ancient religions as <u>idolatrous</u> because the religions incorporated representations of deities.*

new wine into old bottles.[7] This woman had allowed her heathen[8] husband to mutilate her dead child. The child had been declared an *ogbanje,* plaguing its mother by dying and entering her womb to be born again. Four times this child had run its evil round. And so it was mutilated to discourage it from returning.

Mr. Smith was filled with wrath when he heard of this. He disbelieved the story which even some of the most faithful confirmed, the story of really evil children who were not deterred by mutilation, but came back with all the scars. He replied that such stories were spread in the world by the Devil to lead men astray. Those who believed such stories were unworthy of the Lord's table.

There was a saying in Umuofia that as a man danced so the drums were beaten for him. Mr. Smith danced a furious step and so the drums went mad. The over-zealous converts who had smarted under Mr. Brown's restraining hand now flourished in full favor. One of them was Enoch, the son of the snake-priest who was believed to have killed and eaten the sacred python. Enoch's devotion to the new faith had seemed so much greater than Mr. Brown's that the villagers called him the outsider who wept louder than the bereaved.

▶ *What sort of person is Enoch?*

Enoch was short and slight of build, and always seemed in great haste. His feet were short and broad, and when he stood or walked his heels came together and his feet opened outwards as if they had quarrelled and meant to go in different directions. Such was the excessive energy bottled up in Enoch's small body that it was always erupting in quarrels and fights. On Sundays he always imagined that the sermon was preached for the benefit of his enemies. And if he happened to sit near one of them he would occasionally turn to give him a meaningful look, as if to say, "I told you so." It was Enoch who touched off the great conflict between church and clan in Umuofia which had been gathering since Mr. Brown left.

It happened during the annual ceremony which was held in honor of the earth <u>deity</u>. At such times the ancestors of

---

7. **new wine . . . bottles.** Mixing the old and new customs or beliefs. Christ explains that people should not put new wine into old bottles because the bottles will break and the wine will be lost (see Matthew 9:14–17). He says this to explain why his disciples do not fast.

8. **heathen.** One who does not believe in the Christian God; not converted.

words for everyday use

de • i • ty (dē´ə tē) *n.,* god. *Ancient Mesopotamian people believed that the <u>deity</u> Marduke created the world by slaying another immortal, the goddess Tiammat.*

the clan who had been committed to Mother Earth at their death emerged again as *egwugwu* through tiny ant-holes.

One of the greatest crimes a man could commit was to unmask an *egwugwu* in public, or to say or do anything which might reduce its immortal prestige in the eyes of the <u>uninitiated</u>. And this was what Enoch did.

The annual worship of the earth goddess fell on a Sunday, and the masked spirits were abroad. The Christian women who had been to church could not therefore go home. Some of their men had gone out to beg the *egwugwu* to retire for a short while for the women to pass. They agreed and were already retiring, when Enoch boasted aloud that they would not dare to touch a Christian. Whereupon they all came back and one of them gave Enoch a good stroke of the cane, which was always carried. Enoch fell on him and tore off his mask. The other *egwugwu* immediately surrounded their <u>desecrated</u> companion, to shield him from the <u>profane</u> gaze of women and children, and led him away. Enoch had killed an ancestral spirit, and Umuofia was thrown into confusion.

◀ *What unheard-of deed does Enoch commit? In what way does he kill an ancestral spirit?*

That night the Mother of the Spirits walked the length and breadth of the clan, weeping for her murdered son. It was a terrible night. Not even the oldest man in Umuofia had ever heard such a strange and fearful sound, and it was never to be heard again. It seemed as if the very soul of the tribe wept for a great evil that was coming—its own death.

On the next day all the masked *egwugwu* of Umuofia assembled in the marketplace. They came from all the quarters of the clan and even from the neighboring villages. The dreaded Otakagu came from Imo, and Ekwensu, dangling a white cock, arrived from Uli. It was a terrible gathering. The <u>eerie</u> voices of countless spirits, the bells that clattered behind some of them, and the clash of machetes as they ran forwards and backwards and saluted one another, sent

words for everyday use

un • in • i • ti • at • ed (un i nish´ē āt´id) *adj.,* not introduced to the knowledge of something. *To the <u>uninitiated</u>, the Middle English of Chaucer might resemble a foreign language, but it is readily understandable to those who have had some experience with it.*

des • e • crate (des´i krāt´) *vt.,* violate the sanctity of; treat disrespectfully, irreverently, or outrageously. *According to St. Bede, a certain priest of the ancient Germanic religion <u>desecrated</u> a pagan* shrine, going so far as to thrust his spear into it, to demonstrate his conversion to Christianity.

pro • fane (prō fān´) *adj.,* not holy or reverent. *Cows are sacred in India and killing one is a <u>profane</u> deed.*

ee • rie (ir´ē) *adj.,* mysterious; weird. *The dark hallways of the mall after closing had an <u>eerie</u> echo.*

tremors of fear into every heart. For the first time in living memory the sacred bull-roarer [9] was heard in broad daylight.

From the marketplace the furious band made for Enoch's compound. Some of the elders of the clan went with them, wearing heavy protections of charms and amulets. These were men whose arms were strong in *ogwu*, or medicine. As for the ordinary men and women, they listened from the safety of their huts.

The leaders of the Christians had met together at Mr. Smith's parsonage on the previous night. As they deliberated they could hear the Mother of Spirits wailing for her son. The chilling sound affected Mr. Smith, and for the first time he seemed to be afraid.

"What are they planning to do?" he asked. No one knew, because such a thing had never happened before. Mr. Smith would have sent for the District Commissioner and his court messengers, but they had gone on tour on the previous day.

"One thing is clear," said Mr. Smith. "We cannot offer physical resistance to them. Our strength lies in the Lord." They knelt down together and prayed to God for delivery.

"O Lord save Thy people," cried Mr. Smith.

"And bless Thine inheritance," replied the men.

> ▶ For what does Enoch hope?

They decided that Enoch should be hidden in the parsonage for a day or two. Enoch himself was greatly disappointed when he heard this, for he had hoped that a holy war was imminent; and there were a few other Christians who thought like him. But wisdom prevailed in the camp of the faithful and many lives were thus saved.

The band of *egwugwu* moved like a furious whirlwind to Enoch's compound and with machete and fire reduced it to a desolate heap. And from there they made for the church, intoxicated with destruction.

Mr. Smith was in his church when he heard the masked spirits coming. He walked quietly to the door which com-

---

9. **bull-roarer.** Instrument used in religious ceremonies. It is attached to a string or tether that, when twisted, produces a roaring sound.

words for everyday use

am • u • let (am´yü lit) *n.*, object worn on the body for its supposed magical power to protect. *Bart wore an amulet around his neck to protect him from evil spirits.*

de • lib • er • ate (di lib´ər āt´) *vi.*, consider carefully and discuss alternatives. *Let's not spend all night deliberating about where we should eat; I am hungry!*

im • mi • nent (im´ə nənt) *adj.*, about to happen. *The meteorologist said that snowfall was imminent.*

des • o • late (des´ə lit) *adj.*, ruined; devastated. *After the tornado blasted through, our small town was desolate.*

manded the approach to the church compound, and stood there. But when the first three or four *egwugwu* appeared on the church compound he nearly bolted. He overcame this impulse and instead of running away he went down the two steps that led up to the church and walked towards the approaching spirits.

◀ What impulse does Mr. Smith overcome? In what way does he exhibit courage?

They surged forward, and a long stretch of the bamboo fence with which the church compound was surrounded gave way before them. Discordant bells clanged, machetes clashed and the air was full of dust and weird sounds. Mr. Smith heard a sound of footsteps behind him. He turned round and saw Okeke, his interpreter. Okeke had not been on the best of terms with his master since he had strongly condemned Enoch's behavior at the meeting of the leaders of the church during the night. Okeke had gone as far as to say that Enoch should not be hidden in the parsonage, because he would only draw the wrath of the clan on the pastor. Mr. Smith had rebuked him in very strong language, and had not sought his advice that morning. But now, as he came up and stood by him confronting the angry spirits, Mr. Smith looked at him and smiled. It was a wan smile, but there was deep gratitude there.

For a brief moment the onrush of the *egwugwu* was checked by the unexpected <u>composure</u> of the two men. But it was only a momentary check, like the tense silence between blasts of thunder. The second onrush was greater than the first. It swallowed up the two men. Then an unmistakable voice rose above the tumult and there was immediate silence. Space was made around the two men, and Ajofia began to speak.

Ajofia was the leading *egwugwu* of Umuofia. He was the head and spokesman of the nine ancestors who administered justice in the clan. His voice was unmistakable and so he was able to bring immediate peace to the agitated spirits. He then addressed Mr. Smith, and as he spoke clouds of smoke rose from his head.

"The body of the white man, I salute you," he said, using the language in which immortals spoke to men.

"The body of the white man, do you know me?" he asked.

words for everyday use

com • po • sure (kəm pō′zhər) *n.,* calmness of mind or manner. *It is hard to keep your <u>composure</u> in a traffic jam in mid-August; the honking horns and heat can make anyone feel ruffled.*

Mr. Smith looked at his interpreter, but Okeke, who was a native of distant Umuru, was also at a loss.

Ajofia laughed in his guttural voice. It was like the laugh of rusty metal. "They are strangers," he said, "and they are ignorant. But let that pass." He turned round to his comrades and saluted them, calling them the fathers of Umuofia. He dug his rattling spear into the ground and it shook with metallic life. Then he turned once more to the missionary and his interpreter.

"Tell the white man that we will not do him any harm," he said to the interpreter. "Tell him to go back to his house and leave us alone. We liked his brother who was with us before. He was foolish, but we liked him, and for his sake we shall not harm his brother. But this shrine which he built must be destroyed. We shall no longer allow it in our midst. It has bred untold abominations and we have come to put an end to it." He turned to his comrades, "Fathers of Umuofia, I salute you;" and they replied with one guttural voice. He turned again to the missionary. "You can stay with us if you like our ways. You can worship your own god. It is good that a man should worship the gods and the spirits of his fathers. Go back to your house so that you may not be hurt. Our anger is great but we have held it down so that we can talk to you."

▶ How does Okeke interpret Mr. Smith's remarks? Why?

Mr. Smith said to his interpreter: "Tell them to go away from here. This is the house of God and I will not live to see it desecrated."

Okeke interpreted wisely to the spirits and leaders of Umuofia: "The white man says he is happy you have come to him with your grievances, like friends. He will be happy if you leave the matter in his hands."

"We cannot leave the matter in his hands because he does not understand our customs, just as we do not understand his. We say he is foolish because he does not know our ways, and perhaps he says we are foolish because we do not know his. Let him go away."

▶ What do the masked spirits do to the church?

Mr. Smith stood his ground. But he could not save his church. When the *egwugwu* went away the red-earth church which Mr. Brown had built was a pile of earth and ashes. And for the moment the spirit of the clan was <u>pacified</u>.

words for everyday use

pac • i • fy (pas´ə fī´) *vt.*, make peaceful or calm. *The child would not be pacified while in the midst of a tantrum.*

Chapter Twenty-Three

FOR THE FIRST time in many years Okonkwo had a feeling that was akin to happiness. The times which had altered so unaccountably during his exile seemed to be coming round again. The clan which had turned false on him appeared to be making amends.

He had spoken violently to his clansmen when they had met in the marketplace to decide on their action. And they had listened to him with respect. It was like the good old days again, when a warrior was a warrior. Although they had not agreed to kill the missionary or drive away the Christians, they had agreed to do something <u>substantial</u>. And they had done it. Okonkwo was almost happy again.

For two days after the destruction of the church, nothing happened. Every man in Umuofia went about armed with a gun or a machete. They would not be caught <u>unawares</u>, like the men of Abame.

Then the District Commissioner returned from his tour. Mr. Smith went immediately to him and they had a long discussion. The men of Umuofia did not take any notice of this, and if they did, they thought it was not important. The missionary often went to see his brother white man. There was nothing strange in that.

Three days later the District Commissioner sent his sweet-tongued messenger to the leaders of Umuofia asking them to meet him in his headquarters. That also was not strange. He often asked them to hold such <u>palavers</u>, as he called them. Okonkwo was among the six leaders he invited.

Okonkwo warned the others to be fully armed. "An Umuofia man does not refuse a call," he said. "He may refuse to do what he is asked; he does not refuse to be asked. But the times have changed, and we must be fully prepared."

And so the six men went to see the District Commissioner, armed with their machetes. They did not carry guns, for that would be unseemly. They were led into the courthouse where the District Commissioner sat. He

◀ *What makes Okonkwo "almost happy again"?*

---

words for everyday use

sub • stan • tial (səb stan´ shəl) *adj.,* of real value or importance. *The tenth-grade students wanted to do something <u>substantial</u> for a class trip, not just go to the local amusement park as they had for years.*

un • a • wares (un ə werz´) *adv.,* without knowing; unexpectedly; by surprise.

I scared my sister by sneaking up and catching her <u>unawares</u>.

pa • lav • er (pə lav´ər) *n.,* conference; discussion. *After weeks of <u>palavers</u> and meetings, they finally came to an agreement.*

received them politely. They unslung their goatskin bags and their sheathed machetes, put them on the floor, and sat down.

"I have asked you to come," began the Commissioner, "because of what happened during my absence. I have been told a few things but I cannot believe them until I have heard your own side. Let us talk about it like friends and find a way of ensuring that it does not happen again."

Ogbuefi Ekwueme rose to his feet and began to tell the story.

"Wait a minute," said the Commissioner. "I want to bring in my men so that they too can hear your grievances and take warning. Many of them come from distant places and although they speak your tongue they are ignorant of your customs. James! Go and bring in the men." His interpreter left the courtroom and soon returned with twelve men. They sat together with the men of Umuofia, and Ogbuefi Ekwueme began again to tell the story of how Enoch murdered an *egwugwu.*

It happened so quickly that the six men did not see it coming. There was only a brief scuffle, too brief even to allow the drawing of a sheathed machete. The six men were handcuffed and led into the guardroom.

"We shall not do you any harm," said the District Commissioner to them later, "if only you agree to cooperate with us. We have brought a peaceful administration to you and your people so that you may be happy. If any man ill-treats you we shall come to your rescue. But we will not allow you to ill-treat others. We have a court of law where we judge cases and administer justice just as it is done in my own country under a great queen.[1] I have brought you here because you joined together to molest others, to burn people's houses and their place of worship. That must not happen in the <u>dominion</u> of our queen, the most powerful ruler in the world. I have decided that you will pay a fine of two hundred bags of cowries. You will be released as

▶ *What trick does the District Commissioner play on the men?*

▶ *According to the District Commissioner, who rules Umuofia?*

---

1. **great queen.** The queen referred to is Victoria, who ruled Great Britain from 1837 to 1901. During that time the country was, indeed, the most powerful in the world. Benjamin Disraeli, her much favored conservative prime minister, once boasted that the Sun never set on the British Empire.

words for everyday use   do • min • ion (də min′yən) *n.,* governed territory. *The king tried to extend his <u>dominion</u> so that his territory was twice the size of the neighboring country.*

soon as you agree to this and undertake to collect that fine from your people. What do you say to that?"

The six men remained sullen and silent and the Commissioner left them for a while. He told the court messengers, when he left the guardroom, to treat the men with respect because they were the leaders of Umuofia. They said, "Yes, sir," and saluted.

As soon as the District Commissioner left, the head messenger, who was also the prisoners' barber, took down his razor and shaved off all the hair on the men's heads. They were still handcuffed, and they just sat and moped.

"Who is the chief among you?" the court messengers asked in jest. "We see that every pauper wears the anklet of title in Umuofia. Does it cost as much as ten cowries?"

The six men ate nothing throughout that day and the next. They were not even given any water to drink, and they could not go out to urinate or go into the bush when they were pressed. At night the messengers came in to taunt them and to knock their shaven heads together.

◄ Are the prisoners treated with respect? Explain.

Even when the men were left alone they found no words to speak to one another. It was only on the third day, when they could no longer bear the hunger and the insults, that they began to talk about giving in.

"We should have killed the white man if you had listened to me," Okonkwo snarled.

"We could have been in Umuru now waiting to be hanged," someone said to him.

"Who wants to kill the white man?" asked a messenger who had just rushed in. Nobody spoke.

"You are not satisfied with your crime, but you must kill the white man on top of it." He carried a strong stick, and he hit each man a few blows on the head and back. Okonkwo was choked with hate.

As soon as the six men were locked up, court messengers went into Umuofia to tell the people that their leaders would not be released unless they paid a fine of two hundred and fifty bags of cowries.

"Unless you pay the fine immediately," said their headman, "we will take your leaders to Umuru before the big white man, and hang them."

This story spread quickly through the villages, and was added to as it went. Some said that the men had already been taken to Umuru and would be hanged on the following day. Some said that their families would also be hanged. Others said that soldiers were already on their way to shoot the people of Umuofia as they had done in Abame.

◄ What happens to stories that are spread by word of mouth?

It was the time of the full moon. But that night the voice of children was not heard. The village *ilo* where they always gathered for a moon-play was empty. The women of Iguedo did not meet in their secret enclosure to learn a new dance to be displayed later to the village. Young men who were always abroad in the moonlight kept their huts that night. Their manly voices were not heard on the village paths as they went to visit their friends and lovers. Umuofia was like a startled animal with ears erect, sniffing the silent, ominous air and not knowing which way to run.

The silence was broken by the village crier beating his sonorous *ogene*. He called every man in Umuofia, from the Akakanma age group upwards, to a meeting in the marketplace after the morning meal. He went from one end of the village to the other and walked all its breadth. He did not leave out any of the main footpaths.

Okonkwo's compound was like a deserted homestead. It was as if cold water had been poured on it. His family was all there, but everyone spoke in whispers. His daughter Ezinma had broken her twenty-eight day visit to the family of her future husband, and returned home when she heard that her father had been imprisoned, and was going to be hanged. As soon as she got home she went to Obierika to ask what the men of Umuofia were going to do about it. But Obierika had not been home since morning. His wives thought he had gone to a secret meeting. Ezinma was satisfied that something was being done.

On the morning after the village crier's appeal the men of Umuofia met in the marketplace and decided to collect without delay two hundred and fifty bags of cowries to appease the white man. They did not know that fifty bags would go to the court messengers, who had increased the fine for that purpose.

Chapter Twenty-Four

OKONKWO AND HIS fellow prisoners were set free as soon as the fine was paid. The District Commissioner spoke to them again about the great queen, and about peace and good government. But the men did not listen. They just sat and looked at him and at his interpreter. In the end they were given back their bags and sheathed machetes and told to go home. They rose and left the courthouse. They neither spoke to anyone nor among themselves.

◄ Why do you think the men do not speak to anyone or to one another?

The courthouse, like the church, was built a little way outside the village. The footpath that linked them was a very busy one because it also led to the stream, beyond the court. It was open and sandy. Footpaths were open and sandy in the dry season. But when the rains came the bush grew thick on either side and closed in on the path. It was now dry season.

As they made their way to the village the six men met women and children going to the stream with their waterpots. But the men wore such heavy and fearsome looks that the women and children did not say *"nno"* or "welcome" to them, but edged out of the way to let them pass. In the village little groups of men joined them until they became a sizeable company. They walked silently. As each of the six men got to his compound, he turned in, taking some of the crowd with him. The village was astir in a silent, <u>suppressed</u> way.

Ezinma had prepared some food for her father as soon as news spread that the six men would be released. She took it to him in his *obi.* He ate absent-mindedly. He had no appetite; he only ate to please her. His male relations and friends had gathered in his *obi,* and Obierika was urging him to eat. Nobody else spoke, but they noticed the long stripes on Okonkwo's back where the warder's whip had cut into his flesh.

◄ What caused the marks on Okonkwo's back?

The village crier was abroad again in the night. He beat his iron gong and announced that another meeting would be held in the morning. Everyone knew that Umuofia was at last going to speak its mind about the things that were happening.

---

words for everyday use

sup • pressed (sə prest´) *adj.,* held down; subdued. *Carol felt such joy that it could not be suppressed, and a smile burst across her face.*

Okonkwo slept very little that night. The bitterness in his heart was now mixed with a kind of childlike excitement. Before he had gone to bed he had brought down his war dress, which he had not touched since his return from exile. He had shaken out his smoked raffia skirt and examined his tall feather head-gear and his shield. They were all satisfactory, he had thought.

As he lay on his bamboo bed he thought about the treatment he had received in the white man's court, and he swore vengeance. If Umuofia decided on war, all would be well. But if they chose to be cowards he would go out and avenge himself. He thought about wars in the past. The noblest, he thought, was the war against Isike. In those days Okudo was still alive. Okudo sang a war song in a way that no other man could. He was not a fighter, but his voice turned every man into a lion.

▶ What course does Okonkwo want the people of Umuofia to follow?

"Worthy men are no more," Okonkwo sighed as he remembered those days. "Isike will never forget how we slaughtered them in that war. We killed twelve of their men and they killed only two of ours. Before the end of the fourth market week they were suing for peace. Those were days when men were men."

As he thought of these things he heard the sound of the iron gong in the distance. He listened carefully, and could just hear the crier's voice. But it was very faint. He turned on his bed and his back hurt him. He ground his teeth. The crier was drawing nearer and nearer until he passed by Okonkwo's compound.

"The greatest obstacle in Umuofia," Okonkwo thought bitterly, "is that coward, Egonwanne. His sweet tongue can change fire into cold ash. When he speaks he moves our men to impotence. If they had ignored his womanish wisdom five years ago, we would not have come to this." He ground his teeth. "Tomorrow he will tell them that our fathers never fought a war of blame. If they listen to him I shall leave them and plan my own revenge."

The crier's voice had once more become faint, and the distance had taken the harsh edge off his iron gong. Okonkwo turned from one side to the other and derived a kind of pleasure from the pain his back gave him. "Let Egonwanne talk about a war of blame tomorrow and I shall show him my back and head." He ground his teeth.

The marketplace began to fill as soon as the sun rose. Obierika was waiting in his *obi* when Okonkwo came along and called him. He hung his goatskin bag and his sheathed machete on his shoulder and went out to join him.

Obierika's hut was close to the road and he saw every man who passed to the marketplace. He had exchanged greetings with many who had already passed that morning.

When Okonkwo and Obierika got to the meeting-place there were already so many people that if one threw up a grain of sand it would not find its way to the earth again. And many more people were coming from every quarter of the nine villages. It warmed Okonkwo's heart to see such strength of numbers. But he was looking for one man in particular, the man whose tongue he dreaded and despised so much.

"Can you see him?" he asked Obierika.

"Who?"

"Egonwanne," he said, his eyes roving from one corner of the huge marketplace to the other. Most of the men were seated on goatskins on the ground. A few of them sat on wooden stools they had brought with them.

"No," said Obierika, casting his eyes over the crowd. "Yes, there he is, under the silk-cotton tree. Are you afraid he would convince us not to fight?"

"Afraid? I do not care what he does to you. I despise him and those who listen to him. I shall fight alone if I choose."

They spoke at the top of their voices because everybody was talking, and it was like the sound of a great market.

"I shall wait till he has spoken," Okonkwo thought. "Then I shall speak."

"But how do you know he will speak against war?" Obierika asked after a while.

"Because I know he is a coward," said Okonkwo. Obierika did not hear the rest of what he said because at that moment somebody touched his shoulder from behind and he turned round to shake hands and exchange greetings with five or six friends. Okonkwo did not turn around even though he knew the voices. He was in no mood to exchange greetings. But one of the men touched him and asked about the people of his compound.

"They are well," he replied without interest.

The first man to speak to Umuofia that morning was Okika, one of the six who had been imprisoned. Okika was a great man and an orator. But he did not have the booming voice which a first speaker must use to establish silence in the assembly of the clan. Onyeka had such a voice; and so he was asked to salute Umuofia before Okika began to speak.

"*Umuofia kwenu!*" he bellowed, raising his left arm and pushing the air with his open hand.

"Yaa!" roared Umuofia.

"Umuofia kwenu!" he bellowed again, and again and again, facing a new direction each time. And the crowd answered, "Yaa!"

There was immediate silence as though cold water had been poured on a roaring flame.

Okika sprang to his feet and also saluted his clansmen four times. Then he began to speak:

"You all know why we are here, when we ought to be building our barns or mending our huts, when we should be putting our compounds in order. My father used to say to me: 'Whenever you see a toad jumping in broad daylight, then know that something is after its life.' When I saw you all pouring into this meeting from all the quarters of our clan so early in the morning, I knew that something was after our life." He paused for a brief moment and then began again:

"All our gods are weeping. Idemili is weeping. Ogwugwu is weeping, Agbala is weeping, and all the others. Our dead fathers are weeping because of the shameful <u>sacrilege</u> they are suffering and the abomination we have all seen with our eyes." He stopped again to steady his trembling voice.

"This is a great gathering. No clan can boast of greater numbers or greater valor. But are we all here? I ask you: Are all the sons of Umuofia with us here?" A deep murmur swept through the crowd.

"They are not," he said. "They have broken the clan and gone their several ways. We who are here this morning have remained true to our fathers, but our brothers have deserted us and joined a stranger to soil their fatherland. If we fight the stranger we shall hit our brothers and perhaps shed the blood of a clansman. But we must do it. Our fathers never dreamt of such a thing, they never killed their brothers. But a white man never came to them. So we must do what our fathers would never have done. Eneke the bird was asked why he was always on the wing and he replied: 'Men have learnt to shoot without missing their mark and I have learnt to fly without perching on a twig.' We must root out this evil. And if our brothers take the side of evil we must root them out too. And we must do it now. We must bale this water now that it is only ankle-deep . . . ."

▶ What is "after" the "life" of the village?

▶ What action has always been forbidden in the past? Why does Okika believe that the villagers must act differently now?

words for everyday use

sac • ri • lege (sak´rə lij) n., disrespectful treatment of something sacred. *Grave robbers violated the sacred tombs of Egyptian kings even though to do so was considered <u>sacrilege</u>.*

At this point there was a sudden stir in the crowd and every eye was turned in one direction. There was a sharp bend in the road that led from the marketplace to the white man's court, and to the stream beyond it. And so no one had seen the approach of the five court messengers until they had come round the bend, a few paces from the edge of the crowd. Okonkwo was sitting at the edge.

He sprang to his feet as soon as he saw who it was. He confronted the head messenger, trembling with hate, unable to utter a word. The man was fearless and stood his ground, his four men lined up behind him.

In that brief moment the world seemed to stand still, waiting. There was utter silence. The men of Umuofia were merged into the mute backcloth of trees and giant creepers, waiting.

The spell was broken by the head messenger. "Let me pass!" he ordered.

"What do you want here?"

"The white man whose power you know too well has ordered this meeting to stop."

In a flash Okonkwo drew his machete. The messenger crouched to avoid the blow. It was useless. Okonkwo's machete descended twice and the man's head lay beside his uniformed body.

The waiting backcloth jumped into tumultuous life and the meeting was stopped. Okonkwo stood looking at the dead man. He knew that Umuofia would not go to war. He knew because they had let the other messengers escape. They had broken into tumult instead of action. He discerned fright in that tumult. He heard voices asking: "Why did he do it?"

He wiped his machete on the sand and went away.

◀ *How does Okonkwo know that Umuofia will not go to war?*

Chapter Twenty-Five

WHEN THE DISTRICT Commissioner arrived at Okonkwo's compound at the head of an armed band of soldiers and court messengers he found a small crowd of men sitting wearily in the *obi*. He commanded them to come outside, and they obeyed without a murmur.

"Which among you is called Okonkwo?" he asked through his interpreter.

"He is not here," replied Obierika.

"Where is he?"

"He is not here!"

The Commissioner became angry and red in the face. He warned the men that unless they produced Okonkwo forthwith he would lock them all up. The men murmured among themselves, and Obierika spoke again.

"We can take you where he is, and perhaps your men will help us."

The Commissioner did not understand what Obierika meant when he said, "Perhaps your men will help us." One of the most infuriating habits of these people was their love of <u>superfluous</u> words, he thought.

Obierika with five or six others led the way. The Commissioner and his men followed, their firearms held at the ready. He had warned Obierika that if he and his men played any monkey tricks they would be shot. And so they went.

There was a small bush behind Okonkwo's compound. The only opening into this bush from the compound was a little round hole in the red-earth wall through which fowls went in and out in their endless search for food. The hole would not let a man through. It was to this bush that Obierika led the Commissioner and his men. They skirted round the compound, keeping close to the wall. The only sound they made was with their feet as they crushed dry leaves.

Then they came to the tree from which Okonkwo's body was dangling, and they stopped dead.

"Perhaps your men can help us bring him down and bury him," said Obierika. "We have sent for strangers from

▶ *Why has the District Commissioner come to Okonkwo's compound?*

words for everyday use

su • per • flu • ous (sə pʉr´flü əs) *adj.,* more than is needed or wanted; excessive. *That second chicken we ordered for dinner was <u>superfluous</u>, as we barely finished the first one.*

another village to do it for us, but they may be a long time coming."

The District Commissioner changed instantaneously. The <u>resolute</u> administrator in him gave way to the student of primitive customs.

"Why can't you take him down yourselves?" he asked.

"It is against our custom," said one of the men. "It is an abomination for a man to take his own life. It is an offense against the Earth, and a man who commits it will not be buried by his clansmen. His body is evil, and only strangers may touch it. That is why we ask your people to bring him down, because you are strangers."

◀ Why won't Okonkwo's clansmen touch his body?

"Will you bury him like any other man?" asked the Commissioner.

"We cannot bury him. Only strangers can. We shall pay your men to do it. When he has been buried we will then do our duty by him. We shall make sacrifices to cleanse the desecrated land."

Obierika, who had been gazing steadily at his friend's dangling body, turned suddenly to the District Commissioner and said ferociously: "That man was one of the greatest men in Umuofia. You drove him to kill himself; and now he will be buried like a dog. . . ." He could not say any more. His voice trembled and choked his words.

◀ Whom does Obierika blame for Okonkwo's death? Do you feel that Obierika is justified in his claim? Why, or why not?

"Shut up!" shouted one of the messengers, quite unnecessarily.

"Take down the body," the Commissioner ordered his chief messenger, "and bring it and all these people to the court."

"Yes, sah," the messenger said, saluting.

The Commissioner went away, taking three or four of the soldiers with him. In the many years in which he had toiled to bring civilization to different parts of Africa he had learnt a number of things. One of them was that a District Commissioner must never attend to such undignified details as cutting down a hanged man from the tree. Such attention would give the natives a poor opinion of him. In the book which he planned to write he would stress that point. As he walked back to the court he thought about that book. Every day brought him some

---

words for everyday use   res • o • lute (rez′ə lüt′) *adj.,* having a firm purpose; determined. *Cara had always been* <u>*resolute*</u>*; once she set her mind to something she accomplished it.*

▶ Will the Commissioner ever really understand the story of Okonkwo? Why wouldn't that story be told in a paragraph?

new material. The story of this man who had killed a messenger and hanged himself would make interesting reading. One could almost write a whole chapter on him. Perhaps not a whole chapter but a reasonable paragraph, at any rate. There was so much else to include, and one must be firm in cutting out details. He had already chosen the title of the book, after much thought: *The Pacification of the Primitive Tribes of the Lower Niger.*[1]

---

1. **Niger.** River in West Africa that flows through Mali, Niger, and Nigeria

words for everyday use

pac • i • fi • ca • tion (pas´ə fi kā´shən) *n.,* act of calming; appeasement. *After one of the colonists was murdered, the British found the* pacification *of the colonists impossible to achieve.*

Respond to the Selection

Why does Okonkwo feel defeated at the end of the novel? What makes a person like him out of place in the new world brought by the Westerners? Discuss these questions with your classmates.

Investigate, Inquire, and Imagine

Recall: GATHERING FACTS

1a. What does Okonkwo plan to do to establish himself as a great man when he returns to his village?

2a. According to Okonkwo at the end of chapter 20, what keeps the Igbo from being able to "act like one" in response to the coming of the Westerners? What does Okonkwo say is happening to his culture?

3a. What action on the part of Enoch shocks the clan? How does the clan react to Enoch's action? What happens as a result of their reaction?

Interpret: FINDING MEANING

1b. Does Okonkwo, at the beginning of chapter 20, understand the extent of the changes taking place around him? Why, or why not?

2b. Why is it important for a people to "act as one" if they are to preserve their heritage?

3b. Why does Okonkwo take his own life at the end of the novel? What does he think will not happen?

Analyze: TAKING THINGS APART

4a. What new institutions are set up by the Westerners in Igbo territory? How do the beliefs of the second missionary, Mr. Smith, differ from those of his predecessor, Mr. Brown?

Synthesize: BRINGING THINGS TOGETHER

4b. Which person do you most admire, Reverend Brown or Reverend Smith? Why? From your point of view, in what ways did the coming of the Westerners improve life among the Igbo? In what ways did their coming make life difficult or worse for the Igbo?

Evaluate: MAKING JUDGMENTS

5a. What is wrong with calling the people of the lower Niger "primitive tribes"? What doesn't the Commissioner know about the people he is attempting to conquer?

Extend: CONNECTING IDEAS

5b. What other countries around the world—in Africa, Asia, and North and South America—have been colonized by Europeans? How did the colonizers treat the peoples they encountered, and why do you think they felt they had the right to do so? Is the story of the Igbo people a typical one?

Understanding Literature

IRONY. **Irony** is a difference between appearance and reality. Types of irony include the following: *dramatic irony,* in which something is known by the reader or audience but unknown to the characters; *verbal irony,* in which a statement is made that implies its opposite; and *irony of situation,* in which an event occurs that violates the expectations of the characters, the reader, or the audience. Refer to Obierika's comments at the end of chapter 25. What makes Okonkwo's death an example of irony? Why is the title of the District Commissioner's book an example of irony?

TRAGEDY. A **tragedy** is a drama or other work of literature that tells the story of the fall of a person of high status. Tragedy tends to be serious. It celebrates the courage and dignity of a tragic hero in the face of inevitable doom. Sometimes that doom is made inevitable by a tragic flaw in the hero. What tragedy is suffered by Okonkwo? by his people? In what ways does Okonkwo's personality contribute to his tragic downfall? In what ways is his downfall due to forces entirely beyond his control?

THEME. A **theme** is a central idea in a literary work. What do you think the author of *Things Fall Apart* wants to teach us about understanding other cultures? What terrible things happen when people fail to attempt to understand one another but rather try to impose their ways on others?

Glossary of Igbo Words and Phrases

Afo: one of four market days. In order, the days are *Afo, Nkwo, Eke,* and *Oye.* Eke is market day in Umuofia. In Abame, market day was every other *Afo.*

agadi-nwayi: old woman. This is also the name of Umuofia's powerful and fear-inspiring magic, or medicine, which has its origin in a ghostly old woman with only one leg. A shrine is built in the center of Umuofia to honor the *agadi-nwayi.*

agbala: woman; also used disparagingly to mean a man who has taken no title.

Agbala: Oracle of the Hills and Caves. This is a common name for oracles; it is the same as the Igbo word for woman, possibly because oracles, though they themselves are considered to be male, are traditionally served by female priests.

"Agbala do-o-o-o!": "Agbala wants something!" The phrase, called out by Chielo in chapter 11, is especially ominous because the Igbo word *do* literally implies ritual sacrifice.

"Agbala ekeneo-o-o-o! Agbala ekene gio-o-o-o!": "Agbala greets…Agbala greets you!"

"Agbala cholu ifa ada ya Ezinma-o-o-o!": "Agbala wants to see his daughter Ezinma!"

Amadi: goddess of the sky, thunder, and rain.

Ani: the earth goddess, or the Great Earth Mother. Ani was the mother of the ancestors and considered the owner of all human beings.

"Aru oyim de de de dei!": greeting called out by the *egwugwu,* meaning "Body of my friend, greetings!" The *egwugwu* refer to people as "bodies," emphasizing the difference between human beings and the *egwugwu* themselves, who are spirits and no longer have physical forms.

chi: personal god.

"Chi negbu madu ubosi ndu ya nato ya uto daluo-o-o-o!": "God (*chi*) who kills a man on the very day he is the happiest!" This line, uttered by Chielo in chapter 11, is a warning to humans not to be too sure of themselves, since Agbala could strike them at any moment.

Chukwu: creator god and the supreme god of the Igbo.

efulefu: worthless person. During the slave trade, people considered worthless were often sold into slavery.

ege: wrestling technique.

egusi: watermelon seed. It can be dried and roasted and then ground for use in soups.

egwugwu: masked performer who impersonates one of the ancestral spirits of the village. The Igbo believe that during the ritual dramas performed by the *egwugwu*, those who have been dressed up for the masquerade are actually transformed, becoming possessed by the spirits of the ancestors. The *egwugwu* thus become vehicles for communication between the earthly and spiritual realms. Through the *egwugwu*, the ancestors communicate to their children, the people of the community. The term *egwugwu* is also used to refer to any masked dancers. The "dancing *egwugwu*" of Unoka, referred to in chapter one, are simply entertainers who serve no religious purpose. The root of the word is *egwu*, meaning *drum*.

Eke: one of the market days (see *Afo,* above).

ekwe: hollow wooden drum played with another piece of wood. The *ekwe* can be made to "talk."

eneke-nti-oba: swallow, a quarrelsome type of bird. According to the proverb, it is the bird who has learned to fly without perching; according to a folk tale told by Nwoye's mother, it challenged the whole world to a wrestling contest, and was finally thrown by the cat.

eze-agadi-nwayi: teeth of an old woman.

Eze elina...Sala [Ikemefuna's song]: This is the song of Ikemefuna's favorite story "where the ant holds his court in splendor and the sands dance forever." Achebe does not translate the song, probably because it makes no sense out of context.

iba: malarial fever, which is contracted through mosquito bites. *Iba* is often fatal.

Idemili: god of the river. The python, a large nonpoisonous snake, is sacred to Idemili, and therefore, to kill one of these snakes is a grave sin. *Idemili* is also the third-highest honorific title for an Igbo man. In chapter 1, Unoka's friend Okoye announces that he is about to take the Idemili title.

Ifejioku: god of yams. Unoka sacrificed a cock at Ifejioku's shrine every year to help ensure a good crop of yams (chapter 3).

Ikenga: a carved representation of a god.

Igbo: a people native to southeastern Nigeria, and the language they speak. In the past it was commonly spelled *Ibo,* as in this novel; today the *g* is usually added to better represent the correct pronunciation of the word.

ilo: the village playground, where people assemble for games, ceremonies, and dances.

inyanga: showing off, bragging.

isa-ifi: final marriage ceremony in which the groom's female relatives question the bride about her past sexual relations. The bride is not required to be a virgin, but if she has been intimate with another man since the time when the marriage was being discussed and arranged, her bride price may be lowered.

iyi-uwa: stone that is a link between an *ogbanje* child and the spirit world; finding and destroying the stone prevents the child from repeating the cycle of death.

jigida: beads worn around a woman's waist.

kotma: court messenger. The word was formed by shortening and conjoining the English words.

kwenu: shout of greeting used when addressing the united clan, e.g., *"Umuofia kwenu!"*

ndichie: village elders; men of title in the clan. These include the ancestral leaders.

nna ayi: our father. *Nna* means father.

nne: mother. Hence *Nneka,* or "Mother is Supreme," a common given name.

nno: welcome.

nso-ani: serious religious offense, literally, an abomination against the earth goddess.

nza: small bird who, according to the proverb, "so far forgot himself after a big meal that he challenged his *chi*" (chapter 4).

obi: large hut belonging to the head of the family.

obodo dike: land of the brave.

ochu: murder or manslaughter. A male *ochu*, or intentional killing (murder), is more serious than a female *ochu,* which is accidental (manslaughter).

ogbanje: child who repeatedly dies and returns to its mother to be reborn, in a continual cycle of death that can be broken by the destruction of the child's *iyi-uwa,* a stone that connects him or her to the spirit world. This myth probably came about because many children died of sickle-cell anemia, a hereditary disease common among the Igbo.

Ogbu-agali-odu: evil essence or spirit brought into the world when humans tried to work evil magic, or medicines, against their enemies. The feared *Ogbu-agali-odu* roamed at night in the form of a sinister glow, and could kill humans it encountered.

Ogbuefi: traditional title of respect for an affluent person, used like *Mister* before a person's name. Literally, it means "killer of a cow," indicating that the person is rich enough to be able to afford killing a cow for a feast.

ogene: metal gong, used as an instrument of communication as well as a musical instrument. Whenever Igbo elders are to meet, or whenever there is an important occurrence, the people are summoned by the town crier beating on the *ogene.*

ogwu: medicine, or magic (chapter 22).

Ogwugwu: a god who gives life.

oji odu achu-ijiji-o: cow, literally, "the one that uses its tail to drive away the flies."

osu: outcast. *Osu* were people who were considered to be dedicated to a god, and were therefore not allowed to mix with the people of the village. The *osu* condition extended to one's children, so that these people were outcasts for generations.

Oye: one of the four market days (see *Afo*).

ozo: title of honor among the Igbo. Only men of both honor and wealth in the clan could take an *ozo*. Unoka, Okonkwo's father, was called a woman for not having earned an *ozo* title.

tufia: curse meaning "sin" or "abomination," often accompanied by a spit for emphasis.

udu: ceramic percussion instrument, in the shape of an earthen pot, with one or two holes on its side. A flat leather fan is used to beat the holes.

uli: black dye used to draw patterns on the skin.

umuada: gathering of the daughters of a family. For this gathering, the women return to the village where they were born.

umunna: wide group of relatives all descended from a common male ancestor (literally, "children of the father").

uri: one of a series of ceremonies held before marriage, in which the groom-to-be pays the dowry, or bride-price.

Plot Analysis of
Things Fall Apart

A **plot** is a series of events related to a central conflict, or struggle. The following diagram illustrates the main plot of *Things Fall Apart*.

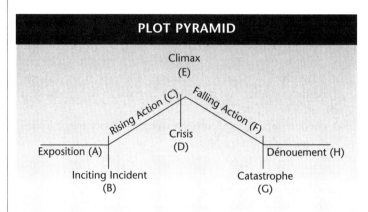

PLOT PYRAMID

Climax (E)

Rising Action (C)

Falling Action (F)

Crisis (D)

Exposition (A)

Dénouement (H)

Inciting Incident (B)

Catastrophe (G)

The parts of a plot are as follows. Note, however, that plots rarely contain all these elements in precisely this order.

The **exposition** is the part of a plot that provides background information about the characters, setting, or conflict.

The **inciting incident** is the event that introduces the central conflict.

The **rising action**, or complication, develops the conflict to a high point of intensity.

The **climax** is the high point of interest or suspense in the plot.

The **crisis**, or turning point, often the same event as the climax, is the point in the plot where something decisive happens to determine the future course of events and the eventual working out of the conflict.

The **falling action** is all the events that follow the climax.

The **resolution** is the point at which the central conflict is ended, or resolved. In a tragedy, that resolution takes the form of a *catastrophe*. The **catastrophe** is the event that marks the ultimate tragic fall of the central character. Often this event is the character's death.

The **dénouement** is any material that follows the resolution and that ties up loose ends.

There are two central conflicts in *Things Fall Apart*—one internal and one external. The internal conflict is Okonkwo's struggle to maintain the perception that he is strong, not weak. The external conflict is the struggle between the Igbo people and the threat of European imperialism. The plot develops both conflicts. It shows how both one individual, Okonkwo, and the Igbo culture in general, fall apart.

Exposition (A)

Part One of the novel can be considered the exposition, because it gives relevant background information about Okonkwo, about life in Umuofia, and about Okonkwo's main conflict: his internal struggle to be everything his father, Unoka, was not. Ikemefuna comes to live with Okonkwo's family and becomes close to his son, Nwoye, and is a positive influence on the boy. Okonkwo violates the Week of Peace by beating his youngest wife, Obiageli. He shoots a gun at his second wife, Ekwefi, narrowly missing her.

Inciting Incident (B)

Word comes that Ikemefuna must be killed; despite being advised to stay out of the matter, Okonkwo participates in the killing. This act introduces one of the two central conflicts of the novel: Okonkwo's internal struggle to avoid being seen as weak. This fear is also Okonkwo's fatal flaw, which will lead to his downfall. The incident sets in motion Okonkwo's personal tragedy; committing such an abominable act will cause terrible things to happen to him. As Obierika tells him, "What you have done will not please the Earth. It is the kind of action for which the goddess wipes out whole families." And indeed, Okonkwo's action leads to Nwoye's eventual betrayal of his father.

A second inciting incident occurs later, in Part 2 of the novel, when Okonkwo learns that Abame has been wiped out by the white man. This incident introduces the other central conflict of the novel, the external conflict between the Igbo and the British colonial forces. This conflict is also foreshadowed at the end of chapter 8, when Obierika brings up rumors about men "as white as chalk" who are as yet unknown in Umuofia.

Rising Action (C)

Okonkwo falls into a deep depression after the death of Ikemefuna. Ezinma, Okonkwo's favorite child, nearly dies of *iba,* or malarial fever; when she recovers, the priestess Chielo comes for her, taking her for a long walk through the night and frightening both Ezinma's mother and Okonkwo himself. At the funeral of a clansman, Ezeudu, Okonkwo's gun accidentally fires and kills Ezeudu's young son. Okonkwo is banished from his village. While in his mother's village of Mbanta, Okonkwo is reminded by his uncle Uchendu of the importance of the female, but the super-masculine Okonkwo does not take this lesson to heart. Christian missionaries come to Mbanta and Nwoye becomes one of the converts. His father disowns him. The villagers ostracize the Christians when one of them is rumored to have killed and eaten the sacred python. Okonwko also hears other news about the white man's presence in Igbo territory. He becomes more and more anxious to return to Umuofia, where he hopes to regain his high status. He is certain that his clan is too manly to allow the white man to take over in Umuofia. However, when he returns, he finds that his town, too, has changed. He wants to fight, but Obierika tells him, "It is already too late." But then Enoch, a zealous Christian convert, unmasks an *egwugwu,* and the villagers burn down the church. For the first time, Okonkwo has hope that his clan might recall its warrior past and fight the white man.

Crisis (D)

The District Commissioner calls the leaders of Umuofia to his headquarters to discuss the incident involving Enoch and the church, but jails and fines the men instead. Court messengers taunt and beat the prisoners until, humiliated, Okonkwo is choked with hate. This crisis marks the turning point for the external conflict: it is now apparent that the British have power over the leaders of Umuofia and are not willing to negotiate.

Climax (E)

After their release, the leaders of Umuofia call a clan meeting. When court messengers come to break up the meeting, Okonkwo beheads one of them with his machete.

Falling Action (F)

The villagers allow the other messengers to escape and Okonkwo realizes that his clan is not willing to fight.

Catastrophe (G)

Okonkwo commits suicide. Because since suicide is an abomination to the clan, the body of this once great man is considered to be evil and his clansmen cannot even touch it. Okonkwo's tragic flaw has led him to this terrible end.

Dénouement (H)

As the Commissioner and his men take Okonkwo's body for burial, the Commissioner reflects that Okonkwo's story might make a nice paragraph in his planned book *The Pacification of the Primitive Tribes of the Lower Niger.* With this detail, Achebe indicates that the British have all but won the struggle to "pacify" the Igbo people.

"Going Home Was a Sad Awakening"
Marjorie Coeyman

ABOUT THE RELATED READING

This article appeared on January 6, 2000 in *The Christian Science Monitor,* an international daily newspaper. Marjorie Coeyman is a staff writer for the *Monitor.*

Living in <u>exile</u>, it is easy to begin to forget the simple things. "The sounds of the morning are different," says Chinua Achebe of the way it feels to greet the day in his native region in Nigeria. "To hear the birds." And, of course, he adds, "To be surrounded by the Ibo language."

These pleasures had not been available to the famed Nigerian novelist, the author of the 1959 classic *Things Fall Apart*—for nine years since leaving his country in 1990.

A serious car accident and the need for Western medical attention first prompted him to leave and then a repressive five-year military <u>regime</u> kept him out.

Shortly after leaving, Mr. Achebe settled in New York's Hudson Valley region where he has since been teaching literature at Bard College in Annandale-on-Hudson.

▶ *What is this article about?*

This summer, however, three months after the inauguration of a new <u>civilian</u> government, Achebe was able to return home for a visit. The journey aroused so many emotions that even Achebe, a man famed for the power of his narratives, says he cannot yet find the words to frame them.

In a dialogue with the Congolese novelist Emmanuel Dongala—also teaching at Bard while he lives in exile from his country's civil war—Achebe spoke recently in front of Bard faculty and students about what he felt and saw while in his homeland.

words for everyday use

ex • ile (eks´ īl´) *n.,* state or period of forced absence from one's country or community. *Poet Pablo Neruda lived for many years in* <u>exile</u> *from his native Chile because as a communist, he feared being persecuted by the Chilean government.*

re • gime (rā zhēm´; ri zhēm´) *n.,* government in power; form of government. *Richard J. Daley, former mayor of Chicago,* *was a controversial figure because of the widespread corruption in his* <u>regime</u>.

ci • vil • ian (sə vil´ yən) *adj.,* non-military; of or having to do with citizens who are not members of the military or police forces. *After years of being run by the military, the country finally returned to* <u>civilian</u> *rule.*

Nigeria has "ceased to work"

"There is great sadness," says Achebe. "This is a country that has ceased to work." And yet, he adds, "I kept fighting to see the good in us as well." Especially at home in his own region, among the Ibo people, he says he found hope and vitality. "The ordinary people are not passive. They are viable, even humorous."

The writer flew into the country's former capital of Lagos, but went almost immediately to his home region 400 miles to the east. He also, at the invitation of the government, traveled to the new capital of Abuja to meet with President Olusegun Obasanjo.

◄ What parts of Nigeria did Achebe visit? With whom did he meet?

Speaking at Bard, Achebe stopped short of wholeheartedly endorsing President Obasanjo. "Writers are not in the business of endorsing anybody," he says. But he did call Obasanjo "the best of the possibilities that we have right now," adding that he is "a bright man," with "many qualifications."

Yet a return to civilian rule is only a beginning point for the troubled country, Achebe points out. "At least now we have turned and are facing in the right direction," he says. "But that is all we have done."

Achebe says it was impossible not to be troubled by the poverty and decay evident in his country. "Even arriving at the airport in Lagos is depressing," he says. "You suddenly felt that something was wrong. There was a lack of smoothness in the runway."

Despite having booked his flight on a respected international airline, Achebe was concerned to realize on landing that there was no wheelchair on board. "Regulations say there should always be a wheelchair on board," he says. "First, you wonder why this airline would disregard the rule on this flight. Then you realize—it is because they are going to Nigeria."

Once off the plane, the drive along a crumbling highway with beggars sleeping by the wayside was also deeply troubling, says Achebe.

But perhaps the point that concerns him most about the future of his country is its unresolved issues of ethnicity and

◄ What troubles Achebe the most about his country?

words for everyday use

vi • a • ble (vī´ ə bəl) *adj.*, capable of working, functioning, and developing adequately; having a reasonable chance of succeeding. *After reviewing thousands of applications, the college admissions board selected the most viable candidates to be admitted to the school.*

en • dorse (in dórs´) *vt.*, publicly and definitely express support or approval of. *Governor Paulsen endorsed Kathy Jones for mayor, saying that Jones was "by far the best candidate for leader of our city."*

the consequences for his people, the Ibo. "There are three major ethnic groups in Nigeria," he explains. "The Hausa, the Yoruba, the Ibo. But the Ibo have been forgotten."

Destruction of native culture

Achebe is the author of five novels, some poetry, and several collections of essays. But he is most <u>renowned</u> for *Things Fall Apart,* a novel that depicts with heartbreaking simplicity the destruction of native culture by the arrival of Europeans. The book has sold 8 million copies, been translated into 50 languages, and is frequently assigned reading in U.S. high school and college classes.

There is today a certain sad irony to the plot of *Things Fall Apart.* The novel's protagonist, Okonkwo, must pass some years in exile from his tribe. When he returns, he finds the old ways have been <u>eroded</u> and that he can no longer find his way without the old customs.

But for Achebe, the relationship with Western culture has always been more complex. He was raised in a family devoted to the Anglican religion[1] and educated in English. While he has sometimes been criticized for the decision to write his novels in English rather than in Ibo—a language he sometimes employs for poetry—he says, "English is the language that was available to me."

He acknowledges, however, that some colleagues disagree with that decision. "I have two hands," he says. "They do different things. Some of my friends think you should cut off one hand out of loyalty to the other."

It has been 12 years since Achebe has produced a novel, and he won't say when another is likely to emerge. "My engagement with fiction is quite interesting, and I don't fully understand it," he says. The next novel "will come when it will come."

As for the future, Achebe has no doubts about the course he would like to follow. When the time is right, he says, "I would like to go back to my village." Although he

▶ *Why did Achebe write his novels in English rather than in Igbo?*

▶ *What would Achebe most like to do?*

---

1. **Anglican religion.** Christianity as practiced in the Episcopal Church of England. King Henry VIII established the Church of England in 1534 when he cut ties with the Catholic Church in Rome.

---

words for everyday use

re • nowned (ri nound´) *adj.,* famous; widely praised and highly honored. *Renowned baseball player Babe Ruth was a hero when my grandfather was growing up.*

erode (i rōd´) *vt.,* diminish or destroy gradually. *The crashing waves eroded the cliff over the years, eating away at the rock to create caves.*

has taught on the university level most of his life, both in Nigeria and abroad, it is not an academic career that Achebe is dreaming of today. "I would like to go back and retire," he says. "What I would most like would be to become an elder in my village."

What happened to our people?

"Perhaps I have been away too long," Okonkwo said, almost to himself. "But I cannot understand these things you tell me. What is it that has happened to our people? Why have they lost the power to fight?"

"Have you not heard how the white man wiped out Abame?" asked Obierika.

"I have heard," said Okonkwo. "But I have also heard that Abame people were weak and foolish. Why did they not fight back? Had they no guns and machetes? We would be cowards to compare ourselves with the men of Abame. Their fathers had never dared to stand before our ancestors. We must fight these men and drive them from the land."

"It is already too late," said Obierika sadly.

      —from *Things Fall Apart* by Chinua Achebe

Critical Thinking Questions

1. How long had it been since Achebe had last visited his home country? Why had he stayed away so long? Where is he living and what is he doing now? What made him decide to visit Nigeria again?
2. How did the reporter get the information she is using to write her article?
3. Why doesn't Achebe endorse the new president, Olusegun Obasanjo? What things did he see on his visit that made him depressed and troubled? What point concerns him most about the future of his country?
4. Why has Achebe's relationship with Western culture been more complex than Okonkwo's? Why does he write in English? Do you think that Achebe should have written in Igbo instead? Is there anything wrong with an Igbo writer using the English language, the language of the colonizers? Explain.
5. Both Chinua Achebe and Okonkwo in *Things Fall Apart* live in exile from their homelands. How does the author of this article compare Chinua Achebe's homecoming to that of Okonkwo? Do you think this is a valid comparison? Explain.

"An African Voice"
Katie Bacon

ABOUT THE RELATED READING

The following is an interview with Chinua Achebe that was published on August 2, 2000 in the online journal *Atlantic Unbound*. Achebe talked to interviewer **Katie Bacon** about his new book *Home and Exile* (2000) and about his classic novel *Things Fall Apart*. In the interview, Achebe explains how Africans like himself took into their own hands the telling of the story of Africa.

This is an excerpt from the interview; you can read the entire transcript at http://www.theatlantic.com/unbound.

Chinua Achebe, the author of one of the enduring works of modern African literature, sees postcolonial cultures taking shape story by story

August 2, 2000

▶ *Why didn't Achebe and his classmates like the novel* Mister Johnson? *What did the novel make Achebe realize?*

Chinua Achebe's emergence as "the founding father of African literature . . . in the English language," in the words of the Harvard University philosopher K. Anthony Appiah, could very well be traced to his encounter in the early fifties with Joyce Cary's novel *Mister Johnson,* set in Achebe's native Nigeria. Achebe read it while studying at the University College in Ibadan during the last years of British colonial rule, and in a curriculum full of Shakespeare, Coleridge, and Wordsworth, *Mister Johnson* stood out as one of the few books about Africa. *Time* magazine had recently declared *Mister Johnson* the "best book ever written about Africa," but Achebe and his classmates had quite a different reaction. The students saw the Nigerian hero as an "embarrassing nitwit," as Achebe writes in his new book, *Home and Exile,* and detected in the Irish author's descriptions of Nigerians "an undertow of uncharitableness . . . a <u>contagion</u> of distaste, hatred, and mockery." *Mister Johnson,* Achebe writes, "open[ed] my

words for everyday use

con • ta • gion (kən tā´ jən) *n.,* contagious disease; poison; corrupting influence of any kind that spreads rapidly. *Crack cocaine was first produced in the 1980s, and its use spread like a <u>contagion</u> throughout the country.*

eyes to the fact that my home was under attack and that my home was not merely a house or a town but, more importantly, an awakening story."

In 1958, Achebe responded with his own novel about Nigeria, *Things Fall Apart,* which was one of the first books to tell the story of European colonization from an African perspective. (It has since become a classic, published in fifty languages around the world.) *Things Fall Apart* marked a turning point for African authors, who in the fifties and sixties began to take back the narrative of the so-called "dark continent."[1]

Home and Exile, which grew out of three lectures Achebe gave at Harvard in 1998, describes this transition to a new era in literature. The book is both a kind of autobiography and a <u>rumination</u> on the power stories have to create a sense of dispossession[2] or to <u>confer</u> strength, depending on who is wielding the pen. Achebe depicts his gradual realization that *Mister Johnson* was just one in a long line of books written by Westerners that presented Africans to the world in a way that Africans didn't agree with or recognize, and he examines the "process of 're-storying' peoples who had been knocked silent by all kinds of dispossession." He ends with a hope for the twenty-first century—that this "re-storying" will continue and will eventually result in a "balance of stories among the world's peoples."

Achebe encourages writers from the Third World[3] to stay where they are and write about their own countries, as a way to help achieve this balance. Yet he himself has lived in the United States for the past ten years—a <u>reluctant</u> exile. In

◀ What did African writers start to do in the fifties and sixties?

◀ Why does Achebe think that writers should stay where they are and write about their own countries?

---

1. **take back the narrative of the so-called "dark continent."** They began to respond with their own narratives about Africa, which Westerners called the "dark continent."

2. **dispossession.** Literally, a depriving of homes, possessions, and security. Here, Achebe uses the word more broadly to refer to how people are deprived of power, of the right to self-govern, and of a political voice in the world.

3. **Third World.** Nations (especially those in Africa and Asia) that are considered economically underdeveloped are sometimes called the "third world." In this world order, the West (Europe and America) are the "first world" and Communist countries are the "second world." These terms reflect the values of the West during the twentieth century and are not necessarily a fair or accurate way to look at the world.

---

words for everyday use

ru • mi • na • tion (rü mi nā´ shən) *n.,* reflection; contemplation. *Grandpa interrupted his <u>rumination</u> about World War II to ask if I was getting bored.*

con • fer (kən fər´) *vt.,* give or bestow upon. *The title of King was <u>conferred</u> upon the prince after his mother, the Queen, had died.*

re • luc • tant (ri lək´ tənt) *adj.,* feeling or showing hesitation or unwillingness. *Bintu was <u>reluctant</u> to join the swim team, but her friends convinced her it would be fun.*

1990, Achebe was in a car accident in Nigeria, and was paralyzed from the waist down. While recuperating in a London hospital, he received a call from Leon Botstein, the president of Bard College, offering him a teaching job and a house built for his needs. Achebe thought he would be at Bard, a small school in a quiet corner of the Hudson River Valley, for only a year or two, but the political situation in Nigeria kept worsening. During the military dictatorship of General Sani Abacha, who ruled from 1993 to 1998, much of Nigeria's wealth—the country has extensive oil fields—went into the pocket of its leader, and public <u>infrastructure</u> that had been quite good, like hospitals and roads, withered. In 1999, Olusegun Obasanjo became Nigeria's first democratically elected President since 1983, and the situation in Nigeria is improving, <u>albeit</u> slowly and shakily. Achebe is watching from afar, waiting for his country to rebuild itself enough for him to return.

Achebe, who is sixty-nine, has written five novels, including *Arrow of God* (1964) and *Anthills of the Savannah* (1987), five books of nonfiction, and several collections of short stories and poems. Achebe spoke recently with *Atlantic Unbound*'s Katie Bacon at his home in Annandale-on-Hudson, in New York.

You have been called the <u>progenitor</u> of the modern African novel, and *Things Fall Apart* has maintained its <u>resonance</u> in the decades since it was written. Have you been surprised by the effect the book has had?

Was I surprised? Yes, at the beginning. There was no African literature as we know it today. And so I had no idea when I was writing *Things Fall Apart* whether it would even be accepted or published. All of this was new—there was nothing by which I could gauge how it was going to be received.

But, of course, something doesn't continue to surprise you every day. After a while I began to understand why the book had resonance. I began to understand my history even better. It wasn't as if when I wrote it I was an expert

<hr>

words for everyday use

in • fra • struc • ture (in´ frə strək chər) *n.*, system of public works for a country, state, or region. *Years of war in Afghanistan had destroyed the country's <u>infrastructure</u>, so that electricity and running water were no longer available to most citizens.*

al • be • it (ȯl bē´ ət) *conj.*, even though. *Shaggy is a lovable dog, <u>albeit</u> slightly cranky at times.*

pro • gen • i • tor (prō je´ nə tər) *n.*, forefather; originator. *Black rhythm and blues artists such as Joe Turner were the <u>progenitors</u> of what would later be known as rock music.*

re • son • ance (re´ zə nən[t]s) *n.*, quality of evoking a response; also, quality of echoing, as in a resonant voice. *The bombing of Hiroshima and Nagasaki at the end of World War II had worldwide <u>resonance</u>.*

in the history of the world. I was a very young man. I knew I had a story, but how it fit into the story of the world—I really had no sense of that. Its meaning for my Igbo people was clear to me, but I didn't know how other people elsewhere would respond to it. Did it have any meaning or resonance for them? I realized that it did when, to give you just one example, the whole class of a girls' college in South Korea wrote to me, and each one expressed an opinion about the book. And then I learned something, which was that they had a history that was similar to the story of *Things Fall Apart*—the history of colonization. This I didn't know before. Their colonizer was Japan.[4] So these people across the waters were able to relate to the story of dispossession in Africa. People from different parts of the world can respond to the same story, if it says something to them about their own history and their own experience.

◀ What audience does Achebe say can relate to the story in Things Fall Apart?

It seems that people from places that haven't experienced colonization in the same way have also responded to the story.

There are different forms of dispossession, many, many ways in which people are deprived or subjected to all kinds of victimization—it doesn't have to be colonization. Once you allow yourself to identify with the people in a story, then you might begin to see yourself in that story even if on the surface it's far removed from your situation. This is what I try to tell my students: this is one great thing that literature can do—it can make us identify with situations and people far away. If it does that, it's a miracle. I tell my students, it's not difficult to identify with somebody like yourself, somebody next door who looks like you. What's more difficult is to identify with someone you don't see, who's very far away, who's a different color, who eats a different kind of food. When you begin to do that then literature is really performing its wonders.

◀ What does Achebe tell his students is "one great thing that literature can do"?

A character in *Things Fall Apart* remarks that the white man "has put a knife on the things that held us together, and we have fallen apart." Are those things still severed, or have the wounds begun to heal?

What I was referring to there, or what the speaker in the novel was thinking about, was the upsetting of a society, the disturbing of a social order. The society of Umuofia, the village in *Things Fall Apart*, was totally disrupted by the

---

4. **South Korea . . . Japan.** Japan ruled Korea from 1910–1945.

coming of the European government, missionary Christianity, and so on. That was not a temporary disturbance; it was a once and for all alteration of their society. To give you the example of Nigeria, where the novel is set, the Igbo people had organized themselves in small units, in small towns and villages, each self-governed. With the coming of the British, Igbo land as a whole was incorporated into a totally different polity,[5] to be called Nigeria, with a whole lot of other people with whom the Igbo people had not had direct contact before. The result of that was not something from which you could recover, really. You had to learn a totally new reality, and accommodate yourself to the demands of this new reality, which is the state called Nigeria. Various nationalities, each of which had its own independent life, were forced by the British to live with people of different customs and habits and priorities and religions. And then at independence, fifty years later, they were suddenly on their own again. They began all over again to learn the rules of independence. The problems that Nigeria is having today could be seen as resulting from this effort that was initiated by colonial rule to create a new nation. There's nothing to indicate whether it will fail or succeed. It all depends.

One might hear someone say, How long will it take these people to get their act together? It's going to take a very, very long time, because it's really been a whole series of interruptions and disturbances, one step forward and two or three back. It has not been easy. One always wishes it had been easier. We've compounded things by our own mistakes, but it doesn't really help to pretend that we've had an easy task.

In *Home and Exile,* you talk about the negative ways in which British authors such as Joseph Conrad and Joyce Cary portrayed Africans over the centuries. What purpose did that portrayal serve?

It was really a straightforward case of setting us up, as it were. The last four or five hundred years of European contact with Africa produced a body of literature that presented Africa in a very bad light and Africans in very <u>lurid</u>

▶ Why is Nigeria still struggling to succeed as a nation?

▶ How did European writers help to justify the slave trade and slavery?

---

5. **polity** (pä´ lə tē). Political organization

words for everyday use   lu • rid (lür´ id) *adj.,* causing horror and revulsion; shocking. *The <u>lurid</u> pictures of the movie star's car crash were published in supermarket tabloids.*

terms. The reason for this had to do with the need to justify the slave trade and slavery. The cruelties of this trade gradually began to trouble many people in Europe. Some people began to question it. But it was a profitable business, and so those who were engaged in it began to defend it—a lobby of people supporting it, justifying it, and excusing it. It was difficult to excuse and justify, and so the steps that were taken to justify it were rather extreme. You had people saying, for instance, that these people weren't really human, they're not like us. Or, that the slave trade was in fact a good thing for them, because the alternative to it was more brutal by far.

And therefore, describing this fate that the Africans would have had back home[6] became the motive for the literature that was created about Africa. Even after the slave trade was abolished, in the nineteenth century, something like this literature continued, to serve the new imperialistic[7] needs of Europe in relation to Africa. This continued until the Africans themselves, in the middle of the twentieth century, took into their own hands the telling of their story.

You write in *Home and Exile*, "After a short period of dormancy and a little self-doubt about its erstwhile imperial mission, the West may be ready to resume its old domineering monologue in the world." Are some Western writers backpedaling and trying to tell their own version of African stories again?

This tradition that I'm talking about has been in force for hundreds of years, and many generations have been brought up on it. What was preached in the churches by the missionaries and their agents at home all supported a

---

6. **fate that the Africans would have had back home.** Some writers said that blacks were better off being slaves in America than living in uncivilized Africa.

7. **imperialistic.** Having to do with imperialism, the practice of extending a nation's power by taking over foreign territories. Britain's "imperialistic need" was to expand its empire by taking over portions of Africa. Literature helped them promote this idea.

---

words for everyday use

lob • by (lä´ bē) *n.*, group of persons engaged in promoting a project or a cause, especially as representatives of a special interest group. *When government leaders wanted to charge television networks for the use of the nation's airwaves, the powerful television broadcasters' lobby pressured them to abandon the idea.*

dor • man • cy (dór´ mən[t] sē) *n.*, quality or state of being dormant, or inactive. *After a winter of dormancy, the grizzly bear awoke and emerged from its cave.*

erst • while (ərst´ [h]wīl) *adv.*, in the past: formerly. *Erstwhile secretary of state for the Kennedy administration, Henry Kissinger is well known in the world of politics.*

certain view of Africa. When a tradition gathers enough strength to go on for centuries, you don't just turn it off one day. When the African response began, I think there was an immediate pause on the European side, as if they were saying, Okay, we'll stop telling this story, because we see there's another story. But after a while there's a certain beginning again, not quite a return but something like a reaction to the African story that cannot, of course, ever go as far as the original tradition that the Africans are responding to. There's a reaction to a reaction, and there will be a further reaction to that. And I think that's the way it will go, until what I call a balance of stories is secured. And this is really what I personally wish this century to see—a balance of stories where every people will be able to contribute to a definition of themselves, where we are not victims of other people's accounts. This is not to say that nobody should write about anybody else—I think they should, but those that have been written about should also participate in the making of these stories.

And that's what started with *Things Fall Apart* and other books written by Africans around the 1950s.

Yes, that's what it turned out to be. It was not actually clear to us at the time what we were doing. We were simply writing our story. But the bigger story of how these various accounts tie in, one with the other, is only now becoming clear. We realize and recognize that it's not just colonized people whose stories have been <u>suppressed</u>, but a whole range of people across the globe who have not spoken. It's not because they don't have something to say, it simply has to do with the division of power, because storytelling has to do with power. Those who win tell the story; those who are defeated are not heard. But that has to change. It's in the interest of everybody, including the winners, to know that there's another story. If you only hear one side of the story, you have no understanding at all.

▶ *Why is it important for everyone's story to be told?*

Critical Thinking Questions

1. Why, according to Achebe, has *Things Fall Apart* had such a lasting impact in the decades since it was written?
2. According to Achebe, why did European authors such as Joyce Cary portray Africans in such a negative light? When did Africans begin to respond with their own stories?
3. Why does Achebe think that Western writers might start trying to tell their own version of African stories again?
4. What does the division of power have to do with storytelling? Whose stories are told? Whose are not told, and why? What does Achebe mean when he says that we need a "balance of stories" in the world?
5. According to Achebe, has Nigeria recovered from the trauma of colonization described in *Things Fall Apart?* Why, or why not?

"The Second Coming"
William Butler Yeats

ABOUT THE RELATED READING

Chinua Achebe took the title for his novel from this famous poem by **William Butler Yeats** (1865–1939). Yeats (pronounced yāts) was an Irish poet, dramatist, and prose writer who was one of the greatest English-language poets of the twentieth century. He received the Nobel Prize for Literature in 1923. **"The Second Coming"** was published in 1921, shortly after World War I and the Russian Revolution. In this poem, Yeats prophesies the beginning of a new and frightening cycle of history. He believed that history occurred in cycles, or *gyres,* punctuated by revolutionary events in which the spirit world intersected this world. To him, the wars indicated that the Christian era, which had followed the era of the ancient world, was about to end, its essential values falling apart.

▶ How does the speaker characterize the times in which he lives?

Turning and turning in the widening gyre[1]
The falcon cannot hear the falconer;[2]
Things fall apart; the center cannot hold;
Mere anarchy is loosed upon the world,
The blood-dimmed tide is loosed, and everywhere
The ceremony of innocence is drowned;
The best lack conviction, while the worst
Are full of passionate intensity.

Surely some revelation is at hand;
Surely the Second Coming[3] is at hand;
The Second Coming! Hardly are those words out
When the vast image out of *Spiritus Mundi*[4]
Troubles my sight; somewhere in the sands of the desert

---

1. **gyre.** Circle or cycle. Yeats pronounced the word with a hard *g.*
2. **falcon . . . falconer.** The reference is to the sport of falconry, in which a trained falcon is used for hunting. The image suggests violence that is uncontrolled by any authority.
3. **Second Coming.** Many Christians believe that Jesus will come again to earth at the end of time as we know it. This event is known as the Second Coming.
4. *Spiritus Mundi.* Latin for "the world spirit," Yeats used the phrase to mean the collective, inherited body of symbols common to all people.

A shape with lion body and head of a man,[5]
A gaze blank and pitiless as the sun,
Is moving its slow thighs, while all about it
Reel shadows of the indignant desert birds.[6]
The darkness drops again; but now I know
That twenty centuries[7] of stony sleep
Were vexed to nightmare by a rocking cradle,[8]
And what rough beast, its hour come round at last
Slouches towards Bethlehem[9] to be born?

◀ What prophecy is implied by the speaker's closing question?

Critical Thinking Questions

1. What picture of the state of the world does the speaker draw in stanza 1? How does the speaker feel about these changes?
2. What does the opening of stanza 2 predict? What shape does the speaker see in a vision? How does this vision differ from the prediction?
3. In the last four lines, what is the meaning of the references to "twenty centuries," a "rocking cradle," and "Bethlehem"? In the final lines, what does the speaker seem to suggest will be the successor to the age begun, two thousand years ago, by the birth of Jesus?
4. Yeats used the term *gyre* to refer to the cycles of history. What three cycles of history are referred to in the poem? How does the speaker feel about the second and third periods? What events might have led to Yeats's feelings?
5. Why do you think Achebe chose to take the title of his book from this poem? How is the world of the Igbo in *Things Fall Apart* similar to the world Yeats describes in stanza 1? What ushers in a new cycle of history for the Igbo?

---

5. **lion . . . man.** The Egyptian sphinx
6. **Reel . . . birds.** Birds are traditionally associated with omens or predictions. Unscientific peoples often observe their behavior to predict the future. The reeling suggests Yeats's gyres.
7. **twenty centuries.** The two-thousand-year period before the birth of Jesus, thought of by Yeats as the Heroic Age
8. **rocking cradle.** The birth of Jesus
9. **Bethlehem.** The birthplace of Jesus

"Lament of the Sacred Python"
Chinua Achebe

ABOUT THE RELATED READING

"Lament of the Sacred Python" first appeared in Chinua Achebe's poetry collection Beware, *Soul Brother* (published in the U.S. in 1971 with the title *Christmas in Biafra*.) The poem mourns the loss of an old religious tradition that was abandoned as the Igbo converted to Christianity. In the past, the Igbo revered the python, a large, nonpoisonous snake, because it was believed to be sacred to the river god, Idemili. Killing the snake was strictly forbidden. But once Christian beliefs became dominant, the python was no longer considered sacred and was killed and even eaten on occasion. In chapter 18 of *Things Fall Apart,* the people of Mbanta become enraged when a Christian convert named Okoli is suspected of having killed a python.

▶ *In the past, how did people react when they saw the python?*

I was there when lizards
were ones and twos, child
Of sacred father Idemili. Painful
Tear-drops of Sky's first weeping
Drew my spots. Sky-born
I walked the earth with royal gait
And crowds of human mourners
Filing down funereal[1] paths
Across lengthening shadows
Of the dead acknowledged my face
In broken dirges[2] of fear.

But of late
A wandering god pursued,
It seems, by hideous things
He did at home has come to us
And pitched his tent here
Beneath the people's holy tree

---

1. **funereal.** Having to do with a funeral
2. **dirges.** Songs of mourning; funeral songs

And <u>hoisted</u> from its <u>pinnacle</u>
A <u>charlatan</u> bell that calls
Unknown monotones of revolts,
Scandals, and false immunities.
And I that none before could meet except
In fear thought I brought no terrors
From creation's day of gifts I must now
Turn on my track
In dishonourable flight
Where children stop their play
To shriek in my ringing ears:
 Look out, python! Look out, python!
 Christians <u>relish</u> python flesh!

And great father Idemili
That once upheld from earth foundations
Cloud banks of sky's endless waters
Is betrayed in his shrine by empty men
<u>Suborned</u> with the stranger's <u>tawdry</u> gifts
And taken trussed up[3] to the altar-shrine turned
Slaughter house for the gory advent
Feast[4] of an <u>errant</u> cannibal god
Tooth-filed to eat his fellows.

And the sky recedes in
Anger; the orphan snake
Abandoned weeps in the shadows.

◀ *What do the children tell the python? What must the python do now?*

◀ *Who eats the god Idemili?*

---

3. **trussed up.** Tied up in preparation for cooking
4. **advent feast.** Christian ceremonial feast

words for everyday use

hoist (hoist) *vt.*, lift, raise up. *A crane was used to <u>hoist</u> the gigantic Christmas tree onto the top of the skyscraper.*

pin • na • cle (pin´ ə kəl) *n.*, highest point. *Martha had reached the <u>pinnacle</u> of success as a professional skater: she had won the gold medal at the Winter Olympics.*

char • la • tan (shär´ lə tən) *n.*, fraud, faker. *The man who claimed to be a medium capable of linking us with the spirit world was actually a <u>charlatan</u> who stole our money.*

rel • ish (re´ lish) *vt.*, eat or drink with pleasure. *After spending a year at college, Randy <u>relished</u> his mom's cooking.*

sub • orn (sə bȯrn´) *vt.*, make [someone] do an unlawful thing. *The senator was accused of having <u>suborned</u> his staff members into collecting illegal campaign contributions.*

taw • dry (tȯ´drē) *adj.*, cheap and gaudy. *Piano player Liberace was famous for his <u>tawdry</u> costumes, and his fans loved to see him prance out onstage covered in silver sequins, feather boas, and glittering fake jewels.*

er • rant (er´ ənt) *adj.*, traveling or given to traveling. *The <u>errant</u> knight traveled all over the land in order to seek his fortune.*

Critical Thinking Questions

1. A myth is a story about how things came to be. What myths are associated with the python?
2. Who is the "wandering god" who has come to pitch his tent beneath the people's holy tree? What does the python think must have caused the god to come there?
3. In Igbo culture, the *ekwe,* or talking drum, was used to alert people of news that was important to the community. Everyone understood what the drum beats meant. How does the church bell in stanza 2 compare to the *ekwe?*
4. What is ironic about the snake's having to turn and flee when it sees children? What used to happen when the snake encountered people?
5. Why do you think the poet calls the Christian God a "cannibal god"? What does the Christian God "eat"?
6. Why is the snake an orphan?
7. Compare the ideas of this poem to those in chapter 18 of *Things Fall Apart.* How do the people of Mbanta regard the python? What would happen if someone dared kill a python?

from *Kehinde*
Buchi Emecheta

ABOUT THE RELATED READING

Buchi Emecheta (pronounced bü´ chē ā mā chä´ tä) is probably the best-known black African woman writer today and, having published thirteen novels and an autobiography, she is also the most prolific. She was born near the city of Lagos, Nigeria, in 1944, and her family kept close ties to their native Igbo village of Ibuza. Like Chinua Achebe, Emecheta writes about the Igbo; however, she gives special attention to what it is like to be a woman in the Igbo culture and in West African society in general. Emecheta's characters are strong, intelligent women who live in an oppressively sexist world, one in which their sexuality and ability to bear children are the only things that matter. Emecheta's best-known novel, *The Joys of Motherhood* (1970) concerns Nnu Ego, the daughter of a great Igbo chief. Nnu's only goal in life is to be a good mother. She channels all her hopes and dreams into her children, and only when they have grown does she realize that she has neglected herself. The novel eloquently shows how African society cripples women by teaching them that they are only good as wives and mothers.

Emecheta, who for many years has resided in London, also writes about the life of African immigrants in England. In *Kehinde* (1994), the novel excerpted here, she gives a view of a clash between British and Nigerian values, one quite different from that portrayed in *Things Fall Apart*. Kehinde, the protagonist of the novel, is a Nigerian wife and mother living in London in the 1970s. Kehinde enjoys an equal relationship with her husband Albert and is relatively happy in her marriage. But things change when Albert decides he wants to move the family back to Nigeria. He goes ahead of his wife, leaving Kehinde to sell the house and keep her well-paying bank job in the meantime. Their son and daughter, Joshua and Bimpe, follow him not long after. Two years later, Kehinde has not been able to sell the house and decides she must join her husband. He seems annoyed that she is coming, but Kehinde doesn't know why. She has no idea what a shock awaits her upon her arrival in Nigeria.

from *Kehinde*

Chapter 11: Arrival

Kehinde waited impatiently at the airport at Heathrow.[1] You could always tell the Nigeria Airways check-in counter, as it was the noisiest and the most chaotic in the terminal. . . .

She hoped that the plane would leave on time, but there was the usual engine trouble, and her anxiety mounted the longer they had to wait. She knew her sister Ifeyinwa and Albert would be waiting for her at the airport in Lagos.[2] One tiresome announcement after another told them it would only take another hour. The hour seemed to extend itself indefinitely. Knowing there was nothing she could do about the situation, Kehinde slept. At 9:30 the following morning, eleven hours behind schedule, they departed.

The journey was uneventful, but by the time they landed in Lagos, relatives who had been waiting all day had gone home. At least they had arrived in daylight.

▶ *How has Albert changed?*

In fact, Albert was waiting, and despite his disapproval over the telephone, he seemed glad to see her. He looked more <u>imposing</u> than the London Albert, in flowing white lace *agbada*[3] and matching skull cap. His skin was darker and glossier, and he <u>exuded</u> a new confidence. Women knew the country did this to their men. There was no doubt about it, Albert was thoroughly at home.

A note[4] <u>discreetly</u> pressed into the palm of one of the men jostling each other to take possession of Kehinde's bags, and the young tough was transformed into the picture of servility and respect. Kehinde, impressed in spite of herself, allowed Albert to take over. It was a long time since she had had the luxury of being looked after. She had arrived

---

1. **Heathrow.** London's main airport
2. **Lagos** (lā´ gəs). Formerly the capital of Nigeria, Lagos is a large port city on the southern coast. A large part of the city is located on an offshore island.
3. **agbada.** Voluminous robe traditional to Yoruba areas, worn by men
4. **note.** Money

---

words for everyday use

im • pos • ing (im pō´ ziŋ) *adj.,* impressive in size, bearing, dignity, or grandeur. *Situated on a hill overlooking the city, the immense domed cathedral was quite imposing.*

ex • ude (ig züd´) *vi.,* display conspicuously or abundantly. *Kathy made a good leader because she exuded confidence and strength.*

dis • creet • ly (di skrēt´ lē) *adv.,* in a way that does not attract attention. "You have a piece of lettuce in your teeth," I whispered discreetly to Matt.*

keyed up and combative, ready to justify herself, but slipped effortlessly back into her old submissive role. Besides, there was something about Albert's new confidence which excited admiration, made him more attractive.

Their old Jaguar did not look old at all compared to the other cars on the Lagos road. Though Albert was a careful driver, Kehinde could detect strange sounds that had not been there before, as old bones creak under the still taut skin that holds them together.

When they were underway, Kehinde felt comfortable enough to ask after the children.

"They're fine. I saw them last Saturday and told them Mama is coming home, and they're waiting for you." Knowing this would please her, Albert gave Kehinde a quick grin, revealing momentarily the old Albert. He had never been an openly demonstrative person, but in the last two years he had acquired a new layer of self-control and <u>detachment</u>.

"Something wrong?" Kehinde asked.

"No, nothing. Why you ask?"

"I don't know. I just feel. . ."

Albert did not help her out, concentrating on the traffic. Kehinde was impressed by what oil had done for Lagos. Beautiful wide roads, elegant individually designed houses, soaring flyovers.[5] It was almost like a developed country. Kehinde filled her lungs with hot tropical air and felt <u>elated</u>.

Perhaps Albert had been angry with her because he felt neglected, even though he had taken the decision that he would go back to Lagos ahead of her. She was to sell the house, and buy more things they would need in Lagos. Albert needed time to find accommodation for all of them. Maybe he had forgotten, and that was why he was <u>sulking</u>. Men! Sometimes they behave just like children. After all, their going home was his idea in the first place, urged on by his sisters.

She tried to bring the smile back to his face by asking, "Aunt Selina and Aunt Mary, do they write you often?"

◄ *What does Kehinde think is causing Albert to act so distant toward her?*

---

5. ˙**flyovers.** Planes overhead

words for everyday use

de • tach • ment (dē tach´ mənt) n., indifference; disinterest. *Everyone on the bus was talking and laughing, all except for Julie, who sat alone with an air of* <u>detachment</u>.

e • lat • ed (ē lā´ təd) adj., joyful. *The new*

father was elated as he held his baby daughter for the first time.

sulk (səlk´) vi., be moodily silent; pout. *Raffi* <u>sulked</u> *like a child when he did not get what he wanted.*

Albert took his eyes off the road and studied her, as if she were someone he had just met. Kehinde was not sure if the sigh that escaped him was one of boredom or pity. He turned his attention once more to the road and replied as if he were addressing the streets that were unfolding before their eyes, "Their generation don't like writing letters much. They are here in the south, visiting. We all came to the airport yesterday, but your plane did not arrive . . ."

"You mean they are all at home, in our house! I mean the bungalow[6] you rented?" Kehinde asked, <u>aghast</u>.

"They are in the south to welcome you and to visit the children at their school. Where do you want them to be?"

Kehinde had harbored the dream of their being alone together for a few days, now that the children were at school. She knew now that she had to nerve herself for a different scenario. Staying in the same house with Albert's sisters was more than she had bargained for.

Suddenly, without warning, they were plunged into a <u>maelstrom</u> of fumes, car horns, careering big yellow buses, minibuses packed to capacity and people: the heart of Lagos, Lagos Island-Eko.[7] Kehinde, unaccustomed to the noise and chaos, was startled, but Albert picked his way <u>adroitly</u> through narrow side roads, cluttered with abandoned cars. They turned at last into a small but freshly tarred road, lined with colorful bungalows. This street was cleaner, though the smell of rotting rubbish coming from the open gutters was suffocating. Albert stopped finally in front of a neat bungalow painted blue and white. Two wide pieces of plank had been nailed together to form a bridge over the gutter which smelt so bad that Kehinde wanted to throw up.

A girl ran out to meet them. "Welcome, Madam, welcome, sah," she greeted, as she pulled the bags out of the boot.[8] Kehinde was <u>maneuvering</u> herself out of the car when her attention was diverted to the main door of the house. A very beautiful, sophisticated, young, pregnant

▶ *Who is standing in the doorway of Albert's house?*

---

6. **bungalow.** House usually with only one level and with a low-pitched roof
7. **Eko.** Lagos
8. **boot.** British word for the trunk of a car

woman, with a baby on her left hip, stood in the doorway, wearing the same white lace material as Albert. Her hair, drawn back and plaited in the latest upside-down-basket style, made her face look narrower, so that her swollen belly was like a badge of womanhood in contrast to her leanness. She <u>scrutinized</u> Kehinde <u>insolently</u>, smiling in a mild and unenthusiastic way. She did not attempt to come and help with the unpacking. Kehinde took it all in, like a film in slow motion.

"Grace! Grace, make you careful with those cases," Albert said sharply, appearing unaware of the drama about to be enacted.

"Yes sah!" the <u>encumbered</u> Grace called over her shoulder, as she staggered across the wooden bridge with Kehinde's case on her head.

Just then, Kehinde was distracted by the arrival of Ifeyinwa, shouting for joy and almost dancing her welcome. A couple of her numerous children followed in her wake, and between the three of them, they almost lifted her bodily from the ground. She found herself for the first time crying tears of joy, mixed with relief at receiving a genuine welcome. By now, almost half the street had gathered to watch and to welcome her. People she had never met were asking her how England was.

Ifeyinwa took control. She ushered her sister inside the large and fashionably decorated living room, tastefully enhanced by the furniture Kehinde had sent home in a separate container after Albert had left London. A part of their old life was there in that room and Kehinde felt a surge of reassurance at the familiarity of it.

Ifeyinwa, who used to be a quiet woman, was talking <u>incessantly</u>. She was thinner than Kehinde remembered, certainly compared with Kehinde's plumpness. She exuded anxiety, tying and retying her top *lappa*[9] in <u>agitation</u>. She seemed bent on protecting her, even from people who came in to say she was welcome.

---

9. *lappa.* Traditional woman's costume, a length of cloth wrapped around the waist

---

words for everyday use

scru • ti • nize (skrü´ t[ə]n īz) *vt.*, examine closely. *Sherlock Holmes <u>scrutinized</u> the scene of the crime for clues.*

in • so • lent • ly (in´ sə lənt lē) *adv.*, boldly; in a way that shows disrespect. *"So what?" Renee asked the teacher <u>insolently</u>.*

en • cum • bered (in kəm´ bərd) *adj.*, loaded down. *The car was <u>encumbered</u> with*

everything we would need for the long trip.

in • cess • ant • ly (in ses´ ənt lē´) *adv.*, endlessly. *The waterfall poured <u>incessantly</u> over the cliff, as it had done for centuries.*

a • gi • ta • tion (a jə tā´ shən) *n.*, anxiety; distress. *Mom noticed my <u>agitation</u> as soon as I walked in the room, and told me to sit down and relax.*

Where was Albert, who should be showing her around, taking her to their room? Instead, she felt Ifeyinwa pulling her. "We're coming," she told a neighbor who wanted to know if Kehinde, by sheer accident, met her sons who were studying somewhere in the East End of London. "I have to take her to her room. You can ask her later. After all, you're neighbors now," Ifeyinwa explained. She pulled Kehinde more determinedly, so she had no choice but to follow.

Ifeyinwa led her to her room. It was clean, simply and neatly furnished with one of the three single beds she had bought in London. Where was the king size bed on which she and Albert had spent a fortune in Harrods[10]? Albert had said in his letter that everything had arrived in good condition. She had never had a separate room from her husband all her married life.

"Little Mother, Ifi, call Albert for me. Where is he?" Kehinde besought[11] her sister.

► Why, according to Ifeyinwa, can't Kehinde call her husband by his name? What does Ifeyinwa call him?

Ifeyinwa opened her eyes in horror. "Sh . . . sh . . . sh, not so loud! Don't call your husband by his name here-o. We hear you do it over there in the land of white people. There, people don't have respect for anybody. People call each other by the name their parents gave them, however big the person. We don't do it here-o. Please Kehinde, don't-o."

Kehinde heard herself laughing mirthlessly. "What are you talking about? I said I wanted Albert. Where is he?" She made her way towards the door, but Ifeyinwa restrained her.

"Where are you going? Come back in, just come back. You will see Joshua's father later. Just come first." Her eyes were red and her voice was _agitated_. "Where do you think you are? This is Nigeria, you know."

"I know that, that's what everybody says. 'This is Nigeria, this is Nigeria,' as if the country were not part of this world."

"Sit down, baby sister. Do sit down. You left home a very long time ago. Here, men move together, you know. We women stick together too."

---

10. **Harrods.** A prestigious London department store
11. **besought.** Begged; past tense of _beseech_

words for everyday use   ag • i • tat • ed (a ́ jə tā təd) _adj._, anxious; troubled. _I was agitated because I had a project due the next day and I had not even started working on it._

192   THINGS FALL APART

"Educate me, please, have I not just got married to Albert and you are now going to tell me what marriage is all about. Where is he, anyway?"

"He knows I'm here and won't barge in like that. He's a cultured man. You must stop calling him by his given name. His sisters are in the front room and so are many of his friends and neighbors to welcome you. You are not going out there shouting his given name as if he is your houseboy; as if you circumcised him. What a cheek! What do you want him for anyway? He'll see you bye and bye. Just get dressed, get ready to go and see those who have been waiting to greet you."

Kehinde looked around her once more. "This is not our room, surely?"

"Our room? This is your room. I chose it for you. Next to Joshua's father's own, this is the best one, even better than Rike's own. She has to share hers with her maid and her baby, and she is next to the room kept for your husband's sisters, who can be very noisy during their visits. You're lucky. Joshua's father allowed me a free hand. He is cultured, that husband of yours."

"You talk about my husband as if he's a stranger to me. We married seventeen years ago and I should be telling you about him."

"That's one of the things you must learn. Stop calling him 'my' husband. You must learn to say 'our.' He is Rike's husband too, you know. You saw her, that shameless one with a pregnancy in her belly and a baby on her hips. Honestly, 'these their acadas'[12] just jump on any been-to[13] man, so they can claim their husbands studied overseas . . ." She trailed on, <u>flailing</u> those annoying arms, and not even standing still. She stopped for breath suddenly, gasping.

Kehinde made as if to stand up, but she pulled her down again. "Sit down and calm yourself."

"I am sitting down. I am calm. You are the one who has been walking up and down like . . . like . . . oh Ifi, I don't

◄ Who is Rike? How does Ifeyinwa feel about her?

---

12. **'these their acadas.'** "These university-educated women." *Acada* is slang for a university-educated person, applied derogatorily toward women.
13. **been-to.** A Nigerian who has been to Europe or America. It is considered a status symbol to have studied overseas.

---

words for everyday use   flail (flā[ə]l´) vt., move, swing, or beat around. *Jason <u>flailed</u> his walking stick around, almost hitting me in the head.*

know like what. Are you trying to tell me that Albert's got another wife, and that he is the father of the baby that woman was carrying?"

Ifeyinwa nodded, mutely, tears rolling down her face. "Her name is Rike. She actually pushed herself on Joshua's father. When I heard she'd had a baby boy, I knew Albert would marry her. Few men would say no to such an educated woman once she'd had a man-child for them. His sisters would not have allowed it, and you yourself wouldn't let Joshua's father throw away a man-child, would you? Then, before we could bat an eyelid, she was carrying another one. But I thank your *chi,* that has made you into such a strong woman, that at least you are the mother of Joshua and Bimpe. This one, with all her bottom power and all her acada,[14] cannot take that from you. This is nothing that has not been seen or heard of before. It happens all the time. My husband has two other wives and we all live in two rooms. At least here you have a whole house, and Albert is in a good job. That one is a big teacher at the university."

Kehinde was kneading one of the pillows she'd taken absentmindedly from the bed. She stared at her sister. She could now see why the two of them had been left alone—so that Ifeyinwa could prevent her from going out and making a fool of herself. Her eyes were red, but there were no tears. Her voice, when she eventually found it, was calm, but came from a distance. "So, Albert married her because she had a baby boy for him, enh?"

The past rolled itself out like a film in Kehinde's mind. Albert had insisted they could not keep the baby because they could not afford it, and yet it too had been a man-child. Was that what her dead parents were trying to warn her in the dream she had had in the hospital? But as she looked at her sister, she knew she could not share this pain with her. Kehinde knew her reaction would be to tell her that God was punishing her for committing such an abomination.[15] Possibly Albert was counting on that too. Meanwhile, Ifeyinwa was crying for both of them. She looked at her sister again and their eyes met. Kehinde tried

▶ Why did Albert marry Rike? What does Kehinde have that ensures she will still be valuable to Albert?

---

14. **all her bottom power and all her acada.** All her power as the younger or "bottom" wife and all her university education. Kehinde has not earned a university degree while Rike has.

15. **The past . . . abomination.** Earlier in the novel, Kehinde ended a pregnancy when her husband told her they could not afford another child. While she was at the clinic, Kehinde dreamt that her child had been a boy, the reincarnation of her father.

to imagine the <u>anguish</u> and helplessness she must have endured these last months, not knowing how to break the news to her. Something inside her advised caution, to act coolly and thank God and her culture for her sister's support.

A loud knock coupled with loud laughter at the door told them that their time alone together was over and the play-acting was to begin. A big woman burst in, a typical successful Nigerian businesswoman, known locally as "tick madam." Not waiting to be invited, she entered with a breezy confidence that indicated unmistakably that the house was hers. She was Aunt Selina, the eldest of the Okolo family, whom Kehinde remembered from her engagement to Albert as a thin woman who had just lost her husband, and had been left with two children of her husband's by another woman to look after. She had no child of her own. Her other relatives, Aunt Mary and the other brother Nicholas, had stood by her, while she quickly sold off all her husband's property and went to stay in the north, away from the harassment of her in-laws. The money had helped to educate Nicholas and paid her passage when Albert sent for her, and her bride price.[16] One could never say to such a woman, "Why don't you wait until I say come in?" She was now known as Mama Kaduna and was the mother of them all. Kehinde had thought at one time when they returned to Nigeria, they would be above all that, and people like Mama Kaduna and Aunt Mary would be kept in their places. Now she knew she had been wrong. They were stronger than she was.

She held Kehinde in a bear hug. "Let me look at you. Let's just look at you. Olisa,[17] thank you for bringing them all home. Look at that tiny girl that a rat would eat and still want some more. Look at her. Has she not grown into a mature woman? Hold your head up! Your chin must always be up. Or don't you know who you are? You are the senior wife of a successful Nigerian man, the first wife of

---

16. **her passage . . . and her bride price.** Aunt Selina paid for Kehinde's trip to England, where Albert was living. She also paid Kehinde's father the bride price, or dowry, traditionally given to the bride's family by the family of the groom.

17. **Olisa.** Probably an Okolo family ancestor

words for everyday use an • guish (an´ gwish) *n.,* extreme pain, distress, or anxiety. *Many people felt a terrible anguish after the events of September 11.*

▶ What flaw does Mama Kaduna seem to notice in Ifeyinwa? What does this scene tell you about standards of feminine beauty in Nigeria?

the first son of our father, Okolo. Olisa, give him peace where he is now, making merry with his age-mates. Our dead father loved beautiful people, and you are beautiful now, my daughter. So cool and round." As she spoke, she shot Ifeyinwa a knowing look, as if to emphasize her <u>deficiencies</u>. Ifeyinwa was even thinner than when she was young, not fashionably so, but worn down by poverty. Ignoring the <u>malice</u>, Ifeyinwa merely responded, "Yes Ma, you're right."

Mama Kaduna turned again to Kehinde for a concluding <u>appraisal</u>: "Ah London suited you, but here will suit you even better," she said, as she swept into the sitting room. She called back over her shoulder, "There are people here wanting to greet you, don't keep them waiting."

When Mama Kaduna was out of earshot, Kehinde asked breathlessly, "Do Joshua and Bimpe know?"

"Of course they know. I told Bimpe not to mention it to you in her letters. She is full of understanding, that girl of ours. I told her it would probably shock you, and that it is very unwise for people living alone to suffer such shocks. It is better to break it to you this way, don't you think? I have noticed that recently, she has accepted Rike too, and understands why Albert had to marry her. She knew her father was lonely, and besides, Rike has been a real little mother to them. She visits them most Saturdays and makes sure they have everything they need. Let's face it, she's been helping you to look after your family, since you could not have been in two places at once."

"But why didn't Albert give me even a hint that this was the way of life he wanted?"

"What rubbish you talk. Men don't say such things. It's like asking why a man did not tell his wife before taking a mistress. But he must have left hints, you must have seen it in his behavior. You were probably too sure of your position to notice, and too busy giving him orders. Why do you think he was not keen on your returning immediately?"

"That was my fault. I wasn't quite sure I wanted to come back just then, and of course there was the house to be sold . . ."

"Ah, you see what I mean. You forgot it was Lagos he was returning to. There are many ways of catching a fish,

words for everyday use

de • fi • cien • cy (di fi´ shən sē) n., inadequacy. *This car's greatest <u>deficiency</u> is its lack of air conditioning.*

ma • lice (ma´ ləs) n., desire to cause pain, injury, or distress to another. *Hue did not break her brother's toy out of <u>malice</u>; it was a mere accident.*

ap • prais • al (ə prā´ zəl) n., evaluation of worth or status. *After a quick <u>appraisal</u> of my resume, the manager said I was hired.*

and Rike used the cleverest. She met Albert when he was low, with neither job nor accommodation, and presented herself as a ministering angel, even taking him to her church. She became so <u>enmeshed</u> in his life that when the children returned, Joshua thought she was one of their aunties. And when he found out, he soon became reconciled to it."

"But what did he say to his father?"

"To his father? What could he say? This is Nigeria; you don't talk to your father anyhow."

"Oh my God, why have I been so blind? How can Albert have changed so fast?"

"I tell you, Rike is a clever African woman, in spite of her book knowledge. But don't worry, you'll soon get used to it, and then you'll be wondering why you were worried in the first place. Albert is a good, hard working man. Just relax and enjoy your life."

Kehinde was too overwhelmed by her sister's news to count how many faces she saw that night, of old friends she had forgotten, people who had been children when she left and were now grown men and women, with families of their own. Her only emotion was one of <u>consternation</u> at how much had changed, but she viewed it all with detachment. That first night reminded her of her first visit to Ibusa,[18] long, long ago, when she was a child. She felt as lost now as she had felt then. Even the way people talked had changed, showing a whole range of jokes and expressions which meant nothing whatever to her.

On the faces of some of the women, however, she could clearly read a combination of helplessness and sympathy. To the one or two who expressed themselves verbally, Ifeyinwa replied: "But now Joshua has a brother, to back him in a fight. Ogochukwu will always be there to support him from the rear," and all agreed that there was nothing as heartrending as a single male defending his father's compound. Though nobody said it directly, the consensus

◀ *How are Nigerian children expected to act toward their fathers?*

◀ *Why does Ifeyinwa say that Rike is a "clever African woman"?*

---

18. **Ibusa.** (Also spelled Ibuza.) Emecheta's hometown, Ibusa is an Igbo village on the western side of the River Niger. Raised in Lagos by her aunt, while still a young girl Kehinde was sent to Ibusa to live with her father, whom she had never seen.

---

words for everyday use

en • meshed (in mesht´) *adj.*, entangled. *The earring became <u>enmeshed</u> in Connie's sweater.*

con • ster • nation (kän stər nā´ shən) *n.*, confused amazement. *Ebere looked at her watch in <u>consternation</u>, unable to believe that five hours had gone by so quickly.*

obviously was that Kehinde should take things as she found them.

She caught sight of Albert once or twice, at the center of proceedings, ordering drinks, seeing to the music, and accepting compliments on behalf of his senior wife.[19] He was remote and distant, as though tradition had put a wedge between them, just as it had apparently between him and Joshua, or Joshua would have protested. He must have learned quickly that here a father was to be respected. Kehinde's heart went out to her children for the adjustments they had had to make.

It was a long time before Kehinde was allowed to leave the party, and she was exhausted. She fell at once into a deep sleep, visited by fragments of the past, as if, in her depleted state, her spirit was seeking solace in its own beginnings.

Critical Thinking Questions

1. What changes does Kehinde notice in her husband when she arrives in Lagos? The narrator says, "Women knew the country did this to their men." Why do you think it is that life in Nigeria has this effect on men?
2. Why does Ifeyinwa pull Kehinde into her room as soon as she arrives? Why does she say that Kehinde must not call her husband by his name? What does she say men and women do in Nigeria?
3. Who is Rike, and what is Ifeyinwa's attitude toward her? Why doesn't Ifeyinwa blame Albert for marrying Rike? What does Ifeyinwa advise Kehinde to do? Why didn't Kehinde's children, Joshua and Bimpe, object to their father's second marriage?
4. Through Ifeyinwa's example, Kehinde learns about social norms in Nigeria. According to Nigerian culture, how should a "cultured man" behave toward his wife or wives? How should his wives address him, and how should they behave toward him? What is the relationship of a "cultured man" with his children?

---

19. **senior wife.** Now that Albert has married again, Kehinde is his senior wife.

words for everyday use

de • plete (di plēt´) vt., lessen markedly in quantity, content, power, or value. *The stream had once been filled with fish, but in recent years, overfishing and pollution depleted it.*

so • lace (sä´ ləs) n., relief from pain or anxiety; consolation. *When he was feeling overwhelmed by stress, Pete found solace in nature.*

5. What does Ifeyinwa think of educated women? Why does Ifeyinwa say that "Rike is a clever African woman, in spite of her book knowledge"? Ifeyinwa says that women in Nigeria stick together. Do you think that is true? How do they support each other? How do they keep each other down?

6. Which women appear to have the most power in the Okolo household? Why does Mama Kaduna say that Kehinde should always hold her head high? Based on what we learn through this excerpt, which women have the most status and respect in a Nigerian family?

7. Compare the Okolo family to Okonkwo's family. What similar values do you see? For example, how is Joshua's new relationship with his father similar to that of Nwoye's relationship with his father?

"Heaven Is Not Closed"
Bessie Head

ABOUT THE RELATED READING

Bessie Head is one of Africa's best-known women writers. She was born in South Africa in 1937, the daughter of a black man and a white woman at a time when interracial relationships were not accepted. Taken away from her mother, Bessie Head was raised by a foster family and then went to a mission school. Trained as a teacher, she taught elementary school for a few years before working as a newspaper reporter in Johannesburg and Cape Town, two of South Africa's largest cities. She later decided to leave her country because she could not tolerate the racism of the South African government. Head moved to Botswana, a country north of South Africa that was formerly a British territory known as Bechuanaland.

Most of Head's writing is inspired by life in Botswana, including the following story, which was published in Bessie Head's first collection of short stories, *The Collector of Treasures* (1977). This story illustrates the difficulty African peoples had in reconciling their own beliefs with the teachings of Christian missionaries. Galethebege, a devout Christian, falls in love with a man named Ralokae, who is an "unbeliever." Galethebege must choose between her religion and her love, then spend the rest of her life praying that she and her husband will be admitted into heaven.

▶ *What did Galethebege do during the last five years of her life?*

All her life Galethebege earnestly believed that her whole heart ought to be devoted to God, although one catastrophe after another occurred to <u>deflect</u> her from this path. It was only in the last five years of her life, after her husband, Ralokae, had died, that she was able to devote her whole mind to her calling. Then, all her pent-up and <u>suppressed</u> love for God burst forth and she talked only of Him, day and night—so her grandchildren, solemnly and with deep

words for everyday use

de • flect (dē flekt´) vt., turn aside from a fixed direction. *In the future, we may use lasers to deflect asteroids that threaten to hit Earth.*

sup • pressed (sə prest´) adj., held back; not expressed openly. *Ekwefi's suppressed anger was apparent through the twitching of her mouth.*

awe, informed the mourners at her funeral. All the mourners present at her hour of passing were utterly convinced that they had watched a profound and holy event. They talked about it for days afterwards.

Galethebege was well over ninety when she died and not at all afflicted by crippling ailments like most of the aged. In fact, only two days before her death she had complained to her grandchildren of a sudden fever and a lameness in her legs, and she had remained in bed. A quiet, thoughtful mood fell upon her. On the morning of the second day she had abruptly demanded that all the relatives be summoned.

"My hour has come," she said, with <u>lofty</u> dignity.

No one quite believed it, because that whole morning she had sat bolt upright in her bed and talked to all who had gathered, about God—whom she loved with her whole heart. Then, exactly at noon, she announced once more that her hour had indeed come and lay down peacefully like one about to take a short nap. Her last words were:

"I shall rest now because I believe in God."

Then, a terrible silence filled the hut and seemed to paralyze the mourners for they all remained immobile for some time; each person present cried quietly because not one of them had ever witnessed such a magnificent death before. They only stirred when the old man, Modise, suddenly observed with great practicality that Galethebege was not in the correct position for death. She lay on her side with her right arm thrust out above her head. She ought to be turned over on her back, with her hands crossed over her chest, he said. A smile flickered over the old man's face as he said this, as though it was just like Galethebege to make such a miscalculation. Why, she knew the hour of her death and everything, then at the last minute forgot the correct sleeping posture for the coffin. Later that evening, as he sat with his children near the outdoor fire for the evening meal, a smile again flickered over his face.

"I am of a mind to think that Galethebege was praying for forgiveness for her sins this morning," he said slowly. "It must have been a sin to her to marry Ralokae. He was an unbeliever to the day of his death . . ."

◀ What does the old man, Modise, think Galethebege was doing just before her death? Why?

---

words for everyday use lof • ty (lôf´ tē) *adj.,* noble; elevated in character or spirit. *The students held the <u>lofty</u> goal of making the world a better place.*

A gust of astonished laughter shook his family out of the solemn mood of mourning that had fallen upon them and they all turned eagerly toward their grandfather, sensing that he had a story to tell.

"As you all know," the old man said wisely, "Ralokae was my brother. But none of you present knows the story of Galethebege's life, but I know it . . ."

As the flickering firelight lit up their faces, he told the following story: "I was never like Ralokae, an unbeliever. But that man, my brother, draws out my heart. He liked to say that we as a tribe would fall into great difficulties if we forget our own customs and laws. Today, his words seem true. There is thieving and adultery going on such as was not possible under Setswana[1] law."

▶ Why did many black people embrace Christianity when Modise was young? Why did Galethebege embrace it?

In the days when they were young, said the old man, Modise, it had become the fashion for all black people to embrace the Gospel.[2] For some, it was the mark of whether they were "civilized" or not. For some, like Galethebege, it was their whole life. Anyone with eyes to see would have known that Galethebege had been born good; under any custom, whether Setswana custom or Christian custom, she would still have been good. It was this natural goodness of heart that made her so eagerly pursue the word of the Gospel. There was a look on her face, absent, abstracted, as though she needed to share the final secret of life with God who could understand all things. So she was always on her way to church, and in her hours of leisure at home she could be found with her head buried in the Bible. And so her life would have gone on in this quiet and worshipful way, had not a sudden catastrophe occurred in the yard of Ralokae.

Ralokae had been married for nearly a year when his young wife died in childbirth. She died when the crops of the season were being harvested, and for a year Ralokae <u>imposed</u> on himself the traditional restraints and disciplines of *boswagadi* or mourning for the deceased. A year later, again at the harvest time, he underwent the cleansing ceremony demanded by custom and could once more <u>resume</u>

---

1. **Setswana.** A language and a people in Botswana
2. **Gospel.** Teachings of Christianity

---

words for everyday use

im • pose (im pōz´) *vt.,* establish or bring about as if by force. *European colonists* imposed *their rules and beliefs upon the people they colonized.*

re • sume (ri züm´) *vt.,* return to or begin again after an interruption. *Mike talked on the phone for an hour, then* resumed *his homework.*

the normal life of a man. It was the unexpectedness of the tragic event and the discipline it imposed on him, that made Ralokae take note of the life of Galethebege. She lived just three yards away from his own yard, and formerly he had barely taken note of her existence; it was too quiet and orderly. But during the year of mourning, it delighted him to hear that gentle and earnest voice of Galethebege informing him that such tragedies "were the will of God." As soon as he could, he began courting her. He was young and impatient to be married again and no one could bring back the dead. So a few days after the cleansing ceremony, he made his intentions very clear to her.

"Let us two get together," he said. "I am pleased by all your ways."

Galethebege was all at the same time startled, pleased, and hesitant. She was hesitant because it was well known that Ralokae was an unbeliever; he had not once set foot in church. So she looked at him, begging an apology, and mentioned the matter which was foremost in her mind.

"Ralokae," she said, uncertainly. "I have set God always before me," implying by that statement that perhaps he too was seeking a Christian life. But he only looked at her in a strange way, and said nothing. This matter was to stand like a fearful sword between them but he had set his mind on winning Galethebege as his wife. That was all he was certain of. He turned up in her yard day after day.

"Hullo girlfriend," he would greet her, enchantingly.

He always wore a black beret perched at a <u>jaunty</u> angle on his head. His walk and manner were gay and jaunty too. He was so exciting as a man that he threw her whole life into turmoil. It was the first time love had come her way and it made the blood pound fiercely through her whole body till she could feel its very throbbing at the tips of her fingers. It turned her thoughts from God a bit, to this new magic life was offering her. The day she agreed to be his wife, that sword quivered like a fearful thing between them. Ralokae said very quietly and firmly: "I took my first wife according to the old customs. I am going to take my second wife according to the old customs too."

He could see the protest on her face. She wanted to be married in church according to Christian custom.

---

words for everyday use

jaun • ty (jȯn´ tē) *adj.*, stylish; lively. *That must be André—I recognize his jaunty stride.*

▶ Why did Ralokae reject Christianity?

However, he had his own protest to make. The God might be all right, he explained, but there was something wrong with the people who had brought the word of the Gospel to the land. Their love was enslaving black people and he could not stand it. That was why he was without belief. It was the people he did not trust. They were full of tricks. They were a people who, at the sight of a black man, pointed a finger in the air, looked away in the distance and said impatiently: "Boy! Will you carry this! Boy! Will you fetch this!" They had brought a new order of things into the land and they made the people cry for love. One never had to cry for love in the customary way of life. Respect was just there for all people all the time. That was why he rejected all things foreign.

What could a woman do with a man like that who knew his own mind? She either loved him or she was mad. From that day on, Galethebege knew what she would do. She would do all that Ralokae commanded as a good wife should. But her former life was like a drug. Her footsteps were too accustomed to wearing down the footpath to the church, and they carried her to the missionary's house which stood just under the shadow of the church.

The missionary was a short, anonymous-looking man who wore glasses. He had been the resident missionary for some time, and like all his fellows he did not particularly like the people. He always complained to his own kind that they were terrible beggars and rather stupid. So when he opened the door and saw Galethebege there his expression, with its raised eyebrows, said "Well, what do you want now?"

"I am to be married, sir," Galethebege said politely, after the exchange of greetings.

The missionary smiled: "Well come in my dear. Let us talk about the arrangements," he said pleasantly.

He stared at her with polite, professional interest. She was a complete <u>nonentity</u>, a part of the vague black blur which was his congregation—oh, they noticed chiefs and people like that, but not the silent mass of humble and lowly who had an almost weird <u>capacity</u> to creep quietly through life. Her next words brought her sharply into focus.

---

words for everyday use

non • en • ti • ty (nän en´ tə tē) n., person of little significance. *Fatai felt like a nonentity at his job—nobody seemed to notice or appreciate the work he was doing.*

ca • pa • ci • ty (kä pa´ sə tē) n., ability; potential. *Hikari's capacity to learn went far beyond what his parents had hoped when they learned he had a disability.*

"The man I am to marry, sir, does not wish to be married in the Christian way. He will only marry under Setswana custom," she said softly.

◀ Why did Galethebege go to the missionary? What did he tell her?

They always knew the superficial stories about "heathen[3] customs" and an expression of disgust crept into his face—sexual malpractices were associated with the traditional marriage ceremony (and shudder!), they draped the stinking intestinal bag of the ox around their necks.

"That we cannot allow!" he said sharply. "Tell him to come and marry in the Christian way."

Galethebege started trembling all over. She looked at the missionary in alarm. Ralokae would never agree to this. Her intention in approaching the missionary was to acquire his blessing for the marriage, as though a compromise of tenderness could be made between two traditions opposed to each other. She trembled because it was beyond her station in life to be involved in controversy and protest. The missionary noted the trembling and alarm and his tone softened a bit, but his next words were devastating.

"My dear," he said persuasively, "heaven is closed to the unbeliever . . ."

Galethebege stumbled home on shaking legs. It never occurred to her to question such a miserable religion which terrified people with the fate of eternal damnation in hell-fire if they were "heathens" or sinners. Only Ralokae seemed quite unperturbed by the fate that awaited him. He smiled when Galethebege relayed the words of the missionary to him.

"Girlfriend," he said, carelessly, "you can choose what you like, Setswana custom or Christian custom. I have chosen to live my life by Setswana custom."

Not once in her life had Galethebege's integrity been called into question. She wanted to make the point clear.

"What you mean, Ralokae," she said firmly, "is that I must choose you over my life with the church. I have a great love in my heart for you so I choose you. I shall tell the priest about this matter because his command is that I marry in church."

---

3. **heathen.** Non-Christian, and therefore considered uncivilized

words for everyday use   in • teg • ri • ty (in teg´ rə tē) n., strict adherence to moral values. *The politician's integrity was called into question when it was learned he had told a lie.*

▶ How did the
missionary punish
Galethebege for
marrying under
Setswana custom?

Even Galethebege was astounded by the harshness of the
missionary's attitude. The catastrophe she did not antici-
pate was that he abruptly excommunicated[4] her from the
Church. She could no longer enter the village church if she
married under Setswana custom. It was beyond her to reason that the missionary was the representative of both God
and something evil, the mark of "civilization." It was
unthinkable that an illiterate and ignorant man could display such contempt for the missionary's civilization. His
rage and hatred were directed at Ralokae, and the only way
in which he could inflict punishment was to banish
Galethebege from the Church. If it hurt anyone at all, it was
only Galethebege. The austere rituals of the Church, the
Mass,[5] the sermons, the intimate communication in prayer
with God—all this had thrilled her heart deeply. But
Ralokae also was representative of an ancient stream of
holiness that people had lived with before any white man
had set foot in the land, and it only needed a small protest
to stir up loyalty for the old customs.

The old man, Modise, paused at this point in the telling
of his tale but his young listeners remained breathless and
silent, eager for the conclusion.

"Today," he continued, "it is not a matter of debate
because the young care neither way about religion. But in
that day, the expulsion of Galethebege from the Church
was a matter of debate. It made the people of our village
ward[6] think. There was great indignation because both
Galethebege and Ralokae were much respected in the community. People then wanted to know how it was that
Ralokae, who was an unbeliever, could have heaven closed
to him? A number of people, including all the relatives who
officiated at the wedding ceremony, then decided that if
heaven was closed to Galethebege and Ralokae it might as
well be closed to them too, so they all no longer attended
church. On the day of their wedding, we had all our own

▶ What did a
number of people in
the community do
when they heard of
Galethebege's
expulsion?

---

4. **excommunicated.** Excluded from the rites of the church
5. **Mass.** Christian religious service during which the Eucharist (the bread
and wine which represent the body and blood of Christ) is served
6. **village ward.** Area of the village: neighborhood

**words
for
everyday
use**

con • tempt (kən tem[p]t´) n., lack of
respect or reverence; disdain. *Queen Marie
Antoinette is famous for the* contempt *she
had for the poor people of France.*

aus • tere (ȯ stir´) adj., somber; morally
strict. *The Tibetan monks lived in a very*

*austere environment, and young Khyentse
was frustrated by all the restrictions.*

ex • pul • sion (ik spəl´ shən) n., act of
expelling. *Holden Caulfield's* expulsion *from
boarding school is one of the events in the
book* Catcher in the Rye.

things. Everyone knows the extent to which the cow was a part of the people's life and customs. We took our clothes from the cow and our food from the cow and it was the symbol of our wealth. So the cow was a holy thing in our lives. The elders then cut the intestinal bag of the cow in two and one portion was placed around the neck of Galethebege and one portion around the neck of Ralokae to indicate the wealth and good luck they would find together in married life. Then the porridge and meat were dished up in our *mogopo* bowls which we had used from old times. There was much <u>capering</u> and <u>ululating</u> that day because Ralokae had honored the old customs . . ."

◄ *Explain why the intestinal bag of the cow was used in the Setswana wedding ceremony.*

A tender smile once more flickered over the old man's face.

"Galethebege could never forsake the custom in which she had been brought up. All through her married life she would find a corner in which to pray. Sometimes Ralokae would find her so and ask: 'What are you doing, Mother?' and she would reply: 'I am praying to God.' Ralokae would only smile. He did not even know how to pray to the Christian God."

The old man leaned forward and stirred the dying fire with a partially burnt-out log of wood. His listeners sighed the way people do when they have heard a particularly good story. As they stared at the fire they found themselves debating the matter in their minds, as their elders had done some forty or fifty years ago. Was heaven really closed to the unbeliever, Ralokae? Or had Christian custom been so intolerant of Setswana custom that it could not hear the holiness of Setswana custom? Wasn't there a place in heaven too for Setswana custom? Then the gust of astonished laughter shook them again. Galethebege had been very well known in the village ward over the past five years for the supreme authority with which she had talked about God. Perhaps her simple and good heart had been terrified that the doors of heaven were indeed closed on Ralokae and she had been trying to open them.

◄ *What questions do the people ponder after hearing the old man's story?*

words for everyday use

ca • per (kā´ pər) *vi.*, leap or prance about in a playful manner. *The young sea lions* <u>capered</u> *about like kittens, chasing each other over the rocks.*

ul • u • late (yül´ yə lāt) *vi.*, howl or hoot. *At the Day of the Dead celebration, we all gathered in a circle to watch the Aztec dancers,* <u>ululating</u> *to cheer them on.*

Critical Thinking

1. What does Galethebege do during the last five years of her life, after her husband's death? What makes her death a "profound and holy event"? Why, according to Modise, was Galethebege praying so fervently on the morning of her death?
2. Compare the attitudes of Galethebege and Ralokae toward Christianity. Why do they feel as they do? What sacrifice does Galethebege make for Ralokae? Do you think it is fair for Ralokae to have allowed her to make this sacrifice? Why, or why not?
3. Analyze the character of the missionary. What is his attitude toward the Setswana people and their customs? What does he not understand about the Setswana marriage customs? Why did he excommunicate Galethebege from the church? Why does the narrator say that the missionary was "representative of both God and something evil"?
4. What do you think about the questions posed at the end of the story? Is heaven really closed to the unbeliever? Or is Christian custom simply so intolerant of Setswana custom that it cannot acknowledge its unique holiness? Is there a place in heaven for Setswana custom? How you answer these questions depends on your personal beliefs—there are no right or wrong answers. You may wish to freewrite about the questions in your journal and keep your answers private.
5. Compare the missionary in "Heaven Is Not Closed" with the characters of Mr. Brown and Reverend Smith in *Things Fall Apart.*

"Should My Tribal Past Shape Delia's Future?"
Dympna Ugwu-Oju

ABOUT THE RELATED READING

This article, which appeared in *Newsweek* magazine on December 4, 2000, depicts a modern cultural clash between the Igbo and the West. **Dympna Ugwu-Oju** lives in Fresno, California. She and her husband are Igbo people from Nigeria, but they have raised their daughter, Delia, in the United States. Ugwu-Oju is torn between teaching her daughter to be an Igbo woman and giving her the independence she craves.

Recently, my 18-year-old daughter, Delia, left for Princeton University[1] to start her college career. Friends worried about the distance between Princeton and our home in California. I reminded them that I, too, had attended college far from my home and family. The distance hadn't hurt me; rather, I became stronger because of it.

In 1974 I traveled to New York for my college education. My home country, Nigeria, was for all intents and purposes as far away as Mars. Back then, it was virtually impossible to reach my family by phone; we could communicate only through snail post[2] and, in an emergency, via telegraph. It wasn't until six years later, after I had completed both my undergraduate and graduate degrees, that I went home for the first time.

I reassure my friends that if I, I tribal African girl, could survive the psychological and cultural <u>rigors</u> of attending college in this country, my American-born-and-bred

---

1. **Princeton University.** A prestigious university located in Princeton, New Jersey
2. **snail post.** Regular mail system, often called "snail mail" because it is much slower than e-mail.

words for everyday use   ri • gor (rĭ´ gər) *n.*, strictness; condition that makes life difficult, challenging, or uncomfortable. *The <u>rigor</u> of military school proved too much for Shawn, and he dropped out.*

daughter will conquer Princeton. What does worry me is how much of her family's beliefs will be left in the Delia who <u>emerges</u> four years from now.

I'm a member of the Ibo tribe[3] of Nigeria, and although I've lived in the United States most of my adult life, my consciousness remains fixed on the time and place of my upbringing. On the surface, I'm as American as everyone else. My husband, who was also raised in Nigeria, and I are both professionals. We live in the suburbs and go to PTA[4] meetings. In my private life, my Iboness—the customs that rigidly dictate how the men and women of my tribe live their lives—continues to influence the choices I make. I see these American and Ibo aspects of my life as distinct; I separate them perfectly, and there are no blurrings. Except for maybe one: Delia.

When I left Nigeria at 18, I had no doubts about who and what I was. I was a woman. I was only a woman.

▶ What did Ugwu-Oju's mother teach her about her role as a woman when she was growing up in Nigeria?

All my life my mother told me that a woman takes as much in life as she's given; if she's educated, it's only so that she can better cater to her husband and children. When I was Delia's age, I knew with absolute certainty that I would marry the Ibo man my family approved for me and bear his children. I understood that receiving a good education and being comfortable in both the Western and the traditional worlds would raise the bride price my <u>prospective</u> husband would pay my family. My role was to be a great asset to my husband, no matter what business he was engaged in.

I understood all of that clearly; I was, after all, raised within the context of child brides, polygamy, clitorectomies and arranged marriages.[5] But then I married and had my own daughter, and all my certainty, all my resolve to maintain my Ibo beliefs, collapsed in a big heap at my feet.

First, my daughter's ties to Ibo womanhood are only as strong as the link—meaning me. Therein lies the problem.

---

3. **Ibo tribe.** Ibo is usually spelled *Igbo* today. Some people, including Chinua Achebe, prefer to call the Igbo a "nation" or a "people" rather than a tribe because the word *tribe* implies that the Igbo are primitive.

4. **PTA.** Parent-teacher association

5. **child brides . . . arranged marriages.** These are practices of traditional African cultures which are challenged today as being unfair to women.

words for everyday use

e • merge (ē mərj´) *vi.,* come out; come into view. *Two figures <u>emerged</u> from the thick fog.*

pro • spec • tive (prə spek´ tiv) *adj.,* expected; likely to be or become. *The university sent forms for all <u>prospective</u> students to fill out in preparation for enrollment.*

I haven't been half the teacher to my daughter that my mother was to me.

I've struggled daily with how best to raise my daughter. Every decision involving Delia is a tug of war between Ibo and American traditions. I've <u>vacillated</u> between trying to turn her into the kind of woman her grandmothers would be proud of and letting her be the modern, independent woman she wants to be. Each time Delia scores an academic or athletic victory, I start to applaud her, but my cheers get stuck in my throat as I hear both her grandmothers' voices warning, "She's only a woman." I know in my heart that her achievements will not matter to her relatives; they will judge her by the kind of man she marries, and the children—preferably male—that she bears.

◀ On what will Delia's relatives judge her?

At 18, Delia knows very little about the rules that govern the lives of Ibo women. She knows just enough about housekeeping to survive. She will most likely not consider my feelings in choosing her spouse. She is not the selflessly loyal daughter that I was to my mother.

I wonder about the implications for people like me, women from traditional cultures raising American-born daughters. Should we limit their opportunities to keep them loyal to our beliefs and our pasts, or should we encourage our daughters to avail themselves of all experiences, even at the risk of rejecting who and what we are?

◀ What question does Ugwu-Oju ask herself?

Maybe what I feel is what parents all over the world feel: that I could have done a better job of instilling my beliefs in my child. Now, it's too late.

Or perhaps I've always known that Delia is her own person with her own life to lead.

Delia called the other night from Princeton. She's coming home soon, and I'm infected by her excitement. But I wonder: will I know the young woman who steps off the plane?

Critical Thinking Questions

1. What expectations does traditional Igbo society have for women? How do these expectations compare with those of modern Western (or American) society?

words for everyday use

va • cil • late (va´ sə lāt) vi., waver in mind, will, or feeling; hesitate. *Leticia* <u>*vacillated*</u> *between going to a large university or starting out at a smaller community college.*

2. Do your parents have expectations for you that you don't agree with? Explain. If your parents are from a different culture, discuss how this affects your relationship with them.
3. What would you do if you were Dympna Ugwu-Oju? What would you do if you were Delia? Do you think it is important for Delia to retain some of the values of Igbo culture? Why, or why not? What do you think about the author's question: Should women from traditional cultures limit the opportunities of their American-born daughters to keep them loyal to their beliefs and their pasts, or should they encourage their daughters to have new experiences, even at the risk of rejecting their mothers' values?
4. How is Dympna Ugwu-Oju's predicament with her daughter similar and different from that of Okonkwo and his son Nwoye in *Things Fall Apart?*

Creative Writing Activities

Obituary

Write an obituary for Okonkwo. An *obituary* is an announcement of a person's death that usually includes a summary of the person's major accomplishments. Consider including his birth date, death date, accomplishments, interests, and testimonials about his life by surviving family members.

Statement of Defense

Imagine that a trial is going to be held before the *egwugwu* to consider the guilt or innocence of Okonkwo in the killing of a member of the clan. You have been appointed to speak in Okonkwo's defense. Write a brief statement that you might make setting forth the facts of the accident. (This assignment applies to chapter 13).

Point of View

The Igbo community depicted in this novel is male-dominated. As a result, the point of view of female characters is somewhat neglected. Take the point of view of one of the female characters, such as Ekwefi or her daughter Ezinma, and retell one of the episodes in the novel, revealing how you feel about the event and about Okonkwo. Your retelling may take the form of a diary entry or memoir, and should be written in the first person, including words like *I* or *me*.

A Son's Betrayal

When Nwoye converts to Christianity, his father sees this as a betrayal, feeling that "to abandon the gods of one's fathers . . . was the very depth of abomination." Imagine that you are Nwoye, and write a letter to your father explaining why you have decided to join the Christians. What makes Christianity appealing to you and to the other Africans who have joined the church?

Critical Writing Activities

An Honest View of a Culture

Chinua Achebe has written that fiction writers have a responsibility to tell the truth. In his novel *Things Fall Apart,* he paints a devastating portrait of how European colonizers destroyed a traditional way of life. However, in his attempt to make that case, Achebe does not simplify or glorify the life of the traditional Igbo, but shows it in realistic, truthful detail, negative aspects as well as positive. Write an essay in which you evaluate the old way of life described in the novel. Explain what elements of the traditional Igbo culture are attractive to you and what elements are not.

Okonkwo as Tragic Figure

Read the definition of *tragedy* in the Handbook of Literary Terms. Then write a paper explaining how *Things Fall Apart* can be considered a tragedy, according to the Aristotelian definition. How does Okonkwo fit the definition of a tragic hero? What is his *hamartia,* or fatal flaw, and how does it show itself in the novel? Do you think that Okonkwo's tragic fall is brought about by a bad *chi,* or do you think it has to do with the choices he makes in life? Give evidence to support your opinion.

The Role of Women in *Things Fall Apart*

In most Western countries today, men and women are treated equally under the law. In the United States, for example, the law requires that women and men receive equal pay for equal work. Is equality among men and women part of the traditional culture of the Igbo, as described in this novel? What is a woman's role in the home and in the community? Who are the strongest women in the novel? Explain, giving examples to support your answer. In your paper, you may also discuss women's roles in contemporary Igbo society as shown in the related readings "Should My Tribal Past Shape Delia's Future?" by Dympna Ugwu-Oju and "The Arrival" from Buchi Emecheta's novel *Kehinde.*

The Economic System of the Igbo

An economic system is a method for producing goods and services to meet people's wants and needs. An important part of every economic system is providing food and shelter for people. In *Things Fall Apart,* Achebe explains the economic system the Igbo had before the coming of the Europeans. How do the Igbo in Achebe's novel get their food? What do they eat? How is their food produced and by whom? What is the sharecropping system, described in chapter 3, and how does it work? Who prepares the meals? In what kinds of shelters do the people live? How do these differ from Western homes? What do the people use for money?

Achebe's Mission

Why did Chinua Achebe write the novel *Things Fall Apart?* How does Achebe's novel, published in 1958, differ from the literature previously written about Africa? Give specific examples from the novel where Achebe seeks to contradict common stereotypes about African people. What is Achebe's mission as a writer, and what does he mean when he says that the world needs "a balance of stories"? In your paper, cite information from the related reading "An African Voice," an interview with Chinua Achebe.

Colonial Attitudes toward African Peoples

By the end of the nineteenth century, the entire continent of Africa had been divided into colonies controlled by European nations. What attitude did the European colonizers have toward the African peoples they conquered? How did they view the Africans' customs, their system of government, and their religious beliefs? Give specific examples from *Things Fall Apart* to answer these questions. Also use examples from "Heaven Is Not Closed" by Bessie Head.

Projects

Proverb Booklet

Proverbs play an important role in the life of the Igbo, for they contain traditional wisdom passed down for generations. Working with other students in a small group, copy down as many proverbs as you can find from *Things Fall Apart,* and gather them in a booklet. You will find some of them listed on page 35, following chapter 5, but there are many more in the rest of the novel. Include with each proverb an explanation of what the proverb means. If you can think of a similar proverb in English, write that down, too. Some students in your group may wish to illustrate the booklet.

Anthology of West African Folk Tales

Folk tales, or myths, play an important role in Igbo culture and in the cultures of many peoples in West Africa. Working with a partner or a small group, visit the library to find books of West African folk tales. Create an anthology of these tales, including the ones retold in *Things Fall Apart.* Have an artistic member of your group illustrate the tales, or decorate your anthology with patterns from West African art copied from books.

West African Visual Art and Music

After reading *Things Fall Apart,* a great example of West African literature, you may be curious about some of the art and music of West Africa. Working with other students, do research on the arts of one or more of the countries of West Africa. Consult art books, geography books, histories, and recordings in your local library to find examples of West African artworks, handicrafts, and music to share with the rest of the class. You may also find information on the Internet. The countries in West Africa include: Benin, Burkina Faso, Cameroon, Cape Verde, Chad, Côte d'Ivoire, Equatorial Guinea, The Gambia, Ghana, Guinea, Guinea-Bissau, Liberia, Mali, Mauritania, Niger, Nigeria, Senegal, Sierra Leone, and Togo.

Postcolonial Literature/Colonies of Africa

Things Fall Apart was the first novel by a black African author to gain international acclaim, and it opened up the field for many other African writers to tell the stories of their peoples. Research an African author other than Chinua Achebe and write a report that includes the following: a short biography; a bibliography (list of works); and a brief history of his or her native country (including when and how it became a European colony). In your biography, include information about the writer's main themes. Some authors you might research include: Mariama Bâ and Léopold Sédar Senghor (Senegal); Ngũgĩ wa Thiong'o (Kenya); Tsitsi Dangarembga (Zimbabwe); Athol Fugard (South Africa); and Ama Ata Aidoo (Ghana). These are just a few of the many African writers who emerged in the twentieth century. For more authors and author information, consult a librarian or search the Internet. Two helpful sites are the University of Florida Africana Collection at http://web.uflib.ufl.edu/cm/africana/contents.htm and "African Postcolonial Literature in English" at http://www.scholars.nus.edu.sg/landow/post/misc/africov.html.

Glossary of Words for Everyday Use

PRONUNCIATION KEY

VOWEL SOUNDS

a	hat	ō	go	ə	extra
ā	play	ȯ	paw, born		under
ä	star	u̇	book, put		civil
e	then	ü	blue, stew		honor
ē	me	oi	boy		bogus
i	sit	ou	wow		burn
ī	my	u	up		

CONSONANT SOUNDS

b	but	l	lip	t	sit
ch	watch	m	money	th	with
d	do	n	on	v	valley
f	fudge	ŋ	song, sink	w	work
g	go	p	pop	y	yell
h	hot	r	rod	z	pleasure
j	jump	s	see		
k	brick	sh	she		

a • bom • i • na • tion (ə bä´ mə nā´ shən) *n.,* anything hateful or disgusting

ac • com • mo • da • tion (ə käm´ ə dā´ shən) *n.,* willingness to adapt and adjust or to reconcile differences

ac • cord (ə kȯrd´) *vt.,* grant; give; allow

ad • her • ent (ad hir´ ənt) *n.,* supporter or follower of a cause

a • droit • ly (ə droit´ lē) *adv.,* skillfully

af • fir • ma • tion (af´ ər mā´ shən) *n.,* positive declaration

aghast (ə gast´) *adj.,* shocked

ag • i • tate (aj´ i tāt´) *vi.,* shake up; disturb

ag • i • tat • ed (a´ jə tā təd) *adj.,* anxious; troubled

a • gi • ta • tion (a jə tā´ shən) *n.,* anxiety; distress

al • be • it (ȯl bē´ ət) *conj.,* even though

al • bi • no (al bī´ nō) *n.,* person whose skin, hair, and eyes lack normal coloration

al • le • giance (ə lē´ jəns) *n.,* loyalty; devotion

am • u • let (am´ yü lit) *n.,* object worn on the body for its supposed magical power to protect

an • guish (a´ gwish) *n.,* extreme pain, distress, or anxiety

an • ni • hi • la • tion (ə nī´ ə lā´ shən) *n.,* complete destruction; putting out of existence

ap • prais • al (ə prā´ zəl) *n.,* evaluation of worth or status

ap • pro • ba • tion (a ´ prə bā ´shən) *n.,* approval; act of approving formally or officially

ar • du • ous (är´ jü əs) *adj.,* hard to accomplish; difficult; strenuous

a • tone • ment (ə tōn´mənt) *n.,* payment given for wrongdoing

au • dac • i • ty (ȯ das´ ə tē) *n.,* boldness; daring

au • di • bly (ȯ´ də blē) *adv.,* loudly enough to be heard

aus • tere (ȯ stir´) *adj.,* somber; morally strict

beck • on (bek´ 'n) *vt.,* summon by gesture

be • get (bē get´) *vt.,* be the father of

be • nev • o • lent • ly (bə nev´ ə lənt lē) *adv.,* in a kind or sympathetic way

be • numbed (bē numd´) *part.,* deadened

blas • pheme (blas´ fēm´) *vi.,* speak irreverently; curse

buoy • ant (boi´ ənt) *adj.,* tending to rise; not easily depressed; cheerful

ca • lam • i • ty (kə lam´ ə tē) *n.,* disaster

cal • low (kal´ ō) *adj.,* young; inexperienced

ca • pa • ci • ty (kä pa´ sə tē) *n.,* ability; potential

ca • per (kā´ pər) *vi.,* leap or prance about in a playful manner

ca • pri • cious (kə prish´ əs) *adj.,* tending to change without apparent reason

cha • os (kā´ äs´) *n.,* extreme confusion; disorder

char • la • tan (shär´ lə tən) *n.,* fraud, faker

ci • vil • ian (sə vil yən) *adj.,* non-military; of or having to do with citizens who are not members of the military or police forces

co • pi • ous • ly (kō´ pē əs lē) *adv.,* abundantly; plentifully

coif • fure (kwä fyür´) *n.,* headdress; style of arranging the hair

com • mu • nal (kə myü´ nəl) *adj.,* shared by a group or community

com • po • sure (kəm pō´ zhər) *n.,* calmness of mind or manner

con • fer (kən fər´) *vt.,* give or bestow upon

con • so • la • tion (kän´ sə lā´ shən) *n.,* comfort; solace

con • ster • nation (kän stər nā´ shən) *n.,* confused amazement

con • sult (kən sult´) *vi.,* ask advice; refer to

con • ta • gion (kən tā´ jən) *n.,* contagious disease; poison; corrupting influence of any kind that spreads rapidly

con • tempt (kən tem[p]t´) *n.,* lack of respect or reverence; disdain

con • vert (kän´ vərt´) *n.,* person who changes from one religion to another

de • bar (dē bär´) *vt.,* exclude

de • cree (dē krē´) *vt.,* order, decide

de • fi • ant (dē fī´ ənt) *adj.,* boldly resisting

de • fi • cien • cy (di fi´ shən sē) *n.,* inadequacy

de • flect (dē flekt´) *vt.,* turn aside from a fixed direction

de • gen • er • ate (dē jen´ ər it) *adj.,* having sunk below a normal condition; morally corrupt

de • i • ty (dē´ ə tē) *n.,* god

de • lec • ta • ble (de lek´ tə bəl) *adj.,* delightful; delicious

de • lib • er • ate (di lib´ ər āt´) *vi.,* consider carefully and discuss alternatives

del • i • ca • cy (del´ i kə sē) *n.,* choice food

de • lir • i • ous (di lir´ ē əs) *adj.,* wildly excited

de • plete (di plēt´) *vt.,* lessen markedly in quantity, content, power, or value

de • ri • sive (di rī´ siv) *adj.,* scornful; ridiculing

de • tach • ment (dē tach´ mənt) *n.,* indifference; disinterest

des • e • crate (des´ i krāt´) *vt.,* violate the sanctity of; treat disrespectfully, irreverently, or outrageously

des • o • late (des´ ə lit) *adj.,* ruined; devastated

des • pi • ca • ble (des´ pi kə bəl) *adj.,* deserving to be despised; contemptible

di • vin • er (də vī´nər) *n.,* person who finds out through intuition or prophecy

dis • cern (di zərń) *vt.,* perceive or recognize

dis • creet • ly (di skrēt´ lē) *adv.,* in a way that does not attract attention

dis • em • bod • ied (dis´ im bä´ dēd) *adj.,* freed from bodily existence

dis • pen • sa • tion (dis´ pən sā´ shən) *n.,* system of management; administration

do • min • ion (də min´ yən) *n.,* governed territory

dor • man • cy (dȯr´ mən[t] sē) *n.,* quality or state of being dormant, or inactive

dregs (dregz´) *n. pl.,* particles of solid matter that settle at the bottom of a liquid

drought (drout´) *n.,* long period of dry weather

dy • na • mism (dī´ nə miz´ əm) *n.,* energy

eaves (ēvz´) *n. pl.,* lower edges of a roof

ee • rie (ir´ ē) *adj.,* mysterious; weird

ef • fem • i • nate (e fem´ ə nit) *adj.,* having female qualities

e • lat • ed (ē lā´ təd) *adj.,* joyful

el • o • quent (el´ ə kwənt) *adj.,* fluent and persuasive

e • lude (ē lüd´) *vt.,* avoid, escape

e • lu • sive (ē lü´ siv) *adj.,* hard to grasp

e • merge (ē mərj´) *vi.,* come out; come into view

em • is • sar • y (em´ i ser´ ē) *n.,* person or agent sent on a specific mission

en • cum • bered (in kəm´ bərd) *adj.,* loaded down

en • dorse (in dȯrs) *vt.,* publicly and definitely express support or approval of

en • meshed (in mesht´) *adj.,* entangled

en • thralled (en thrȯld´) *part.,* fascinated; held as if in a spell

er • rant (er´ ənt) *adj.,* traveling or given to traveling

erode (i rōd) *vt.,* diminish or destroy gradually

erst • while (ərst´ [h]wīl) *adv.,* in the past: formerly

es • o • ter • ic (es´ ə ter´ik) *adj.,* understood by a chosen few

es • py (e spī´) *vt.,* catch sight of

es • teem (e stēm´) *n.,* great regard or respect

e • van • ge • list (ē van´ jə list´) *n.,* preacher who holds public services to spread Christianity

ex • ile (eks´ īl´) *n.,* state or period of forced absence from one's country or community; banishment

ex • pe • di • ent (ek spē´ dē ənt) *adj.,* useful for causing a desired effect; advantageous

ex • pul • sion (ik spəl´ shən) *n.,* act of expelling

ex • ude (ig züd´) *vi.,* display conspicuously or abundantly

fare (fer´) *n.,* food.

feign (fān´) *vt.,* pretend

fer • ment (fər ment´) *vt.,* chemically change into an alcoholic substance

fes • tive (fes´ tiv) *adj.,* merry; joyous

fi • brous (fī´ brəs) *adj.,* tough; stringy

flail (flā[ə]l´) *vt.,* move, swing, or beat around

for • sake (fȯr sāk´) *vt.,* give up; leave; abandon

griev • ous • ly (grēv´ əs lē) *adv.,* severely

gut • tur • al (gut´ ər əl) *adj.,* harsh; throaty

hag • gard (hag´ ərd) *adj.,* tired; worn

har • bin • ger (här´ bin jər) *n.,* person or thing that comes before to announce or give an indication of what follows

hoist (hoist´) *vt.,* lift, raise up

hu • mil • i • at • ed (hyü mil´ ē ā təd) *part.,* hurt in pride or dignity

i • dol • a • trous (ī däl´ ə trəs) *adj.,* blindly worshiping objects or images

im • pend • ing (im pend´ iŋ) *adj.,* about to happen

im • pen • e • tra • bly (im pen´ i trə blē) *adv.,* incapable of being passed through

im • pe • ri • ous (im pir´ ē əs) *adj.*, overbearing; arrogant

im • pose (im pōz´) *vt.*, establish or bring about as if by force

im • pos • ing (im pō´ ziŋ) *adj.*, impressive in size, bearing, dignity, or grandeur

im • po • tent (im´ pə tənt) *adj.*, lacking strength; powerless

im • prov • i • dent (im prä´və dənt) *adj.*, failing to provide for the future

im • pu • dent (im´ pyü dənt) *adj.*, shamelessly bold

in • ad • vert • ent (in´ ad vərt´ ´nt) *adj.*, unintentional.

in • cess • ant • ly (in ses´ ənt lē´) *adv.*, endlessly

in • cip • i • ent (in sip´ ē ənt) *adj.*, in the first stage of existence

in • dig • ni • ty (in dig´ nə tē) *n.*, something that humiliates, insults, or injures self-respect

in • dul • gent • ly (in dul´ jənt lē) *adv.*, kindly; leniently

in • fra • struc • ture (in´ frə strək chər) *n.*, system of public works for a country, state, or region

in • i • ti • ate (i nish´ ē āt´) *vt.*, admit as a member; teach the fundamentals

in • so • lent • ly (in´ sə lənt lē) *adv.*, boldly; in a way that shows disrespect

in • teg • ri • ty (in teg´ rə tē) *n.*, strict adherence to moral values

in • ter • val (in´ tər vəl) *n.*, space; gap

in • tone (in tōn´) *vi.*, speak or recite in a singing tone

ir • rep • a • ra • ble (ir rep´ ə rə bəl) *adj.*, unable to be repaired or remedied

jaun • ty (jȯn´ tē) *adj.*, stylish; lively

lam • en • ta • tion (lam´ ən tā´shən) *n.*, expression of grief

list • less (list´ lis) *adj.*, spiritless; with no interest

lob • by (lä´ bē) *n.*, group of persons engaged in promoting a project or a cause, especially as representatives of a special interest group

lobe (lōb´) *n.*, rounded, projecting part

lof • ty (lȯf´ tē) *adj.*, noble; elevated in character or spirit

lu • rid (lu̇r´ id) *adj.*, causing horror and revulsion; shocking

lux • u • ri • ant (ləg zhür´ ē ənt) *adj.*, growing in great abundance

mael • strom (māl´ strəm) *n.*, turbulence; anything that is like a whirlpool in its furious activity

ma • lev • o • lence (mə lev´ ə ləns) *n.*, spitefulness; ill will

ma • lice (ma´ ləs) *n.*, desire to cause pain, injury, or distress to another

ma • neu • ver (mə nü´ vər) *vi.*, move into or out of a position, often requiring skill to do so

man • i • fest (man´ ə fest´) *adj.*, apparent; obvious

mar • row (mar´ ō) *n.*, soft tissue inside bones; innermost, essential part

mirth (mərth´) *n.*, high spirits or gladness accompanied by laughter

mirth • less (murth´ lis) *adj.*, humorless; sad

mis • cre • ant (mis´ krē ənt) *adj.*, evil

mo • lest (mə lest´) *vt.*, attack; cause harm to; annoy

mul • ti • tude (mul´ tə tüd´) *n.*, large number

non • en • ti • ty (nän en´ tə tē) *n.*, person of little significance

or • a • tor (òr´ ət ər) *n.*, public speaker

or • dain (or dāń) *vt.*, establish; order; decree

os • tra • cize (äs´ trə sīź) *vt.*, banish; exclude; reject

pac • i • fi • ca • tion (pas´ ə fi kā´ shən) *n.*, act of calming; appeasement

pac • i • fy (pas´ ə fī´) *vt.*, make peaceful or calm

pal • ate (pal´ ət) *n.*, roof of the mouth

pa • lav • er (pə lav´ ər) *n.*, conference; discussion

pan • de • mo • ni • um (pań də mō´ nē əm) *n.*, scene of wild noises and confusion

parched (pärcht´) *part.*, dried up; very thirsty

per • pen • dic • u • lar (pur´ pən di´ kyə lər) *adj.*, at a right angle to a given line

per • turb (pər tərb´) *vt.*, cause to be alarmed or upset

pes • tle (pəs´ təl) *n.*, tool for grinding or crushing

pin • na • cle (pin´ ə kəl) *n.*, highest point

plain • tive (plān´ tiv) *adj.,* expressing sorrow

plum • age (plüm´ ij) *n.,* feathers of a bird

pre • scribe (prē skrīb´) *vt.,* set down as a rule

pres • tige (pres tēzh´) *n.,* reputation; power to influence

pro • fane (prō fān´) *adj.,* not holy or reverent

pro • found (prō found´) *adj.,* deep; intense

pro • gen • i • tor (prō je´ nə tər) *n.,* forefather; originator

pro • spec • tive (prə spek´ tiv) *adj.,* expected; likely to be or become

prow • ess (prou´ is) *n.,* bravery; skill

pul • sa • tion (pul sā´ shən) *n.,* rhythmic beating

qua • ver • ing (kwā´ vər iŋ) *part.,* trembling; shaking

re • buke (ri byük´) *n.,* reprimand; scolding

re • coil (ri koil´) *vi.,* retreat; shrink back

ref • uge (ref´ yüj) *n.,* shelter; protection

re • gime (rā zhēm ; ri zhēm) *n.,* government in power; form of government

rel • ish (re´ lish) *vt.,* eat or drink with pleasure

re • luc • tant (ri lək´ tənt) *adj.,* feeling or showing hesitation or unwillingness

rend (rend´) *vt.,* tear; split

re • nowned (ri nound) *adj.,* famous; widely praised and highly honored

req • ui • site (rek´ wə zit) *adj.,* required; necessary

res • ig • na • tion (re´ zig nā´ shən) *n.,* acceptance; submission

re • sil • ient (ri zil´ yənt) *adj.,* recovering strength quickly

res • o • lute (rez´ ə lüt´) *adj.,* having a firm purpose; determined

re • son • ance (re´ zə nən[t]s) *n.,* quality of evoking a response; also, quality of echoing, as in a resonant voice

re • strain (ri strān´) *vt.,* hold back; contain

re • sume (ri züm´) *vt.,* return to or begin again after an interruption

rev • el (rev´əl) *vi.,* take intense pleasure

ri • gor (ri´ gər) *n.*, strictness; condition that makes life difficult, challenging, or uncomfortable

rouse (rouz´) *vt.*, cause to come out of a state of sleep

ru • mi • na • tion (rü mi nā´ shən) *n.*, reflection; contemplation

sac • ri • lege (sak´ rə lij) *n.*, disrespectful treatment of something sacred

scru • ti • nize (skrü´ t[ə]n īz) *vt.*, examine closely

sed • i • ment (sed´ ə mənt) *n.*, matter that settles to the bottom

sen • ior • i • ty (sēn yȯr´ ə tē) *n.*, status, priority

sin • is • ter (sin´ is tər) *adj.*, wicked; evil; dishonest

so • lace (sä´ ləs) *n.*, relief from pain or anxiety; consolation

sol • i • tar • y (säl´ ə ter´ē) *adj.*, alone, single

spe • cious (spē´ shəs) *adj.*, not genuine

sub • mis • sion (sub mish´ ən) *n.*, act of yielding; surrendering

sub • orn (sə bȯrn´) *vt.*, make [someone] do an unlawful thing

sub • side (səb sīd´) *vi.*, become less intense

sub • stan • tial (səb stan´ shəl) *adj.*, of real value or importance

sulk (səlk´) *vi.*, be moodily silent; pout

sul • len • ness (sul´ ən nəs) *n.*, resentment; gloominess

su • per • flu • ous (sə pᵾr´ flü əs) *adj.*, more than is needed or wanted; excessive

sup • pressed (sə prest´) *adj.*, held back or held down; also, kept from public knowledge

taw • dry (tȯ´ drē) *adj.*, cheap and gaudy

ten • ta • tive (ten´ tə tiv) *adj.*, timid; uncertain

teth • er (teth´ ər) *vt.*, fasten with a rope or chain

thatch (thach´) *n.*, woven plant material often used to make a roof

trans • fix (trans fiks´) *vt.*, make motionless

trem • u • lous (trem´ yü ləs) *adj.*, shaking, quivering

tri • fle (trī´ fəl) *n.*, something of little value; trivial matter

trill (tril´) *n.*, warbling sound made by birds or insects

tri • pod (trī´päd´) *n.*, three-legged stand

tu • ber (tü´ bər) *n.*, thick part of an underground stem

tu • mult (tü´ mult´) *n.*, commotion

ul • ti • ma • tum (ul´ tə mä´ təm) *n.*, final offer or demand

ul • u • late (yül´ yə lāt) *vi.*, howl or hoot

un • a • wares (un ə werz´) *adv.*, without knowing; unexpectedly; by surprise.

un • can • ny (un kan´ ē) *adj.*, mysterious; unfamiliar

un • in • i • ti • at • ed (un i nish´ ē āt´ id) *adj.*, not introduced to the knowledge of something

va • cil • late (va´ sə lāt) *vi.*, waver in mind, will, or feeling; hesitate

val • e • dic • tion (val´ ə dik´ shən) *n.*, farewell

val • or (val´ ər) *n.*, courage or bravery

vi • a • ble (vī ə bəl) *adj.*, capable of working, functioning, and developing adequately; having a reasonable chance of succeeding

vi • brant (vī´ brənt) *adj.*, pulsating with life

vig • or (vig´ ər) *n.*, strength; intensity

vol • u • ble (väl´ yü bəl) *adj.*, talkative

wail • ing (wāl´ iŋ) *n.*, crying

wil • y (wī´ lē) *adj.*, sly; crafty

wrath (rath´) *n.*, rage; fury

wrought (rȯt´) *vi.*, (*alt. p.t.* of work) done

zeal (zēl´) *n.*, intense enthusiasm; passion

Handbook of Literary Terms

ALLUSION. An **allusion** is a rhetorical technique in which reference is made to a person, event, object, or work from history or literature. There are many allusions to the Bible in *Things Fall Apart*. Most of these are explained in footnotes.

CATHARSIS. The ancient Greek philosopher Aristotle described tragedy as bringing about a **catharsis**, or purging, of the emotions of fear and pity. Some critics take Aristotle's words to mean that viewing (or reading) a tragedy causes a person to feel emotions of fear and pity, which are then released at the end, leaving the viewer (or reader) calmer, wiser, and perhaps more thoughtful. The idea that catharsis calms an audience has been contradicted by recent psychological studies that suggest that people tend to imitate enacted feelings and behaviors that they witness. Much of the current debate over violence on television and in movies centers on this question of whether viewing such violence has a cathartic (calming) or an arousing effect on the viewer.

CHARACTERIZATION. **Characterization** is the use of literary techniques to create a character. Writers use three major techniques to create characters: direct description, portrayal of characters' behavior, and representations of characters' internal states. When using direct description, the writer, through a speaker, a narrator, or another character, simply comments on the character, telling the reader about such matters as the character's appearance, habits, dress, background, personality, motivations, and so on. In portrayal of a character's behavior, the writer presents the actions and speech of the character, allowing the reader to draw his or her own conclusions from what the character says or does. When using representations of internal states, the writer reveals directly the character's private thoughts and emotions, often by means of what is known as the *internal monologue*.

CONFLICT. A **conflict** is a struggle between two forces in a literary work. A plot involves the introduction, development, and eventual resolution of a conflict. One side of the central conflict in a story or drama is usually taken by the main character. That character may struggle against another character, against the forces of nature, against society or social norms, against fate, or against some element within himself or herself. A struggle that takes place between a character and some outside force is called an *external conflict*. A struggle that takes place within a character is called an *internal conflict*. Okonkwo experiences both external and internal conflict in *Things Fall Apart*.

FOLK TALE. A **folk tale** is a brief story passed by word of mouth from generation to generation. See *myth* and *oral tradition*.

FORESHADOWING. **Foreshadowing** is the act of presenting materials that hint at events to occur later in a story. One example of foreshadowing in *Things Fall Apart* is Unoka's statement to his son that "it is more difficult and more bitter when a man fails *alone*." This foreshadows Okonkwo's lonely defeat and death at the end of the novel.

IRONY. **Irony** is a difference between appearance and reality. Types of irony include the following: *dramatic irony,* in which something is known by the reader or audience but unknown to the characters; *verbal irony,* in which a statement is made that implies its opposite; and *irony of situation,* in which an event occurs that violates the expectations of the characters, the reader, or the audience. An example of irony in *Things Fall Apart* is when Okonkwo names one of his children *Nneka,* or "Mother is Supreme." It would appear from this choice that Okonkwo has respect for mothers. In reality, Okonkwo honors only those attributes that he considers masculine—power, authority, status, strength, and fierceness in battle. Therefore, his choice of the name is ironic. An example of irony of situation occurs at the end of the novel, when Okonkwo—who longed to be a great man in his clan—is so far from being great that even to touch him is an abomination.

MOOD. **Mood,** or **atmosphere**, is the emotion created in the reader by part or all of a literary work. The writer can evoke in the reader an emotional response—such as fear, discomfort, longing, or anticipation—by working carefully with descriptive language and sensory details.

MOTIF. A **motif** is any element that recurs in one or more works of literature or art. The idea of a *chi,* or personal god, is one motif in *Things Fall Apart*. This motif appears again and again to suggest that Okonkwo is struggling against a bad *chi,* or bad fate.

MYTH. A **myth** is a story that explains objects or events in the natural world as resulting from the action of some supernatural force or entity, most often a god. Every early culture around the globe has produced its own myths.

Myths and science have a lot in common because both offer explanations of natural phenomena. One example of African myth is the story of how Tortoise got his patterned shell, which Ekwefi tells in chapter 11 of *Things Fall Apart.*

ORAL TRADITION. An **oral tradition** is a work, an idea, or a custom that is passed by word of mouth from generation to generation. Materials transmitted orally may be simplified in the retelling. They also may be sensationalized because of the tendency of retellers to add or to elaborate upon the materials that come down to them. Often, works in an oral tradition contain miraculous or magical elements. *Folk tales, myths,* and *proverbs* are all part of the rich oral tradition of the Igbo people.

PLOT. A **plot** is a series of events related to a central conflict, or struggle. A typical plot involves the introduction of a conflict, its development, and its eventual resolution. See page 166 for a description of the elements of plot and an analysis of the plot of *Things Fall Apart.*

PROVERB. A **proverb**, or **adage**, is a traditional saying, such as "You can lead a horse to water, but you can't make it drink." Proverbs play an important role in Igbo culture.

SETTING. The **setting** of a literary work is the time and place in which it occurs, together with all the details used to create a sense of a particular time and place. The setting of *Things Fall Apart* is an Igbo village in the 1890s. In the novel, Achebe includes many details about traditional Igbo culture to help create this setting.

SUSPENSE. **Suspense** is a feeling of expectation, anxiousness, or curiosity created by questions raised in the mind of a reader. For example, in chapter 11 Achebe creates suspense about what will happen to Ezinma.

SUSPENSION OF DISBELIEF. **Suspension of disbelief** is the act by which the reader willingly sets aside his or her skepticism in order to participate imaginatively in the work being read. In chapter 22, the narrator tells us that "the Mother of Spirits walked the length and breadth of the clan, weeping for her murdered son." Readers may not believe in spirits, but they must be willing to suspend disbelief in order to get the full effect of the story.

SYMBOL. A **symbol** is a thing that stands for or represents both itself and something else. The locusts that come in swarms to Umuofia in chapter 7 symbolize the European colonists who will later descend upon the clan.

THEME. A **theme** is a central idea in a literary work. One theme of *Things Fall Apart* is the struggle between tradition and change.

TRAGEDY. A **tragedy** is a drama or other work of literature that tells the story of the fall of a person of high status. The Greek philosopher Aristotle described tragedy as a serious work that celebrates the courage and dignity of a tragic hero in the face of inevitable doom, doom often made inevitable by a tragic flaw, or *hamartia,* in the hero. Aristotle identified the most common *hamartia* as *hubris,* or arrogance resulting from excessive pride. *Hubris* is the flaw that brought about the downfall of many heroes of Greek tragedy, including Oedipus. Aristotle claimed that watching a tragedy gave audiences the chance to cleanse themselves of the emotions of pity and fear, in other words, to "get those feelings out" through their pity for the hero and their fear at the thought that such a tragedy could happen to them. He called this cleansing a *catharsis.* *Things Fall Apart* can be considered a tragedy, with Okonkwo as its tragic hero.

TRAGIC FLAW. Called *hamartia* by the Greeks, a **tragic flaw** is a personal weakness that brings about the fall of a character in a tragedy. The most common tragic flaw is that of *hubris,* or arrogance resulting from excessive pride.

TRAGIC HERO. A **tragic hero** is a character of high status who possesses noble qualities but who also has a tragic flaw, or personal weakness.

Acknowledgments

The Atlantic Monthly Group. "An African Voice" from *Atlantic Unbound*, August 2, 2000. Copyright © 2000 by The Atlantic Monthly Group. All rights reserved. Material obtained from *The Atlantic Unbound* at www. theatlantic.com.

The Christian Science Monitor. "Going home was a sad awakening" by Marjorie Coeyman. This article first appeared in *The Christian Science Monitor* on January 6, 2000 and is reproduced with permission. Copyright © 2000 *The Christian Science Monitor*. All rights reserved. Online at csmonitor.com.

Bessie Head Estate. "Heaven Is Not Closed" from *The Collector of Treasures and Other Botswana Village Tales* by Bessie Head, published by Heinemann Educational Books Ltd., 1977. Copyright © Bessie Head Estate, reprinted with permission by John Johnson Limited.

Heinemann Educational Publishers. "Arrival" from *Kehinde* by Buchi Emecheta. Copyright © 1994 by Buchi Emecheta. Reprinted by permission of Heinemann Educational Publishers.

Newsweek. "Should My Tribal Past Shape Delia's Future?" by Dympna Ugwu-Oju from *Newsweek* December 4, 2000. Reprinted by permission of *Newsweek*. All rights reserved.

Random House. "Lament of the Sacred Python" from *Christmas in Biafra and Other Poems* by Chinua Achebe, copyright © 1973 by Chinua Achebe. Used by permission of Doubleday, a division of Random House, Inc.

Simon & Schuster. "The Second Coming" reprinted with the permission of Scribner, a Division of Simon & Schuster, Inc., from *The Collected Works of W. B. Yeats, Volume 1: The Poems, Revised*, edited by Richard J. Finneran. Copyright © 1924 by The Macmillan Publishing Company, copyright renewed © 1952 by Bertha Georgie Yeats.